GLIMPSE

THE TESLA EFFECT
BOOK 1

JULIE DREW

RING OF FIRE PUBLISHING

ISBN-13: 978-0692234235
ISBN-10: 0692234233

Glimpse (The Tesla Effect, Book 1)

Published by
Ring of Fire Publishing
Seattle, Washington, U.S.A.

Caitlin Wilson, Editor.
Cover images by Augustino, wavebreakmedia, and Pakhnyushcha.
Cover design by Julie Drew and Stephen Penner.

Acknowledgements

The idea for *The Tesla Effect* trilogy began to take shape when I went to a talk at Kent State University given by Dr. Ronald Mallett, Professor of Physics at the University of Connecticut. Dr. Mallett's presentation was essentially my favorite thing: taking science and technology on the one hand, and narrative and character and empathy and drama on the other, and mashing them up into something exciting and accessible. His story of how he became interested in time travel and eventually became a physicist is fascinating and inspiring, and the time machine that appears in my books is based on his description of his own experiments in this field. In addition, I read a whole host of explanations of quantum physics and time travel theories from a wide variety of sources, in print and online, some of which I partially grasped. Heaps of gratitude to all those writers who attempt to translate the work of scientists for the rest of us.

Creative work takes a village. A fearless publisher and a talented editor turned this story I spun in my head and on my hard drive into a book. Support from the Department of English and Buchtel College of Arts and Sciences at the University of Akron allowed me time to write and meet my deadlines. Add to that my friends and colleagues who are writers and artists—generous and interested and encouraging and supportive, all—and you get the kind of environment that nurtures and sustains not just the creative impulse, but the daily grind of bringing a project to fruition. Priceless, and so very much appreciated. Thanks to Jan Bean and

Lauren Scarpa, in particular, who read early drafts and whose comments helped make the book a better read.

Mostly, though, it's on family. Nobody could ask for a more supportive bunch than mine, and lucky for me, they come with quite a bit of expertise, as well. Thanks to Philip Anderson and Amber Genuske for brainstorming with me on plot lines and cover art, and in advance for the upcoming research trip so integral to the sequel. And apologies to Brian Anderson and Casey Shevlin for my inability to fully express how much your input, from character development and back stories, to dialogue, pacing, and plot structures—I'm sure I've left things out—helped to shape this book and series. I honestly don't think Tesla would have seen the light of day without you. Your enthusiasm never waned, your notes were always honest and spot-on, and Brian's always made me laugh, to boot. You guys are the best. And last but not least, thanks to my husband, Bill Lyons, who never wavers in his astonishing commitment to make my writing a priority in his life, thus freeing me up to write books, and to do so without guilt or regret. You.

For my niece, Katy Drew

When I was a child, I caught a fleeting glimpse,
Out of the corner of my eye.
I turned to look but it was gone.
I cannot put my finger on it now.
The child is grown, the dream is gone.

— Pink Floyd, *Comfortably Numb*

PROLOGUE

The intruder picked up the journal off the desk in the girl's bedroom with a latex-gloved hand. So far, nothing in the house had offered even a hint to suggest how she fit into this assignment, but recent developments suggested the girl was involved. And it was the intruder's job to find out what her involvement entailed—a job that could end very, very badly if answers weren't found soon. The pages of the girl's journal, filled with an immature, rounded script, passed quickly by as the intruder thumbed through them—until a particular phrase in the middle of a random page caught the intruder's eye:

…documenting his secret experiments…

The intruder snapped to attention, all business now, and turned pages backwards, to find the start of the entry.

There.

October 23. Why can't my life ever be normal? Like my mom having died when I was a kid hasn't been bad enough, now I have a heartbeat that's screwed up? High school is totally ruined for me—oh my

God, what if I have to wheel around an oxygen tank and wear a mask strapped to my face?!

Impatient, the intruder scanned down the page, desperate to find something relevant.

Plus, I think I might be crazy. Either that, or there's something else at work here. Something I can't explain. But since there's no lightning bolt on my forehead, and there aren't any sparkly vampires at my school (I think I would have noticed), whatever this is, I figure I'd better write it down. I'm not my dad, compulsively documenting his secret experiments on quarks, and wormholes, and electromagnetic whatevers, but I do have sense enough to make a record of this weirdness.

I mean, I might be dead tomorrow, and this could be important.

With a hand that now trembled, the intruder turned the page to read more but found only the silence of uninterrupted white space, page after page of it, until there were no more, then held the book by its binding and shook it to dislodge any loose, folded papers that might have been inserted into the journal.

Nothing.

The girl's bedroom had been scoured, the house had been thoroughly searched and professionally wiped—there was no indication that anyone had been in the home at all. The girl might have destroyed her later entries, the intruder mused, or perhaps thought better of the dangers involved in leaving a record, but this was, of course, merely conjecture.

Still, it was a clue—months old now, but experience told the intruder that this was the thread that needed to be pulled to unravel the whole cloth.

The intruder walked back down the stairs into the living room, then slipped quietly out the back door and walked leisurely toward town in the warm sunshine, having reached the conclusion least desired but, in the end, unavoidable. Clearly, it was time to take a more aggressive approach to this assignment, one that would require face-to-face time with the girl. And however regrettable it might be, she would find the experience terrifying.

CHAPTER 1

The bass thumped and spilled out the doorway in sharp contrast to the soft glow of muted lamps. The heavy throb seemed to pound her body from the inside as Tesla walked up the sidewalk toward the Victorian house just east of the center of campus. The party was visible—and certainly audible—from a block away, which was right about the time Tesla started to feel like maybe this wasn't such a good idea.

Keisha sensed her friend's hesitation. "Try not to be a freakshow."

"Oh, nice. Thanks," Tesla said.

"Look, my cousin lives there. It's a birthday party for one of his roommates. I told you, it's cool."

Tesla stopped in the middle of the sidewalk and turned to face Keisha head on while she enumerated her concerns on her fingers, one by one. "First, your cousin doesn't know me, and we weren't invited. Second, we'll both get in trouble if we get caught—at least I will, you know how pissed my dad was after we went to that frat party last month. *'You're seventeen,'*" she said in a deep voice, clearly mocking her father. "*'You've got no business at a college party!'* Third—"

"Look, I'm sure your dad's forgotten all about that by now. Besides, this is totally different. We're just going to my cousin's place. He hasn't been back in the States that long. Isn't it natural that I'd want to hang out? Think of it as a family obligation, and you're here to help. Plus—and most importantly—*I* am eighteen."

Tesla considered Keisha for a moment, the dark hair that fell in smooth waves to her chin, those incredible cheekbones, and legs that looked a mile long beneath her short skirt. With a slight frown, Tesla turned and walked toward the house again, Keisha by her side.

"Yeah, I know," Tesla grumbled. "You remind me constantly, which, by the way, is hardly the mature behavior of an eighteen-year-old. And just so you know, no one—especially my dad—will buy that family obligation line." She paused, aware that Keisha was waiting for more. "And I'm not drinking."

"Hey, nobody said you had to drink," Keisha replied quickly. The advantage was clearly hers now, but she didn't want to blow it. "I probably won't either."

"At least you have the option," Tesla pointed out. "My dad loves to lecture me on the potential dangers of anything that would put 'undue pressure' on my heart."

"Actually, we all get that lecture, just without the heart condition part tacked on as extra incentive. Mine are all, '*Think about your future, Keisha!*'"

"Maybe," Tesla conceded. "But it still sucks."

"Well, yeah. But nothing has happened since you were in the hospital, right? And it's been, what, like six months now? You're still here." Keisha clearly wanted Tesla's mood to improve before they got to the party.

Tesla relented. "Actually, it's been eight months. And, yeah,

I'm still alive."

"And you're back on the court again, and so far a little ball hasn't killed you, right?"

"Right."

"So come on," said Keisha. "What do you say?"

They both paused at the steps that led up to the front porch of the old Victorian mansion that shook with the beat of unseen woofers, the ornately carved trim around the edges of the roof and the spindly porch railings just visible in the gloom. *Six steps*, Tesla thought automatically. *Porch is forty feet long, eight feet deep. Twenty-six posts, spaced exactly twenty-four inches apart, hold up the railing.*

Tesla raised her voice so Keisha could hear her above the din of club music, laughter, and the general sounds of partying, and gave her friend what she wanted. "Fine. We worked hard enough to look this good, let's not waste it."

"Exactly," said Keisha, satisfied at last. She checked to make sure her skirt was straight and then eyed with approval her best friend's skinny jeans and tissue-thin, white embroidered top she'd gotten in Mexico last year. Tesla had, as always, a worn black messenger bag slung across her body, but Keisha had long since given up any attempt to persuade her to trade it in for an actual bag with some semblance of style. She focused instead on Tesla's wild array of curls, red-gold shot through with honey, cinnamon, and pumpkin-orange, so bright and multi-faceted that Keisha still had her doubts that it was natural, especially in full sunlight. "You look totally hot—in that tomboy, white-girl kind of way. Except for the eyes, of course. Stunning. Let's go get 'em."

The two made a striking pair, the tall, mahogany-hued black girl and the slim white girl with riotous red hair and pale skin like heavy cream. Keisha usually got the second looks until the viewer got close to Tesla and saw her eyes: one startlingly poison-green, the other a clear, bright blue, both fringed by dark auburn lashes. It was her strange, mismatched eyes, Tesla had always thought, that made people notice her, and while she wanted to be noticed—at least sometimes, and by some people—those eyes made her feel self-conscious rather than confident, and confidence was what she was after.

The girls climbed the stairs to the deeply-shadowed porch, where they encountered more people as they got closer to the front door. A logjam of indistinguishable bodies and voices that spoke and laughed and called out to one another hit them like a wave that broke upon the threshold of the house. The music shook the walls as they made their way inside. Keisha, as usual, led the way.

The old house was a throwback to some Edith Wharton novel. *Max would love this*, Tesla thought. She tried to take it all in to tell him about later. The large, open room just inside the door was twenty-eight by thirty-four, she noted with a glance, and featured a chandelier that hung from the high ceiling and shone directly onto a round, polished wood table with a huge crystal vase of fresh flowers on it. Three arched, open doorways led off in different directions, and between these were soft lamps and comfortable sofas and chairs in intimate little seating arrangements, like a posh hotel lobby. Thirty-two people stood, sat, or lounged around the room and Tesla glimpsed more through the doorways that led to other rooms in the enormous old house. Everybody had a red plastic cup in hand, and the air was heavy with smoke—some of it from cigarettes—and the smell of spilled beer. Tesla was hemmed in as she and Keisha joined the throng headed for the doorway directly opposite the front door, caught between the press of bodies to her right and a red velvet sofa with a rounded, carved back immediately to her left. She felt someone touch her hand, and looked down at a couple wrapped around each other on the sofa, mere inches from where she stood. The guy looked right at Tesla, his eyes open while he kissed the heavily made-up girl in his arms. He touched Tesla's hand again, a light caress, while he stared intently at her.

"Seriously?" Tesla said. She moved away as much as she could in the press of bodies, which was only three and a half inches, and even that required her to lean into Keisha. The guy shrugged, closed his eyes, and returned his attention to the girl whose mouth he had his tongue in.

"That's just wrong," said Keisha.

"Right?" Tesla agreed, relieved as they finally began to move forward.

They slowly made their way into what they could now see was the kitchen, a bright, old-fashioned space with windows instead of upper cabinets on the far wall that had nonetheless been outfitted with huge, modern stainless steel appliances and butcher block countertops.

Keisha looked around, pleased. "It's like IKEA exploded in here." Then she gripped Tesla's hand, hard. "Hot Asian guy, just enough hair gel, six o'clock."

"Keisha, he's at twelve o'clock. Do you even know what a clock face looks like?"

"Whatever, dude. He's over by the keg. What do you think?"

Tesla looked. "Yeah, he's cute." The boy in question—the man in question, she corrected herself—had a beautiful face, saved from femininity by a square, masculine jaw and decent biceps under his *Frack You, Gaius* T-shirt. "Uh-oh," she warned, as Keisha pulled her toward the keg. "Sci-fi geek alert. He's a *Battle Star Galactica* fan."

"Hey, it works for you," said Keisha, undeterred.

"It most certainly does not," said Tesla hotly. "Do you see any guys around me? Ever?"

Someone stepped in front of Tesla and blocked her view of Keisha's target *du jour,* so suddenly that she actually ran into him: yep, he was tall, *solid,* clearly a guy. It felt like she had hit a wall, but before Tesla could say anything to him about his unfortunate blindness or willful rudeness, he could take his pick, he grabbed Keisha by the arm and snarled, "What the hell are you doing here, Keisha?"

"What?" Keisha asked defensively.

Tesla looked up at the angry guy whose shoes she practically stood on. Six one and a half, exactly, with broad shoulders and an easy, athletic build. He was a study in browns: shoulder-length dark hair shot through with gold fell in soft, springy ringlets to frame his face. Warm, deeply tanned skin, slightly lighter than Keisha's, lay smooth and taut over muscled forearms, and light, golden-brown eyes narrowed as he glared at Keisha. Neither his angry frown nor the scruffy start of a goatee could disguise his full, sensual mouth. His white tee-shirt had a small rip on the shoulder seam, and Tesla stared at his coppery-brown skin just visible through it.

Keisha shook off his hand. "We're hanging out, Finn. Back off!"

Keisha's cousin, thought Tesla, shaken by the sudden volatility in the air.

"You shouldn't be here," Finn growled.

"What is your problem?" Keisha demanded. "It's barely ten o'clock! And family legend has it that you were hardly an angel when you were my age."

"This is not some stupid frat party, and you are both obviously in high school." He glanced at Tesla briefly, then jerked a thumb in her direction. "Jesus, Keish, she looks like she's fifteen years old!"

"I'll be eighteen in October!" Tesla protested, stung by this insult, but both Finn and Keisha ignored her.

"Well, we can't leave yet," Keisha said, and her voice took on that I-will-brook-no-argument tone Tesla knew all too well. "We're supposed to meet our friend Malcolm, and it would not be cool if we left before he gets here."

Finn rolled his eyes. "Fine," he snapped. And then he turned to Tesla, "But get out as soon as he arrives. You can't be here tonight." His bright, burnished eyes bore straight into Tesla's and, much to her surprise, he made no comment about hers. He didn't even seem to notice that they were, to say the least, unusual, and she was inexplicably offended by this show of disinterest. She glared back at him, her usual shyness around boys nowhere to be found. For a moment she was aware of nothing but the intensity of his stare, and in her peripheral vision his wild, unkempt hair, the grim set of his mouth. And then he turned and was gone before she could think of a single, scathing retort.

"What the hell?" Tesla asked.

"Finnegan thinks he's the shit," Keisha answered with a dismissive wave of her hand. "He figures he can tell me what to do because he's older than me—*barely* older. Just ignore him."

Tesla certainly intended to ignore him, but she was curious. "Why is it such a big deal that we're here? We can't be the only ones here underage."

"I doubt it's about that," Keisha said slowly. She paused, and her frown made it clear to Tesla that it was not easy to explain Finnegan Ford. "He's had a very cool—but very weird—life, and it's made him kind of a pain in the ass."

"What do you mean? Cool and weird how?"

Keisha pulled Tesla back into the line of people moving toward the keg, and spoke over her shoulder. "Cool in that he's lived in a bunch of different countries, Europe mostly, but weird in that he was stuck in boarding school a lot. He's been on his own, really, his whole life, no siblings and not much contact with his parents since he started school."

"Shit," said Tesla.

"Yeah. He's used to being the boss. Of himself and—he thinks—of everyone else, too," Keisha said, at the keg at last. The hot Asian guy, whose expression had been decidedly bored up till now, looked anything but as he watched the girls approach. Keisha, for her part, had lost all interest in Finn's unusual childhood.

Unnoticed by either of the girls, Finn stood in the opposite doorway, just close enough to hear the conversation as he watched his cousin flirt with his best friend. She could lay it on thick, and despite his apprehension about what this evening might bring, Finn couldn't help but be amused. Joley might be a little older, and more experienced, but Keisha was a force to be reckoned with, and Finn wished him luck. Keisha giggled, flattered Joley, and looked away in faux confusion, but despite her amusing, over-the-top performance, Finn's interest was drawn from his cousin to the redheaded girl who stood next to her.

It was fanciful, of course, but it seemed that all the light in the room was pulled toward the girl in the white embroidered shirt, the pale gleam of her arms reflecting back the light and illuminating everything around her. Her thick, fiery hair curled over her shoulders and down the thin, white shirt she wore in stark contrast to the long line of her throat. His eyes traveled down her slim body, until she laughed and his eyes snapped back up to her face, animated with humor and intelligence and a soft, wide mouth framed by dimples.

He forced his attention back to Keisha, anxious to get the girls out of the house.

Joley was leaning in, foolishly, like a fly buzzing around one of those carnivorous plants. "So, Keisha, love, you still haven't told me—what year are you? I most certainly haven't seen you around before, and it's a rather small campus."

"I haven't seen you either, we must not have had any classes together," Keisha said. "I love your British accent, I feel like I'm on *Downton Abbey*. Tell me how you pronounce your name again?" She looked up at him from under her lashes—not something she was able to do often, given her five-foot ten-inch frame.

"Ah, yes—the BBC has been a brilliant wingman for me these past two years. My name is Zhou Li. It's Chinese, and it's pronounced *Joe-Lee*."

"Joley," said Keisha slowly. She turned the radiance of her most seductive smile on him—which was hard to resist, as Keisha herself was well aware. "I like it."

A silvery-blonde, lightly tanned boy approached Tesla and tugged gently on her sleeve, so gently that she missed it at first. Relief washed over her expressive face as she looked at the boy and smiled.

"About time you got here," Tesla said. "I've had to bear witness to Keisha's charms for, like, two hours. I'm exhausted. And a little skeeved."

"It's been five minutes, tops," said Keisha. "And you're just jealous."

Joley stared expectantly at the three of them and Keisha, who had no choice now, made the introductions with a vague wave at Tesla and the blonde boy. "Friends, Joley. Joley, friends."

"Yeah, nice to meet you," said Joley, peering closely at them in the bright kitchen lights. Then he looked at Keisha, clearly puzzled, and Finn, still eavesdropping, almost laughed out loud. He knew exactly where this was headed.

"You're all students here, right?" asked Joley. "I mean, you *are* in college?"

Tesla looked at Mal, Mal looked at Keisha, and Keisha looked at Joley. There was an awkward pause, and then Keisha mumbled, "Not in the technical sense."

Joley looked amused now, too, but far less flirtatious than he had only seconds before. "What other sense is there, love?"

"Look," said Keisha, the shy pretense gone. "We're almost finished with high school, Tesla's dad is a professor here, and we've spent so much time on campus we probably know it better than you do."

"Perhaps," said Joley. "But I'm far too good looking to go to jail, even for something as crucially important as serving you alcohol."

"Liability? Seriously? Look, Joley, no one has a drink, see?" Keisha indicated the absence of beer cups within their small group.

The blonde boy flicked his straight, silvery hair out of his eyes and tentatively raised his hand. "I was actually just about to…"

Tesla put her hand on his arm. "No, we were just about to leave. We promised Finn."

Joley looked startled. "You know Finn, do you?"

"He's my cousin," said Keisha with a shrug. "He lives here."

"I know," said Joley. "What did you say your friends' names were?"

"Malcolm and Tesla," Keisha said, and Joley's eyes snapped to Tesla's face.

"I can't believe—why would he bring you here?"

"Well, he didn't exactly invite us," admitted Keisha

reluctantly. "I heard there was a party tonight. One of the girls mentioned it today after practice, and I wanted to check it out."

Joley was clearly agitated. He looked around the crowded room for something or someone, the worried look on his face reminiscent of Finn's reaction when he'd first seen the girls tonight. It was a look that acknowledged the potential for catastrophe.

"You should really go now," Joley said, his tone urgent. He moved his hands as if to herd them toward the back door that opened up off the kitchen.

"Hey man, what's up?" said a deep voice just behind Tesla's shoulder. "Is there still beer in the keg?"

Finn craned his head around the doorway to get a look at the two guys who had approached, and he tensed with the onrush of sudden adrenaline.

Tesla moved closer to Mal to make room for the newcomers. She and Mal and Keisha had to press tightly together to accommodate the two giants—football players in all likelihood, with their ham-sized hands, powerful shoulders, and disturbing absence of neck.

"Well, hey, sweet thing," said the guy closest to Tesla as he peered down at her. His eyes raked her body before he turned to the keg and bent low to pump it, an empty red cup in his other hand.

Tesla looked down at the top of the guy's head, which was already balding at the crown. *Geez, how old are these guys, anyway?* she thought.

"C'mon, Tesla, let's get out of here," said Malcolm. "I'm hungry."

A loud *thump*, followed immediately by a grunt of pain and several excited voices yelling encouragement from the parlor caught Finn's attention. He glanced back over his shoulder and saw two idiots pummeling each other. They swung wildly, with little effect but the almost certain outcome of crashing into Lydia's antique table and flower-filled vase.

He would have to take care of it.

He glanced back briefly at the tableau by the keg and cursed the piss-poor timing of all drunks and their inexplicable need to show each other their beer muscles, and sprinted away to break up the fight.

CHAPTER 2

"C'mon, Tesla, let's get out of here," Malcolm said. "I'm hungry."

Tesla jumped, just a little, as the big blond hulk straightened up quickly and loomed over her, his beer still unpoured.

"Tesla?" he asked sharply as he stared at her, hard. "What's your last name?"

Tesla felt the jolt of an unnamed fear that hit her stomach, traveled to the tips of her fingers and toes, and left her breathless. She said nothing, only returned his stare.

"Who wants to know?" asked Keisha as she stepped up next to Tesla.

"I'm sure all the guys want to know," said the other giant, his short dark hair cut close to his head as well. "What's your name?" His voice was sharp, too, his eyes as hard and bright as a bird of prey, not at all like the lazy, hazy voice of some beer-soaked jock.

Both men seemed to lean in closer, to cut off Tesla's air supply and shrink the space around her until she was wedged in, trapped by the bodies, the keg, and the walls of the kitchen. She took a step back—approximately six-point-three inches. She knew instinctively that this would allow her to clear Malcolm's body and make a straight line to the arched, interior doorway and the big, hotel-lobby-like room they'd been in earlier, which would be the shortest route of escape, even if only by a little over three feet. The back door was closer, of course, but she'd have to get past these two guys to reach it.

Before she could react to his sudden movement, Tesla's wrist was caught in the blond giant's fist. "Let's talk," he said softly, and it wasn't a question. "Out back where it's quiet and we can get to know each other."

Tesla leaned away from him as he began to pull her toward the back door. "No, I don't think—" she began, but was cut off by Keisha's outraged voice.

"What the hell do you think you're doing?" she demanded loudly. "Let go of her!"

The other man ignored Keisha, as well as Tesla's struggles against his partner, and stepped quickly to the back door and opened it. The unlit night was revealed as the man stepped outside, the sound of his footsteps sharp against the wooden stairs, and was swallowed by the darkness. The blond one, Tesla's wrist still in his vice-like grip, walked toward the door with Tesla in tow, her feet actually sliding across the hardwood floor. She frantically tried to peel his fingers from her wrist with her other hand, but they were like iron bands.

At exactly the same moment, Joley and Malcolm stepped in front of him, tried to block his way, and Mal cried, "Let her go!" though his voice cracked a little on the last word.

"Beckett! A little help here, please!" Joley yelled.

Immediately a girl stepped into the room and planted herself in front of the man who held Tesla by the wrist, her back toward the open door through which the other man had disappeared. She wore tailored trousers, an untucked white button-down shirt that fit close to her curves, and a man's tie loose around her neck, her long, honey-colored hair pulled back in a tight ponytail.

"What's up?" she asked. She stood lightly, easily, though her body blocked the way to the back door and her eyes never left the huge blond man who held Tesla's wrist in his meaty fist. Her question, however, was directed at Joley.

"This Neanderthal and the bugger outside have not observed good party etiquette," Joley said calmly. "This one has decided to take Tesla here out back for a chat, whether she wants to go or not." Joley's explanation was factual, but Tesla sensed a strange emphasis in his words that she didn't understand.

"Tesla?" asked the girl, her voice suddenly sharp. Her gaze darted momentarily to Joley before it locked back on the man in front of her.

"Indeed. Friend of Finn's cousin, here, Keisha. Also in bloody high school." He pointed at Keisha.

"Well, that's unexpected. And you need to leave," the blonde girl said quietly to the man who held Tesla's wrist.

"Out of the way, little girl." He raised his free hand as if to move her aside while he began to pull Tesla toward the door again.

But the girl Joley had called Beckett grabbed the creep's enormous hand with her own small one and turned her wrist in a deceptively gentle motion until the man cried out, his arm now bent awkwardly, elbow up, his wrist somehow turned backward in an unnatural and painful way. As Beckett lowered her own hand, the guy's knees bent, and he slowly moved toward the floor to alleviate the pressure she exerted on his wrist.

He had no choice. He let go of Tesla, and she was free.

"Harper!" called the guy loudly, on his knees now, his face dark red and his wrist still twisted under Beckett's hand.

They all heard the thunder of feet on wooden stairs as the second man ran back up the steps from the yard into the kitchen. He completely filled the doorway as he blinked in the bright light and took in the scene in an instant, like the professional he was.

"Get the girl!" said the one on his knees, his voice tight with pain.

But as the second man made a move forward, toward either Beckett or Tesla—no one was sure which—and Mal and Keisha moved in close to Tesla, shocked at the violent turn of events, Finn ran into the room and barreled through the three friends as he rushed at the man in the doorway. He would have knocked Tesla to the ground if she hadn't seen him move and leaned exactly fifteen degrees to her right, no more and no less than was needed to avoid a collision. Finn slammed his shoulder into the solar plexus of the dark-haired man, which propelled them both out the door and down the steps. Everyone in the room froze as they heard the *thud* of something heavy land outside on the lawn, followed immediately by the sound of a very large person desperate to suck in oxygen because he's had all the air expelled from his lungs.

Finn came back in the door, a small cut over his right eye, but he seemed otherwise all right—in fact, Tesla thought, he actually looked happy, and more than a little bit pleased with himself. When he touched Beckett's shoulder she immediately released the thug on his knees in front of her. The blond man slowly got to his feet, but his injured arm hung uselessly by his side.

Finn spoke quietly, his voice matter-of-fact, while a thin thread of blood followed the line of his eyebrow and moved slowly down his temple. "The cops are on their way. Pick your friend up off the ground outside and don't come back."

A siren sounded in the distance, as if on cue.

The injured man looked at Beckett, took in her trim, athletic frame and unperturbed gaze. "We're not finished," he said quietly, and then looked back over his shoulder at Tesla. "And we will have that talk, Tesla Abbott. Count on it." He moved slowly toward the door, his arm cradled in his uninjured hand, and when Finn didn't move to get out of his way he was forced to walk around him, out the back door, and into the night.

It was only in the silence which followed that Tesla realized the techno-beat of the music had disappeared, and that all sounds of the party had gone right along with it. The kitchen was empty but for the six who had witnessed the recent excitement and now stood between the back door and the abandoned keg. Through the arched doorway, Tesla could see a girl with spiky black hair close the front door on the last partiers as they quietly left.

Keisha and Malcolm looked at Tesla with concern. "I'm fine," she said.

"Can we sit for a minute before we leave?" Keisha asked Finn, despite Tesla's assurances.

Finn said nothing, but turned and led them all back into the big lobby-like room they'd first entered, where they joined the spiky-haired Goth girl, who sat on the edge of a huge overstuffed sofa upholstered in black and cream stripes. Tesla took a chair and Malcolm sat on the floor at her feet. Keisha hovered protectively nearby as Joley, Beckett, and Finn took the other chairs.

"Well, that was fun," said Tesla.

"No, that wasn't fun at all, actually," said Finn in a tight voice. "You guys should never have come here tonight."

"Well, everybody's okay, that's what counts," said Malcolm, reasonably, but then his face was split by a grin as he stared with open admiration at Beckett. "Well, everybody except that talking mountain. You kicked his *ass!*"

"The point is that those idiots would've probably drunk our beer and left, but they saw you guys as easy targets," said Finn. "You shouldn't be at a college party, and that's exactly why."

"Wait a minute," said Tesla, stung by this faulty logic. "You can't seriously blame us for this! The fact that we are seventeen instead of eighteen is irrelevant."

"Well, only you and Mal are seventeen. You know, factually," Keisha reminded her, and Tesla shot her a hateful look.

"I'm sixteen," piped up Goth girl, "and nobody bothered me."

Tesla indicated with a wave of her hand that Goth girl's comment was exhibit A, and sent a raised-eyebrow look in Finn's direction. "My point exactly. If the cause of their behavior had been our age, they would have bothered this girl. They didn't, because our age had nothing to do with it."

"Thanks, Bizzy, that's not exactly helpful," said Finn with a frown for the Goth girl. "And now that you've reminded us of your youth, why don't you go upstairs and go to bed like a good girl."

"Wait, you live here, too?" asked Keisha, glancing at the Goth girl—at Bizzy—in surprise.

"Yep," said Bizzy. "I'm a senior. Physics and Astronomy, double major." She grinned, and her lovely smile undercut the intimidation her darkly outlined eyes and spiky black hair were supposed to inspire. "And this was my birthday party."

"You're a college senior and you turned sixteen *today*?" asked Mal. "How is that possible?"

"Must be she's a fracking child prodigy, mate," Joley offered good-naturedly, and Tesla glanced pointedly at Keisha. *See? Geek.*

Beckett, who up until this moment had offered nothing to the conversation, said, "If the excitement is all over, I'm heading up.

My workout is insanely early tomorrow." She turned and walked toward the elegantly curved staircase at the far right of the room. The lamplight reflected off her hair, not a single strand of which was out of place. "And it's not her birthday," she said to the room at large.

Tesla, Keisha, and Mal looked confused.

"Um, hey, thanks!" Tesla called after Beckett. "You know, for saving our lives and stuff."

Beckett raised a hand in acknowledgement and let it drop back by her side as she ascended the stairs and never once looked back.

"Who *is* that?" asked Mal.

"That's Beckett. Beckett Isley. She lives here, too," said Bizzy. "She grew up in Singapore. Thailand too, I think. She knows some martial arts."

"Some?" said Mal, who couldn't help a quick glance back at the stairs, though Beckett was long gone.

Keisha turned to Joley, a trace of her earlier, flirtatious tone back in her voice. "That's weird, I would've thought you'd be the Kung Fu master."

"What, because I'm Chinese?" asked Joley with a grin. "I grew up in Kensington and went to boarding school. The only 'wax on, wax off' move I've got is the one I use when I polish the Porsche."

Keisha laughed, and Joley looked at her with a comical leer. "I'd be delighted to show you all the moves I *do* have, however."

"Joley. Focus." Finn was seriously out of patience.

Joley had the grace to look a little shame-faced, and Finn stood up and glanced pointedly at Malcolm. "Like he said, everybody's fine, and that's what counts. Sometimes parties get crashed, sometimes drunks are jerks. It happens. You kids should go home now, it's all over."

"For the record, my name is Malcolm, and I am not a kid," Mal said, clearly offended.

Bizzy giggled, and Malcolm blushed.

Tesla looked at Keisha, who nodded, and they both stood up. "Okay, well, thanks for the hospitality, I guess," Tesla said to no one in particular. "We'll hope for something a little duller next time." She turned and began to follow Keisha and Malcolm out the door.

"There won't be a next time," said Finn, who had moved quickly to her side. "I don't want to see you here again." He had leaned down to whisper in her ear and his breath moved the hair on her neck. She shivered as if she were freezing, though she could feel the heat that radiated off his body.

And then they were on the porch, just Mal, Keisha, and Tesla, the door to the old Victorian house shut firmly behind them. They stood for a moment, undecided, until the porch light went off and left them in darkness. Keisha looked up the street in the direction they'd come only an hour earlier, and sighed dramatically before she walked down the steps with Malcolm toward the sidewalk.

"Hey, Mal, didn't you say something about food?" Keisha asked.

"I did, indeed," said Mal. "Who wants Thai?" He turned to Tesla, who was still on the porch, in the shadows where her friends could not see her face. "You coming?" he asked. "C'mon, you know you want a big bowl of noodles."

Tesla shook her head, as if to wake herself up. "Yeah," she said quickly, then ran down the steps to join them. She had been stunned by two realizations as she stood there on the porch. The first was that for the past hour she'd forgotten to remember that she was The Girl Whose Mom Had Died—a reality that had long ago become a part of her, who she was and how she saw herself. And the second was that even though no one had said her last name out loud, those two creepy guys who'd tried to drag her outside had known it anyway.

CHAPTER 3

Tesla removed one earbud when Max positioned himself directly in front of the couch so she couldn't ignore him. "What?" she asked, the tinny sounds of *Dark Side of the Moon*, piped from her iPod to her headset, adrift in the air around them.

"I said Dad'll be home soon. Did you wrap his present?"

"What present?" Tesla asked.

"Tesla, it's his birthday!" said Max, his exasperation plain.

"No kidding. You've told me every five minutes this whole week."

"So you didn't forget," he accused her as he pushed his glasses up further on the bridge of his freckled nose. Her little brother looked like Tom Sawyer would look, she thought, his blue eyes mischievous, his wavy carrot-orange hair falling over his forehead and ears. Only his wire-framed glasses, which were often lost or mangled seemingly beyond repair, suggested the intellect that hid behind his decidedly non-intellectual looks.

Tesla shrugged and put the earbud back in her ear as Max stomped toward the kitchen, his shoulders tense. She felt a familiar pang of concern and irritation, both of which were the product of the many years she'd felt responsible for him. *This isn't his fault*, she thought. *It's Dad's.* She had been mad at her father for as long as she could remember. Max tried to buffer the tension between them but his interventions accomplished little and never lasted.

Tesla put her iPod and headset on the coffee table once she'd made up her mind to go and talk to her brother, but then she heard the back door open and shut.

"I'm home, and I've got pizza!"

Immediately irritated, Tesla reluctantly walked into the warm, sunny kitchen.

"I thought you'd be late," said Max, the pizza box in his hands already open. "Aren't you right on the verge of something big?"

"Yes, but 'on the verge' could mean months, even years. I decided to come home and hang out with you two, like I said I would," said their still-youthful father as he glanced at Tesla.

Dr. Greg Abbott—a physicist—had light brown hair, curly like his daughter's. It looked a bit thin on top, Tesla thought, as the kitchen lights glinted off of his tortoise shell glasses. The glare hid his eyes completely, but they were a pale, powdery blue, like sun-bleached denim. Tesla supposed he was an okay-looking man for forty-two—no, scratch that, he was forty-three now—but all she could see when she looked at him was the black hole right next to him where her mother ought to be.

"All anybody at the lab can talk about is that gala for the new Director of the Physics Institute, anyway," her father was saying. "I couldn't get out of there fast enough."

"What, you aren't psyched about the big party?" Max asked. "The paper's done a story on the Institute twice this week, and they mentioned the gala on NPR this morning."

"Well, of course I'm delighted that we were able to get Van Alden as the new director—he's done some very important work in the last three or four years, and I've never met him. But I hate parties, and I'll have to wear a tuxedo," Greg Abbot confided to his son, his tone tinged with just enough horror to suggest that this was a nightmare of epic proportions.

"I suppose having to wear a suit isn't the worst thing in the world," he conceded when Max laughed. "But I don't intend to suffer alone—I got tickets for all of us."

Tesla looked away, her face carefully blank, and sat down at the kitchen table, determined not to get sucked into the conversation. Just because her father was willing to pretend they were one big happy family rather than this barely held together threesome living under a cloud of grief, didn't mean she was going to help him do it.

"So, what's up around here?" Dr. Abbott asked after a moment.

Max shrugged and chewed the pizza in his mouth. "Finished *Wide Sargasso Sea* this morning. It was okay. Clever conceit, but it's no *Jane Eyre*." He drank deeply from his glass of root beer until a wet, foamy soda-ring sat above his upper lip like a bad pre-teen moustache. "I'm not wild about the trend where authors take classic literature and write new back stories, or side stories, or whatever. Or those weird mash-ups of horror and nineteenth-century novels. Get your own characters, you know? It's called writing."

Clearly amused, Greg Abbott looked at his son with great affection. "It's June, Max—summer vacation. Have some fun. Have a childhood."

Tesla hid her smile behind her napkin as she pretended to wipe her mouth.

"Dad, we've been over this," Max explained patiently. "This *is* fun."

"Yeah, Max, we know. You slogged through Shakespeare's comedies last summer when you were *eight*," said Tesla. "Your third-grade teacher thought you were a freak, you know."

"Mrs. Timken loved me. Besides, you're the freak, not me," Max said defensively. "You're the one who can do calculations as easily as most people breathe, but you fail your math and science classes just to make a point—"

"I do not!" Tesla interrupted, but her father intervened.

"Let's not argue," he said. "I thought after dinner maybe we could play—"

The sound of the doorbell cut him off, and Max leapt up from his chair and raced for the front door.

"—Bananagrams," Dr. Abbott finished lamely. "I was going to insist, as the birthday boy, on a *Star Trek* theme," he muttered to himself.

Tesla glanced at her father, who had picked up the newspaper she knew he had already read this morning before work. She looked down at her plate and said nothing as the front door slammed.

"It's for you, Dad," Max said as he hurried into the room. He handed the flat, square package to his father. "UPS. Looks like a birthday present," he added triumphantly, with a huge grin aimed pointedly at his sister.

"Oh?" asked Dr. Abbott, genuine surprise on his face. "I've already talked to Aunt Jane today, and she'll be here next week. She said we'd celebrate my birthday then." He frowned and turned the package over so he could read the shipping label, and then looked at Tesla. "It's from you."

Taken completely by surprise, Tesla could only stare as her father tore open the package.

The brown paper drifted unheeded to the floor as her father

opened the cover of a photo album. He was clearly shocked by the first page of photos, and the look of both pleasure and pain on his face made Tesla recoil.

They sat at the table, all three of them silent and still as Dr. Abbott slowly turned the leaves of the album. The overhead light glinted off of the clear, plastic-film-covered photographs.

"Tesla, this is quite a gift," he said. He looked up from the album and Tesla noted with panic that he had tears in his eyes.

"I don't know what to say, these pictures are wonderful."

Max had risen from his chair and stood behind his father to peer over his shoulder at the album. He pointed at the open page. "Hey, that's us." Then he frowned. "I don't remember these pictures."

"You wouldn't," Dr. Abbott said. "You were too young. That's you in your crib, and this one is Tesla's old sandbox. Your mom built it for her."

"No, Dad, I know that's us in the pictures. I mean I haven't seen these specific photographs before. Where'd you get them?" Max asked his sister.

Tesla finally found her voice. "I have no idea."

"Actually," their father said, clearly puzzled, "I don't remember these from the family albums, either. Where did you find them?"

Tesla spared only the briefest glance at the album as she got up from the table and stood by her chair, poised for flight. "I didn't *get* them anywhere," she said. "I don't know anything about that photo album."

Dr. Abbott looked confused. "It says right here—" he broke off and rummaged on the floor for the scrap of paper that held the shipping label. "Here it is," he said, the torn label in his hand turned toward her so she could see. "Tesla Abbott is listed as the sender, from this address. Three days ago."

Thanks she saw Max mime in her direction, but she ignored him. "Sorry Dad; I did *not* send you this. I—I didn't do anything for your birthday."

She thought he looked hurt, but for such a brief instant she decided she'd imagined it.

"Well, no big deal," he said evenly. "I suppose it's a mystery." He got up and moved to the counter for more soda.

"Not really," Tesla hissed at Max, her voice low with suppressed outrage. "I can't believe you got Dad a present and sent it to him from me. That is *so* not cool!"

"I didn't—" Max began, but she got up in a huff and marched out of the room.

Upstairs, Tesla lay on her back on the bed. She stared up at the ceiling and fumed while the blades of the fan slowly turned to generate a faint stir in the air. *This is a bad idea*, she thought. To lay flat on her back in bed, do nothing, and feel like the unluckiest girl in the world could only remind her of that excruciatingly long week in the hospital last fall, and the humiliating event that had put her there. She had been right in the middle of two-on-two after school— she was literally on the court playing before varsity practice started and Keisha would have to go—when it happened. Tesla and Keisha were running the same pick-and-roll they'd done a thousand times together, perfectly in sync, the echo of the ball as it pounded the hardwood and the squeak of rubber soles on the polished floor so familiar she barely noticed them. And then suddenly Tesla had been slammed in the chest, but from the inside: dizzy and disoriented, her heart had tried to pound its way out of her body. She dropped the ball, stopped dead in her tracks, and her defender actually ran into her, instead of into Keisha, as planned, and had to grab Tesla hard to keep them both on their feet. Tesla heard the coach's whistle from the other court, where the freshman girls' team was busy with a three-on-two drill, but it sounded like it was a long way off, or as if she were in a tunnel. She put her hands on her knees and bent forward, her eyes closed, as she tried to breathe and fight the dizziness while sweat poured off her body.

"Tesla? You okay?" asked Keisha as she approached, and if Tesla hadn't felt like she would hurl any minute she certainly would have ridiculed the unusually gentle and timid tone of her best friend's voice. Keisha could make money as a female power-and-assertiveness trainer. The fact that she sounded so un-Keisha-like at that moment gave Tesla some idea of what she must look like: pale, damp with sweat, eyes closed and short of breath, none of which was due to her drive to the hoop.

Coach Winters had walked over from the sidelines, put her hand on Tesla's shoulder, and asked if she was okay. Tesla opened her mouth to speak, glanced up at the coach, and immediately closed her eyes again, tight, as she fought off another wave of dizziness.

Great, Tesla had thought. *Maybe I'll puke right here, with half the guy's basketball team watching from the bleachers. That will really make my junior year complete.*

Coach Winters put Keisha in charge of drills and walked Tesla to the office with her arm wrapped tightly across her shoulders. Each of the coach's hands had gripped one of Tesla's arms to steady and support her as the shaken girl made her zombie-like way out of the gym and down the hall. Once they were in the office, Tesla slumped into the nearest chair while the coach conferred with the secretary and the principal, Mr. Dietrich. They spoke in low voices, with an occasional glance in Tesla's direction, but she was still dizzy, with an odd buzz in her head. Her stomach lurched threateningly. She couldn't have deciphered the words—or their meanings—if she'd wanted to. All she could think about was how soon she'd be able to lie down, keep her eyes closed, and do nothing while her heart slowed to normal and her head and stomach quit with the gymnastics.

"Miss Abbott? How do you feel?" asked a woman's voice.

Tesla turned her head, slowly and carefully, and squinted up at the woman. Gray-streaked brown hair in a poofy style, a suit jacket over a frilly, high-collared blouse. And garish lipstick, the only off-note in an otherwise completely repressed look. Mrs. Babbit, the high school guidance counselor. The one whose job was to understand the students, relate to them on their own terms.

Brilliant staffing decision, Tesla thought.

She closed her eyes, put her head in her hands again and swallowed once, loudly. "I don't feel very well," she managed.

"I can see that. Do you have any flu-like symptoms? Fever, sore throat, muscle pain, headache?" Babbit leaned in, too close, and peered at Tesla.

Tesla shook her head gingerly, unsure if she'd moved it enough for Babbit to get that her answer was *No*.

"Then I have to ask…have you taken anything you shouldn't? Smoked some marijuana maybe, swallowed some pills?"

Tesla couldn't help it, she had to look at Babbit, even if she threw up. "Are you serious?" she asked, incredulous. She swallowed again to keep the bile down. "I was playing basketball when this happened. No, I'm not high."

Babbit patted Tesla's knee, her pudgy fingers alarmingly, unnaturally orange against the girl's milk-white skin.

Gross. Mrs. Babbit in a tanning bed, Tesla thought, immediately desperate to get the image out of her head.

"Of course not," Babbit said. Then another idea occurred to

her. "Could you be pregnant?"

Tesla was certain the woman sounded hopeful. "No, I couldn't be pregnant," she snapped. "Can I go home now?"

"Well, actually, given your symptoms we really are required to administer a drug test, so if you could take this specimen cup and…"

"I will not pee in a cup for you!" Tesla said too loudly, as she stood up too quickly. She couldn't breathe, and a wave of dizziness washed over her, a loss of all orientation, as if she spun slowly and unstoppably through space. She remained conscious just long enough to marvel at the sensation. Her vision went to black from the outside in, and the last thing she remembered was the floor rising up to meet her.

Tesla had woken up in the ambulance, though it had taken her a minute to realize where she was. She had a mask on over her nose and mouth, and her wrist was held gently by a paramedic who looked rather like Peter Petrelli on *Heroes*, his thick dark hair parted on the side, old-school—*rakish*, Max would have said.

The paramedic reached out with his other hand and pulled the mask up to rest on top of her head.

"Great hair," she said weakly, immediately horrified as she heard herself. She had definitely not meant to say that out loud.

"Thanks," he said. He flashed a crooked, totally hot smile. "How do you feel?"

"Okay. Weird."

"That's to be expected." He pulled the rubber-capped ends of the stethoscope up from around his neck and placed them in his ears. "I'm going to listen to your heart now. Try to relax."

He deftly maneuvered the cold metallic end of the stethoscope underneath the rounded neckline of Tesla's sleeveless basketball jersey, her lucky number twenty-three from the King

James days of the Cavs. The paramedic frowned, and Tesla had a moment of panic. *What if he can't hear my heart through my sports bra?* she thought. *What if I have to take it off?*

"What?" she asked, alarmed.

"Do you have a heart condition?"

"No," she said immediately. "I'm perfectly healthy."

"Okay, good," the paramedic replied. "We're almost at University Hospital, and they'll run some tests to determine why you fainted."

"I fainted?" Tesla asked. Her voice sounded young and pathetic, even to her.

"Yup. Passed out cold in the principal's office. You landed on your face—there's a nasty cut over your eyebrow. You need stitches, and they'll want to look at you for concussion, too."

He turned then to talk to the driver, and Tesla slowly moved her hand up to her face to touch her forehead. The thick gauze bandage there couldn't conceal the egg-sized lump over her eye. It hurt to touch and, unexpectedly, tears sprang to her eyes. *Because I'm not already embarrassed enough*, Tesla thought, *clearly I need to cry in front of the cute paramedic to round out this perfect day.*

The ambulance slowed perceptibly and came to a stop just before the doors were opened from the outside. Tesla felt like she could probably walk now, since the dizziness had subsided a bit, but that was apparently not an option. She remained strapped to the gurney as the paramedic waved goodbye after he'd briefed the triage nurses and handed Tesla over, along with some paperwork, and then someone in green scrubs wheeled her in through the automatic doors in the ambulance bay. She closed her eyes against the sudden glare of fluorescent lights overhead, as bright and omnipresent as the sun a few months earlier when her dad had made her and Max go to Mexico with him for some scientists' conference. The gurney's industrial-size wheels clacked rhythmically down the hall, but they had seemed to Tesla to have nothing to do with her, lying there in the Acapulco sun. She felt disconnected from the bed beneath her, in need of no material support as she glided along on thin air.

Wait, she remembered thinking. *That can't be right. I'm not in Mexico, and that's not the sun.*

And yet she had floated into the hospital, moved through space and time upon the very light that seemed to suffuse every particle of the universe.

CHAPTER 4

After what felt like half a day, but was probably less than an hour of self-pity over that awful day, Tesla opened her bedroom door cautiously and listened.

Silence.

No sound of movement or conversation, no sound from the TV in the family room. She started down the staircase and, when she encountered no one, entered the kitchen. Both her dad and Max seemed to have deserted her, which worked well for everyone. Half of the pizza was still in the box on the table, cooled but perfectly acceptable, and Tesla took a slice—she had eaten nothing earlier— and bit into it while she stood next to the chair her father had so recently occupied.

With a casual flip of the photo album's cover, she absently turned the pages while she chewed. *Me and Dad,* she thought, surprised at how young and happy he looked as he watched her little-girl-self build a castle in the sandbox. *Max, still in diapers—and Dad making some goofy face at him. God, what a dork. Me, peeking at Max between the bars of his crib.* Tesla felt a sense of familiarity as she looked at the furniture, the pictures on the walls, and the yard in the old photos, though she had no clear memories of them. It was more like she remembered that she used to remember that house, the house across town no one ever mentioned. The house they'd lived in when there were four of them. She turned the last page and froze, the pizza halfway to her mouth. A single photo held the place of honor, the last picture in the album, centered on the final page.

Her mother. Dr. Tasya Petrova-Abbott, a physicist, like her husband. Dead at thirty four, eight long years ago.

Tesla put her slice of pizza on top of the box and slid down into the chair, her eyes fixed on the picture of her mother. Like her father, she didn't remember this photo, but she couldn't seem to dwell on the questions that raised, not while the hole in her gut she'd thought had closed opened again into a bright blossom of pain. Tasya Petrova appeared unaware of the photographer's presence as she stood in a white lab coat, the chalk in her hand half raised to the blackboard in front of her as she contemplated a string of mathematical equations that made no sense to Tesla, though she was something of a math wiz. Her mother's straight, chin-length auburn hair hung softly by the sides of her face, tucked behind her ears for convenience rather than beauty. But a beauty she was, with her high cheekbones and firm jaw, her wide-set green eyes behind black-framed glasses whose heaviness served only to highlight her soft mouth, lips slightly parted as she concentrated on the problem in front of her.

Her mother had been beautiful, and brilliant. People said Tesla looked like her, but she rarely saw it, except for their similar coloring. They both had unusually fair skin, without a freckle or a hint of ruddiness, though Tesla's hair was a much lighter, brighter red, thick and curly, not fine as silk like her mother's had been. Tesla's curls were her father's contribution to the gene pool, which gave her one more thing to resent him for; she would have preferred Tasya's smooth, deeply auburn hair, her chiseled, Eastern

European bone structure and slightly hooded eyes the color of lichen in a cool, primeval forest. Tesla's differently-colored eyes were a genetic mutation, and she never could settle on whether she liked them or not, since people told her they were beautiful, but strange. Those eyes might have been a bonus if the rest of her face looked like her mother's, but she was unhappily aware that her carrot-top hair and oval, child-like face made her look even younger than she was, and she feared the strange eyes thrown into that particular mix just made her odd at best, comical at worst.

Tesla closed the album, sick of herself, sick of these thoughts. She felt restless and depressed by both the pictures and the way she'd left things with Max. She hated to fight—even with her dad, and wished everyone would just leave her alone. Live and let live, that was what she usually tried for, but tonight—tonight, with these unexplained photographs, with this particular photograph—her usual restlessness was cranked up to eleven. She put the leftover pizza in the fridge and folded up the cardboard box for recycling, perhaps as a gesture of apology—it was likely the only one she would offer her father. When she moved the flattened box toward her, however, she saw that her father had left her a note, partially hidden beneath the box.

Tesla, sorry for the misunderstanding about the photo album. It's probably from Aunt Jane, she was around a lot back then, and often with a camera in her hand. And the shipping label was probably a simple mistake by some clerk. I brought work home—I'll be upstairs grading papers unless I have to go back to campus. We can talk in the morning. Dad

At the sound of footsteps, Tesla looked up from the note and saw Max in the doorway with a backpack slung over his shoulder.

"Dad's upstairs working," he said, his face and voice

carefully neutral.

Tesla gently waved the paper in her hand. "Yeah, he left me a note. Where are you off to?"

"Spending the night with Dylan. His mom's on her way to pick me up."

"Oh," was all she could muster in response. She knew it was contradictory, but despite her desire for solitude, Tesla felt decidedly abandoned.

"So, see you later," Max said. He hesitated, half-turned to walk out the front door.

"Don't forget to brush your teeth—and don't stay up too late," she said automatically. "And try not to crush Dylan so badly in Warcraft. He won't want to play with you anymore."

"Okay," said Max, happy again. A car horn sounded from the driveway and he left, a sharply off-key whistle forced through his front teeth as he shut the front door.

Tesla finished the dishes, put the cardboard pizza box, along with the paper napkins and her father's note, which she had wadded up altogether in a ball, into the recycling bin. She wandered into the living room. *What a weird couple of days,* she thought. *First those creeps at that party, and Keisha's cousin Finn being such a jerk, and now this birthday present for Dad, and nobody knows where it came from....*

"I need to get out of the house," she said aloud, pulling her phone out of her back pocket.

Keisha's cell went right to voicemail, so Tesla tried Malcolm. He picked up on the first ring.

"What's up?"

"I'm bored, plus cabin fever, plus a big fight with my dad and Max."

"I have just the cure," he assured her.

"Pizza?"

"Pizza."

"I actually already had a slice," she said reluctantly.

"So? What's that got to do with it?"

Tesla considered that for a moment. "True enough. Angelo's in ten?"

"Meet you there," he said, and the line went dead.

Malcolm and she had been friends forever—he wasn't Keisha, but then, nobody was. Both of the girls could always count on Mal, and he was really upbeat—annoyingly so, sometimes. He had an *indefatigable* spirit, as Max would say, whose word-of-the-day calendar that Aunt Jane had given him last Christmas had become a gift the whole family got to enjoy. Every. Single. Day.

Tesla had met Keisha and Malcolm in third grade when she'd had to transfer to another school, and they had become immediately inseparable—until freshman year when Malcolm had stopped being a part of their frequent sleepovers. The parents of all three of them had seemed to agree at the same precise moment that they were too old for co-ed slumber parties. Consequently, the girls had gotten closer the last few years, with Malcolm sometimes like a third wheel. Still, nobody knew Tesla the way her two best friends did, and if Keisha wasn't around, Malcolm was hands-down the next best thing.

Cheered up by the anticipation of being cheered up, Tesla walked the three blocks from her house to the town square which, as was typical for an old but thriving university town, had been charmingly refurbished and was now totally gentrified. There was a gazebo in the open park at the center of the square where live music was often staged, and an eclectic collection of businesses in the old brick and stone buildings that surrounded it on all four sides. There were coffee shops, bookstores, bars, vintage clothing stores, and a dozen ethnic restaurants, including several vegan options.

Angelo's was their preferred hangout.

The tiny pizza shop was an institution; it had been in business since before Tesla was born and, as far as she knew, had always looked exactly the same as it did now. She opened the glass front door and took in the familiar sight of the crowded room, the smells of garlic and sharp cheeses, bubbly tomato sauce and spicy meats. There were only a few tables up front by the door, and a counter with three barstools that ran along the front glass-paned wall and faced the square, where one could simultaneously perch, munch on a slice, and people-watch. Most of the room was taken up by an open kitchen, and customers lined up, single file, and pointed out what they wanted as they moved their trays along the high counter. The servers lifted each wide, over-loaded slice onto a wooden paddle and slid it into the oven until it was crisp and melty, then plated it and laid it on the counter under the glass partition for the customer to take and move on.

Tesla spotted Malcolm just as he saw her at the door, and they both got in line.

"What's up?" asked Malcolm. "Big fight, or small one?"

"Small, I guess," Tesla admitted. "But it always seems like a big one in the moment. Plus," she added, "my dad got an old photo album with pictures of us all—my mom, too—from UPS today. The label said it was from me, which it wasn't, and nobody remembers any of the pictures."

"That is weird," said Malcolm. "You didn't send it?"

"I'd certainly remember if I'd mailed my dad a birthday present. From our house, to our house, no less."

"Order?" barked the young man behind the counter. The employees at Angelo's hated to have to ask for an order, especially from regulars, who should know better.

"One slice of chicken-bacon-ranch," said Tesla.

"Make it four," corrected Malcolm, who added "I haven't had anything to eat since lunch," when Tesla looked at him.

They redeemed themselves in the eyes of the pizza gods by having their money out and their drink orders ready at the register, and then Tesla and Malcolm sat down at the only unoccupied table. It was stuck in the corner up near the front, wedged between the end of the kitchen and the rest of the tables that were not against the wall. Nineteen people stood, ate pizza and talked, or headed toward the counter again. Once Tesla and Malcolm sat down, neither of them could see much beyond the bodies that crowded around their table. This human wall effectively blocked the view and created a false sense of privacy.

Malcolm picked up his first slice. "So," he began. "Weird party the other night, huh?"

"I'll say," Tesla agreed. "The house was weird, the people who live there were weird. Those creepy orc-guys were weird."

Malcolm chuckled appreciatively while he ate. "Saruman orcs, or Sauron orcs?"

"Okay, you're as big a dork as Max is."

"Hey, you referenced the trilogy, not me," he pointed out, his gray eyes opened wide under suddenly arched brows.

"Seriously, though, what do you think that was all about?"

Malcolm shrugged. "Who knows? They were idiots. They took a shine to you."

"Oh, thanks. How flattering. And 'took a shine' to me?" She laughed, and a deep dimple appeared in each of her cheeks.

"Yeah, you know. You're cute." Malcolm shrugged, his eyes on his pizza

"What'd I miss?" asked Keisha, who had suddenly materialized beside their table.

"Mal broke his own record. He's eaten five pounds of food in just under three minutes," Tesla offered. "So far."

"I'm a growing boy," Malcolm protested.

Keisha grabbed an empty chair from a nearby table and deftly wielded it in front of her, which forced several people to move aside and left room for her to sit.

"You hungry?" asked Malcolm. "I can head up and get you a slice."

Tesla laughed. "You know he wants to go back up himself, and you're just an excuse so he doesn't look like a pig."

Mal tried—and failed—to look offended.

"Nah, I can't stay," said Keisha. "Saw you two from the window. Thought I'd say hi—I haven't seen you since the party."

"The birthday party that wasn't a birthday party, you mean?" said Mal, popping the final bite of his second slice into his mouth. He dusted off his hands with finality.

"Yeah, exactly," said Keisha. "What's up with you, T?"

Tesla told Keisha about the photo album and the fight with her dad and Max, but while she talked she couldn't help but notice that her best friend seemed distracted—hardly listening at all, actually, and then Keisha stood up abruptly.

"That's weird about the pictures, for sure, but I gotta go. Glad to see you're okay after the other night—no adverse effects from all the excitement. I'll call you later."

Confused, Tesla watched Keisha weave her way toward the door. The crowd parted suddenly in one of those random movements that seem orchestrated and Tesla found herself with a brief, clear view of the front window of the pizzeria and the barstools that stood at the counter and overlooked the town square. The stool on the far left, just like the others, was occupied, but unlike the others, its occupant faced inward toward the restaurant rather than toward the window.

It was Finnegan Ford. He stared right at Tesla as Keisha walked by him, lightly bumped his fist with her own, and walked out the door.

CHAPTER 5

Tesla got up from the table and headed straight for Finn. "Why are you here?" she demanded.

Finn raised an eyebrow. "Dinner. You?" His slight smile mocked her.

"Yeah, I'm here eating, and so's Malcolm," Tesla replied. She scowled at Finn and hooked her thumb back at Malcolm, who sat right where she'd left him. Mal grinned sheepishly and waved at Finn, who ignored him.

"Are you following me?" Tesla asked.

Finn put his pizza down on the paper plate, wiped his mouth and hands with his napkin and—finally—looked at Tesla in amusement. His brown curls sprang out in every direction, his eyes, golden-bronze, were hard and bright and clearly amused. "I'm sure you do it for the high school boys, but—seriously. Get over yourself."

Tesla could feel the blood suffuse her face and she silently cursed him for his ridiculously good looks, his overblown confidence. She felt like the village idiot by comparison. *Focus*, she thought. *Something's not right here.*

"I didn't mean—I saw Keisha—oh, forget it." Tesla turned

on her heel to go back to her table, a big incoherent ball of humiliation and anger. She mumbled under her breath something that sounded suspiciously like *d-bag*.

She heard Finn laugh behind her as she stomped over to her chair and sat down opposite Malcolm, who looked confused.

"What was that all about?" he asked as he drained the last of his soda.

"I don't know." She pushed her plate away in irritation.

"What'd Finn have to say?" he persisted.

"Nothing," she said. "Nothing except that I'm not his type, and that I should 'get over myself' for thinking he was following me." She fumed and waited for Mal to jump in on her side.

"You think he's following you?" asked Malcolm.

"No, Mal." Tesla picked up her plastic fork and stabbed the crust on her plate for emphasis. "I *asked* him if he was following me. A question is not a statement. Totally different things."

"You can't be serious," Malcolm said. "Why would he be following you?"

"I don't know," Tesla wailed. She leaned forward, her eyes lowered miserably to the tabletop so that all Malcolm could see was the thick, dark fringe of her eyelashes against her skin, still warmly pink from embarrassment. "Keisha breezed in and right back out, and she was so distracted, and then she walked past Finn like she didn't see him, but I know she did, and…what about that party the other night?" Tesla stared at him, dared him to contradict her. "There was something off. And there's something off about Finn. I know it."

"Well, he's gone now, so forget about it," Malcolm assured her.

"He is?" Tesla craned her neck to see through the crowd.

"Yeah, he left before you even got back to your chair. You

seem disappointed," he added, his voice carefully noncommittal.

"No, I'm relieved. I think he's a jerk," Tesla stated emphatically.

They sat for a few more minutes, until Tesla sighed. "I better head back home," she said. "I didn't tell anyone I was headed out."

"Do you usually?" asked Malcolm, flicking his silvery bangs out of his eyes.

"I usually text my dad. If he wonders, he can just check his phone. Saves us both from an actual conversation."

"Text him, then. Tell him you're with me."

"No, I'm gonna go. I guess I still feel bad about the fight earlier."

Malcolm shrugged. "Okay. I'll see you." When they got outside he turned to head back to his house, which lay in the opposite direction of Tesla's.

"See you," Tesla called after him.

She had only gone seventeen steps, however, had just passed the front of Angelo's and the red brick of the bookstore next door, when she heard a voice from the shadows under the store's awning.

"Tesla," said Finn as he stepped into the light. "Over here."

"What do you want?" she asked, startled.

"Just wanted to say sorry for my 'd-bag' behavior." It was an apology, technically, but he was clearly laughing at her. "You surprised me, that's all," he continued. "I'm usually not that rude."

"Could've fooled me." Tesla increased her speed and walked past him.

Finn was beside her in an instant and his long legs kept her pace effortlessly. He wore fitted, skinny black jeans, a worn pair of Adidas Sambas, and a black T-shirt. His arms swung easily by his side, and Tesla wondered if he ever felt even slightly self-conscious, under any circumstances. His cool confidence was *not* attractive, she told herself, it was an irritation—almost as much of an irritation as her own hyper-awareness of the mere eight and a half inches that separated them.

"I wasn't following you, but I was glad to see you at Angelo's. I've been worried about you since the other night," he said. "Those guys must've shaken you up. And—for the record—I asked Keisha to check on you just now."

Tesla hesitated, though she was relieved to learn her suspicions of Keisha were unfounded. She'd already learned not to be candid with Finn or he'd turn it against her, make her feel like a fool.

"Yeah," she shrugged. "I'm fine. Nothing happened, really."

Finn glanced at her as they walked. "Good," he said. "I thought you might not be, ah, up to that kind of excitement."

Tesla stopped and turned on him, her eyes narrowed. "What's that supposed to mean?"

Finn raised his hands, his palms up in surrender as he tried to back-pedal. "Nothing—man! I wasn't insulting you, or making fun of you—not this time, anyway—it's just that I noticed that Keisha and that other kid—"

"—Malcolm," Tesla inserted.

"—and Malcolm," Finn continued smoothly, "seemed concerned about you, and you looked kind of shaky and pale."

"I'm always pale," said Tesla.

"No, you're always fair-skinned," he countered. "But your cheeks are kind of pinkish, right there." He made as if to touch her face, and Tesla snapped her head back two inches, just out of his reach. "The other night you were pale," he explained, but he dropped his hand back down to his side. "There's a difference."

Tesla could feel herself blush and began walking again,

looking straight ahead and hoping the dusk in between the now-lit lampposts along the sidewalk hid this fact from Finn, who stayed right beside her.

"Maybe I just seemed that way compared to you and Keisha," she mumbled.

"Well, obviously," he said. "The black girl and her biracial cousin make you seem even lighter. But that's not the point."

When she didn't reply, Finn changed the subject. "So, what's your story? There is a story, right?"

They had stopped again, beside a wrought iron and wood-slat bench on the edge of the park in the center of town. The bench was nestled cozily between blooming hydrangeas, the deep purple-blue bunches of flowers like party balloons in the summer night. Two lampposts, twenty feet away on either side of the bench, cast a soft light that didn't quite reach them.

Finn gestured toward the bench, and after a brief hesitation, Tesla sat down and Finn joined her, his arm along the back of the bench, his fingers three inches from Tesla's right shoulder.

"Yeah, there's a story, but it's not that interesting," she began hesitantly.

"I'll find it interesting," he said, his voice serious for the first time.

Tesla thought for a minute. She could feel the pulse in her throat and Finn's eyes on her face as he waited. "Long story short, I have an arrhythmia—an irregular, too-fast heartbeat. I found out in October. I couldn't play basketball for a while, which I used to do a lot—with your cousin—but nothing has happened since, so I'm allowed to do the stuff I did before. Or at least work back up to it." She hated to seem fragile or weak. "It's no big deal."

"But you have to be careful, right? Because it *could* be a big deal." When she looked at him with suspicion, he hurried on.

"Keisha told me a little about it, last fall when it happened."

Tesla searched his face, but could see no sign of ridicule. All she saw were warm, sympathetic brown eyes focused intently on her own. The slight flick of his gaze moved from one side of her face to the other. Searching.

"Yup, that's me," she said lightly. "I need to ask the wizard for a heart."

Finn was quiet for a moment. "And your mom died, right?"

"How do you know that?" she asked slowly.

"Keisha."

"Why would Keisha talk to you about me?" she demanded, her body tensed in preparation to leave.

"Whoa, whoa," said Finn, hand out to stall her. "She doesn't, at least not any more than she mentions stuff about anybody. It's not gossip, you're her best friend. And I'm pretty sure she only told me that about you because it's something we have in common."

"Your mom died, too?" Tesla asked as surprise trumped anger.

"No, not exactly. My dad—he's not dead, at least as far as I know, but he's never been a part of my life. And my mom works internationally, so I've spent a lot of time alone. I know what it's like to not have your parents around."

"Oh." For the life of her, Tesla couldn't think of a single thing to add.

"Not that I don't enjoy the freedom," he said, that faint swagger back in his voice. "No bedtime when I was a kid, and no curfew later when I got older. Totally worth it."

He seemed to be bragging, but Tesla didn't buy it.

"Sounds lonely," she said. "So where are they—your parents?"

"My mom's in Kenya, I think. She works for the World

Health Organization. And Daniel Finnegan—the sperm donor, basically—lives in Ireland. Dublin," he added with a shrug.

"So that's where—"

"Yeah," he said, but his sudden smile held neither warmth nor humor. "That's where my name comes from. Finnegan's not exactly a typical name in the black community. He and my mother met twenty years ago somewhere, were together for a couple of weeks, and the rest is history. She saddled me with his name— evidence that she has a sense of humor, if nothing else—and then took off to save the world as soon as I was old enough to go to school. I know, I know, it's heartwarming—you're jealous, aren't you?"

Beneath the sharp quips Tesla sensed a depth of sadness in him that she could not even begin to address, and hastened to bring the story back onto solid ground. "So your mom and Keisha's mom are—"

"—sisters," he finished for her, and then they fell silent for a moment. "They both went into medicine. Keisha's mom's a surgical nurse, as you know, and my mom's a doctor. Infectious diseases. She works mostly in Africa. I went to school all over the place, but I did most of secondary school—high school—in London. That's where I met Joley. He decided to come here for undergrad and law school, and I tagged along. He's family, for me. And Keisha's here, so I figured, why not?"

Tesla weighed his words and heard the things he didn't say—that he didn't want to drift anymore, maybe even that he wanted to belong to someone.

"That's pretty much my whole story," he concluded lightly, in control of the moment again so quickly that Tesla wondered if she'd imagined his vulnerability. "How about you—what's with your name?"

"What do you mean?" Tesla asked, confused.

"I mean, what is 'Tesla'—does it mean something?"

"Kind of," she said. "My mom was Russian, and her father was a physicist in St. Petersburg—it was Leningrad, then. She grew up with stories of European scientists like most people grow up with stories about their crazy Aunt Alice. She always liked Nikola Tesla, a Serbian guy, I think, who did a bunch of groundbreaking work with electromagnetism."

"Really," said Finn, a puzzled look on his face. "Most people get named after a grandparent or a movie star."

Tesla smiled, and her dimples dug deep into her smooth cheeks. "I know. Not us, though. I was named Tesla Nikola Petrova Abbott. By the end of his career, Nikola Tesla was pretty much insane, so you can imagine how thrilled I am to be named after him. My mom used to sit with me on her lap and tell me that Tesla successfully took a picture of the bones of his hand before the X-ray was invented. And that he destroyed his own skin from exposure to various kinds of radiation. Gross, huh? My little brother Max's full name is Maximilian Planck Petrova Abbott." She shrugged, anticipating Finn's laughter. "They are—were—a little odd, my parents."

"Planck, the quantum mechanics guy?" Finn asked, no trace of laughter in his voice.

"Yeah," she said, still unsure whether she should trust him not to make fun of her. "I think Einstein based some of his work on Planck."

The conversation seemed to have died a natural death, but it didn't feel particularly uncomfortable to Tesla, which surprised her. She didn't really sit still much, even conversationally—she was restless by nature and preferred to keep moving.

The occasional pedestrian, alone or in a small group, strolled by or cut across the park. They added a soft murmur of footsteps and muted voices to the evening, which had cooled considerably. Tesla shivered in her sapphire blue tank top as a breeze played gently with the ends of her hair, making them dance around her shoulders. She wrapped her arms around herself and hugged her elbows in tight.

"Cold?" Finn asked. He moved his hand from the back of the bench to her shoulder. The skin of his fingertips felt hot against the edge òf her collarbone.

"No, I'm good." Tesla dropped her hands into her lap and leaned back until his hand fell away.

"So what was it like when you first found out about the arrhythmia—in October, you said?"

"Why do you want to hear about this?" She asked, relieved to feel suspicious again. She felt better when she was at odds with him. "You were a total jerk when I met you, you know. You snarled at me to get lost, told me not to come back, and then *deliberately* misunderstood me tonight so you could make me feel like an ass."

"Okay, I deserve that, I guess," he conceded. He rubbed his hand over the stubble on his chin. "It's possible I wasn't at my most charming when we met the other night—usually, everyone loves me immediately." He paused, just long enough for her to snort in derision. He smiled and continued. "I had a lot on my mind, and I took it out on you guys. But I am interested. In your story," he added quickly. "I'm a journalism major."

"What, you're writing a term paper on the lives of teenaged girls?" she asked.

Finn threw his head back and laughed with genuine spontaneity. His smile flashed in the dusk, and Tesla realized that until this moment she had not seem him relaxed or lighthearted. Despite his composure, his cool-guy smoothness, he carried a tension in his body, a mental or psychological seriousness of some kind that was as pitiable as it was intriguing.

"No," he said, still chuckling. "I just meant I like true stories. I like to know what makes people tick, why they do what they do. If you understand people's motives and histories, there's very little you can't figure out."

"Well there's nothing to figure out here." She hoped he would grow bored and change the subject. "I passed out while I was playing basketball after school—not what you want to do in a gym full of people, most of them athletes, when you just play a little for fun. I'm not even on the team. It was totally humiliating, and I wound up in the hospital for a week."

"Wow. How long were you unconscious?" Finn asked.

"Well, actually, I just felt dizzy in the gym. I fainted in the principal's office, not on the court. I had to go to the hospital, and they kept me overnight, at first just for concussion. I got stitches, see?" She moved her hair and turned her face just slightly into the faint light behind Finn so he could see the fine white line that ran into the dark, silky auburn of her eyebrow.

"Yeah, I see," he said softly. He moved his hand slowly toward her face, then ran his thumb along her brow, over the scar, the tips of his fingers just touching the side of her face for the briefest of moments.

"Then they detected the heart problem," she rushed on, "kept me longer for tests, discovered the arrhythmia, blah blah blah. Turns out my dad knew about it, but I guess the pediatrician when I was a baby said it was no big deal. End of story."

"Huh," Finn said, apparently deep in thought.

"I told you it wasn't much of a story," she said quickly, confused by his nearness, the ease with which he touched her, the intense response she felt when he did.

"No, actually it is," he assured her. "But I suspect there's more. What was it like in the hospital? I've never had reason to go." He knocked on the wooden seat of the bench for good measure.

Tesla shrugged. "I was bored, mostly. I watched *Gilmore Girls* reruns and slept a lot. My head hurt. The concussion made me...I don't know," she said, hesitant. "It was just weird."

"How do you mean?" Finn leaned in toward her.

"At some point in the middle of the night after I was admitted, I did something really stupid."

"I doubt that—you seem like a reasonably intelligent person."

"Gee, thanks," she said. "I guess it wasn't my fault—I did have a concussion—but it makes me feel stupid now. Or maybe I was a little bit crazy that night. The world seemed...I don't know. Different."

In fact, Tesla had awoken around three o'clock in the morning, when the whole world is asleep and it feels daring just to be awake. No longer disoriented, she felt strong, clear-headed, even.

"The doctors had at that point found some problem with the electrical activity in my heart," Tesla continued. "They said I'd have to stay for a few days while they ran more tests and figured out what it all meant. They told me to rest, to let them get to the bottom of it."

"Sounds like a good plan," Finn encouraged.

"Yeah, well. I'm not always good at following directions," Tesla admitted. She missed the smile that pulled one side of Finn's mouth up for just a moment.

"So what was the stupid thing you did?" he asked.

Tesla not only didn't like to talk about it, she didn't like to think about it—but did, far too often. The puzzle of it all nagged at her, hung around at the edges of her consciousness. That night in the hospital she had felt that her perceptions were sharper, more accurate. She sensed, rather than heard, the few people who padded along on rubber-soled shoes as they carried out their silent, night-shift duties. She felt the weight of the entire building around her, the floors above, and below. The mechanics of it all thrummed along, the ductwork and the ventilation, the generators and the electricity that powered the lights and machines, while the sensors hooked up to all the sick people monitored their vital signs, the beep and hum and whir of them like so many sleeping children.

"You have to understand, my head wasn't right," she said quickly. "I was hooked up to this machine, a heart monitor, and the wires seemed like tentacles attached at my neck, my chest, my temple, my thigh. It was alive and we were, you know, plugged in to each other. *Symbiotic.* The monitor was small and portable, the size of one of those old clock radios, and bolted to a wheeled pole like the ones they hang I.V. bags on. It was powered by an ion battery so I could get up and move around. I woke up in the middle of the night, and I felt great. I had this sudden urge to get out of my room, to find the heart of the giant, pulsing hospital, and my monitor was on wheels, so why not, I thought?"

Finn was silent, and Tesla tried to explain what even she found inexplicable. "It all seemed so perfectly natural, like that's what I was *supposed* to do. I felt this energy in and around me from everywhere at once. I can't explain it."

I can *explain it,* she thought, though she would never say it out loud. *That energy—it called to me. I had to answer.*

CHAPTER 6

Tesla paused, distracted when Finn waved a hand to shoo a mosquito that buzzed around his ear. It was so dark now that his face was in shadow, though the lamplight from behind him had turned his wild hair into a shimmering halo around the edges. She wondered if this story made her seem even younger or sillier than he already thought her.

"I know this is crazy," she said. "It sounds crazy, doesn't it?"

"Actually, it sounds like an incredible experience," Finn said.

"No, it sounds crazy," she corrected him. "I've only told Keisha what happened that night, and never all of it, even to her. I mean, how could I know perfectly well that I had a concussion—which definitely messes with your head—and simultaneously believe that what I thought and felt were real?"

"Not everything can be neatly explained," Finn said. He reached up and absently caught one long tendril of her hair that had been caught by the breeze and blown toward him. He held onto it, tethered her to him.

Breathe, Tesla reminded herself. She wondered why he had such an effect on her, and then Finn released her hair, their connection broken.

"What happened then?" he asked.

Tesla closed her eyes. Remembered. She had peeled back her covers and sat up, slowly, looked toward the half-closed door of her hospital room where the bright light of the hallway sliced into the darkness. The light had looked strange, diffused. "I put on my favorite robe—"

"I thought you came in an ambulance straight from school. You had your favorite robe?" Finn asked, and Tesla saw that he was, indeed, a journalist.

Unexpectedly, she grinned. "Keisha brought it to me from my house the second she got out of school. She said some perv designed hospital gowns so that sick and doped-up people, who maybe wouldn't notice, would have horrifying wardrobe malfunctions all over the hospital for the amusement of the interns."

"That's Keisha, alright," Finn said, his affection for his cousin apparent in his voice.

"Anyway, I wanted to get out of that room, but I didn't want to get caught. I was supposed to stay in bed." When Tesla's feet had touched the icy, polished floor that night, the cool, solid texture against the soles of her bare feet braced her. It had felt marvelous just to be upright again. She took hold of the pole with the heart monitor and made her way to the door.

"I peered around the doorjamb and saw that the nurses' station was pretty far down the hall to the right," she said, "but just a few feet from my room on the other side was the elevator and, across from that, the door to the stairwell. I didn't see a soul, except for the bent head of someone who sat at the nurse's station." Tesla felt again the excitement of that moment, the thrill of escape. The beep of her heart monitor had been so soft she had felt certain no one would hear it.

"I made my way toward the elevator, but just before I pressed the Down button I realized that when the elevator arrived it would *ping*, and the nurse at the station would probably look up. So I decided to take the stairs."

"Pretty impressive presence of mind with a concussion," Finn commented.

"I know, right?" said Tesla, clearly proud of her Jason Bourne moment, despite the fact that she had already characterized the escapade as stupid.

"I got the door open and closed again behind me," she continued. "Then it was just me and my machine in the stairwell. That soft beep echoed around in the narrow space, and down I went. I was a little confused by how much of the building seemed to be underground. I mean, there are usually only one or two basement levels, right? But I walked down two hundred and eighty steps with my monitor before I started messing up the count. And by then my feet were really cold and I had to hold onto the railing. I was tired. I lost track of time, which is unusual for me." Unaware that her voice had changed tone, that she sounded anxious, even afraid, Tesla didn't notice Finn's intense look, she just stared at her hands in her lap.

"What happened?" he asked.

Tesla shrugged. "And then I was just at the bottom. There was a heavy, windowless metal door, wide open like I was supposed to go in, one of those key pad security system panels on the wall right next to it, and no one in sight."

They both heard the breathlessness in her voice, and Finn waited, expectantly.

"I paused for a sec, and then I walked right through the door."

"Nice," he said, approval and admiration clear in his voice.

"What was on the other side of the door?"

"That's when it all gets a little fuzzy. I stood for a minute and looked back up the stairs, confused. I couldn't really remember why I had come down there. I was just inside the open door and at the beginning of a hallway that couldn't have been there, because my hospital room was the last one on my floor in the corner of the building, and the stairwell was right next to my room."

"How could you be sure? Remember, you had a concussion," Finn pressed her for details, pushed her to remember, to think it through.

"I know. But I've been over it and over it, and concussion or not, I know where I was. I have a, um, highly developed sense of direction and spatial relationships," she added self-consciously.

"Spatial relationships?" he repeated, amused by her again. "Who says that? I'm not even sure I know what it means."

"You do, too," she said impatiently. "And it's not that hard to figure out if you don't."

"Explain it to me, this gift of yours," he said.

"I never said it was a gift," she said quickly.

"Still. Give me an example."

"Well, like with basketball," she said reluctantly, thankful that the gloom concealed her. "I'm no athlete—not like Keisha—but I—"

"But you what?" he encouraged when she hesitated.

"I just seem to know, instinctively I guess, where I am in relation to whatever is around me." *There*, she thought. *I said it.*

"How do you mean?" he asked.

"I never miss a shot," she said softly.

"Ever?"

"Ever." She looked at her hands in her lap. She downplayed this stuff with Keisha and Max, scoffed and denied when they couldn't help but comment on what they saw her do, consistently, over time. She was *not* a freak. And she had never—not even once—tried to tell anyone about this stuff. She had refused to try out for the team, despite Keisha's harangues their freshman year. She wasn't sure why she had decided to spill it to Finn, whom she didn't even know, but somehow it had just become part of the story that she was, for good or ill, telling him now.

"I can miss, of course," she said quickly. "But not if I really try. And I don't mean easy stuff—I'm talking hard shots. Impossible angles. Of course, if I'm too far away, if I don't have the upper body strength to actually get the ball to the hoop, I can't do it. Like I said, I'm not really an athlete. But my aim—my perspective and my depth perception and my calculations of distance, speed, arc—well, they're good, and they're sort of, um, instantaneous. I don't have to think about it, I just *know*."

Finn sat back and considered her for a moment. "Well, that's pretty cool," he said. "We'll have to play sometime."

Tesla smiled, a bit tentatively, but it was clear that she appreciated that he hadn't made a big deal out of it. "So where was I?"

"I think you were under the hospital. The corridor continued on even though you knew you were at the end of the building."

"Right. So after twenty feet or so the hallway should have ended and turned 90 degrees, because it had hit the exterior wall—you know, the end of the hospital building itself—just like every other floor on the South side." She paused and frowned. "So, clearly my story has no credibility, because it's impossible that that hallway continued."

"How do you know?" Finn asked.

"Because right next to the hospital is a huge green space, the university's quad, which is empty. There are no structures there.

And then, across the quad, a good two hundred yards away, is the physics building—I've been there a thousand times. My dad's classroom lab is there, his office, too, and I could navigate it, the hospital, the library, and student union with my eyes closed. I grew up here," she answered with absolute certainty.

"You're the one who said it couldn't have happened, not me," Finn pointed out.

Tesla cocked her head slightly to the side, considering this, and then nodded. "My concussion must have been worse than the doctors let on. It's the only explanation."

The darkness hid Finn's face from her, but she sensed his excitement, the breath he kept in check. She viewed her story as similar to the stories of dreams you have that, while perhaps exciting for you because you experienced it, not so much for the listener, who knows from the start that it was all a figment of your imagination. She was surprised that Finn was so caught up in it.

"What did you do?" he asked.

"I looked at that long, empty hallway that could not possibly be there," Tesla continued. "I knew I should go back to my room. I didn't know where I was. My head hurt. I was clearly in some kind of restricted area."

"So you went back to your room?"

"No. I began to walk down the hall."

"I see what you mean about not following directions,'" Finn said dryly.

Tesla ignored him. "It was a while before I realized that the sounds of the hospital were gone; there were no vibrations, no sense at all of the pervasive energy field I'd imagined myself a part of. There was only the sound of my heartbeat from the monitor, which glided along silently on the concrete floor. I passed no doors, no signage of any kind. The gash in my forehead throbbed, and then I came to the end of the hallway. On my left was a single, unmarked door with a simple lever-handle. I pushed it down, the door clicked, and swung inward without a sound. I walked through, wheeled my machine with me, and the door closed behind us."

"And?" Finn encouraged when she paused.

"And I stood there, shocked. I was in a huge, airplane-hanger size room, with scaffolding and lights above that were mostly off. Just like the hospital it seemed to be shut down for the night, though there was a small glow that came from the far right corner of the enormous space."

Tesla stopped then, unsure how to continue with the story, or even if she should. She remembered how she had walked toward the light and realized only when she was very close that it came from another structure within the massive cave, a low ceilinged room within the larger, cavernous space. The light came from a doorway, and she hadn't hesitated at all, but had walked right through it. Her way had been blocked by a huge piece of glass, semi-transparent, and turned at an angle. She walked around it, and when she did she saw herself reflected in the weak, see-through mirror. She stood for a moment and looked at that girl. Her face was alarmingly pale where it wasn't bruised and swollen, and there was a huge bandage on her forehead. Her hair was a tangled mass of flame that curled and moved around her head and shoulders with a life of its own. She lifted her hand automatically to smooth it down, but when she saw how badly that girl's hand shook she snatched it back.

She had turned away from herself and looked at the empty room, a square space about the size of her bedroom at home, but with huge, reflective mirrors angled toward the center at each corner. She walked into the middle, slowly turned around and took in the bare, smooth walls, the low ceiling, the inexplicable, but somehow purposeful mirrors while her heart beeped quietly by her side.

And then, from nowhere and everywhere she had heard the amplified sound of her father's voice as it echoed in the strange chamber.

"In five. Four. Three. Two. One."

The light of a thousand, thousand suns hit her face and blazed through her head and she was blinded in a pure white nova, the monitor's dutiful amplification of her accelerating heartbeat the only sense of her physical self that remained to her, until the pain in her chest hit her like a truck and she fell, once again, into darkness.

"So, what was in the smaller room?" Finn asked, and Tesla was pulled back into the present.

"Nothing, really," she said quickly, suddenly wary. She dreamed of that night sometimes, and always woke in a clammy sweat. Whatever had happened—or whatever she imagined had happened—continued to make her afraid, all these months later.

"You can't just stop there, Tesla," he said casually, but his voice was too intense, he was too interested in what was supposedly a chance conversation and she knew he had manipulated her into telling her story, *this* story, though for what purpose she could not imagine.

"Look, I need to get home, it must be late—" she said as she reached into the side pocket of her messenger bag for her cell and realized that it wasn't there. "Great. I left my cell at Angelo's. I gotta go." She was already on her feet and had begun to jog back the way they'd come.

At Angelo's she pushed the glass door of the pizzeria open and made her way toward the table she'd occupied with Malcolm, though she held out little hope her phone would still be there. The crowd was a lot worse at this hour, and the noise of conversations and the TV that blared from its mount on the wall were hardly conducive to ambient dining. She gently pushed between two people to get a clear view of the table and saw, to her astonishment, her cell phone right in the middle of the table, between and among the plates and glasses and red pepper shakers that cluttered its surface.

"Hey, I left my phone here," she said loudly to the four students who sat there eating, and one of the guys indicated without a word that she should take it. "Thanks," she said, grabbed it and turned to go.

"Tesla," Finn said, suddenly by her side in the crowd, but before he could say more there was a shout.

"Turn it up—shut up everybody, check it out!"

The girl at the register had picked up the remote and turned up the volume on the TV, and every head in the place turned to face the screen. The ticker tape feed at the bottom read, "Breaking News: explosion on university campus," and the live video showed smoke and fire billowing out of a large, cream-colored building, a dozen fire trucks and ambulances parked nearby. Red lights flashed, reporters stood with mics in the glare of studio lights positioned by their crews, and dozens of people watched from behind yellow tape barricades.

"Tesla," Finn said again, his voice loud and his hand on her arm. "We need to talk."

"I can't!" she said, and the panic in her voice was unmistakable as she shook his hand off her.

He tried to follow, overcome by frustration, as she pushed her way through the bodies. Tesla was desperate, panicked. "Move!" she shouted repeatedly as she slipped further away from him and burst out of the door of Angelo's.

Finn shoved someone into a chair by the door in order to catch her before she got away. "Tesla, stop! What the hell?" He was outside, finally, and he grabbed her arm again, tried to fix her to this moment, to him.

She pushed him away from her, harder than he would have thought she was capable, and he staggered back a step. "That explosion—it was the physics building," she yelled. "I need to make sure my dad's at home!"

Tesla turned before he could say a word and sprinted toward her house as fast as she had ever, in her seventeen years, moved.

CHAPTER 7

Tesla rounded the corner by the tall hedge of the next-door neighbor's house and was suddenly yanked back on her heels by Finn, who had caught up to her.

She turned on him, her eyes narrowed to furious slits. "Get the hell off me, Finn!"

"Wait, wait, wait," he hissed. He pulled her back into the thick, solid wall of greenery. "Slow down. Tell me what's going on, I can help." He was winded—she had said she was no athlete, but the girl was *fast*.

She squirmed and twisted, tried to break free from the tight grip he had on her, but his hand around her bicep would not yield. "Let me *go!*" she whispered fiercely, her voice low, but she stopped struggling. Finn's hushed voice, his attempt to hide them both in the dark shadows of the hedge, had begun to affect her own behavior. She leaned toward him and whispered, "I need to find my dad—"

"Shhh," he suddenly cautioned, his mouth by her ear, as he pulled her deeper into the greenery and pointed at her house. "Look." He felt her labored breath, the adrenaline-fueled tremors that shook her body. They melted into the hedge, safely hidden in the shadows that were even darker than the night that had descended fully since they'd left Angelo's. *A lifetime ago*, Finn thought as he slowly, carefully leaned his head out from the hedge. Tesla immediately followed suit, just enough to get a glimpse of the front of the house.

They stood still and peered through the dark, barely breathing. There was no movement, no noise at all on the quiet residential street. But just as Tesla opened her mouth to tell Finn she didn't see anything, they both stiffened and stared, mesmerized by the ghostly vision they could just make out through the gently blown, sheer curtains of the open living room windows.

A light moved along the interior walls of the house and made its way up the staircase to the second floor.

"*Shit!*" Finn said quietly to himself as Tesla darted out from behind him. She stuck close to the dense leaves and branches that formed a wall on her right as she began to walk quickly toward the backyard of her house.

He caught up with her under the big maple half a dozen yards from the back of the house where Tesla had paused in the shadow of its thick, gnarled trunk. He stood just behind her, put a hand on her shoulder and leaned down. "What, exactly, are you doing?"

"I need a better vantage point," she whispered back.

"There's somebody in your house, Tesla, and I don't think it's a member of your family. You can't go in there. C'mon, let's go. Leave it to the professionals."

"Good. You call the police. The physics building—where my dad works—blew up tonight and now somebody's *in my house*." She stared him down, her eyes disconcertingly clear, blue and green even in the darkness. And then she walked swiftly toward the backdoor.

I didn't mean the police, he thought, as he hurried after her and cursed himself for not realizing before just how reckless she was.

"The lock's broken?" Finn whispered behind her, just as Tesla reached the door and began to turn the handle.

"No. We never lock it."

Finn shook his head in disgust. *Brainiacs,* he thought. *How do they dress themselves in the morning?*

He cringed at the *click* of the screen latch as it closed behind him, and then followed Tesla across the kitchen floor. She paused in the wide, arched doorway that led to another room, and he came up close behind her. He put his hand on the small of her back, aware of how close she was, the faint lemony smell of her hair, the top of her head just under his chin.

"Tesla, we have to go," he whispered in her ear. "Now. This is dangerous." *Although it's anybody's guess where the danger is coming from,* he thought grimly.

Tesla surprised him again when she suddenly reached behind her, grabbed a handful of his T-shirt, and began to inch her way forward. She pulled him along behind her and he did not resist. He could not know that he would regret his acquiescence in this moment for a very long time.

They inched forward, Tesla in the lead while Finn followed blindly behind her in the dark. They both froze at the sound of a creaky floorboard on the stairs; it served to remind them, viscerally, that they were not alone. No other sound followed, as if the entire house held its breath. And then a dark shape was in front of them. Finn was behind Tesla, unable to act as she was suddenly pulled forward into the wide expanse of the room. His hands reached out in front of him and found only air. The streetlights outside were inexplicably off and Finn was left to grope in the dark of an unfamiliar room. In the split second that it took for Tesla to be yanked away from him he understood what it meant to be helpless.

He followed her momentum forward a step or two but stopped, afraid to go further and somehow make the situation worse, his body tense as a boxer's. Within seconds he heard a crash and Tesla cried out—once, agonizingly—in pain.

Finn turned his head left, then right. He attempted, as an act of will, to force his other senses to make up for his inability to see in the dark. He heard a hurried footfall close by, sensed someone move just out of reach, and he lunged to his left, relieved to be able to act, to set his body in motion and damn the consequences. He felt his shoulder connect with a very large, rock-hard torso.

Finn and the man he had tackled fell to the floor. They rolled and clutched each other tightly in the dark, neither of them able to punch the other, as their arms strained to get a purchase on a largely unseen opponent. Finn felt the weight of the man on his chest and his right arm was pinned to the floor by the guy's knee, meaning he was only seconds away from defeat—and then Tesla would be alone with their assailant. With the speed of desperation, Finn threw his head forward and connected with the man's face, a dim shadow above him. Confusion reigned as he heard, simultaneously, the sound of shattering glass just above him and felt the sharp, feather-light shards of whatever had broken land in his hair and on his face. Warm blood was in Finn's eyes—he wasn't sure whose it was—and he blinked furiously to clear them, but the grunt of pain and sudden absence of pressure as the man slid off of him told him that the other guy had gotten the worst of it.

Finn rolled away from the man who no longer pinned him to the floor, the man who now moved slowly, groggily, to his knees by the sound of it. He was just about to grab for the man again and finish it, anything to get some lights on and see what the hell had happened, when he heard Tesla moan somewhere behind him. He paused for only a fraction of a fraction of a second, uncertain whether to secure the man's capture or go to Tesla, and realized immediately that even pausing to consider the question gave away the answer. He turned away from the injured man, whoever he was, and made his careful way toward the sound Tesla had made. He felt the air in front of him so as not to run into her, or over her, and though he clenched his jaw when he heard the heavy footsteps of the man he'd grappled with move away from him, cross the room, and then the slam of the backdoor, Finn remained undeterred until he heard Tesla whimper right in front of him, low to the ground.

"Tes, it's me, are you okay?" He wondered suddenly if there might be more people in the house when he heard the backdoor close again, gently and quietly this time.

"Max?" Tesla asked, her voice thin and reedy.

"No, it's Finn. Are you hurt?" He crouched down and felt along the floor in front of him. And then his hand was in her hair, spread across the hardwood floor, and he followed it with his fingers to find her head, her shoulders. "Can you sit up?" he asked.

"Yeah, I think—" she began, and he could feel her move to brace her hands against the floor and push herself up, but then she gave a cry of pain and fell back to the floor.

"Fuck this," Finn said through clenched teeth. He crawled a couple of feet away until he found a table leg, which turned into a table, upon which his scrabbling hands found a lamp. He flipped the switch on its base and the room was flooded with light. He squinted in the sudden glare and turned to find Tesla on the floor about four feet away from him. She lay in a fetal position, legs drawn up, head down, the long, bright waves of her hair tangled across her face so he could not see her expression, or even if her eyes were open, and she cradled her left arm against her body with her other hand.

Finn scrambled over to her, still on his knees, and gently brushed her hair back from her face—and immediately wished he hadn't. She turned stricken, drenched blue-green eyes toward him, bright as polished beach glass, all of her pain and fear right there for him to see, and when he went to reach for her, to offer whatever comfort he was capable of, she said, "Did you see my dad?"

"No, I didn't see him. And I think it was just the one guy, and he's gone—your dad would certainly have heard the noise if he was here. Where are you hurt?" He wanted to touch her, as he had since he'd seen her up close for the first time, at the botched party, but unlike in the park earlier tonight, he was afraid. His hand hovered an inch above her shoulder as he waited for her to tell him what to do.

"My arm," she said as she closed her eyes, her wet lashes jet black against her cheeks. One tear squeezed out from under her eyelid, and Finn felt a rush of such tenderness and rage that he was paralyzed for a moment—not by the rage, which he had long ago grown accustomed to, but by the tenderness, unfamiliar and unwelcome.

"Let me see." He gently but firmly moved her hand away from the arm she held close.

He had to quickly swallow the shocked gasp he would have otherwise made and turn back to her face, away from her already swollen forearm, the hand and wrist at a sickening angle. The end of a clearly broken bone pressed tightly against skin that was already a deep, angry purple, but at least the skin wasn't broken—it wasn't an open fracture. The pain must be unbearable.

"Is it bad?" She looked at him with those eyes, summer sky and swimming pools and new leaves in the spring.

"No, not really. Probably a sprain," he assured her, the lie calm and sure. "Still, we should get it looked at. Can you stand up if I help?"

"I think so," she said, and he moved to get behind her, to offer his support so she wouldn't need her injured arm, already swollen beyond recognition, and cradled in her other hand, up by the elbow. Slowly, carefully, Finn took most of her weight and they got her up on her feet. She shook uncontrollably, but she said she thought she could walk.

With one arm around her waist to keep her steady, they made their way to the front door. Finn opened it—it was also unlocked—and they stepped out into the night. Tesla asked no questions as he walked her up the street toward the edge of campus, but he heard her suck in her breath whenever her steps jarred her arm. They were almost to the old Victorian house when Tesla stopped, and Finn, though his arm was tight around her waist, could feel her sway on her feet.

"Tes, we're almost there," he said. "Hang on, okay?"

Tesla turned her head to assure him she could make it, but just as she opened her mouth to speak, her eyes fluttered and her knees gave out. Finn felt her slump against him, her dead weight more than he could support with one arm. He turned her body awkwardly, tried not to touch her injured forearm as he picked her up, her head fallen back over his arm. The vulnerable, pale flesh of her throat was revealed, the sharp little V of her chin he felt he already knew, as he'd seen it thrust out toward him in defiance on several occasions. Every muscle in his back and shoulders was tensed as he carried her up the steps to the front porch of the old house and leaned his shoulder into the buzzer.

The door opened almost immediately, and he met Lydia's eyes with their fine web of lines at the corners, as her sharp, observant intelligence shone out from behind her reading glasses.

"We've got a problem." Finn stepped into the parlor as Lydia held the door wide and moved out of his way. He carried the unconscious girl into the house and Lydia looked up and down the dark, quiet street of the sleepy college town before she shut the massive oak door. The sharp, metallic sound of a deadbolt as it slid into place echoed ominously down the sidewalk, just before the porch light went off and plunged the house into darkness once more.

CHAPTER 8

"What do we do with her?" asked a girl's voice.

"Beats me," replied another girl. "I don't know why he brought her here in the first place."

"He brought her here because she needed sanctuary, and a doctor—a doctor who would not involve the police. As you both well know," said a third woman who was clearly neither as young as the first voice, nor as snotty as the second.

Tesla lay perfectly still, her eyes closed. She did not know where she was, or who these people were, but she felt, oddly enough, okay with that.

"Finn should be back by now, shouldn't he?" asked a man's voice, one that Tesla thought sounded vaguely familiar. "Perhaps I'll just pop over there, see if he needs anything."

"No," said the woman who sounded older and more authoritative than any of the others. "We'll give him a little more time. Besides, if we decide to send someone, Joley, it'll be Beckett, not you." There was a faint, but discernable trace of amusement in her last comment.

Joley, Tesla thought. *And Beckett. I'm at Finn's house?* Her forehead wrinkled in concentration as she remembered the explosion she'd seen on the TV at Angelo's, her race home, Finn's urgent whispers in her ear, the powerful hands that had grabbed and thrown her across the living room and the unbelievable pain that had exploded in her arm and shoulder.

"I'm not entirely useless, you know," Joley said, and Tesla realized by the sound of his footsteps and voice that he had moved closer. "Look sharp—she's awake," he said, and everyone fell silent.

Tesla opened her eyes, and the blurry details of the room came slowly into focus. It felt like the old Victorian house, but this was a room she hadn't seen at the party. She lay on a sofa with some kind of soft beige upholstery, a pillow under her head. To the left of the sofa was a fireplace with a huge oak mantle, covered with framed photographs and candles. Joley stood with one hand on the mantle as he looked at her. Opposite the sofa were two overstuffed, leather club chairs, Beckett in one with that Goth girl, Bizzy, perched on the arm. An older woman with gray streaks in her brown hair, cut in a plain, practical bob, sat in the other. The woman peered at Tesla over the tops of her glasses.

"How do you feel?" she asked, not unkindly, but without a smile.

Tesla swallowed once, and licked dry lips before she could answer. "Okay. Good, actually."

The woman smiled then, briefly. "Yes, the doctor gave you some pain medication. That was a nasty break, clean through. The doctor set it, said you'd be fine. A few weeks in a cast."

Tesla was content to say nothing. She thought, suddenly, that she should feel awkward, reclined on a sofa in front of these people she didn't know, that maybe she ought to sit up, but she couldn't really make herself care, let alone actually do it. Painkillers, indeed.

"Is my dad—" Tesla began, but stopped, not quite sure what

question she wanted to ask.

"Finn has gone to Dr. Abbott's lab to see what he can find out," the older woman said. "He brought you here about," she paused and glanced at the clock ticking away on the mantle, "about two and a half hours ago."

"Did I go to the hospital?" Tesla asked. "I don't remember."

"That's because you fainted," said Bizzy. She spoke cheerfully, her short, jet-black hair cut in uneven chunks and spiked all over her head. She stared at Tesla with undisguised interest, her eyes heavily rimmed in black. "Finn carried you here. We have—we found a doctor who makes house calls."

"Yes, it was all very romantic," said Beckett pleasantly enough. "Finn burst in through the door, the damsel in distress in his arms in the classic movie pose, wan and pathetic in a dead faint, or an attack of the vapors, or whatever it's called."

Tesla opened her mouth to retort, but stopped. She felt like she hadn't even been there, so how could she argue? Maybe she *had* been pathetic.

"Very dramatic, Beckett," said the older woman from her chair. "Though I'm not sure I'd describe a person who has passed out from the pain of a serious injury as 'pathetic.'" She turned back to Tesla. "I am Lydia, by the way. We haven't actually met yet. I own this house, and rent rooms to these young people."

"Nice to meet you," Tesla replied.

"Finn said you surprised a burglar at your house," Joley said.

"I guess," said Tesla. "Whoever it was threw me into a table and ran out."

"Yeah, Finn said that's how you broke your arm," said Bizzy. "He said you were trying to find Dr. Abbott—your dad— 'cause you'd seen the explosion on TV."

"Do you know what happened?" Tesla asked. "At the physics building? My dad works there, he has an office and lab, and I couldn't tell from the news shot where the fire was, and he wasn't home when we were there—" Tesla stopped in midsentence as she heard the rising panic in her own voice. She waited a moment, her eyes closed, and breathed deep before she continued. "I can't believe all this happened at the same time—who would break into our house? Thank God Max is spending the night with Dylan." She struggled to sit up. "I really can't stay here, I need to see Max—and I have to find my dad."

"Because the first time you went looking for him turned out so well?" Beckett asked.

"Excuse me, do I know you?" Tesla responded, sitting up at last but feeling weird, slightly addled from the painkillers. The low tone of her voice had a decided edge. "He might be in trouble, Beckett, and I'm not going to just sit here and do nothing." Tesla's chin jutted out and her eyes blazed blue-green fire.

Beckett sat, slouched and relaxed. She fairly oozed condescension.

"Understandable, of course," Lydia announced. "But you'll get better results this time if you think before you act, my dear. As for your brother, might I suggest that you text his friend's mother, ask her to keep the news of the explosion and your, ah, accident, away from him for tonight, and then talk to him about it tomorrow when you have more information?"

Tesla agreed. There was no sense scaring Max at this point, he'd only worry and wonder, much as she was doing now, and there was nothing he could do. She might as well let him enjoy his sleepover at Dylan's, where she knew he was safe. Everyone waited while she sent the text, painstakingly tapping the touchscreen of her cell that she balanced on her knees, her left hand completely useless.

"Should Finn be back by now?" Tesla asked suddenly. "How long has he been gone?"

"That's in the category of 'need to know,'" Beckett said with a smirk, but her mouth snapped shut abruptly when Lydia looked at her.

"We've been following the news and so far no injuries have been reported. No one can get into the building while the explosion is investigated, but Finn has a press pass that allows him some access, particularly on campus. He went right to your father's lab once you were safely here and the doctor was on the way," Lydia said. She indicated with a wave of her hand Tesla's arm, which was encased in a brand new, neon-turquoise cast all the way up to her elbow.

"I picked out the color," said Bizzy with a grin. "It matches your eyes. You know, together. Blue and green."

Beckett rolled her eyes.

Tesla paused and took in the odd group that surrounded her. She remembered well the party a few days ago and now this bizarre turn of events. Was it all, somehow, connected? She had to ask.

"Who, exactly, are you people?"

The other four exchanged brief looks with one another, and then Lydia spoke.

"Of course you've begun to wonder," she said. "We had hoped to avoid this—your father, in particular, didn't want you to know—but it seems we have no choice now. It begins with Elizabeth, who is one of your father's prized students. She is his research assistant, a position that has never been given to an undergraduate. That should indicate his level of confidence in her current abilities, as well as her potential as a scientist."

"Elizabeth?" Tesla asked, confused. She looked at Joley, who pointed at Bizzy.

Bizzy grinned from her perch on the arm of Beckett's chair and waved. Her spiky hair and heroin-chic eyeliner, the nose stud and row of tiny eyebrow barbells, her underfed, hipster body did not shout 'physicist,' Tesla thought, but you never knew.

"So we are, in a sense, familiar with your father and his work," Lydia said.

"Okaaay." Tesla drew the word out. She didn't get it.

"Everyone here has different areas of interest, of expertise," Lydia continued patiently. "Finn is a journalist, Joley is going into law, Elizabeth is a physicist, and Beckett is in philosophy and comparative religions."

"Really?" Tesla glanced at Beckett, surprised by what seemed to her an odd fit.

"Yeah. Really," Beckett assured her.

"I still don't understand," Tesla said. "How are you all involved with my dad, or with his work?"

"We weren't until recently," said Joley. He stepped away from the fireplace and began to pace the room, no longer the laconic rich boy with a quirky love of sci-fi. His energy and sense of purpose were apparent for the first time. "Not all of us, at any rate. The situation has evolved, you might say, and Lydia has hand-picked each of her tenants. Bizzy was recruited—was offered a room here first. She started to work with your dad this past year, and recently—the last couple of months—we've all become interested in his project, for different reasons, and we've all moved in here. Now it seems other people have become interested in your dad's work as well, and—well, that's where we come in."

"You've lost me," Tesla said with complete candor. "So Bizzy works in my dad's lab, and talks to you guys about his current project." Everyone nodded in unison, which would have been funny in other circumstances. "Joley's in—what, pre-law? So he's interested in the legal aspects of my dad's work. Finn cares about the news-value, I suppose, and Beckett—" here Tesla paused and turned to Beckett herself. "Why do you care about this, exactly?"

"I'm interested in belief systems, particularly fundamentalism," Beckett said, as if that explained it.

"And?" Tesla asked, her patience having worn thin.

"And, religious fundamentalism—you know, there is only one Truth, and only a select group of believers knows what it is— doesn't really play well with experimental physics. Or evolutionary biology, or most of the humanities, for that matter. I'm interested in those tensions, and how they get played out in the world."

When Tesla just looked at her, no trace of comprehension on her face, Beckett spoke slowly, the insult apparent. "Your dad's work pisses a lot of people off."

"Oh," Tesla said. "I guess I never thought—are you saying that someone—or some group—is out to get my dad?"

"That's not clear yet," Lydia said, "but tonight's events would suggest that it is at the very least a strong possibility." Lydia watched Tesla to gauge her reaction to this.

"And you guys are—" Tesla began.

"Watching his back," Bizzy finished triumphantly.

Tesla looked around the room. "You have got to be kidding. The League of Extraordinary Undergrads?"

"Tesla, I know this is all new to you," Lydia said kindly. "But we have had your father under surveillance for quite some time now. And, I should add, you and your brother, more recently."

Another surprise, Tesla thought. "What, like—you guys watch us?"

"Only in the most unobtrusive way," Lydia assured her.

"We need to know whether anyone else is watching you."

"Don't worry," said Beckett snidely. "It's a pretty dull assignment—trust me."

"Beckett," Lydia said, once and without inflection, and the blonde fell silent immediately. Apparently they didn't mess with Lydia.

"And *is* anyone else watching us?" Tesla asked.

"Yes, but we believe it began only a few days ago," Lydia said. "We're not sure yet who they are, or what their purpose might be or, even, if they're connected to one another."

"But we intend to find out, love," Joley said. He stopped at the far end of the couch where Tesla lay and looked at her kindly. "We tried to keep you out of it."

"So, when we showed up at Bizzy's birthday party—" Tesla began.

"We tried to get you to leave," he said.

"And it wasn't really my birthday," Bizzy confided. "We wanted to flush them out, whoever's been watching you, make them feel like they'd never be noticed in a drunken crowd, see if they'd try to pump me for information."

"So those two guys were actually after my father?" Tesla asked, alarmed.

"Well, they were interested in information about him and his work," Lydia said smoothly. "Let's not overstate the case. I doubt they expected Dr. Abbott's daughter to be there, served up on a silver platter, as it were."

"Our plan was to try to bring the bad guys in a little closer— they would certainly know that I was your dad's assistant. We hoped to create an opportunity for us to observe them, let them think the whole thing was their play when it was actually ours. They would assume we were just some random college students, and while they were trying to get information out of me, we'd be working on our own agenda. Finn is the master, he can get people to spill anything, and they have no idea what happened," Bizzy said.

No wonder Finn was so angry when we showed up, Tesla thought. *And that explains why that gorilla knew my name.* She shivered as she recalled her fear as the man had dragged her across the kitchen floor.

"Does my dad know you watch him?" Tesla asked.

"Yeah, we decided early on to tell him," Bizzy said. "He's my boss and my major professor, and I thought he should know. Lydia said okay, so we brought him in."

"He didn't like it at first, any more than he liked it when we suggested keeping an eye on you and Max, either, but when he realized you might be at risk he seemed happy to have us nearby," Joley said.

Tesla was startled by his casual use of her brother's name and she felt her stomach muscles tighten in dread. This felt far more invasive than the abstract notion that she'd been under surveillance. Her ever-present sense that she must protect Max had not been diluted at all by the pain meds.

"Finn should be back by now," Beckett said. "I'll head over to the lab."

"Not yet," Lydia said. "If he's found something, he'll want to follow up immediately. Let him do his job."

At that exact moment, the front door opened and shut below with a bang—Tesla realized for the first time that they must be in a room on the second floor—and everyone turned toward the open door. They heard his footsteps on the staircase, and then Finn walked into the room.

Tesla felt overwhelmed by his presence. His face looked

serious, older than she'd thought before, and she could see that a purplish bruise had already appeared on his cheekbone.

His warm, gold-brown eyes went immediately to Tesla, then slid to Lydia.

"How is she?" he asked, as if Tesla wasn't even in the room.

"I'm okay, thanks," Tesla retorted before anyone else could speak, annoyance plain in her voice. In her peripheral vision she noted the sudden grin on Joley's face. "Any sign of my father?" she continued, this time without the sarcasm.

"No," Finn said. "But I couldn't get in the building, and the police and fire marshal aren't saying anything yet about what happened and why." He paused, as if he was unsure how to proceed, and though she didn't really know him, even Tesla knew this was highly unusual.

"There's something else," she said tersely. "Tell me."

He looked at her for a moment. "Keep in mind that we don't know if your dad was even there tonight—as far as we know he was at home. But I spoke to the two campus security guys on duty tonight, and we pieced together, based on the floor plan of the building, where the explosion occurred. It was your dad's office."

Lydia smoothly took over before Tesla could respond. "We'll likely hear from him tomorrow. My guess is that he saw the explosion on television and realized that it might have been intended for him, as a warning at least, and he has gone into hiding, temporarily, for everyone's safety. He knows your brother is safe with friends, and he has confidence in you not to panic—he knows that you saw him at home, and there is no reason to assume he was anywhere else. I see this as a very good sign."

"Maybe," Tesla said uneasily. "But didn't you have someone on the house tonight, watching it? Watching him?"

Finn's head whipped around toward Lydia, and she put up

a hand to stop him.

"Finnegan, we've explained the basics to Tesla. She had a right to know," she added firmly when Finn began to protest. "We've told her we watch over her family, due to the sensitive nature of her father's work, and that others are watching as well." She turned, then, to Tesla. "We had actually called it a day, dear, as we thought all three of you would be in for the evening, celebrating his birthday. No one was watching the house once your father got home this evening."

"Well, you obviously had the right idea spying on us, even though it didn't work in the end," Tesla said.

No one responded, though Bizzy looked down at her shoes and Joley seemed to be inordinately interested in the photographs on the mantel. Tesla sighed. *I guess I can't be mad at them for watching us and mad at them for not watching us at the same time.*

"How long have we been under this microscope—Max and I?" she asked Lydia.

"Less than two weeks," Lydia answered without hesitation. "And it hasn't been around the clock, obviously. When your father's at the lab Elizabeth is usually there anyway, so he's almost always covered. Once you're all in the house at night we don't always stay, but when we do, we're focused on the house more than you, anyway. We don't really get that close, my dear."

"Finn won't let anybody else watch you," Bizzy said with a wide grin. "Ow!" she suddenly exclaimed when Beckett punched her in the arm. "Well, it's true!" she hissed.

"Who are you people?" Tesla asked again, inexplicably angry, a feeling she had already come to associate with Finn and his friends. "I mean, if there are bad guys out there who want the scientist's top-secret work or whatever, why haven't you called the police, or the FBI, or, I don't know, Jack Bauer?"

Bizzy laughed, but no one else did. "Tesla," Lydia said calmly. "I understand the shock of all this. You're still reeling from the incident at your house earlier tonight—and medicated on top of everything else. We don't want to alarm you. It would have been better if you could have gone on blissfully ignorant, but at this point we have no choice. We don't contact the police or the FBI because I am already on the job. I work for the government, and I've been assigned to your father for some years now. These young people work for me. Believe me, we are on top of this."

Tesla closed her eyes. She needed a moment to process this craziness, not to mention shut out the sight of every single set of eyes in the room searching her face to see—what, exactly? If she would cry? Run from the room in fear, unable to handle it? Did they assume she'd be a total narcissist and focus on the creepiness of being spied on by strangers (because that actually was pretty creepy)—that she'd only care about herself, not about her dad or Max, or the larger issues that were obviously at work here?

She looked right at Finn, then, sick and tired of being out of the loop, treated like a fragile child, because of her heart, because of her age, because of her lack of experience. Because her mother had died. She was worried about her dad, but these people seemed to think he was okay. She wasn't sure what she should do next, but before she got to any of that, Tesla had to ask what seemed the most fundamentally important question at that moment.

"What, exactly, is my father working on?"

Before Lydia could stop him, Finn stepped forward, crouched down in front of the sofa so his eyes were on a level with Tesla's. In the split second before he spoke she wished she could take back the question, but it was already too late.

"Time travel," Finn said.

CHAPTER 9

Bizzy reached up to twist the tiny silver stud pierced through the delicate flesh of her left nostril while she watched Tesla. The redhead was always so explosive, so *pissed* at everyone, and Bizzy was not inclined to miss anything she might do or say because of some archaic, Miss Manners rule about staring.

Lydia frowned. "We should have talked about this first, Finnegan."

Finn sat on the couch next to Tesla and faced Lydia. He said nothing, merely raised an eyebrow at her, waiting. Joley stopped pacing and stood in front of the fireplace, arms crossed over his chest. Lydia drummed her fingers on the cracked, fat brown arm of her leather chair, then appeared to come to some sort of decision.

"Tesla, we'll have to trust that you can handle this, and that you can absolutely, without any room for error, keep your mouth shut."

Everyone looked at her expectantly, and Tesla nodded. "Yeah, I can do that."

Lydia looked at her a moment longer. The woman's eyes did not waver, as though they could see right through the injured girl. Then—satisfied, it seemed—Lydia nodded. "There are aspects of your father's work that we haven't been able to piece together, and you may be able to help."

"Well, if my dad couldn't help you, I can't believe I would be able to," Tesla began as her gaze darted about the room. She seemed nervous, jumpy.

"No, that's not what I mean. Your father is of course the scientist, and this is about the project he's been immersed in for nearly two decades. But while he's willing to have us around to keep you and Max safe, he does not, by any stretch of the imagination, share that work with us."

"What about you, Bizzy?" Tesla asked, and the goth girl jumped at the sound of her name. "You're there, in the lab, every day. Don't you know what's going on?"

"Well, yes and no," Bizzy said, surprised and chagrined to find Tesla's attention so fully hers—she was far more comfortable observing than being observed. "I got this research assistantship in the spring semester, so I haven't been there that long. And Dr. Abbott doesn't really include me—or anybody else—in every aspect of his work. I work on some discrete pieces of the project, but he's the only one with the big picture." Bizzy chewed on her lower lip for a moment, lost in thought. "Whatever this is all about, the only thing I'm sure of is that it's connected to your mom."

"Wha—my mom's been dead for almost eight years." Tesla's voice shook.

"I know, sorry, that was too blunt, wasn't it?" Bizzy said. "But I've seen some notebooks he keeps locked in his desk. They were your mom's. He's still working on the stuff she was doing before she died." Bizzy spoke quickly, not at all surprised that she was messing this up. She wasn't very good with people—some of the things she'd seen and done in foster care, and the things that had been done to her—she was just much better in a lab, and far more comfortable.

"I don't know anything about my mom's work," Tesla said, her eyes on the cast in her lap. "She was so young—Max was a baby—I mean I know she was a physicist, and she and my dad met in college, but I never thought about her work, really."

"I think it's a bad move to bring her in like this," Beckett said suddenly. She had been watching Tesla carefully since she'd woken up. "We've had a while to become a team, and we work well together—and, importantly, for us this isn't personal. She's too involved, too emotional. I think this will put her at risk, as well as us. We're not even sure what we're up against, other than that there are some dangerous people involved."

Undeniably practical, and yet still bitchy, Tesla thought as she turned to consider Beckett. "I'm actually right here," Tesla said. Her eyes flashed and a deep, antagonistic crease appeared between her dark red eyebrows, but Lydia put up her hand, and even Tesla obeyed the implicit order.

"Your point is well-taken, Beckett, but we can't undo what's been done. And now that Tesla is aware, we'll just have to make it work. For all our sakes." Lydia paused then turned back to Bizzy. "Elizabeth, why don't you fill Tesla in on what you know from the lab and Dr. Abbott, and what you've surmised based on the notebooks."

Bizzy nodded, and paused for a moment to gather her thoughts. "Well, basically your dad has built a time machine."

"That sounds...crazy," Tesla said rather weakly.

"Not really," Bizzy assured her as she twisted one of her hair spikes that poked straight out from her temple. It's about light—lasers—and speed and gravitational fields and—black holes, of course."

"Elizabeth, please," said Lydia, her tone that of a TV mom,

sick and tired of the mud her kid tracks across the kitchen floor. "We've talked about this. You must try to remember what you didn't know before you were a physicist. Explain it to *that* person. Layman's terms."

"Oh, right. Sorry." Embarrassed, Bizzy rolled the stud that pierced her tongue across her front teeth as she wondered how to explain time travel to people who knew virtually nothing about science, especially when she already struggled to imagine how other people's minds worked on the most mundane, everyday matters.

"Okay," she said, finally. She looked up and met Tesla's gaze with determination. "Imagine that time is not a straight line, with the past behind us and the future in front of us. Instead, it's a series of closed loops, the past and future connected, like this." She made a closed circle of her thumb and forefinger.

Bizzy was about to move on but Tesla looked back at her blankly.

"Sorry, but 'huh'?" Tesla said.

"Eloquent," quipped Joley, who shushed immediately when Lydia gave him the look.

"Try to picture it," Bizzy continued. "Time is a closed loop. Black holes create a tunnel through which we can move from one point in time to another. From one point on the closed loop to another point. That makes traveling backward or forward in time possible."

Bizzy paused, hopeful despite herself. "Are you with me so far?"

"I think so," said Tesla. She rolled the shoulder of her broken arm, just slightly, and winced as dull pain radiated up the muscles of her arm.

"Okay, so black holes—which rotate—affect time, but they

also affect space. Think about a vanilla milkshake, and you drop a big blob of chocolate syrup into it. You start to stir it with a spoon, in one direction only, and what will you see?"

Tesla just looked at her, so Finn stepped in. "You'd see an unbroken swirl, like a nautilus shell, as the chocolate followed the wake of the spoon around and around in the vanilla."

"Exactly," Bizzy said, glad she'd had to try and explain this stuff before to the others, who were much better than she with metaphors. "Rotating black holes do the same thing, they create a kind of invisible wake that drags space around behind it, in a swirl, pulling everything into the tunnel. It's called 'frame-dragging.'"

"Okay," Tesla said. "I think I understood that."

"Well, now it gets complicated," Bizzy said. "Let's back up a minute and remember what we know about gravity."

"It's a bitch?" asked Joley, and Finn rewarded him with a grin, that flash of even, perfect teeth that drew Tesla's gaze to his mouth each time she saw it.

"Boys," Lydia said, though Tesla detected affection in her voice more than exasperation.

Bizzy continued, undeterred. "For a long time we thought space wasn't really anything, that gravity was the attraction of less mass to more mass. Newton's apple falls to the ground because of the gravitational pull exerted on the apple by the much larger—more massive—planet Earth. But Einstein changed all that by suggesting that space and time are a singular and inextricable thing—fabric, kind of, like a rubber sheet that the planets sit on. The sun is so massive that it weighs down the rubber sheet, bends it to create a slope that the smaller, less massive planets slide down into. The rubber sheet is invisible, so it looks to us as though the heavier object attracts or pulls the lighter object, even though that's not what's really happening."

"I feel smarter already," Joley joked.

"Well, you're not," retorted Bizzy.

"Bizzy," he replied, a hand over his heart and a pained expression on his face. "I'm wounded."

"Whatever," she said, though she couldn't hide her smile. "Anyway, along comes Stephen Hawking, who puts quantum mechanics and black hole theory together, with some pretty astonishing results."

"Such as?" Finn prodded helpfully, and Tesla wondered if they'd rehearsed this. When she smiled, Finn looked at her with mock seriousness. "What? I'm her lovely assistant. I make science look good."

"Such as, black hole theory had always assumed that after a star's collapse, matter is trapped forever inside the black hole, an assumption based on the classical notion of matter, what it is and how it behaves. But Hawking pointed out that if the matter inside the black hole obeys the laws of quantum mechanics, which says very different things about what matter is and how it behaves, then we have a whole new ballgame."

She paused, as if for dramatic effect, but when no one spoke, she continued, slightly deflated.

"For a long time, all we had was particle theory: you know, matter cannot be created or destroyed, it exists in a particular moment in a location that can be known. But wave theory—quantum mechanics—says that the best we can do in determining the location of matter is to calculate the probability of either when it is, or where it is. That we can't know both the location and the motion of a particle, just one or the other, and then beyond that there are simply a host of limitless possibilities."

"I think I got that, except for the last part," Tesla said with some hesitation. "Limitless possibilities? Is that even possible?"

"That's funny," Bizzy said, clearly startled. A grin stretched her mouth wide, but then she stopped. "Wait, were you trying to be funny?"

"Not really," said Tesla.

"Biz, seriously. Nobody does quantum mechanics stand up," said Finn gently.

"Fine," said Bizzy, grumpy for the first time. "If it was a serious question, here's a serious answer: the idea of limitless possibilities is nothing more than math. Math and imagination," she corrected herself. "If we want to calculate where an object is—which means, because of Einstein, that we combine space and time into spacetime—we have to calculate where and when that object is. At that point, we are in the realm of quantum mechanics. There's an uncertainty principle at work, which limits what we can know. We can only know where it *might* be, and it might be lots of places. If I throw a tennis ball at the wall, it might hit the wall and bounce back, but it also might tunnel through and appear on the other side of the wall."

"Um, I don't think so," said Tesla. "That couldn't happen."

"Mathematically, it could," Bizzy insisted. "Therefore, it actually could."

"Yeah, I don't get it," said Tesla.

"Me either, and I've heard it before," admitted Finn. "It makes my head hurt."

"That's because you're lazy," said Bizzy, once again amazed by how slow otherwise intelligent people could be. "It's pretty simple, really. You know how the speed of light is always really important in science fiction?"

Tesla nodded.

"That's because it's really important in actual science. Einstein's theories of relativity prove that time slows down for a moving clock—which we can think of as the time traveler—the closer the clock gets to the speed of light. Speed and gravitational fields—these are the two things that make time travel possible. Follow me?"

"I think so," said Tesla. Her arm, hand, and shoulder had begun to throb. She couldn't concentrate very well, and this stuff was hard to understand under the best circumstances.

"So gravity—the bending of spacetime—creates closed time loops and black holes create tunnels through those loops. But energy—light—can *also* bend spacetime, create those loops and tunnel through them. When matter circulates, like at the edge of a black hole, it can become a source of gravity—it bends spacetime, creates frame-dragging. Your dad, and I guess your mom, too, developed a time-machine based on a circulating light source."

"Theoretically," added Finn.

"Yes, theoretically," agreed Bizzy. She turned to Tesla. "Your dad has been focused on photonics for years now—"

"On what?" Tesla interrupted.

"Photonics. Lasers. By circulating two light beams in opposite directions, spacetime is twisted in a loop, and the loops are stacked up like a spiraling helix—"

"Like a slinky?" Tesla asked.

"Exactly like a slinky!" Bizzy said, clearly relieved. "Relativistic time-dilation, it's called. The frame dragging that creates the spiraled, stacked time loops allows us to move from one point to another, rather than having to follow the line around and around and around at what is for us a normal pace, the past behind, the present now, the future up ahead. We can skip around."

"Okay, so are you saying that it works? That this is real, and my dad can, like, travel in time?" Tesla felt like a fool the moment she asked, but no one in the room seemed to think it was a silly question.

"No," Bizzy said. "This is all very new, very theoretical—in scientific terms, that is. When I say 'new' I mean that your dad's only been on this for like fifteen years. That's nothing. So far we've focused on subatomic particles only, and we're limited even there. We can only move objects backward in time, not forward, and the apparatus itself has to continually function—it serves as its own destination—for the future object to travel back to. So, the object could never travel back further than when the time machine was up and running. The machine creates the tunnel, the wormhole that allows you to get from point A to point D without the need to go through B and C to get there."

"Soooo," Tesla said, "if I build a time machine right now, turn it on and leave it on for a hundred years, someone a hundred years in the future could come back to here, right now, to my time machine, because it's still on?"

"Yup, that's pretty much it," Bizzy said.

"So my dad's time machine," Tesla asked slowly. "How long has it been running?"

"Very, very good, Tesla," Lydia said quietly, as if to herself.

Finn looked at Beckett, one eyebrow raised, but she ignored him.

"Well, we're certainly not surprised that Tesla's smart," Joley said. "What we need to do now is get her to help us figure out how this hinges on her. If, in fact, it does."

"Sorry, what?" Tesla asked. "Hinges on me how?"

"We were actually hoping you could answer that," said Joley.

Lydia took over. "Tesla, Elizabeth has had two very brief opportunities to see your mother's journals. Your father keeps them under lock and key."

"If my dad doesn't want you to see them, why did you look?" Tesla asked Bizzy. "Is that why you took the job in his lab? So you could spy on him?"

"No!" Bizzy said quickly. "He left the notebooks out, but it was an accident. The first time I saw them I didn't know what they were. The second time, I did." She paused and her hand moved up of its own volition to pull her hair spikes out straighter, to touch the row of five tiny rings that pierced the rim of her ear, all her armor intact. "I could tell you he trusts me, and that I have the run of both labs and his office—which is all true—but no, he didn't intend for me to look at them. And I did it anyway."

Tesla was impressed, despite herself, by the girl's honesty. "So what did you see?"

"The first time, I saw a crude sketch of the apparatus your father has built in his lab here. Much smaller scale, but clearly the prototype."

"And the next time?" Tesla asked.

"I saw a phrase that stood alone on a page. Before I could read more, a couple of his grad students came in the door and I had to close the book. Dr. Abbott has been really careful since, and I haven't gotten another chance."

"What was the phrase?" Tesla wondered why the other girl was so hesitant, and why the air felt suddenly charged with tension.

"It said, *The Tesla Effect.*"

CHAPTER 10

There was silence in the room.

"The Tesla Effect," Tesla repeated. "What does that mean?"

"You don't know?" asked Finn.

"No, of course not." Tesla shifted on the couch. The ache and throb that ran down the length of her arm from just above her elbow had intensified. "Should I?"

"Well, we had hoped," Joley said. "That's what we need to bloody figure out."

"But why?" Tesla asked. "I don't understand."

Lydia intervened. "We think your parents were working on time travel, together, and that they had a major breakthrough when your mother was still alive. The most obvious explanation for 'the Tesla effect' is that it has something to do with the work of Nikola Tesla, since he was instrumental in the early phases of quantum mechanics. But other than that general connection, we need to know if there is another layer of meaning, one that is much closer to home. We know your father has continued his and your mother's work, and we want to know if somehow their theory or concept is connected to you."

"But," Tesla began, and stopped. "I mean, wouldn't I know if I knew something?"

"Okay, that one *had* to be on purpose," Bizzy said.

Tesla scowled at her. "You know what I mean," she said. "And regardless of what I might know, why don't you just ask my dad?"

"He doesn't know." Finn got up from the sofa and joined Joley by the fireplace. "We don't know why there's a gap between what your mom was working on when she died, and what your dad knows about that work, but there is."

There was a moment of silence for Tesla, for her parents, for the tragedy they'd all dealt with so long ago.

"You were just a kid when your mom died, weren't you?" Joley asked.

"Yeah, I was nine," Tesla said. *And I don't even know what happened*, she thought. *Dad won't talk about it.*

"So it's unlikely she told you something complex, not at that age. But she might have recorded something for when you were older. In a book, or maybe a video? Anything like that ring a bell?"

They all looked at her. Hopeful, expectant. "No. Sorry."

"We didn't actually think you'd have the answer on the tip of your tongue," Lydia assured her. "Don't worry. But we will work with you to see if we can't jog a memory, stumble upon something you don't realize you know."

"Okay." Tesla lifted her cast with her right hand and gently repositioned it on her lap.

Lydia looked at her watch. "You should take another pill," she said. "It's time."

"These?" asked Finn as he picked up a prescription bottle and a glass of water on the little table at the end of the sofa where Tesla sat. At Lydia's nod, he shook out one pill into his hand and gave it to Tesla, along with the glass of water.

Beckett got up and stretched, lean and cat-like. "I'm done. You don't need me for anything?" she asked Lydia.

"No, dear, sleep well," the older woman said over the top of her glasses and Tesla wondered if Lydia's wasn't the best disguise ever for some kind of secret, government agent. No one would ever suspect her.

Bizzy settled deeper into her chair, Joley took Beckett's seat, and Finn remained at the fireplace. He seemed to have too much energy to sit still for long, and Tesla thought several times that he looked at her. But every time she glanced over at him he was looking away and she felt both jittery and annoyed by it.

"So, what happens next?" Tesla attempted to sound business-like. "What is it about all of this that requires some kind of secret government organization? I'm still a little confused, despite all of Bizzy's information."

"Understandable," said Lydia with a small smile. "These are complex issues."

"Tesla," Joley said as he leaned forward in his chair, elbows on his thighs, his face intent and focused on hers. "Think about it. Why would time travel be controversial?"

Tesla did think about it, and everyone else remained quiet. "Well," she began hesitantly. "I suppose it could be profitable. Like in those old *Back to the Future* movies, where that guy bets on sports whose outcomes he already knows and he makes a fortune. It's cheating."

"Absolutely," said Lydia, "although in addition to those forms of chance there are those who fund scientific research and development. There is corporate espionage, investments in new technologies, and the absolute lack of any risk if one knows the outcome ahead of time."

"So money would make a time machine pretty desirable," said Tesla.

"Desirable, but also a potential threat," said Finn quietly. "Think of the advantages one corporation might have over all the competition, if it knew what advances would be made in the next couple of years. Imagine you knew before it happened what Apple or Google would become."

Tesla nodded, already way ahead of him. "What about politics? I mean, governments watch governments, they spy and compete over stuff like weapons and natural resources, right?"

"They most certainly do," said Lydia quietly. "Imagine if a foreign government hostile to our own, for example, knew who our next four presidents would be? Or if our government knew that another country, hostile to ours, would develop nuclear capabilities in five years?"

"Oh," said Tesla, overwhelmed by the possibilities. "That kind of information could stop a war."

"Or start one," Finn said.

"And we can't forget there are a lot of people whose first priority is a narrow set of religious beliefs and an uncompromising morality," Joley continued. "Some of those people—some of those groups, or organizations—feel the kind of research your father does is literally a sin. The very questions such research asks are considered a direct attack on their faith. Some believe themselves at war with such research—at war with the people who conduct the research."

Tesla's head had begun to ache, whether from the attempt to digest all this new information or from her broken arm, she didn't know. "So, are you saying that all this is happening? That corporations, governments, religious extremists—are after my dad?"

Lydia looked at her with some sympathy. "We are saying they are interested in the work that your father does. That for the most part they don't want it to wind up in the hands of anyone but themselves. Whether to use it for their own ends, or to destroy it, depends on the group, as do the lengths they are willing to go to to achieve their goals."

Lydia noted how pale Tesla was, and the dark circles under her strange, mismatched eyes, so startlingly bright against her skin. "What we don't know," the older woman said gently, "is how many such groups, and which ones, in particular, are currently in play."

"Well, we do know a little more than just those generalities," Finn said pointedly.

"Yes, but we haven't been able to draw any firm conclusions, and Tesla looks like she's had about as much handed to her tonight as she can take," Lydia said.

"No, really, I'm fine," Tesla assured her. "We don't know where my dad is, and I haven't seen Max since—well, since all this happened tonight. I want to know who's a threat, and what kind of a threat, exactly, they pose."

Finn gave her a swift look of approval. "I've been digging around for a while now, and we've got some solid leads. First, your dad and mom had a friend in grad school, Sebastian Nilsen. The three of them were pretty close as far as I can tell, and did their coursework and some of their research projects together. I've interviewed classmates, pored over their college records, photographs in the school newspaper, conferences they attended, whatever I could find. They did everything together, until your parents broke all ties with Nilsen in your mother's final year of her doctoral program—shortly after you were born—and it looks like they haven't been in communication with one another since."

"I don't really know anything about when they were in

college," Tesla said.

"Has your dad ever mentioned Nilsen?" Finn prodded.

"No," Tesla said. "I don't think so. Why don't you just ask him?"

"He refuses to discuss Nilsen," Finn said quietly. "I don't know why, but I will go where the information leads me, regardless."

"What does that mean?" Tesla said, aware that Finn had just possibly threatened her father. "How is this relevant?"

"It's necessary background," Lydia said. "Nilsen was passed up for an important fellowship that went to your mother and father jointly, and he resented it. The funding was substantial, and the prestige even more so. There was a controversy soon after when Nilsen published a paper that was suspected by many to be based on data stolen from your parents' lab. Nothing was ever proven, but Nilsen was effectively ostracized from the scientific community. What had once been a deep friendship had become an intense and bitter rivalry."

"Nilsen bounced around job-wise for a couple of years after leaving here. He was denied tenure, which essentially ended his academic career. He became a mercenary," Finn continued.

"I thought he was a scientist," Tesla said.

"He was—he is," Lydia said. "But he began and continues to work for the highest bidder, without loyalty to any government or set of professional ethics, and without any oversight. Nilsen seems to have amassed a considerable fortune, as well as ties to some powerful and ruthless people—although much of this is speculative, he has been linked to several instances of corporate and military espionage for rogue governments, and he has proved to be rather elusive when it comes to records of virtually every kind."

"Sounds like he's broken plenty of laws," Tesla said. "Why

doesn't the government just arrest him?"

"First of all, he's not a US citizen," Joley said. "There has been some precedent in the international courts. I'm working on that angle for a term paper in International Law and Intellectual Property, but I'm not there yet. And the government would still have to build a case against him, and then there's extradition—which brings me to the second problem: no one knows where he is. He operates internationally, and resources, financial and otherwise, are not a problem. He hasn't been positively identified in years—the last published photo of him that Finn has been able to unearth is twelve years old. We don't even know what he bloody looks like now, and we haven't been able to trace him financially, either."

"Okay," Tesla said as she stifled a yawn. Her arm felt a little better as she slipped back into that comfortable euphoria she'd experienced when she first woke up on this couch. "I don't know how to address any of that, but maybe I can begin work on the phrase you saw in my mother's notebook. *The Tesla Effect*. Maybe I should go to my dad's lab and see if that jogs a memory—if that part of the building is accessible after the blast, I mean." She felt the fear for her father creep back in, despite the pain meds. "I can't believe his office was blown up."

"We're not interested in his office anyway," said Bizzy, who had been so quiet Tesla had forgotten she was still in the room. The others had long ago grown used to Bizzy's penchant for silent observation, but Tesla felt startled.

"We're not?" she asked.

"No. His office and the labs are for general coursework and research, not for Dr. Abbott's big project, which has tens of millions of dollars in external funding and has a bunch of security measures attached to it. His time machine is in the Bat Cave."

Tesla laughed, but then stopped as a thought occurred to

her.

"A cave?" she asked.

"Well, it's not really a cave, it's a huge underground facility. We just call it the Bat Cave," Bizzy said.

"A big cavernous structure? With steel beams way high up?" Tesla asked. "And another, regular-sized room in the middle of it all, with mirrors in the corners?" Tesla felt strange. Her breath grew short and two spots of deep pink stained her cheeks. Her eyes were too bright, too green, too blue. She had begun to look feverish.

"Yeah, that's it," said Bizzy, clearly puzzled. "That facility requires a high security clearance, I'm surprised Dr. Abbott would tell you about it."

"He didn't," Tesla said, her right hand over her chest where she felt the rapid rate of her heart. "I think I've been there."

"I think you have, too," said Finn. His eyes were locked on hers and a sense of excitement permeated the air around him, as though he'd kept it in check until this exact moment. "Keisha told me you'd had some weird hallucination about a giant underground room, and from what you told me tonight, you were definitely there."

"Yeah, but I didn't finish the story," Tesla began somewhat breathlessly. "I've seen that cave, and that room."

"That room," Bizzy said slowly, "is the time machine."

Tesla's world had begun to spin out of control and she knew she might not be able to get a firm grip on it again. Her eyes sought Finn's and this time he was looking right at her, pinning her to the sofa.

"I think I've done it," Tesla said quietly, her eyes wide open and fixed on the tall boy by the fireplace. She was afraid to blink, afraid to upset the fragile balance suggested by the comfortable room.

"What do you mean, you've 'done it'?" asked Lydia sharply as her hands gripped the arms of her chair tightly.

Tesla took a deep breath. "I think I traveled through time."

CHAPTER 11

"Do you think you really time-traveled, then?" asked Joley, who walked beside Tesla, with Finn and Beckett right behind them. They were all headed toward the Abbott house.

Tesla swallowed, hard, then cleared her throat. How could she be sure? What she remembered—what she had been sure, up until last night, had been hazy, concussion-induced dreams—made no more sense in the light of day than they had at the time. Despite her announcement last night at Lydia's house—which she'd made on painkillers, Lydia had been quick to remind everyone—she really wasn't certain.

"I don't know," Tesla finally answered.

"It might help if you told us the story," Joley said, somewhat aggrieved. "I know you've been through bugger-all, and Lydia was concerned for you last night when she sent you to bed before you could give us any details, but it was bloody frustrating for the rest of us."

"In other words, despite the drama of last night, we don't know any more than we did before you showed up," said Beckett.

Tesla didn't turn around. For the life of her, she couldn't figure out what she'd done to make Beckett despise her.

The four walked the tree-lined block in silence after that. Lydia had said they would all meet again this afternoon and hear the rest of her story, but Tesla wasn't sure she even *knew* the story—some of the details of that night in the hospital were fuzzy at best. And she still felt a little shaky—due in part to the pain pills she was on—but better than she had the night before. She'd slept until noon, a heavy, dreamless sleep, and woken up on the couch, covered by a soft cotton blanket. The first thing she'd seen when she opened her eyes was Bizzy, who watched her from the leather chair Lydia had occupied the night before. After Tesla had eaten the bowl of cereal Bizzy offered, washed her face and used the new toothbrush the goth girl waved at her, they had walked down to the kitchen in silence while Tesla wondered if Bizzy applied black eyeliner the moment she woke up each day, or if she actually slept in it. Downstairs, the others leaned or sat on the counters, clearly waiting.

"I think you should go to your house first," Lydia had said without preamble. "Look around, go get your brother, and see if, given the information you now have about your parents' work, you are reminded of a memory, an event, anything that might be relevant. By then we'll likely have heard from your father."

"I don't like that he hasn't called," said Tesla, cradling her cast with her right hand and holding it protectively to her chest. She'd checked her cell first thing, but her father had neither called nor texted. It was an unwelcome, but hauntingly familiar sensation, to be unmoored, adrift in the world, as if she and Max were utterly alone. She'd hoped to never feel again that sense of abandonment she'd experienced after her mother died.

"I don't see any need to worry at this point," said Lydia briskly. "I expect to have more information about the explosion very soon. Elizabeth will go to the lab—the lab and the Bat Cave—

and she'll report back when she returns. I've got to check in with another field agent. We'll meet back here later, and we'll hear the rest of what you remember about that night."

Tesla wasn't quite sure what she was supposed to do, other than pick up Max from Dylan's house, but she figured she could just go with it for now, since she was clearly not in charge. One corner of her mouth quirked upward wryly as she considered what her reaction would be to this type of dependency and passivity without the painkillers she was taking. She loathed being told what to do.

Tesla's arm didn't hurt, thanks to those pills, although she could already feel the strain on her shoulder, as if she carried a ten-pound hand weight around with her all the time. She resolved to rig up a sling after she got home and everybody else had left.

A slight breeze lifted Tesla's hair to cool her neck and shoulders as she walked, and she closed her eyes, just for a moment, the sun warm on her head. She loved summer, despite her propensity to burn. Behind her, Finn watched her bright hair twist and move in the air, red and orange and honey strands woven together, and caught a glimpse of the back of her neck as the breeze blew among and around them.

As they turned the corner and her house came into view, Tesla came to an abrupt stop, suddenly reluctant to go any further.

"Now what?" asked Beckett, annoyed to have almost run into Tesla.

"Nothing," said Tesla. She walked on again despite her reluctance to go home.

"I'm sure it's fine," Finn said as he jogged a couple of yards to take the lead. "But I'll go first, just in case. No arguments, Abbott."

No one caught the brief smile that played around Tesla's

lips. She had no intention of arguing, but it was nice of him to help her save what little face she had in this strange group, especially in front of Beckett Isley. Perhaps he wasn't such a pain in the ass, after all.

As they approached the front door of Tesla's house, Finn glanced briefly at the open windows. The curtains blew gently in the breeze just as they had the night before when he and Tesla had hidden in the shadows of the neighbor's hedge. He saw nothing out of the ordinary now, however, and continued up the front steps. "Becks, after you," he said as he opened the still-unlocked front door.

Beckett moved swiftly and purposefully up the steps and through the front door, her feet in soundless black ballet flats, her body deceptively relaxed. She was a coiled snake, ready to strike. Her right hand was held loosely at waist-level, her left hand down by her thigh, where its open palm faced the others who stood just behind her. Tesla did not need to be told that that open palm meant they should wait, and be quiet. The lithe blonde moved slowly into the foyer. She stepped lightly, carefully, turning her head in a new direction with each step.

In under two minutes—though it seemed much longer— Beckett was back in the doorway. "The first floor is clear, but be on your guard," she said. "I'll check upstairs."

Tesla stood in the living room and stared at the wreckage. The coffee table was upside down, the magazines that had been on top of it scattered across the floor. A few pages fluttered in the summer breeze. The lampshade on the little table next to the sofa was crooked, and a delicate bottle-green glass vase that had sat beside that lamp for years was smashed into one hundred fourteen discernible, razor-sharp pieces on the floor. Several dark spots, large enough to be identified as blood from where she stood, had dried on the carpet among the shards of glass.

"You okay?" asked Finn, right beside her.

"Yeah," she said, a little surprised to find that it was true. She indicated the blood on the beige carpet. "Did you get cut last night?"

"No, just this." He gingerly touched his bruised cheekbone.

"Yeah, me either." She stepped toward the bloodstain and squatted down to sit on her heels, her head cocked slightly to the side as she took a closer look. "Maybe it was the other guy. The burglar."

"Maybe," said Finn, and something in his voice made Tesla glance quickly at his face, but she could not read his carefully blank expression.

"Don't touch anything," said Joley, who now stood beside Finn and surveyed the room. "Lydia will have a team here shortly, and they'll dust for fingerprints, take the blood from the carpet, run everything through their databases."

"Should we call the police?" Tesla asked.

"Let's hold off on that," said Finn, "at least until we determine the extent of the damage, and what might have been stolen. You ready to do a walk-through?"

Tesla nodded. "I'll take a look here, why don't you start upstairs. I'll be up in a minute." She felt okay, but it was weird to stand here in her living room, blood and broken glass on the floor. Perhaps all she needed was a minute alone, to feel comfortable in her own house and like she wasn't under surveillance. For a change.

Joley donned latex gloves and went to work in the kitchen, but Finn didn't move.

"It's weird, standing here, isn't it? After last night," he said absently. He figured Tesla had to be shaken up, being here where she'd been attacked just a few hours earlier. He felt it himself, and he hadn't even been hurt.

"Yeah," she said. "I don't really remember what happened. Just bits and pieces."

"I can sum it up," Finn said in a clipped, cold voice. "Some asshole broke your arm and I didn't get a chance to return the favor. Yet."

Fists balled up tightly at his sides, Finn turned and climbed the stairs without another word.

What the hell? Tesla thought. *He sounds like he's mad at me.*

Upstairs, Finn turned into the first open doorway and found Beckett going through the papers and books on the desk of what must be Tesla's bedroom, if the posters of LeBron and Zack somebody—a young actor whose name he couldn't remember— were any indication. There were two basketballs on the dresser, a very old, very used, one-eyed teddy bear on the windowsill, and a short stack of theoretical math books on the bedside table. Crumpled clothes were strewn everywhere, books and magazines lay open, facedown on the carpet, and the bed was a rumpled mess. At least half a dozen dirty glasses cluttered every available surface.

"She's really a slob, isn't she?" he asked, astonished and amused.

"Yes, she is," said Beckett. "A slob and a little girl. Can you believe the tweeny crap all over this room? She's probably got a *Team Edward* shirt in every color."

"What is your problem, Becks?" Finn asked.

"What do you mean?"

"I mean, what is your problem with Tesla? You're not typically warm and fuzzy, but you're downright hostile where she's concerned." Finn had moved into the room and stood in front of the window, only a few feet from Beckett.

"You're right, I have been kind of nasty," she said, her voice pitched softly, her hesitation clear.

Finn felt wary; Beckett didn't do soft and hesitant.

She took a step closer to him, reached out and touched his hand, and he had no choice but to remember the other time they'd been this close. "I guess it's harder to be around Tesla than I thought," she admitted. "Hard to be constantly reminded how lucky she is and how I grew up—always the foreigner, with a family more concerned about the plight of strangers than their own daughter."

Finn knew Beckett's story. He knew she'd had to become tough—and done a damn good job of it—to survive her years in several developing countries. An only child and then, years later, in charge of a younger sister, with missionary parents who'd home-schooled her and left her to explore the streets of Singapore, Bangkok, Xi'an and Beijing on her own, she knew how to take care of herself, but she didn't know much about how to make friends.

"Yeah, I get it, Becks. Sorry if we've been oblivious, but you know it's not because the group doesn't care, right?" Finn was careful to make this about all of them, not just Beckett and him. There was no Beckett and him, despite what had happened between them.

And then somehow, Becket was in his arms, her own arms wrapped tightly around his waist, her head buried in his shoulder. He put his hands lightly on her shoulders in an attempt to comfort her, and looked awkwardly out the window as if he might escape through it. Beckett was a mass of intriguing contradictions, smooth and shiny to the touch but deadly sharp underneath. Whatever she might truly care about was buried under a layer of biting wit and nonchalance. She was brutally sarcastic and, frankly, hot as hell—an appealing combination, at least to those who imagined themselves up to it. But Finn had decided months ago he didn't want this entanglement. He didn't want *any* entanglement.

"Thanks, Finn; you always did know how to make me feel better," Beckett purred suggestively, and then she reached up and kissed him on the mouth.

Downstairs, Tesla closed her eyes and breathed deeply. She exhaled and let herself remember the fear and the pain, the hands that had grabbed her in the dark and thrown her across the room, her intimate knowledge of the placement of furniture and uncanny spatial awareness absolutely useless as her body was propelled forward, unchecked. She had crashed into the coffee table with enough force to break the bones in her arm—not just crack them, but break them clean through, and she remembered it as sensation and image, unconnected, nightmarish fragments. She had little recollection of what came after, just a hazy sense of Finn's face close to hers, his brown eyes dark with concern, not a trace of his usual mockery when he looked at her. She remembered the cool night air as they made their way outside and the sudden realization that she would pass out. She knew nothing more until she woke up on Lydia's couch.

Of course I don't remember at all that Finn carried me down the street and into the house, she thought, her eyes suddenly open again as she laughed softly to herself.

Clearly the best way to deal with trauma was to focus on the nearest cute guy.

She turned from the room and quietly made her way up the stairs. She unconsciously skipped the third stair from the top, as she always did, because the boards under the carpet groaned whenever someone put their weight on them. She had never thought to wonder why she tried to glide through the house, unseen and unheard, why she didn't want to call attention to her presence in her own home.

Tesla covered the six feet of hallway to her open bedroom door and stopped, mouth open and breath stilled. Finn and Beckett Isley stood in front of the window beside her unmade bed while the sheer, white curtains billowed around them in the warm breeze. Beckett's arms were wound tightly around him, her head pressed against his shoulder, an unreadable expression on her face as the two girls looked at each other. Finn's hands were on Beckett's shoulders, his face turned toward the open window.

"Thanks, Finn, you always did know how to make me feel better," Beckett said. She tipped her chin up to look at Finn and as he turned toward her, Beckett rose up on her toes and kissed him.

Tesla turned on her heel and moved as quickly and quietly as she could past the bathroom she and Max shared to her little brother's bedroom. She went inside and closed the door, wincing at the faint *click*. The last thing—the very last thing—she wanted was for Finn to know she'd seen him kiss Beckett, seen how comfortably they fit into each other's arms, proof positive that they knew each other very, very well. Her face burned with humiliation as she buried her face in her hands.

Surprise—and pleasure—kept Finn from pushing Beckett away immediately. But push her away he did, only a moment later, gently and without ambiguity. "Becks. C'mon. We tried this once, remember? We're better as friends." He stepped back from her embrace. "Let's get back to work."

Becket looked stunned for the briefest of moments, and then she shrugged. "Sure," she said. "I'm done in here anyway."

CHAPTER 12

Tesla looked up quickly when she heard the door open.

"What are you doing in here?" Finn asked. She could see Beckett right behind him. The blonde girl peered over Finn's shoulder, and Tesla was sure she had a smirk on her face.

"What do you think I'm doing?" Tesla snapped, her humiliation instantly turned to anger. "I'm looking through Max's stuff to see if there's any hint of where my father might be. You remember my father—the one you're supposed to protect?"

If Finn was stung by her tone, he didn't show it. He looked at her for a moment, his expression unchanged. "Of course I remember. What did you find?"

She felt a pit in her stomach as large and hollow as the house. "Nothing. I want to go get Max. Now."

"Okay," Finn said, no questions asked. "Beckett and Joley can finish up here."

Without another word to either of them, Tesla got up from the bed and walked down the stairs, across the living room, and out the front door, where Finn caught up to her. She was aware of his occasional, sideways glance in her direction as they walked, but she didn't return his look.

"Does your arm hurt?" he asked.

"No," she said curtly.

Finn scowled as he felt a trickle of sweat run down between his shoulder blades. They walked for another minute in silence. "What is up with you?" he finally asked.

Tesla stopped and turned to him on the sidewalk, her eyes squinted against the bright sun, a mere hint of blue and green from between dark lashes. "Well, let's see, my father's office was bombed, he's apparently in danger from I don't know who, and now he's missing. Someone vandalized my house and broke my arm. And a bunch of people I don't even know have been watching me for weeks. I guess that's what's up."

"Okay, I get it," Finn said, angry at last. "But it doesn't explain why you're mad at me."

"I'm not mad at you." She spoke the lie lightly, infuriatingly nonchalant, and felt a sharp little pang of satisfaction when he pressed his lips tightly together, a soft, frustrated exhalation of air escaping his flared nostrils.

"Forget it," she said then, her fleeting sense of triumph gone as quickly as it had arrived. The worry and fear for her dad, and the absurdity of feeling rejected by this guy she barely knew all came together into a lump in her throat. Her eyes stung sharply with tears she refused to shed in front of Finnegan Ford, so she turned away from him and said, "This is the house. I'm gonna get Max."

Before she could get to the front door, however, Max had flung it open and raced down the porch steps and stopped right in front of her. Tesla knew he had been about to hug her, to throw his arms around her, but had caught himself just in time, and she couldn't help but smile.

"You okay?" she asked as she clutched his shoulder with her uninjured hand.

"Yeah," Max said. He pushed his glasses up higher on his nose and spoke quickly, excitedly. "Dylan's mom said I couldn't go home, and she's been so weird, and nervous, and—what happened to your arm?"

Tesla grabbed his hand, sat down on the first step of Dylan's front porch and pulled her brother down to sit beside her. Finn watched quietly, a few feet away on the sidewalk. Tesla still held Max's hand, which he appeared not to notice.

"I broke it last night—just an accident. But I have to tell you something, Max. Dad is—"

"Your dad is just fine, I'm sure of it," said a very assured, and unusually low-pitched woman's voice from the doorway behind them.

Tesla turned her head quickly toward the sound. "Aunt Jane? What are you doing here?" She looked up at the brunette woman who stood on the porch a few steps above her, noted the familiar short haircut, clipped up over her ears like a boy's, the long bangs that brushed the top of her eyelashes. She was dark and elfin, her age difficult to guess.

"I'm here for you and Max, of course," said Aunt Jane. She wore a smile geared to reassure, but somehow it didn't quite reach her eyes, which remained far too serious to match her light tone.

"What do you mean, you're here 'for' us?" asked Tesla. She stood up slowly. For some unfathomable reason, she needed to feel bigger.

Aunt Jane quickly walked down the steps to stand beside Tesla, and Finn noted that with Jane's heels the two were exactly the same height.

"Tes, why don't we go back to the house and talk," said Aunt Jane. She reached out to touch Tesla's arm but stopped as she took in the cast. "We clearly have a lot to catch up on."

Tesla took a step backwards. "You know about Dad. Tell me."

Aunt Jane glanced quickly at Max. "Let's talk later." She was a petite woman with a voice that suggested she gave orders easily and often. Finn guessed she only had to give them once.

Tesla reached down and found Max's arm, and her eyes never left Aunt Jane's. She pulled Max up from the step where he still sat, brought him in close and clutched him tightly to her side. "Tell us now," she said, and her voice sounded remarkably like her Aunt's.

Aunt Jane hesitated for only a moment as she took in the tableau of Tesla and Max, who held onto each other for support. They stood braced, the weight of all they'd lost—could still lose—clearly upon them.

"Tesla—Max—your father may have been kidnapped."

Thirty minutes later, Tesla, Max, Aunt Jane, Finn, and Becket sat on the grass under the maple in the Abbotts' backyard. The house had been commandeered by Lydia's people—and Joley, who said he loved all things CSI and didn't want to miss a single carpet-fiber removal.

Tesla sat quietly next to Max. Her broken arm rested on her bent knees while her right hand absently pulled up handfuls of grass.

Aunt Jane, who had not yet expounded on the matter of Dr. Abbott, watched Tesla's angry face and Max's uncharacteristically close proximity to his sister, and began.

"Your dad hasn't been seen for almost twenty-four hours. I don't have to tell you that this is unusual behavior for him. We know that he's almost always at his lab or here, at home, with you."

In the pause that followed, Tesla looked up at Jane. "First, how do you know what his usual behavior is? You haven't been here for like a year." Tesla was surprised by her own accusatory tone. Why was she mad at Aunt Jane?

Aunt Jane smiled, and this time it softened her face considerably. "I may not be here as often as I'd like," she said, "but I keep in pretty close contact with your dad."

Tesla looked down at her feet again, and Aunt Jane continued. "You said 'first,' Tesla. What's 'second?'"

"Second, who is 'we'?"

Tesla caught the swift glance between Beckett and Finn, and wondered why she was surprised. "Wait, don't tell me. You're some kind of secret agent." She vaguely remembered that she'd sworn to Lydia that she could keep her mouth shut, but at the moment she didn't care.

"Well," Aunt Jane began with some hesitation, "I wouldn't put it that way, exactly—"

"What the hell?" Tesla cried as she hugged her legs tighter. "You're supposed to be some kind of business consultant, my mom's best friend from college. You've been an aunt to us our whole lives—you're Max's godmother! You're a spy? Did my father know about you—" Tesla clapped her hand tightly over her own mouth, horrified to realize that she had begun to speak of her father in the past tense.

"Tesla, honey, your dad's okay," Aunt Jane assured her as she stood and went to Tesla and Max, crouched down, and lay a hand on each of their shoulders. "It's possible that he has decided to stay hidden to keep himself, and you two, safe, but after this long without word it's more likely that he's been taken—and if so, whoever is responsible wants him alive, I assure you."

Tesla took a deep breath, let go of her tight grip on Max's arm, and shrugged off Aunt Jane's hand on her shoulder. She stood up and looked down at Jane, whom she'd known all her life, and her eyes were cold and without a trace of the love and trust she'd always felt for the woman she called her aunt.

"I want to know it all, and I want to know it right now. Nothing happens until you have spilled every goddamn detail about my parents, their work, who you are, and what has happened to my father."

Aunt Jane stood, her eyes never leaving Tesla's, and they sized each other up. Then the older woman nodded. "Fair enough. But Max—"

"Max stays," Tesla interrupted. "No more secrets. From us, or between us." She looked down at her little brother, who met her eyes without fear. "Max and I are a team," she finished.

"I understand that you've been told about your parents' work on time travel," Jane began after a moment, her deep voice displaying no sign of emotion whatsoever.

"You 'understand'?" Tesla said, the scorn clear in her voice. "Let's be clear. You were told that I was attacked in our house the same night Dad disappeared, and so I had to be brought in."

"Yes, Tesla, that's right."

"Then just say so! And tell me who told you—what part of 'tell us everything' do you not get?"

"Sorry," Jane said, and her voice actually sounded it. "Force of habit. Yes, Lydia and I know one another, and we have been in periodic contact about your father and his work the last few years. We do not work for the same agency, but our employers have agreed to coordinate on this case for various reasons. We keep each other in the loop."

"So you know these guys, that they've been watching us," Tesla said, indicating with her hand those assembled, and more.

"Yes, although I've only just met everyone involved here,

except for Lydia."

Tesla didn't mean to, but she couldn't help it: she glanced at Finn, her belief that he had betrayed her—again—by keeping this from her plain on her face. Finn, to his credit, did not look away.

She turned back to Jane. "What do you think has happened to Dad?"

"We believe that he has experienced some kind of breakthrough in his work, and that someone, or some group, who has watched him in anticipation of just such a breakthrough, has kidnapped him in order to steal his work."

"Steal the ability to time-travel," Tesla corrected her.

"Wait, what?" said Max, who had been silent until this moment.

"Yeah, Max, this was what Dad and Mom worked on, together, and Dad has continued since Mom died. He's really close. *Really* close," she repeated.

"Yes, and we need to talk about that," said Finn. "This has all started to move quickly and we don't want to lose sight of what you might be able to tell us—your experience could be directly connected to your dad's disappearance."

"I know, but wait," said Tesla as she turned back to Jane. "Who do you think has Dad?"

"There are several possibilities," said Jane in her clipped, low voice. "We're aware of both groups and individuals who have an interest in this, for profit or ideology."

"And which do you think it is?" Tesla pressed.

"I think it's someone who wants to profit from the technology, and I think it's a personal issue as well."

"Sebastian Nilsen," Tesla said quietly.

"Who?" asked Max.

"Dr. Sebastian Nilsen," Jane repeated. "He went to college

with us—with your mom and dad and me. I went on to study politics and history, but your parents and Sebastian earned doctorates in physics. They were friends. Close friends."

"So why would he kidnap my dad?" Max asked. "There has to be more to the story, something specific that has motivated him. Jealousy, money, something. But I don't think friendship is a part of it—or at least not anymore."

"Max, I thought you were just hearing about this for the first time?" Jane said.

Max shrugged. "It's a narrative, and there are a limited number of possible motivations for the characters in any story, right?"

"That's right," said Finn. "I think I came to that realization like, six months ago, and only through advanced courses in literature, narrative theory, and social psychology. Good job, man."

Max grinned at Finn, and they quietly fist-bumped.

The back door banged shut and everyone who sat under the tree in the Abbott backyard turned as one and watched Joley approach.

Finn, who knew him very well and could see the suppressed excitement on his face, stood up. "What is it?" he asked.

Joley focused in on Tesla as if he spoke to her alone. "We found something."

CHAPTER 13

By dinnertime Tesla was back at Lydia's house to unpack the bag she had hurriedly thrown together. Bizzy had taken her and Max upstairs to show them two small bedrooms on the third floor and an adjacent bathroom they could use before she left them to get settled.

"Can I come in?" asked Max from the doorway.

"Yeah," Tesla said. She did not look up as she shoved two tanks and a pair of khakis into the open dresser drawer.

Max came in and sat on the edge of the bed. "Are you mad?"

Tesla didn't answer. She zipped up her now empty duffle bag and tossed it onto the floor in a corner.

"Are you mad at me?" Max asked. He picked at the bedspread and pushed his glasses up higher on his nose with the other hand.

Tesla closed her eyes and exhaled slowly. Then she sat down on the bed, too. "No, Max, I'm not mad at you. I'm not very happy at the moment, but of course I'm not mad at you."

"Who are you mad at?"

"No one. Everyone. I don't know," Tesla said. "I'm worried about Dad. And I don't want to be here. And I'm not sure why we have to do what any of these people say."

Max took his usual time to think the situation through, unlike his sister, who seemed to prefer to fly off the handle at the least provocation. "Well, since you're only seventeen, we probably can't be totally in charge of ourselves," he reasoned. "And if Dad was here, don't you think he'd say we have to listen to Aunt Jane?"

Tesla's scowl didn't diminish, but she had to admit he was right. "Yeah, probably. But I want to be at home, in our house. We don't really even know these people, and they've all ganged up on us."

Things had not gone well back at the Abbott house after Joley came outside and announced that Lydia's team had found additional writing on the back of the note her father had written, the one he'd left for Tesla underneath the pizza box. One of Lydia's people had gone through the trash and found Dr. Abbott's note to his daughter and turned it over. The words, handwritten just as the other side had been, read, simply, *Don't be afraid—keep trying.*

The note was a puzzle they had yet to decipher, and the afternoon waned as they had discussed it endlessly. Tesla's arm had begun to throb painfully. They asked her the same questions, over and over again, maybe because they didn't like her answers, but she didn't know what she could do about that. *No, she hadn't thought to turn the paper over when she'd found her father's note. No, she didn't know what he meant by it.* Finally, she'd had enough. She needed some down time and a chance to talk all this craziness over with Max.

"Um, not to kick you guys out, but maybe we could pick this up tomorrow? Max and I will come over to Lydia's as soon as we wake up, but right now I'd kind of like to order some Chinese and go to bed. I'm wiped out."

"You can't stay here," Finn had said matter-of-factly.

"Of course I can," Tesla responded.

"Tesla, we don't know who was in your house yesterday—remember the guy who attacked you? We don't know if and when he'll be back. It would be stupid to let you and Max stay here."

"Well then it's a good thing you're not in charge, isn't it?" She snapped back. "This is where we live. We'll lock the doors. End of discussion." *How dare he tell her what to do, like she was Max's age, like he was her father*, she thought, and was immediately swamped with guilt.

"Sorry, Tesla, but Finn's right," Aunt Jane had said, the regret plain in her voice. "I've got to follow up some leads on your dad, and I'm not sure how long I'll be gone. When I get back, I can stay here with you, but for now I need you and Max to stay at Lydia's. You'll be safe there."

"Don't worry, Jane," Beckett said. She stood up and brushed the grass and whatever off her skin-tight jeans. "We'll protect the kids while you're gone."

Tesla looked daggers at her. She was so angry she couldn't trust herself to speak, and she felt the flush of helplessness suffuse her face—she would not concede.

Jane glanced at Tesla and sighed. She knew her well enough to recognize the signs of imminent battle. "Tesla," she said in her low, deep voice. "What's important right now is that we work together to find your father. We all have to do what we can to make sure we get him back quickly and unharmed. Which means you and Max need to stay with Lydia—I need you to work with them as much as I need for you to be safe, so I don't have to worry about you while I'm gone. You'll get more accomplished if you stay there. For now, Lydia's house is command central."

And now here she was for an indefinite stay with these spies who'd watched her do and heard her say God knows what. Half of them didn't even like her, and the jury was out on the other half. And they all made her feel like a little kid, a burden. She tried to let it go so she could focus on her dad, on the ill-defined work that lay ahead of her to figure out what it all meant while the clock ticked away.

When Max left, clearly excited to explore the house a bit, Tesla realized that she should go downstairs as well, so they could all work out a plan for how to proceed from this point. Jane had said she would be over, briefly, before she left town, as soon as she'd made travel arrangements. Tesla took one of the pain pills Bizzy had brought up with them, picked up the long, green cotton scarf that she'd brought with her from home, and tossed it onto the bed. With her right hand she folded the scarf so it was narrow and long, and then sat down on the bed to try to rig some sort of sling for her broken arm. She put one end of the scarf in her mouth, and wound the thicker mid-section of the fabric underneath her cast. Then she picked up the other end, and brought it up toward her shoulder from the other side—and stopped, the scarf in place, but with one end in her mouth and the other end in her uninjured hand. She had no idea how she could even begin to tie it with only one hand.

"Want some help?" asked Finn, who had appeared silently in the doorway.

She dropped the end that she held between her teeth and spoke in the coldest voice she could manage. "No thanks."

"Could you possibly be more of a pain in the ass?" he asked conversationally as he walked into the room anyway. He sat down where Max had sat, on the edge of the bed next to Tesla, and got to work. He watched his hands, not Tesla's face, and talked while he settled her cast, at exactly the right angle, into the scarf and tied the soft fabric in a square knot at the back of her neck.

"You know, you're not here because anybody is trying to punish you," he said. "This is dangerous stuff, and you'd be here if you were ninety years old." His hands were behind her neck as he tied the knot, while Tesla held her long hair up with her good right hand. She could feel his fingers, warm and sure, on her skin and see, for the first time, that the light brown of his irises were shot through with flecks of gold.

"Well, if I was ninety, I hope you wouldn't put me on the third floor," she said lightly. "That would just be mean. You know, with my walker and all."

Finn stopped and their eyes met. They sat close together, and he had leaned in toward her to fix the sling. "I'd still put you up here." He finished off the knot, slowly and deliberately. "It would take you awhile to get up and down the stairs, but we'd know where you were. It's probably the only way we could keep you out of trouble."

Tesla felt her heart beat loudly, certain he could hear it, too. Finn wasn't looking at her anymore, he was focused entirely on tying her sling, but all she could think was that his mouth was six and a quarter inches from her own. It was all such a mess—she was angry and resentful, sick of everyone telling her what to do, she'd been attacked and spied on and Finn treated her like a child, she was nothing but a pain in the ass to him, and she wanted to be—she didn't know what she wanted to be.

"All this is not my fault, you know," she began, her face hot and her voice unsteady. "I don't *mean* to get in trouble, but I—"

Finn suddenly moved forward those last few inches and pressed his lips, softly, to hers.

The very air she breathed tipped Tesla toward him—the weight and pull and curve of it led, inexorably, to his warm mouth, and the points of contact where they touched became all that was left of her physical self: her mouth against his, the tender skin of her neck under his fingers. Her body flooded with heat as he paused, his mouth on hers, as if he were surprised. Both his hands were now behind her head and he pulled her in closer, deepening their kiss.

It lasted a second, maybe two, a month, a year. And then he moved away and left her with lips slightly parted, eyes wide open. He smiled and stood up, shoving his hands into his pockets.

"Yeah, I know," he said. "You just can't help it. See you downstairs."

Lydia poured freshly steeped black tea into the bone china cup, then looked over at Tesla. "Milk? Lemon?"

Tesla looked up, puzzled, as if she'd forgotten where she was. "Um, lemon, I guess. Thanks."

Finn watched her from his customary position in front of the fireplace as he drank his tea—black and hot enough to scald. It had taken them all awhile to get used to this little quirk of Lydia's, her insistence that they have afternoon tea, but he now looked forward to it, and not just because it meant a decent snack in the middle of the day. It was a chance to sit and chat, to catch up, in addition to whatever business related to the Abbott case they might all have to discuss. Everyone in the house knew each other a little better because of these teas, and that meant they functioned more efficiently as a unit.

Lydia picked up a fresh slice of lemon with little silver tongs, placed it carefully on the saucer, and then handed it to Tesla, who sat in a chair by the coffee table. Tesla seemed unsure what to do. Her eyes darted around the room—landed on Finn then hastened away again—until she scooted out to the edge of her chair so she could set her cup and saucer on the corner of the table, just inches away from where Lydia was doing the honors.

After she'd served everyone else, Lydia proceeded to make her own cup which gave Finn a moment longer to watch Tesla from beneath his hooded eyes. He stood casually, lazily, his legs crossed at the ankles and his shoulders slouched as he leaned up against the fireplace—a deliberate contrast to his silent anger. He was furious with himself for that kiss—he circled back to it again and again. He could still feel her soft mouth, the faint scent of soap on her skin, the inevitability of the way she had moved toward him. The memory was a scourge with which he lashed himself, without pity.

Lydia sat back, took a sip of her tea, and closed her eyes for a brief moment, a relaxed smile on her face. And then she opened her eyes and spoke, and everyone remembered what she did for a living.

"Tesla, we have new information on your father," she began without preamble. "His credit cards have not been used since he disappeared, his car is parked on campus near his office, and we have a team there now to gather any forensic evidence."

Tesla glanced at Max, who swallowed visibly. Neither of them responded.

"His cell phone records indicate that he made only one call that night, to your house phone—and he left a voicemail message. He called the house—importantly, a few minutes *after* the explosion at his office. Which of course is excellent news."

Tesla sat up very straight. "What did the message say?"

"It's very brief, and we have a copy here." Lydia turned to Joley. "Can you play it for Tesla, please?"

Joley didn't answer, but held up his iPhone and played an MP3 file, the volume up high enough for everyone to hear.

"I had to go out, kids, so do me a favor and clean up the kitchen from our pizza party. Oh, and DVR that TV show we want to watch, the

one with the really high ratings. I'll be home as soon as I can."

"What does it mean?" asked Tesla. Like everyone else, she had already learned to look to Lydia for answers. Her father's voice had sounded normal, she thought, maybe a little excited. Surely that was a good sign?

"There is still some question about what he might have meant, but we've got some ideas," Lydia said, then looked to Finn with a slight nod.

"First, he sounds good: strong, lucid." Finn watched Tesla's face as he spoke. Her expression reflected quite clearly what she thought and felt—he couldn't remember what it was like to be that open to life—that open to being hurt—if, indeed, he had ever been.

"I think so, too," she said quickly. "He doesn't sound like he's scared or—or hurt."

Finn nodded once. He would not allow himself to smile at her, encourage her—about her father's situation or about that kiss. He didn't think either was good for her, and didn't want to be responsible for where either might lead. "And let's assume that his voicemail is supposed to send you, and us, a message that no one else would understand," he continued smoothly. "First, his voicemail tells us that he's alive and well. He didn't text, he wanted you to hear his voice. It also tells us that he was able, at least, to make that phone call—he is not gagged, and his hands aren't tied."

"Or at least that wasn't the case at that time," Beckett corrected him.

Tesla swallowed, hard. Gagged and tied? What kind of a world did she now live in?

"Third," Finn said. "We should assume that every word was deliberate—he said *I should be home soon.* He doesn't want you and Max to worry about him. And finally, we have what appear to be two coded messages, which we hope you two can decipher." He paused and looked from Tesla to Max. "He asks you to clean up from a pizza party, and to record a TV show you are all interested in."

Tesla looked at Max, who shrugged, and she looked back at Finn. "I'm not sure," she began, but Lydia interrupted.

"We think his request that you clean up refers to the note we found yesterday at your house, which seems to be an attempt to make up after the argument you had." She paused in order to let Tesla weigh in.

Tesla frowned. "Yeah, I guess so. That's certainly what I thought when I read it."

"What about the reference to a TV show?" Beckett asked without malice or sarcasm. She was a professional, at least for the moment. "Has your family talked about a new show, one you all wanted to watch?"

"No," said Tesla. "We really don't watch the same shows, and actually my Dad hardly watches TV at all. I like science fiction and the occasional reality show, and Max likes stupid stuff."

"Oh, because *The Bachelor* is an intellectual and artistic tour de force?" Max said.

Finn jumped in. "So your dad didn't mean it literally, then. What TV shows right now are highly rated? Maybe the name of a show, or an actor, will be a clue."

Joley had already googled *highly rated TV shows* on his phone, and he began to read aloud from the screen as he scrolled down. "In May, *Game of Thrones* received the highest Nielssen rating—"

"Nielssen—Nilsen!" Bizzy said excitedly. "Sebastian Nilsen! You were right, Lydia!"

Everyone began to talk at once, and it took a moment for

Tesla to realize that Aunt Jane had entered the room and set a nondescript overnight bag at her feet.

"That's right," Jane said, and everyone quieted down. "Nilsen has kidnapped Greg Abbott. We just got confirmation, a phone call was made to the local FBI ops office from a burner."

"A burner?" Tesla asked.

"A prepaid disposable cell phone, untraceable," Joley answered. "Doesn't anybody watch *The Wire*?" he asked as he turned to Finn. They both shook their heads in disbelief.

Everyone began to talk again, but Lydia held up her hand and silence dropped on the room like a blanket. "Hello, Jane. Nice to see you."

Finn was surprised by the lack of warmth in Lydia's voice, her stone-cold expression as she spoke to the younger woman.

"Lydia." Jane nodded at the woman seated behind the tea pot. There was an odd tension in the room, and everybody else looked as confused by it as Finn felt. Everyone but the two women, that is. They looked calmly at each other, and Jane Doane appeared slightly amused.

"What else do we have from the phone call?" Beckett asked. "Who called, and from where? Is there a ransom demand?"

"No ransom demand yet. We're triangulating tower signals now to narrow down the call's point of origin, which appears to be Niagara Falls on the Canadian side. The voice was altered and our voice recognition software came up with nothing. We need someone from an agency that operates internationally on this, so I'm on my way up there now. Hopefully the trail isn't too cold."

Lydia nodded. "I'll carry on here," she said vaguely.

"Good. I'll check in with you after I've arrived and catch you up." Jane took two steps and leaned down to give Max a hug where he sat on the couch, and then she turned to Tesla. "Tesla, try not to worry. If there's one thing you and Max can trust it's that I want to get your father back."

Lydia moved suddenly, a quick jerk of her hand that seemed unintentional, and Tesla's cup and saucer, filled with now-cold tea, crashed to the floor and broke into several large, sharp pieces of china as the dark liquid seeped into the thick rug beneath the coffee table.

"Oh, how clumsy of me," said Lydia. "I don't know what I was thinking." She dabbed at the wet mess at her feet with a linen napkin, her face hidden from sight as she attempted to clean it up. Jane watched her for a moment, then grabbed her bag and walked out the door.

Lydia set the broken pieces of china on the coffee table and put the tea-soaked napkin beside them. "We still have a lot to discuss," she said to the room at large. "Tesla, if you're up to it, I believe you left your story unfinished. Let's hear that first."

All eyes turned to Tesla. "Should we maybe get Aunt Jane back in here first?" she asked. "She hasn't heard any of this either, and it might be important."

"We'll catch her up later," Lydia assured her.

CHAPTER 14

Tesla began her story, hesitatingly at first, but with increased confidence as she relived that strange night at the hospital. She went back over what she'd already told Finn about her concussion and exploration of the subfloors under the hospital last fall, about her assumption that what happened had been a head-injury-induced hallucination.

"So, you found yourself in this room, and you heard your dad's voice do some sort of countdown, then bright lights and you passed out," Finn summarized. "Then what?"

"Then I dreamed—I thought I had dreamed—but maybe I woke up."

"Well what happened?" Bizzy asked, too excited to sit cross-legged on the floor any longer, so far away from Tesla. She had sort of walked on her knees over to where Tesla still sat, in the chair by the sofa, and plopped down right in front of her to sit on her heels. "What happened when you woke up?

"It was kind of awful—I'm not really claustrophobic, but I woke up and I was sort of curled up in a ball on my side, my knees up by my face, and it was completely dark. For a second I wondered if my eyes were still closed."

Finn noted the tension in Tesla's voice, but she didn't sound scared, as she had when she'd started to tell this story to him the first time. She had clearly begun to adapt to the fear and the danger, and it had given her confidence. Time alone would tell if, like Finn, she would find it addictive.

"My eyes were open, but I couldn't see, it was too dark— and I could hardly move. I was packed into a space that was barely big enough for me, and something hard and sharp pressed into my back…. It was like those scary stories you tell at camp when you're a kid, the one where someone wakes up to find they've been buried alive in a coffin."

Tesla paused a moment, and no one said a word. They knew exactly what she meant.

"So I tried to move, arms and legs, head, and there were literally only a few inches at various points where I wasn't pressed up against a hard, smooth wall, but I had about six inches above me. That same hard, smooth material made a solid ceiling on top of me."

Lydia handed Tesla a new cup of tea, without the saucer this time, and Tesla took it and sipped, gratefully. The strong brew, with just a hint of tangy citrus, was delicious and gave her a chance to pause and remember.

"That space above me was enough, so I started to push against the ceiling with my legs and my shoulder," she continued. "I was afraid I was completely sealed in, but once I started to push it was clear it was movable, latched but not locked. Once I popped the latch with one good shove of my shoulder I could see light, so I moved the top up until it clicked. It was hinged on one side, like a lid or a door. I sat up and looked around."

"Tell us what you saw—and take your time, don't leave out any details," Lydia encouraged her.

"I was in a room, not really dark, there were a couple of dim lights on." Tesla closed her eyes and tried to visualize it all over again. "I was in a rectangular box, four by three feet, two and half feet deep. Once I sat up I could see that this box—with me in it—sat on a large metal table, right in the middle of what was clearly a lab." She opened her eyes then, and looked right at Bizzy, who looked like she wanted to ask a question. "I've been in and around labs all my life, Bizzy, and there's no question what this place was."

"Okay, so you passed out and woke up in a box in a lab," said Beckett. "Weird, but okay. Then what?"

"Well, my head was killing me, and I felt a little dizzy, and—you're right, this is weird—my heart monitor and the wheeled-pole it had been attached to were in the box with me, but the pole was bent, a perfect ninety degree angle, to fit in the box. The monitor still beeped and my heart sounded and felt normal." Tesla stopped and looked at Finn, and he felt his own pulse in response. "I told you this would sound crazy."

"Tes, we're talking about time travel—I think we can agree that at this point there's no such thing as crazy," he said.

"Good point," she conceded. "So I sat there and looked around at this lab. Most of the lights were off, no one else was there. There were no windows, and just the one door, which was closed. I needed to figure out where I was and what had happened, so I peeled off the various sensors taped to me so I was disconnected from the monitor, climbed out of the box and down from the table. I'd just decided that I would go to the door and look out, see if I could figure out where in the hospital I'd wandered off to—after I checked to make sure I still had my robe on over the hospital gown—" Tesla said as she flashed a quick smile at Finn, her dimples deeply embedded in each cheek—"and then—"

"Wait, what?" Bizzy asked, clearly confused.

"My cousin," Finn said, relieved to look away from Tesla and ignore the urge to smile back at her. "Not important."

"But before I could, the door opened," Tesla continued. "I saw some guy silhouetted in the light from the hallway, lit from behind so I couldn't see his face."

"Disaster," said Joley.

"Well, I was... I mean, it wasn't really a well-trained, spy-quality reaction.... I said, 'Who's there?'"

Lydia and Bizzy smiled sympathetically, but Beckett, Joley, and Finn laughed out loud.

"What? I assumed I was in the hospital, and had just wandered into some basement lab. I had a concussion!" Tesla reminded them.

"Go on," Lydia said.

"Well, whoever it was flipped on the light switch, and it was pretty bright, and it took a second for my eyes to adjust. And, it was just some guy. He wore a worker's uniform, blue pants and shirt, and carried a bucket filled with cleaning supplies."

"Did you know him—had you seen him before?" Lydia asked.

"No, I didn't know him," Tesla said. "He shut the door and asked how I'd gotten in. He walked toward me and said 'Who are you?' As he got closer I could see he was young, my age, so I figured I couldn't be in too much trouble."

"'Who are *you*?' I asked him back."

"Brilliant," said Joley.

"Yeah. Well, he pointed to his name tag. 'I'm Sam,' he said. 'I'm the night janitor. You're not supposed to be in here—how did you get in?'"

Tesla paused and looked down at her lap, at the fingers of her right hand that picked at an imaginary thread on the leg of her jeans.

"And?" Beckett asked impatiently. "Do we have to drag this out of you?"

"Beckett," said Lydia, though her eyes never left Tesla.

Beckett rolled her eyes, but sat back in her chair and waited with everyone else.

"Sorry," said Tesla. "It's just weird to think that this might have really happened, and plus, I'm a little embarrassed by some of it."

"Don't worry," Lydia assured her. "Go on."

"Okay. I said, 'I'm not sure how I got in here. I think I'm lost.'" Tesla waited for the snickers, but when she heard none she continued. "I told him I had been brought into the hospital earlier, that I had a concussion, and that I thought I'd passed out and wasn't sure how I'd gotten in here, or where 'here' actually was, for that matter, but apparently I'd managed to get in this box and shut myself inside it. I asked him if he could help me find my way back to my room."

"What was his response?" asked Finn.

"He looked strange, actually," Tesla admitted. "Like I'd shocked him. He was quiet for a minute, just looked at the box I'd climbed out of on the table, and that made me glance at it, too, and with the lid propped open I noticed for the first time those same sort of mirror things in the corners of the box, you know the mirrors that were in that room, the one inside the big cavern. Only in miniature. I had no idea what that meant and, well, we just sort of stood there."

"Well he had to have said more than that," Bizzy said, but Tesla was already shaking her head no.

"I didn't really give him the chance," she said again. "I confessed."

Beckett snorted, and Tesla was tempted to ask her if she'd like a bag of feed or maybe a sugar cube, but ignored her instead to go on with the story.

"I told him exactly what had just happened, and—you might be interested to know—he didn't laugh. Not once. He looked amazed, impressed even, and then he said—"

"He said what?" Lydia asked. Even she was impatient now.

"He said I had to go back, before anyone else knew, and that he could help me."

"And you believed him? Janitor-boy?" Beckett said, incredulous.

"Yes, I did," Tesla answered. "He was nice, and he seemed totally honest and sincere."

"And cute, right?" Bizzy said. "I'll bet he was cute." She grinned, and her nose stud twinkled in the room's soft lamplight.

Tesla chose to ignore her. "He helped me back into the box, arranged the monitor and pole around me, and he—well, he shut the lid again," Tesla finished.

"You let him put you back in that coffin? You're mad," Joley muttered.

"Well, I did, and I'm not sure what happened after that, I must have fallen asleep, but it seemed like just a moment later I was curled up in a ball on the floor, with the heart monitor and bent-up pole next to me, but there was no box. I was back in that room with the mirrors. All the lights were off, there was no voice on the intercom, nothing. I was totally alone."

Tesla shrugged when she realized that everyone still waited. "That's it, guys. I left the room and walked back across that giant airplane-hanger cave, found the door and the hallway, made my way back up the stairs and into my room, and as far as I know, no one saw me. I had to carry the monitor because the pole was bent and the wheels didn't work anymore, and it was kind of heavy, and all those wires and patches I'd taken off just sort of dangled off it. I got back in bed and I was out. The nurse woke me up in the morning and asked me what had happened to my monitor, and I just kind of blanked and said I had no idea. And that's it. I just thought it was a freaky dream."

"And now?" Lydia asked intently. "What do you think now?"

"I think it happened, and I think—" but she stopped herself, bit her lip in worry. She caught Lydia's eye, and the woman nodded once in encouragement, so Tesla opened her mouth to say she had travelled back in time, and that if this was a part of the mystery of her father's kidnapping, of what this guy Nilsen wanted, she probably ought to try to do it again—

She stopped as the roar in her ears drowned out every other sound in the room, the voices that vied for her attention, asked her to finish her sentence, but this new thought had just sliced through it all, and the fuzzy memories, the uncertainty of what had happened to her, were gone. All of it simply fell away. She looked up at Lydia and said, instead, with a crisp confidence that could not be mistaken, "I need to see that note you found today at my house."

Everyone looked at her, stunned into silence, until Lydia said softly, "Joley." He left the room quickly and came back, a piece of paper encased in a clear plastic bag in his hand. Without a word he handed the bag to Tesla, who reached for it as if it were made of spun glass.

She slowly brought the bag up closer to her face, but before she could actually read it she noted the handwriting, recognized it—*she recognized it*. She read the words written there in rounded script:

Don't be afraid—keep trying.

Tesla looked hard at the shape of the letters, the familiarity of the cursive style, and knew that the world had just changed, had always, already been changed.

"My father did not write this note," she said in a voice of absolute, unquestionable certainty. "I did travel back in time, and I'm going to do it again."

Even Lydia was shocked. Her mouth hung open, eyes wide. "How do you know?" she asked. "How can you be sure?"

"Because I wrote the words on this side of the paper," Tesla said as she stared at the sealed, pizza-stained note. "I don't know how—or when—but I wrote this note so that I would see it now, and use my dad's time machine again."

CHAPTER 15

After a very awkward shower the next morning, for which she had to wrap her cast in a plastic garbage bag Max pilfered from the kitchen, Tesla felt decidedly better. Rested, and seemingly past the worst of the physical and emotional exhaustion that apparently resulted when you were viciously attacked, had your arm broken by said attacker, had your dad kidnapped by an evil, probably mad scientist—oh, and realized that you had travelled back in time. She looked at the bottle of pain pills beside the sink and opted not to take any more of them. The pain was manageable and she had already grown tired of the buzz.

She dressed in her rather beat-up, but most comfortable khaki shorts, despite the frayed pockets and hem, and a tight little tie-dyed T-shirt of greens and purples, a major operation that had taken, unbelievably, fifteen solid minutes to accomplish. Disgusted by how slow and awkward she was, Tesla slipped on her Teva sandals, grabbed her scarf-turned-sling, and headed downstairs to do something—anything—to help find her dad.

In the kitchen she found Bizzy, Joley, and Max. They leaned or sat on the countertops while they ate cereal. "Don't you people have a dining room? You know, with a table and chairs?" She poured Cornflakes into the bowl that Joley pointed to with his spoon while he chewed.

"Yeah," Bizzy said, "but it's too much trouble."

Tesla shrugged. It seemed rude to comment on the contradiction between that British tea thing they did every afternoon and this makeshift, stand-up breakfast in the kitchen. Whatever. "You sleep okay?" she asked Max as he rinsed his bowl at the sink.

"Yeah, great," he said. "When do we go to dad's lab? Or should I say when *did* we go to dad's lab?" He pondered this for a moment. "So. Weird. And having watched *Loopers* a dozen times, turns out, is no help at all."

"Not until tonight," said Finn as he walked into the room, answering Max's original question and ignoring the rest.

"Why wait?" Tesla asked, anxious to get started.

"Because if it's ten o'clock in the morning here then it's probably ten o'clock in the morning there. When you did it before, Tesla, it was the middle of the night in the hospital, and when you found yourself in that box, and met that janitor, it was still the middle of the night. He said he was the night-shift, didn't he?"

"Oh," Tesla said. "Right. I didn't think about that."

"We don't really know what to expect," he explained, "but we should try not to arrive there in the middle of a busy workday."

"Okay," Tesla said. "I guess we should sit down and think this through before I go. Should I bring some stuff with me? *Can* I bring stuff with me?"

"Let's all slow down a little," Finn said. "Lydia's in the library, she wants to talk to us as soon as you're all finished in here." His condescension started a tight little ball of resentment forming right behind Tesla's eyes. *He's not so much older,* she thought. *Barely two years. But he acts like he's in charge of everyone and everything. Ass.*

"What about you?" Bizzy asked, just before she tipped her cereal bowl up to her lips and drank what was left of her milk.

"I've been up for a while. I already ate," he said over his shoulder as he walked out of the room.

Ten minutes later, after Bizzy had helped Tesla retie her sling, Tesla and Max followed the others out of the kitchen and down a long, wide hallway, at the end of which were two closed, massive oak doors. Joley knocked, once.

"Come in," Lydia called from inside.

Joley grabbed the slightly tarnished brass knobs of each door and slid them silently apart and into the hidden pockets on either side of the doorway, which was eight-feet wide once the doors were pushed back into the wall. Tesla and Max gaped at the massive library. Floor to ceiling built-in bookcases comprised three of the room's walls, with a circular, wooden staircase leading up to a railed balcony that ran along all three walls and provided access to the open second floor of books.

"Whoa," said Max, just behind Tesla, who couldn't help but turn and grin at her little brother.

"Dream come true for you, right?" she said quietly.

"I can't believe you guys get to live here," Max said to Bizzy, who stood right next to him.

"Yeah," she agreed, "this is pretty awesome. And Lydia shares—we have access to all the books, whenever we want."

The fourth wall of the library, to the left of the doorway where they stood, was an exterior wall, painted a deep, hunter green. There was an enormous oak fireplace in the center of the wall and a portrait of some old guy hung over the mantle. The red of his jacket and his white, curly wig contrasted nicely with the dark wood and green wall. Two deep, worn brown-leather chairs sat in front of the fireplace with lamps and small tables beside them. The room was filled with natural light from the huge windows on either side of the fireplace, each of which was exactly ten feet tall.

"Come in and sit," said Lydia at the head of the conference table made out of a massive slab of deeply polished wood. The table sat in the center of the room and was so long that ten upholstered chairs were pulled up to it, with plenty of room to spare. Finn was already seated at Lydia's left, and as the others moved to take seats at the table, Beckett came in behind them, her hair still wet from the shower.

"How was your workout?" Bizzy asked as she took the chair next to Finn.

"The usual," Beckett said, and then grinned at the goth girl. "I'm getting a little better."

Bizzy rolled her eyes.

"Beckett trains with a UFC fighter," Joley explained as he sat next to Tesla on the other side of the table. "Mixed martial arts. A couple times a week they just have a really scary, no-holds-barred death match."

"I hope you never get mad at me!" Max said as Beckett walked past him toward the other end of the table to sit opposite Lydia.

"No worries, little man," Beckett said with a sweet, genuine smile as she ruffled his hair. "I'd never hurt you."

"Even though you could," Joley pointed out.

"Even though I could," Beckett agreed.

"We're all here now," Lydia began, "and we need to tackle a few issues. Finn?"

Everyone turned to look at Finn, and they all seemed surprised, which surprised Tesla. Usually, she was the only one in this group who needed someone to explain or translate.

Finn hesitated—another surprise—then cleared his throat. "As you all know, we've agreed to attempt to use Dr. Abbott's time machine today, on the assumption that Tesla used it successfully a few months ago, though she's only just realized that. Our hope is to figure out both how the technology works—and Tesla's role in that—and where Dr. Abbott is so we can rescue him from Nilsen. We're really in the dark here, but as Nilsen is untraceable in our current time, our hope is that in the past, where he is known and locatable, we can learn something that will help us find him now, in our time. And thus, of course, find Dr. Abbott."

They all sat quietly as they waited to see where this was headed.

"There's little doubt that Nilsen wants the Abbott technology, so that's where we have to start. The machine is set to the time in Tasya Petrova's journals, about eight years ago, where we see detailed diagrams and specs of the prototype time machine, when that first version of it was up and running—that's our destination place-time." Finn paused and drummed his fingers nervously on the table. "I imagine everyone assumes that Tesla will be the one to attempt to go back in time. But I've persuaded Lydia that I should go instead." He had deliberately not looked at Tesla while he spoke, until now, and she correctly read the challenge in his eyes.

"I'm going, Finn, this is not your call," Tesla said, her voice low and dangerous.

"No, it's not," Lydia agreed, cutting Tesla off before she could really get started. "But it is mine, and I have agreed—somewhat reluctantly—that Finn should be the one to attempt this."

"But I've already done it, and it's my dad who's been kidnapped. My parents designed and built the time machine in the first place!" Tesla argued, but Lydia's face remained serene and unmoved.

Lydia let her speak for only a moment, then she held up her hand and Tesla stopped, despite herself. "I'm sorry, Tesla," Lydia said quietly. "You certainly have the stronger claim, but that is not the issue here. Finn has made some excellent points, and once you hear them, I think you'll agree that this is the best decision."

"I can't believe you'd do this to me," Tesla said quietly to Finn, directly across the table from her.

He looked at her calmly, which made her even angrier. "I know," he conceded, "and I'm sorry. But you need to think here, Tesla. Your mom is gone, your dad has been kidnapped, and you are all Max has left."

Tesla stopped dead with a sharp intake of breath, as if she'd been struck. She hadn't thought of Max, but Finn had, *damn him*. How could she argue with him now?

"There was no catastrophe when I did it before," she said half-heartedly.

"That's true, but we don't really know how this works," he countered, maddeningly sure of himself. "Bizzy may be brilliant, but she's sixteen, an undergraduate. She certainly doesn't know all that your dad knows and she's the one who will have to run this little experiment. It might not be the same this time, or you might not be able to get back—have you thought of that?"

"No, but—"

"Tesla," Lydia interjected. "Given your responsibility to Max, and the fact that we need you here to figure out what your mother meant in her journal when she connected you to the time machine, not to mention your heart condition…."

Tesla sat silently as the others tensed for her furious response. It was over, and she knew it. She had already lost. She took a deep breath, let it out slowly. "Fine," she said, after a moment. "What can I do to help?"

Everyone at the table looked at her, the shock registered clearly on their faces, but Beckett's face actually made Tesla want to laugh. *Note to self*, she thought. *Beckett hates it when I am reasonable and mature, so do that as often as possible.*

"Thank you, Tesla, I appreciate your cooperative attitude," Lydia said, ever gracious.

"I just want my dad back," Tesla said quietly, and out of the corner of her eye she could see Max nod in agreement, which confirmed that this was, indeed, the right decision.

"Alright then," Lydia said. "We'll meet at the East entry door to the Physics building on campus at nine o'clock tonight. Bizzy will let us in, and we'll head down to the underground lab—yes, Bizzy, I know, 'the Bat Cave'—together. Between now and then, we have much to do."

Joley had a yellow legal pad in front of him on which he had written continuously throughout the meeting. His pen was poised as he waited for Lydia to speak again. Tesla wondered idly if he was the official secretary for the group, if he took minutes for some sort of record, or if he was just an unbelievably nerdy, albeit stylish and totally hot guy. The quirky contradictions she always saw in him brought a smile to her face.

"What's funny?" asked Finn, who watched her.

Her smile was instantly eclipsed as Tesla turned icy blue-green eyes on him. "Nothing," she said with great dignity. She hoped her disdain would crush him, but he laughed out loud, amused by her instead. God, she *hated* him sometimes!

Meanwhile, Lydia marshaled the troops. "Bizzy, you'll be at the lab all day to check the equipment and make your preparations. Please be sure that none of Dr. Abbott's other students or colleagues will be around tonight."

"Yeah, I've got that covered," Bizzy said. "The lab's been locked up tight since the explosion, and most people are gone for the summer anyway—nobody in the department even knows that Dr. A is missing, at least not that I can tell. And of the relatively few people who know about the Bat Cave, I'm one of only two that have the access codes. No one will be there."

"Good." Lydia nodded, but they could all see that she was worried. "Finn and I will go over every possible contingency for tonight. I want him to be prepared for whatever he might find when he—when he makes the jump to the past? I'm not really sure what we call this, either." She paused a moment to smile conspiratorially at Max. "Anyway. As for the rest of you. Beckett, the lawn needs to be mown and Joley, please take Max with you to the grocery store. There's a list on the kitchen board, and Max can help you choose items he and his sister might like while they're with us."

Tesla couldn't believe it. "Seriously?" she asked. "Housework? Shouldn't you guys be, I don't know, headed to your weapons room to gear up, Matrix-style?"

"This is real life, Tesla, not a movie," Lydia said dryly. "Real life is filled with the everyday details of actual living—and without somebody to take care of those details, the desired outcome is far less likely to happen. We are not a group of violent crime fighters. There are a few, very discrete things we can do to help the larger effort, and that's our focus." She paused a moment, and looked over the tops of her glasses at Tesla with some amusement. "You can vacuum the downstairs; you only need one hand for that."

Still in shock, Tesla got up from the table along with everyone else, as Lydia said in parting, "And you're all on your own for dinner, the Landlady is far too busy with espionage and time travel experiments to cook tonight."

"Come on," said Bizzy at Tesla's side, "I'll show you where

the vacuum cleaner is before I head over to campus."

At twenty minutes after nine that night, Tesla found herself racing over the lawn of the hospital, across the open quad, and toward the Physics building. She had fallen asleep in the lazy heat of the afternoon, up in her third floor bedroom, though she'd only intended to lie down and rest for fifteen minutes or so. When she'd woken up, the streetlights were on and a lovely, cool breeze blew a light summer rain through her open window. She'd panicked when she checked her phone and saw that it was after nine, thrown on the faded boyfriend jeans that lay crumpled on the floor, grateful that she still wore the sports bra and tie-dyed spandex T-shirt she'd had on all day—it took way too long to change her shirt and re-sling her arm without help, so she'd just left it all as it was, slung her messenger bag across her torso, and run out the door.

She sprinted across the quad, her worn running shoes familiar and effective in the wet grass, her arm pressed in tight to her torso to minimize impact. *Stupid stupid stupid* went the litany in her head as it kept time with her steps. *How could you have slept so long*? She wondered if she was too late and picked up speed as she turned the corner of the physics building. She came up short, however, when she saw that Finn stood in shadows at the door underneath the massive outdoor light fixture that Bizzy had disabled in the hope that no one would see them sneak in. There was just enough moonlight to see Finn's broad shoulders outlined against the cream-colored building, and to see that he was alone.

Finn looked up and she walked the twenty feet that stood between them.

"Did you just get here, too?" she asked, hands on her hips as she caught her breath from the run.

"Yeah," he said, "At the last minute I remembered I needed

to go by the Bio-Med department first." His hand moved unconsciously to gently touch the cargo pocket of his loose-fit khakis. "I guess everybody else was here on time and they've gone down to the Bat Cave already. I called Bizzy's cell, but I doubt there's any reception down there."

Tesla didn't respond—there seemed no need to—and instead watched him in the gloom, as easy in his skin as always. She was nervous, aware of his nearness, and he seemed completely unfazed, she thought, as if he hadn't kissed her, then acted like it never even happened, and then plotted behind her back to use the time machine himself. She couldn't figure him out, couldn't figure herself out when it came to him. He was beautiful, even in the dark, the shape and breadth of his shoulders, his hands held loosely by his side, his entire demeanor lithe, athletic, prepared. She hated the contrast between her nervous tension and his cool, easy stance.

"You know I didn't do this to piss you off," he said, as if he could read her mind. "It's about Max."

"Yeah, I know," she said, though she hated to admit it. "I forget sometimes how young he is."

"So you don't hate me, then." He spoke in his usual, mocking tone, but for the first time Tesla wondered who, exactly, was the object of his near-constant derision.

"I don't hate you, Finn," she answered. "I hope you realize, though, that whatever risks there might be in this for me, they're the same for you."

"I suppose," he said, distracted by her hair that fell around her face like the evening, damp from the rain that could not mute its color, warm as embers at dusk. He caught a fiery strand of it in his hand, moved it off her face and tucked it behind her ear. "But I don't have a little brother, or anybody who needs me—"

Before he could finish his thought, which he might have

begun to articulate in the vague hope of just such a reaction, Tesla took that last step in, put her right hand behind his neck, and drew herself up on her toes to kiss him, her lips opening, just a little, against his. When his tongue touched hers he felt her indrawn breath, and then she tightened her hold on him and deepened their kiss.

He crushed her against his body, his earlier pledge to stay away from her, to just do his job and not complicate matters, abandoned in an instant.

Neither of them heard the door open, but they broke apart and stepped quickly back from one another at the sound of a deliberate cough only a few feet from where they stood.

"Gross," Beckett said. She tried to sound blasé but the attempt was an utter failure. She was furious. "In case you've forgotten, we have work to do. Everyone's downstairs."

"The door was locked. What were we supposed to do while we waited?" Finn asked, cool and amused.

Tesla couldn't read him. Was he embarrassed to be caught, and caught by Beckett, whom he had kissed just the day before? *God, how could I have forgotten that,* she berated herself, *and now I've practically jumped him myself.*

"I suppose more loathsome things than this have been done out of boredom," Beckett said. "Let's go." She turned and led the way down a flight of steps that began just inside the door, but Tesla got a glimpse of her face as she turned toward the stairs.

No. Effing. Way. Beckett Isley was jealous.

Finn glanced at Tesla and wondered just how angry she was—he assumed she was angry, in no small part because she was pretty much always angry if he was in the room, but now Beckett had managed to include him in her little insult of Tesla. He was resigned to her anger as he registered the flush on her cheeks, the tension in her body, and then she flashed him a radiant smile like sun sparking off water. Her eyes crinkled at the corners, dimples cut into her perfect cheeks, and her mouth—her mouth—

He held the door for her to indicate that she should go first, and when she passed him he smelled the rain-wet of her hair and caught the sound of the faintest nervous giggle as she started down the steps after Beckett, as if they'd been caught together ditching history class.

It was all he could do not to grab her and kiss her again, kiss her until the laughter in her eyes had turned into something else, but he dutifully closed the door and followed the girls down flight after flight of stairs to the Bat Cave.

CHAPTER 16

Twenty minutes later Tesla stood behind Bizzy's chair in what was clearly a control booth of sorts. Several monitors in front of them showed Finn from different angles as he stood in the center of the room that she now knew was actually a time machine. The cameras and monitors were a new addition to the lab, Bizzy explained, since Tesla had wandered into it months earlier. The tiny control booth was clearly not meant to hold six people—it had only two chairs, and Lydia sat in one, right next to Bizzy. No one had volunteered to wait outside and leave more room for the others, so Beckett, Joley, and Max—and now Tesla—filled up what little space remained, and everyone stared at the monitors.

"Okay, Finn, can you hear me?" Bizzy spoke into a small microphone that sat in a stand on the desk immediately in front of her.

"Roger that, ground control" Finn replied, one eyebrow arched and a lopsided grin on his face.

"Okay, relax, Major Tom," Bizzy said.

Finn laughed, and Tesla felt her breath catch as she saw that smile, his head thrown back, from half a dozen screens in the room. Whatever risk this little escapade might pose, you'd never know it from Finn's demeanor. He was excited, happy—giddy, even. This was so clearly what he wanted to be doing.

"I ran multiple tests today, and the equipment is all good," Bizzy was saying. "I'll count down, and then I'll activate the lasers; you should close your eyes, the light will be really bright when it hits the mirrors. Okay?"

"Yup," he said. "Got it."

Lydia leaned toward Bizzy's microphone. "Finn, are you quite sure you're ready for this?" she asked.

"Definitely," Finn said.

"I can't say I'm surprised," she said dryly. "And Finn— remember: if you don't find the young janitor, hide yourself until he comes in to clean and give him the same story Tesla did so he can send you back. It's a dubious coincidence, but that boy's confusion really can't be our concern right now. Be careful."

"You can count on it," Finn said. He looked intently at the camera, right at the small knot of people crowded into the control booth. "Things have just started to get interesting."

"Here we go," Bizzy said into the microphone as Lydia sat back, tense but satisfied. "In five, four, three...."

Tesla felt a chill crawl up her spine as she remembered these same words spoken in her father's voice, only it was Tesla in the time machine then, not Finn, and she had had no idea what it meant. Finn closed his eyes, his arms hanging loose by his sides, and Bizzy threw a switch on the panel in front of her. A white-hot light filled the room and made it impossible to see Finn, or anything else, in the monitors.

They all leaned in closer as Bizzy watched the digital counter on the panel, her hand poised to flip the switch off again as soon as thirty seconds had passed, just as she said Dr. Abbott did in each of their experiments. As the digital numbers rolled from twenty-nine to thirty, Bizzy firmly toggled the switch that killed the lasers—the lasers that had sent Finnegan Ford back through time in a wormhole.

Except that Finnegan Ford stood in the center of the room, his image reflected on the monitor screens in front of them. He blinked and looked around.

"Finn?" Bizzy said into the microphone. "You okay?"

"Yeah, fine," he said. "What happened?"

"I don't know," she said. "It didn't work."

"That much I had figured out."

"Let me run another check, sit tight," she said. She consulted a notebook and began to check the various readouts that flashed in incomprehensible digits on the panel in front of her.

In ten minutes Bizzy had checked and rechecked all the equipment and found no malfunctions. It should have worked, she concluded, and so they tried again. And failed. And tried again. By midnight Beckett and Joley no longer even watched the monitors as Bizzy counted down yet again and threw the switch on the lasers, only to find, thirty seconds later, that Finn still stood in the center of the time machine. Frustration mounted, and everyone felt it, except perhaps Max, who had fallen asleep in the corner, curled up on the floor.

"Let's take a break," Lydia said. "Stretch our legs." They left Max to sleep and walked out of the control booth and down the metal-grated stairs that led into the Bat Cave and the entrance to the time machine.

"I say we call it," said Beckett without preamble. "We have other leads to follow. In my opinion, we should have focused our energies on what Jane may have found in Canada. We need a hard trail that will lead to Dr. Abbott, and all of this is guesswork anyway."

"I agree," said Joley as he stifled a yawn. "Besides, we all probably have radiation poisoning at this point from all this laser activity."

Bizzy was incensed. "We do not! Dr. Abbott is scrupulous about exposure. We're all totally safe."

"Yes, well, you'll be singing a different tune I expect when I'm trapped in an isolation booth, making the Vulcan sign against the glass, telling you I am, and always will be, your friend—oh yes, Elizabeth, you'll be sorry when I'm gone, mark my words."

"Children," Lydia chided, but her heart wasn't in it. "You may be right, Beckett, but I'm not sure we should give up just yet. Elizabeth, dear, unfortunately you're the only one who knows enough about all of this to determine what else we might do to make it work. We can only follow your lead here."

"Yeah, I know." Bizzy chewed on her lower lip as she thought. "There's so much here that we don't understand. The one thing we do know, however, is that it worked before, when Tesla jumped. We have to focus on what's different this time."

"Bizz," Finn began, but Lydia put up her hand to stop his protest. "Let her finish," she said quietly, but firmly.

"I know you disagree, Finn," Bizzy said in a rush, "but you've got to admit it: Tesla has already jumped. The technology worked for her. We may not know what that means, but I think we should let her try it again."

"We've already been through this," Finn said. He looked at Lydia as he spoke. "There are too many reasons not to send Tesla back. You agreed."

"True," said Lydia slowly. "But that was when we thought it would work with you. I still believe it's vital we try this; it was less important who went, before, when we assumed that it would work with anyone. If that's not the case, and Tesla is our only option, I am inclined to agree with Bizzy. Better to send Tesla, even with the risks that entails, than to be unable to send anyone at all."

All eyes were on Tesla, who could feel her heart thump. "I agree," she said. "I'll go."

It took just under ten minutes for Bizzy to reset the controls and for Lydia and Beckett, who seemed rather subdued, to join Joley, who was already up in the both with Bizzy. Finn lingered, the last one in the time machine with Tesla.

"Finn, you know I have to do this."

"I know, I know," he assured her. "I won't argue."

"Oh. You won't?" she asked, unsure how to proceed in a conversation with him that wasn't based on an argument.

"No. I just wanted to say be careful. Be alert. Gather details, remember it all. And come back safe."

"I will," she said. "Things have just started to get interesting."

She laughed, then, in response to the surprised look on his face and she felt, for once, like she had it all under control.

"Finn," said Lydia from the booth. Her amplified voice echoed in the room where Tesla and Finn stood and their faint, watery reflections peered back at them from the four semi-translucent mirrors stationed at each corner. "Get up here."

"Right," Finn said. He turned to go, and then stopped before he'd taken two steps. "Almost forgot," he said quietly as he turned back to Tesla and stood so that their bodies blocked the camera sightlines. "Take this with you." He unzipped the cargo pocket on the leg of his khakis, reached inside, and gently extracted a tiny brown mouse whose nose and whiskers twitched inquisitively, and put it firmly into her hand.

"He's so tiny," she whispered, then closed her fingers gently but firmly around the creature. "But what...."

"I got him from Biology. They've got lots of them in the lab over there," Finn said quickly. He started to back away toward the door. "It occurred to me we might want to know if someone else can survive the jump besides you—if maybe this little guy might get pulled along with you when you go back in time. When you went before, your clothes and the heart monitor went with you; they were in contact with you, so they travelled with you. But we don't know if living, organic tissue will go, too. Or if it does, if it will survive."

"Right," said Tesla. She carefully lifted the flap of her messenger bag and gently placed the mouse inside.

"Right," Finn repeated unnecessarily. "So I'll see you when you get back."

"Yup," she said, and knew he heard the false bravado in her voice. "And Finn," she faltered. "Max...."

"Don't worry," he said, and his clear brown eyes held hers steadily. "I've got Max."

And then he was gone, and she was alone, once again, in the time machine.

Tesla patted the messenger bag at her hip. She felt somehow reassured by the tiny presence in there, and shrugged a little to adjust the green scarf wrapped around her cast and tied behind her neck. She stood in the center of the room while the now-familiar sound of Bizzy's voice counted down from five in the sterile space, and she closed her eyes just as the light of a thousand suns filled the room.

CHAPTER 17

They were once again blinded by the white light that filled the screen of each monitor until Bizzy's sure hand on the switch killed the lasers. The group stood silently as they stared at the empty time machine from every camera angle.

"It may have worked this time," said Joley in an attempt to lighten the heavy atmosphere.

"I don't think there was ever a malfunction," said Bizzy quietly. "I think it works for Tesla. Or *with* Tesla. I think that's how it was designed, though Dr. Abbott seems unaware of it. And I am completely clueless about how that is even possible. I think when we figure it out, we will have figured out what *the Tesla effect* is."

"Tesla changed her mind, huh?" asked Max, who had woken up while Bizzy did the countdown. The others turned to face him.

"It was more like we all changed our minds, once we realized that it wouldn't work with me," said Finn. "It works for your sister—maybe only for her. We're not sure."

"It's okay, I know she wanted to go," said Max in an attempt to reassure him, which is of course what Finn wanted to do for Max.

"She's pretty brave, and plus she really wants to get your dad back." Finn had made a promise to look out for Max and he was determined not to break it.

"Yeah, I know," Max said. "She'll be okay. She's smart."

"Yes she is," said Lydia. "So we've got to trust her, and remain confident that she'll be back very soon. But in the meantime, we can't sit idly by. Your father is in the hands of a very dangerous man, Max, and time is not on his side. I don't want to frighten you, but whatever Nilsen wants from him, the longer Dr. Abbott holds out, the more frustrated—and desperate—Nilsen will become. We want to find him before that happens."

Finn looked at Lydia, surprised she would be so candid with the boy.

"I've said all along we should have focused on Jane's leads," Beckett said. "It's certainly not too late to do that now. Have you had an update from her?"

"Yes," said Lydia. "She's in Canada, but it's unclear yet if any of her leads will pan out. I don't know the details—in fact, I know very little of her work. Her reputation suggests she doesn't always follow protocol."

"Shouldn't we also update her?" Finn asked. "She's not just an agent, she's a close family friend of the Abbotts. I'm sure she'll want to know that Tesla's made the jump."

"Yes, of course," said Lydia as she moved toward the door. "I'll take care of that, if I can reach her. I imagine she has her hands full right now and won't welcome any distractions, however. As Beckett said, Jane may very well be the one to solve this case. She's very good at her job," she added, almost to herself. She smiled then, as if she'd just remembered they were there. "I suggest we return to the house and get some sleep, in shifts. We want to be here if— excuse me, *when*—Tesla returns."

"I'll stay," Bizzy said. "I'm way too keyed up to sleep."

"I'll stay with you," said Finn. "You okay to head back to the house with Joley?" he asked Max, who nodded.

Once she was alone in the control booth with Finn—her favorite among the housemates—Bizzy exhaled, long and loud. She felt like she was still in shock. "I can hardly believe it," she said. "I mean, I know that it works in theory, but I thought I'd be lucky if we had some small success with subatomic particles. And then suddenly, *this*. I mean, she's just gone. It's so weird."

"Completely weird," Finn agreed.

Bizzy glanced at him, a sudden grin on her face. "So you two seem to be, ah, friendlier."

"Why Elizabeth, what do you mean?" Finn asked archly.

"Becks said she caught you guys making out when she opened the door."

Finn shrugged, his mouth tipped up on one side. "That might be a bit overstated," he said evasively. He didn't have a clue what this was between him and Tesla Abbott, but he wasn't about to work it out with Bizzy, who was like a younger sister.

"I like her." Bizzy offered her unqualified stamp of approval despite Finn's refusal to discuss it. "But don't get your hopes up, Finn. Don't you think she seems annoyed with you? A lot?"

"Yeah, she does," said Finn, and his grin now matched Bizzy's. "It's all part of my charm."

Bizzy shook her head at his delusions. "She's odd, though, don't you think?"

"How do you mean?" Finn asked, wary.

"I don't know. Not in a bad way. She's just hard to understand—I know, I know, I don't understand anybody. But this is different. She's shy, but she's always pissed and flying off the handle. And she's not exactly a supermodel, but once you see her— really look at her—it's like she's the only one in the room. And even though she looks—soft, I guess—she's incredibly stubborn, she's smart and obviously brave. She's nothing but contradictions."

"Why Bizzy, I do believe you're in love," Finn teased.

Bizzy blushed. "All I mean is that she's interesting," she tried to explain, at a loss, as usual when it came to verbal communication. She tried a different tack. "She's colorful," she suggested.

Finn was about to laugh at her again, but he was suddenly caught by the image of Tesla walking to her house in the brilliant sunshine, nervous about returning to the scene of her attack, starting and stopping on the sidewalk as they walked. "That's true," he said. "She's always on the move, in this abrupt sort of way—she's like a hummingbird. Quick, hard to catch—you get a flash of blue and green and red and she's gone."

"Why Finn, I do believe you're in love," Bizzy said, laughing at him in turn as she spun around and around in her chair at the control panel.

When Tesla felt the pressure of a solid wall up against her back, and the sense of her entire body cramped and confined, she knew it had worked. Without the sense of panic she'd felt last time, she waited only a few seconds before she began to push up on the lid of the much smaller time machine that she now thought of as 'the coffin.' She had only just begun to push upward with her shoulder when the lid swung swiftly upward and she blinked in the sudden glare of the fluorescent lights of the lab and stared into the very dark, very liquid eyes of Sam the janitor.

"Holy shit," he breathed. His black hair fell into his eyes, and a nervous laugh escaped his lips. "Ho. LEE. Shit."

"Yeah. Can you help me out of here?" Tesla asked as she looked pointedly at her casted arm.

"Oh. Yeah. Of course," Sam said quickly as he helped her sit up.

"Oh, hang on a sec," she said while she rummaged in the messenger bag in her lap.

Sam saw the smile that lit up her face as she looked up and pulled a small object out of the bag with her good right hand. It was a mouse, held gently in her palm. His twitchy pink nose poked out from between her fingers.

"This is—Schrödinger," said Tesla, naming him on the fly. "Alive and well."

"Whoa. You brought him with you?" Sam asked, but Tesla didn't respond.

"Can we put him somewhere secure?" she asked.

Sam looked around until he saw a rectangular cardboard box with a lid, the kind that held reams of copy paper. He removed the paper, brought the box over, and Tesla put Schrödinger inside. Sam took his keys, punched some air holes in the lid, and placed the box on a nearby desk.

"I knew you'd be back," Sam said triumphantly, as if he had single-handedly made this happen.

"You... you know what's happened here?" Tesla was very much aware of the promise she'd made to Lydia. The more people who knew about this time travel stuff, the more danger her dad was likely to be in.

"Yeah, I keep my eyes open," he said. He backed up a step as Tesla climbed the rest of the way out and then hopped down from the table to stand in front of the boy—he was, clearly, a boy, younger than she was, now that she had a chance to really look at him.

"And what have you seen?" she asked casually.

Sam looked at her intently. Tesla could read the quick intelligence in his inky eyes, and silently approved his caution, which appeared to match her own.

"I'm interested in the work the docs do around here," he said with a shrug. "And of course I remember that I helped you a couple of months back. When you wandered in here with a concussion and I found you hidden in there." His hand gestured vaguely to the table and the coffin, directly behind her. "So. Are you lost again?"

"Not so much lost this time... more like I've retraced my steps," said Tesla. She was surprised to find this cryptic conversation so enjoyable. It seemed as clear to Sam as it was to her, though if she was wrong she had actually told him nothing.

"Want a soda?" he asked suddenly, and then blushed at the surprised look on Tesla's face. "I mean, I was actually just going to get one when I saw... when I realized you were here. Wanna walk down the hall and get a drink?"

"Sure," said Tesla, who thought she might as well go with every little bit of bizarre that this experience had to offer.

She followed Sam out of the lab and they walked in silence for a couple of minutes through long, echoing hallways until they came to an open area with a few small tables and chairs, and several vending machines.

Tesla sat at one of the tables and Sam walked to the closest machine. "Coke?" he asked, his back to her as he dug quarters out of his pocket.

"Root beer, actually."

He bought the two sodas and sat down in the chair across from Tesla, and they looked at each other in silence.

"So," he began, and then stopped, not sure how to proceed.

"Yeah," she said, and they both laughed. "Look, Sam, don't ask me about this, but...." Tesla hesitated, but it was where she knew she had to start. "What's the date today?"

Sam looked at her and cleared his throat. "It's Monday. June twenty-seventh." Tesla continued to look at him expectantly and he was the first to blink. "Two thousand and four."

Tesla closed her eyes and felt her heart beat strong and sure in her chest. *Holy shit is right*, she thought. *Exactly eight years ago.*

She opened her eyes and found Sam's gaze fixed on hers. "You okay?" he asked.

"Yeah," she said, but it came out as barely a whisper. Then louder, "Yeah, I'm fine. What about you?"

"I'm good," he assured her. "But I think the docs who run this place would be, um, more than a little surprised by your visit."

"I'll bet," Tesla said with a grin. "I guess that's why the box is so small: they don't think anyone would use it to, ah, hide in."

"Exactly," Sam said. "Although they hoped that somebody would some day, of course. Especially Dr. Petrova—"

Tesla was suddenly on her feet, her chair pushed back with such force that it crashed to the linoleum floor. "What did you say?" Her voice was the barest whisper.

"Dr. Petrova," he repeated, eyeing her warily. "This is her lab, hers and Dr. Abbott's. And that—box—is their work...." Sam stopped and a worried frown creased his forehead. "I thought we were on the same page, but maybe you'd better tell me who you are and what this is all about. I'm not with security—and I don't understand most of what goes on here. But I owe the docs a lot and I'm not going to say any more until I get some answers."

CHAPTER 18

Tesla licked suddenly dry lips. *Why didn't I anticipate this*, she wondered. But it didn't matter, nothing mattered, really, except what this boy had just told her.

"Tasya Petrova and Greg Abbott are my parents," she said slowly. "I'm Tesla Petrova Abbott. And my mother is alive...."

Several hours later they still sat in the lab's break room, their sodas long gone. They leaned back in their chairs and just looked at each other. They had talked furiously after Tesla's admission of who she was, talked over each other and, more than once, got up to pace the floor as the story in two parts unfolded. Sam had run his hands through his hair at various points in agitation, and now it stuck up on end all over his head. He knew that if he were a real scientist he wouldn't just accept that this was real, he would need controls, data, the same results repeated over and over again. But right here, right now, he knew it was true. The girl who sat across the table from him had just arrived—for the second time—from eight years in the future.

"I've met you, you know," he said suddenly.

"What? What do you mean?" Tesla felt like her head was filled with a constant buzz—her mind raced as she tried to adjust to this world in which she could jump back and forth in time.

"Like, a week ago," he said. "You were—you are—a little kid. You have a baby brother. Your dad brought you guys in to try to persuade your mom to knock off for the night. She was here really late—my shift had already started. You were too shy to talk to me, you hid behind your dad and stared at the floor. The baby grabbed my finger and kind of drooled all over himself."

"This is too bizarre, I can't get my head around it. So right now, in this time and this place, it's 2004 and I'm nine years old. Max is a baby. And my mom is alive."

"Yeah, you said that," said Sam. "Why wouldn't she be?"

Tesla paused. How much could she share with Sam? They had established that time travel had occurred, that she was here from the future, and that was about it. That much had taken them long enough, as they'd carefully avoided any statements that might reveal what they both understood as a very secret project.

"She's no longer alive eight years from now," she finally said simply. Her head swam with all sorts of dire possibilities, most of them, to her chagrin, from sci-fi horror stories about time travelers who go back and accidentally step on a butterfly or something, and then back in their own time it's all changed and they can never get the world back to what it was. She didn't want to make any mistakes that she might regret later.

"Oh, man. Sorry," said Sam. "This must be so weird for you."

"Yeah, you might say that."

Sam glanced at the clock on the wall and stood up. "My shift is just about over. I need to clock out. We have to figure out what to do with you—people will be coming in soon. We can't risk sending you back right now."

Tesla thought for a minute. "I know. It's okay. Can you give me twenty-four hours, and then help me get back tomorrow night, like you did before?"

Sam looked at her and weighed what he saw. Clear, *amazing* eyes, one blue and the other green, that he tried not to stare at. Seventeen, she'd said, and they were about the same height, even though Tesla was two years older than he was. Crazy, wild red hair framed her face, and her cheeks dimpled when she smiled. If he hadn't felt totally outclassed, he would've fallen hard for her. But since there was no way she'd ever look at him like that—he felt like an awkward kid next to her—he was able to relax. He had absolutely no shot, and it released him from all the effort and anxiety of hope.

"Okay," he said. "What do you need to do, and how can I help?"

"I need to keep a low profile," she said, "that's first. You saw *Back to the Future*, right?"

"Yeah, of course. I get it. We'll keep you out of sight as much as possible."

"I need to do some research. At the library."

"You can come to my house, no one will be there. It's only five a.m., the library's not open yet, but I can take you there at seven. We're on the campus of a university, so that's no prob—"

"Yeah, I know," she said. "I live on campus. I mean, I *will* live on campus. I know where the library is."

Fifteen minutes later, after they'd put some potato chips in Schrödinger's box and the lid from Sam's soda bottle filled with water, Sam clocked out and changed in another room into jeans, sneakers, and a Jimi Hendrix T-shirt that had seen better days. They walked outside into the pre-dawn. The sky *felt* like it was almost day rather than looked like it, as Sam stopped at a small Honda motorcycle chained to a pillar of the physics building and pulled a helmet out of the backpack he carried.

"You ride a motorcycle?" Tesla asked, surprised. "I didn't think you were old enough to drive."

"Thanks," said Sam, stung a bit.

"Sorry. No offense."

"Don't worry about it." He unlocked the bike, and by the time he stood up again, he was over it. "I'm fifteen and three quarters, which is old enough in this state to get a motorcycle permit if I need it to work. Which I do."

"Oh," said Tesla as she tried not to smile. "Cool."

"Put this on." He handed her the helmet.

"What about you?" she asked, the helmet awkwardly held in her right hand. It was heavier than it looked.

"I only have one, and you're going to wear it."

"Oh," Tesla said. She sounded like a monosyllabic idiot as she looked with some doubt at the helmet in her hand.

"Here," Sam said. He took the helmet from her and put it on her head. "Chin up," he ordered, as he fastened the buckle and made sure it was secure. Then he threw one leg over the bike and sat down on the leather seat, turned on the engine and revved it once.

"Get on," he commanded, and she climbed up behind him. He showed her the tiny bars for her feet, and told her to hang on.

"I only have the one arm, you know," she warned, and he laughed. The predawn air was cool on her face and as they drove onto one of the main streets through campus, everything still dark and not a soul awake, Tesla realized that she felt great. *Really* great. Strong and whole and hopeful. She had work to do, she knew, and she had to be careful. She had to go back to her own time and help fix this whole mess. But right here, right now, her dad hadn't been kidnapped by some lunatic, and her mom was alive, somewhere in this town, peacefully asleep in her own bed, and none of the terrible events that seemed to Tesla to define her life had ever happened.

By the time they'd driven through campus, across town and underneath the old freeway overpass (which she did not tell Sam would be torn down in just a few years), Tesla felt comfortable on the back of the bike, her right arm around Sam's waist, her left arm comfortably in front of her, supported by her sling and both their bodies. The breeze was chilly as they drove, and she shivered a little as they turned from an old business district, with easily half of the stores boarded up and graffiti tags sprayed across the empty display windows, and onto a short, dead-end street with half a dozen tiny, identical cinderblock houses.

Sam pulled into the dirt driveway of the second house on the left and turned the engine off. "This is it," he said, and Tesla could tell he was embarrassed.

"Thanks for bringing me here," she said. "You didn't have to, I know. It's what a good friend would do, and you just met me." She didn't want to be fake, tell him how lovely his house was; that would just embarrass them both. He was poor, the house looked it. But none of that was the point. He *had* gone above and beyond, and she wanted him to know that that's what she saw.

He shrugged. "No problem." Tesla got off the bike first, carefully, and then Sam followed suit. She handed him the helmet, and they walked inside.

The house was dark, and he flipped a switch on the wall that illuminated the room from a plain, round ceiling fixture that cast a harsh light over them. He put his keys on a table by the door and walked into what Tesla could see was a cramped kitchen.

"I'll make us some food," he called.

The worn sofa was clean and had once been a cheerful brown and yellow striped pattern, though it was faded beyond hope of cheerfulness now. A faux-leather recliner, a coffee table, and a TV on a low dresser completed the room's decor. Tesla noted the framed photographs on the wall over the sofa, and went closer to examine them.

She assumed the two adults in the largest picture were Sam's parents. The man had a kind face and gentle eyes above his enormous black moustache. He had begun to bald. The woman who sat beside him had an oval face and black, soulful eyes just like Sam's. She wore a headscarf over her hair and pulled snug up under her chin, and a cream-colored, crew-necked sweater that matched the ones her husband and children wore. There were two children in the photo who sat in front of and just below their parents. The boy—obviously Sam—was younger in the photograph than he was now, and Tesla suddenly longed to see Max as she looked at this little boy's face in the family portrait, the big eyes, the tousled hair. The girl, a teenager, also wore what Tesla assumed was a Muslim headscarf. She stared defiantly at Tesla from her place on the wall, her eyes stormy.

"Is this your sister?" Tesla called without turning around.

"Yes," Sam answered quietly, right behind her.

Tesla jumped and turned quickly to face him. He stood very close to her, their eyes level. He's not as tall as Finn, she thought, the comparison automatic. She felt inexplicably nervous.

"Her name is Haleh. She goes by Hallie. She's in college. In Boston."

"Haleh's a pretty name," she said smoothly as she stepped to the side and walked around him, toward the kitchen. "How come she doesn't like it?"

He shrugged, noncommittal. "I didn't say she didn't like it, but everybody mispronounces it. Maybe she wants to fit in."

Tesla retreated to safer territory. "Did you say something about food?"

"Yeah, scrambled eggs and toast. That okay?"

"That's great, thanks," she said airily. She wanted to regain the composure she felt was her right as the older of the two. He was just a kid, after all.

Tesla stood quietly in the kitchen while he scooped eggs from the pan onto two chipped plates, and buttered toast that had already popped up from the toaster. They stood in the kitchen and ate in silence.

"Is Sam your real name, or a nickname like Hallie?" she finally asked, unable to stop herself, apparently, from being an idiot.

Sam looked at her as he chewed and waited a moment before he answered. "My 'real' name is Sam, because I say it is."

Tesla blushed and didn't answer.

By the time they'd finished, the sun had begun to rise and ease into the day. "Once the library's open, I'd like to head over there," Tesla said.

"I'll take you," Sam said, "but I've got to just drop you."

"Hot date?" Tesla asked. She was a little horrified to find that she wanted him on the defensive, and she had no idea why.

"No, second job," he answered evenly.

"Wow, you work two jobs and you're not even sixteen? What's up with that?" she asked.

"My parents both work, and I work after school. When I'm not in school for the summer, I work two jobs. They don't make a lot of money, and it's not cheap to live, or to send your daughter to college. So I help."

Tesla felt the blush creep up her neck and suffuse her face. She looked down again, ashamed to reveal how lucky she was, how much she took for granted, how easy her life was in so many ways. She had never really questioned the self-pity she so often indulged in, the sense that she deserved special consideration because her mom had died. She had forgotten that there were other forms of hardship, maybe even worse ones.

After they'd washed the dishes together, dried them and put them back in the cabinets, they left the house and climbed back on the motorcycle. Tesla wore the helmet, her right arm wrapped lightly around Sam's waist. "So where's your other job?" she asked.

"Pizza shop," he said curtly, and she wondered if he was angry because she was such an insensitive clod. "Angelo's."

"No. Way," she said, and somehow this was the biggest surprise of all. "That is by far the best place in town. I go there all the time, chicken-bacon-ranch is my favorite."

"Chicken-bacon-ranch?" he asked. "That's a new one."

"No, they've had it forever," she assured him. "It's fantastic. With shredded basil under the cheese."

They retraced their route from a few hours before and made their way back to campus as they passed through the little refurbished downtown with the grassy public square and the gazebo. Tesla noted that not all of the storefronts had been redone yet, but Angelo's was still there and it looked exactly the same. They passed two dorms and some student apartments, and were soon in the thick of classroom and administrative buildings. Sam pulled up in front of the library, and Tesla climbed off the back of the motorcycle. She unbuckled her helmet, pulled it off, and handed it to him.

"I've got a long shift," he said. "Sorry to leave you alone for so long, but it can't be helped. I'll pick you up here a little after four."

"Okay, thanks."

"Are you gonna tell me what your research is for?" he asked.

She looked at him for a moment. "No, I don't think so," she said. "I don't want to step on any butterflies."

"If you don't tell me that could be the death of the butterfly," he pointed out. "There's no way to know."

"That doesn't make it easier, you know," she said.

"Who said I wanted to make it easier?" Without waiting for her to answer he turned and rode away.

When he was gone Tesla looked up at the university library, at the wide, formal steps that led to its entrance. It was time she began her research, began to dig into her parents' work, and the rivalry they had had with Sebastian Nilsen. It was time to look for clues—anything at all—that would help Lydia's people identify Nilsen in the future and provide some clue as to where he might take her father eight years from now. And then she turned away from the library, which would be of no use to her, and cut across campus toward the physics building and her father's office.

Though it was a bit risky to take the elevator up to the fourth floor and just walk right into the physics department, Tesla thought she'd be safe enough. It was only eight o'clock in the morning, and it was summer; the campus was pretty quiet, with only a fraction of the usual number of students, faculty, and staff around. And as unlikely as it was that she would run into anyone she knew, if she did, the odds that they would somehow recognize her were negligible. If anyone here knew her at all, it would be as a little kid, not as her nearly-grown-up self. When the elevator doors opened, Tesla walked out, turned left, and walked into the department as if she had every right to be there, though she threw the occasional guilty look over her shoulder.

"Can I help you?" asked the middle-aged woman behind the desk, and Tesla visibly relaxed when she realized she did not know the woman.

"No, thanks, I just need to drop off a late paper for my professor." Tesla smiled, patted the messenger bag at her side, and walked by without pause in an effort to discourage further conversation.

She held her breath for a moment, but let it out again when the woman did not follow or call out to her. When the hallway made a ninety degree turn, the front office was lost from view altogether. She checked the name plates on each door as she went, but stopped unexpectedly at the one right before her father's office. *Dr. Tasya Petrova*, she read, as her fingers moved lightly over the raised letters of the name plate. She sighed wistfully, then remembered that she hated overt displays of sentimentality and moved on. Tesla looked back down the hall to make sure no one watched her, then took the key to her father's office that she'd taken from the house, slid it into the lock and opened the door, thankful that her father had never thought to request a bigger, better office as the years had passed and his career had advanced. She closed the door behind her and relaxed when she heard the click of the automatic lock slide into place.

She was in, she was alone, and no one knew she was here.

Tesla carefully passed the heavy strap of her messenger bag over her broken arm, over her head, and then laid it on the desk. She sat down in her father's chair and began to search his desk drawers. A small twinge of guilt pricked her conscience, but it wasn't like she didn't have cause, she reasoned. *Where are you, Dad?* she wondered silently. She felt the paralysis of fear creep up on her and shook it off to focus on the task at hand.

The shallow, center drawer held exactly what she'd expected: pens, pencils, a couple of scientific calculators, a ruler, a stapler, and various other mundane office supplies. She shut that drawer and opened the first of the three drawers to the left of her chair. A tape dispenser, an unopened bag of cheap pens, a heavy 3-hole punch and more of the same were all she found, so she started on the next one and was surprised to discover that what appeared to be a middle and lower drawer was, in fact, one deep drawer that served as a filing cabinet.

Tesla began at the front and worked her way to the back of the drawer, reading the labels on the file tabs. *Grad School Teaching Evals, Thesis Notes, Qualifying Exams, Dissertation Committee Notes, Research Agenda for Job Apps*. It seemed clear that these were old files filled with papers from her father's graduate work. She took each one out, quickly perused the pages, realized quickly that they were not helpful, and moved to the drawers on the right, only to find that they were locked.

There was no place to insert a key, even if she'd had one, and for a moment Tesla panicked. This must be where he kept sensitive material, exactly the stuff she probably needed, but she couldn't open it. *Calm down*, she thought to herself. *Think!* Obviously her dad could open the drawers, and unless there was some kind of sophisticated remote device that wasn't on the premises, she would figure it out in this room. She began with a close examination of the drawers themselves, but this only confirmed that there was no keyhole of any kind on the smooth metal surface of the drawers. She pushed back her chair, slid down to the floor, and crawled into the knee-space of the desk. It was much darker here, and she couldn't see very well, so she ran her uninjured hand lightly across the inside surfaces. She was just about to give up and had already turned her thoughts to where in the office she might look next, when the very tip of her index finger touched a raised, rough area on the interior wall of the right hand desk drawers.

Tesla scrambled out from under the desk and jerked the center drawer open. She pawed through the pens and markers in the hope that her not-always-practical father might just have—and there it was, a small flashlight. She grabbed it, ducked down and crawled back into the space beneath the desk, the flashlight's thin beam trained on the six-figure combination lock she had felt.

She sat for a moment and stared. Six numbers. What numbers would her father choose? The commonplace approximation for the speed of light? *186000*. She spun the numbers. Nope, probably too obvious. The first six digits of pi, maybe. *314159*. Fail. Maybe the golden ratio, her dad loved the Greeks. *161803*. Wrong again. Wait, what about *e*, Euler's number; her mother had been all about order and chaos and randomness! Euler's number was irrational, significant because it was crucial for probability calculations—what were the numbers again? She turned the tumblers with her right hand and held the flashlight in her mouth to illuminate the lock. *271828*. Just as she dialed the last tumbler into position, she heard a soft click, and the drawers on the right side of the desk slid open an inch.

Okay, I. Am. Awesome, she thought.

She grabbed the flashlight out from between her teeth, ducked and stood up from underneath the desk—and promptly smashed her head into the center drawer she'd left open. The pain brought tears to her eyes for a moment, and she gingerly touched the top of her head and felt the stickiness of blood. *Maybe not entirely awesome*, she thought. *What would Finn say now about my talents with spatial relationships?*

She squatted to pick up the pens and other crap that had flown out of the drawer when she hit it, scooped them up, quickly returned them to the drawer and then slammed it shut, harder than was strictly necessary. *Stupid drawer.* Then she sat back down in her father's chair and scooted in so she could fully open and peer into the two drawers that had unlocked when she'd hit upon the right combination.

The first drawer held a stack of papers, some stapled or paper-clipped together, and a couple of old cassette tapes, unlabeled. She left the tapes and grabbed the stack of documents and put them on her lap to flip through them. The first was a copy of the abstract of her mother's dissertation—but Tesla frowned. The *blah blah blah* of adult conversation about scientific research that had swirled around her all her life made her certain that her mother had done her doctoral dissertation on wave-particle duality. The abstract Tesla held in her hand, however—signed and approved by her four committee members—was titled, "The Multiverse: Probability Theory, Randomness, and Wormholes." Those areas of research were connected, of course, but this title suggested a very different project.

She must have abandoned this project for the one she eventually submitted and, later, published. Why had her father kept it? It certainly didn't seem important enough to lock away, but Tesla had already moved on to the pages beneath the abstract. A photocopy of an article published in 1994 in one of the most prestigious theoretical physics journals, with a hastily drawn circle in red pen around the title and an angry exclamation mark next to it, looked up at her. The title was "Time Travel and Patterns in Random Sequences."

The author was Dr. Sebastian Nilsen.

Tesla's heart beat faster with excitement. Nilsen's infamous article, the one that had ruined his career and caused the rift with her parents! The title was so close to her mother's abandoned dissertation title, it wasn't much of a leap to conclude that when Nilsen stole her data and published it, Tasya Petrova had changed her dissertation topic. *She should have brought him up on charges, the scumbag*, Tesla thought.

She had just moved to slide the article underneath the pile on her lap so she could examine whatever was next when someone knocked sharply on the office door.

"Dr. Abbott?" said a crisp, insistent woman's voice.

Tesla froze and held her breath.

"I heard somebody in there just a few minutes ago," someone else said, a man.

The knock came again. "Dr. Abbott, are you in there?" Tesla and the woman only a few feet away from her listened intently from their respective sides of the door.

"Sorry," the woman said. "You must have heard a noise from one of the other offices. He's not usually here this early. You'll have to come back later to have him sign your drop/add form." Her voice faded as she walked away.

Tesla waited another few seconds before she allowed herself to exhale, but her hands shook now. She realized that the longer she stayed here, the greater the chance she'd be caught, and she couldn't even begin to think of what would happen if her father himself came in before she left. She gathered the stack of papers on her lap and shoved them into her messenger bag, which was not easy with one arm in a cast. She had ransacked her father's office, and he would discover the theft—but surely he had already discovered they were gone, back in two-thousand-and-four, right? Had she always already stolen them—did she even have a choice now?

Tesla moved to shut the drawer and, at the last minute, grabbed the cassette tapes and threw them in her bag as well. She was scared now, completely overwhelmed by the unanswerable question of whether this act in the past would change the future, or if she chose *not* to act in the past, whether that omission would change the future. She wished, suddenly, that Bizzy was here with her, or Finn or Lydia, even Max, to help her figure this out. How could she know? She was blind, just like everyone else, to the future, but she was also blind to the past and the two were interdependent—and of course, though she had tried to avoid thinking about it, this was all tied to her mother. Her mother, who right now, in this time, would be dead in a few months. If she could somehow warn her, let her know about the car accident that would end her life, she could save her—or perhaps set off the very chain of events that would lead to her inevitable death. How could she know? And just like that, she couldn't breathe. Panic began to set in, and she was so agitated, so desperate to get out of there *and not have to decide* that she could not take even one more minute to look in the second, lower drawer which remained slightly open. Without a second glance she shut it firmly and slung her bag over her head and across her body. At the door she stood still for a moment, her ear pressed to the door, and listened. She heard nothing, but she feared the carpet in the hallway would effectively muffle the sounds of anyone who walked by or, worse, waited outside to catch her. When she opened the door she might come face to face with—well, it could be anyone, a student, another physics prof, the secretary, who would probably call the cops, or even her father. She finally just had to open the door and look out.

The hallway was empty.

Tesla took a deep breath, stepped out into the hall and shut the door softly behind her, and then she let herself out the side door of the department, found her way to the elevator and left the building like an apparition, a mere suggestion of the person she would be in another time, another place.

CHAPTER 19

At 4:10 Sam rode up to the library and stopped right next to the sidewalk. Tesla leaned in so he could put the helmet on her, and then she climbed on the back of the bike, both of them oddly comfortable in the routine they'd established only a few hours earlier.

"How did it go at the library?" he asked, his face turned to the side so she could hear him over the sound of the engine, which rumbled low as it idled.

"Good," she answered hastily, not eager to remember that she had lied to him earlier. "I found some stuff that might be useful, and I took some notes, so I guess it was a good day."

Sam nodded. "Where to?" he asked.

"Can we just drive around a bit?" she asked, hesitantly. "I don't want to put you out, but this is kind of cool for me, you know, to be here."

"Sure," he said easily. "We've got time to kill. We can't go back to the lab until nine, when my shift starts."

"When do you sleep?"

Sam laughed. "Tomorrow. You caught me on a weird day. I don't usually work a double like this."

He drove away from the curb before she could respond, turned left at the stop sign, and headed down University Boulevard, which cut directly through the center of campus.

"There's physics," he said.

"Oh, yeah," she said weakly and resolved to become a better liar.

They rode slowly, and Tesla was able to look both left and right as they went. She noted how much—and how little—had changed over eight years. Sorority and fraternity row was exactly the same. The student recreation center was older and smaller than it would be in 2012, though Tesla could not remember when the newer one, which she was familiar with, had been built. The student union was the same, few of the classroom or administrative buildings had changed, and the open green spaces, where students played Frisbee or sunbathed while they read, their heads pillowed on their backpacks, all made her feel like she hadn't travelled in time at all, that then was now and now was then, and she could ride up to her house and find Max in front of the TV with his X-Box.

When they rode past Angelo's Sam reached down and squeezed her hand, and she smiled, though she faced his back, glad to feel less alone on this strange mission. An ice cream parlor that no longer existed, but was clearly in operation now, jolted Tesla with a sudden, unexpected memory in which she held her mother's hand as they walked into that shop, a little string of bells on the door announcing their arrival with a jingle that sounded, somehow, like strawberries and rainbow-colored sprinkles. She clutched Sam's shirt front, leaned into him and craned her neck to say in his ear, "Take a right on Webber."

He did as she directed, and they left the town square behind them for this quiet, shady street of old trees and neat, modest homes. Sam did not need to be asked to slow the bike to barely a crawl, just fast enough to keep it upright, as Tesla stared intensely at a whitewashed house with a red brick chimney dominating one side and towering over the roof. She held Sam's shirt tightly in her fist, though she did not know it, and the arm she held rigidly across his torso was tense and brittle and reminded the boy that she was breakable.

As they neared the house, Tesla gasped audibly when a pale young girl with spindly legs and fiery-red curls that waved madly all over her head ran from around the side of the house, barefoot and shrieking. A man followed close on her heels, a garden hose in his hand as he chased her and roared in mock rage. He held his thumb over the open nozzle of the hose as he attempted to spray the little girl with water. His own hair was sopping wet, water poured in rivulets down his face, and the front of his shirt was soaked.

The motorcycle pulled even with the house, and as if in slow motion, Sam and Tesla turned their heads to watch the man and the little girl, and with a shock of recognition that she felt to her very core, Tesla's eyes met those of Greg Abbott as he watched them in turn and raised a hesitant hand to wave.

They passed the house and the end of the street forced them to turn, so Sam went left, and it was over.

Tesla was damp with sweat, every muscle tensed and held beyond its endurance. Her legs shook with such force she doubted they would hold her if she had to get off the motorcycle. She tried not to cry, and berated herself for having to try. It wasn't as though she didn't know her father was here, in this time, years younger, or that she herself was here, a nine-year old girl. And when she told Sam to turn down the street where they used to live, it was obviously because she wanted to get a look at her old life which, for her, had always been about the mother she no longer had. What she had not expected—what wrecked her now—was the sight of her father and her younger self at play. They had been happy.

She had known for eight years that she'd lost her mother, but somehow, somewhere, she had lost her dad along the way, too.

Sometime later, when she felt less vulnerable, Tesla noticed they were on a two-lane road, clearly outside of town, and the sun was below the treetops.

"Hey—" Tesla said as she leaned into Sam so he could hear her. "Um, sorry about that."

Sam didn't answer. *He must be really pissed*, she thought, *that I asked him to drive down that street, that my dad saw me.* She couldn't begin to understand the ripple effects that must have already begun, now that her father had seen her here, in the past.

The motorcycle slowed as it rolled off the two-lane, paved road and into a field of tall grass and wildflowers. Once it had stopped, and they were a good twenty yards from the road, Sam turned the motor off and they sat there until the silence of the field, and the sudden lack of motor sounds gave way in their consciousnesses to the twitter of birds settling in for the night. Sam pushed the kickstand down with his foot and then slid off. He stood next to the bike, his hands shoved into the pockets of his faded jeans.

"What are you sorry for?" he asked as she took off the helmet and felt the breeze lift her hair as it spilled out, down and around her shoulders. It took her a moment to remember that she had apologized to him. She felt numb, in shock, unable to focus.

"Isn't it obvious?" she said. "It was a stupid risk to take. I let my dad see me. Oh God, Sam, what will he do? For my father to know at this point that time travel works, that *I'm* the one who's done it—"

"Tesla," Sam interrupted. "He didn't see you. He waved at

me—he knows me, I work for him, remember? He only saw you as someone on the back of my bike—the helmet and visor covered your hair and face. There is no way he jumped to the conclusion you're afraid of, he doesn't know, I promise."

Sam was right. She felt the blush on her cheeks, the visible heat that was always as much of an embarrassment to her as whatever it was that made her blush in the first place. "Oh," she said. "Right." She looked away as the shadows crawled across the meadow toward them. Tesla felt oddly deflated, rather than relieved. "I guess I just freaked out a little."

"Who wouldn't?" he said as he took a tentative step closer, his eyes still on hers.

She shrugged and shifted her gaze away from him again. "I guess."

"What are you embarrassed about?" he asked suddenly. "You don't seem shy, exactly, but you won't ever look at me."

"I look at you," she answered hotly. She felt like she was the younger one instead of him, and she didn't like it. "I blush easily, and I hate it, that's all. It makes me self-conscious. And, you know. My eyes."

Sam shook his head in disbelief. "Man, girls are weird."

"Oh, right, and guys aren't."

"What I meant was, you're crazy."

"Is that supposed to be less of an insult?"

"You blush because you feel things," Sam said simply. "And I won't even respond to the comment about your eyes. I don't know if you're an idiot or you want compliments, but I'm not encouraging you, either way."

Tesla smiled, she couldn't help it. Her dimples bit deep, her cheeks moved up into tight, round apples that were softly, beautifully pink.

"Okay, whatever," she said as she swiped her hand in the air as if to disperse the conversation like so much smoke. "We should probably head back. It'll take us awhile to get back to town, and I want to jump back—ahead, I guess—to my own time as soon as possible."

Sam's disappointment showed plainly on his face, but he immediately climbed back on the bike and started the engine. He drove slowly and carefully over the bumpy meadow as the long grass whipped at their legs and the smell of crushed flowers wafted up in their wake, until they were on pavement once again. The night air was chilly, and Tesla shivered once, glad Sam was in front of her to shield her from the wind. They didn't attempt to speak as they drove through the dusk and the stars came out to wink and watch without comment as life unfolded below.

By ten o'clock Tesla and Sam were back in the lab. They'd snuck in, and Sam had Tesla hide in a small maintenance closet until he'd gone through every room on the floor and confirmed that they were alone. They went to the lab, then, which was quiet and dark until Sam shut the door and turned on the lights.

Tesla walked over to the coffin, in its customary spot on the table. "You know, you should suggest to your boss that he make this a little bigger," she joked. "It's not all that comfortable as a mode of travel."

"Yeah, I'll get right on that," he said. "I'm sure the docs will take a suggestion from the sixteen year old janitor very seriously."

"Fifteen," she corrected, and immediately regretted it. She *hated* it when Keisha did that to her.

"Fifteen and three quarters," he countered, not in the least bothered. "And let's not forget that I am actually older than you are—you being seventeen in this time is cheating, so it doesn't count."

"It so counts, and you know it," she said. "Nice try." She hopped up to sit on the table, happy to feel a bit more coordinated than she had since her arm had been broken. She was used to a sense of her own agility, and the clumsiness of the cast and the inability to use her arm had become an irritation. "So what do you have to do to send me back?"

"Not much. I just flip the switch here." He pointed to a control panel that looked to Tesla like a high school science fair project. And not a first place entry, either.

"Really?" she asked, her nose wrinkled. "That's it?"

"Yeah, it turns the lasers on."

"So how do you know how to do it?" she asked, her eyes narrowed to blue and green slits. "Do you fool around with the equipment when you're here at night?"

"No," he said hastily. "Not exactly."

Tesla merely raised an eyebrow.

"Sometimes Dr. Petro—your mom works late, and, you know, I hang out in here. We talk. I'm interested, and she likes to explain stuff."

"Oh," said Tesla, at a loss for words. Sam knew her mother. Better than Tesla would ever know her. "I should go," she said quickly. "And I need Schrödinger."

Sam walked over to the metal table and held out his hands for the messenger bag, which Tesla took off and handed to him. "Heavier than when you came," he observed. "Still room in there for the rat?"

"He's not a rat, and yes, there's room." Tesla put her hand in Sam's as she got her feet under her and stood up on the table to step into the coffin. She lay down and curled up on her side and Sam placed her bag, with Schrödinger inside, in the space between the backs of her calves and the rear wall of the box.

"Ready?" he asked, his hand on the lid.

Without much room to maneuver, Tesla could only glance at him, but the one dimple he could see flashed as she smiled at him. "Guess so," she said cheerfully.

He began to lower the lid, but just before the latch clicked he lifted it again, just enough so that they could see each other.

"Come back soon," he said simply.

"Oh, sure, make me do all the work," she joked, and then she was shut inside and slipped from the world in a brilliant swirl of light.

CHAPTER 20

Finn jerked his head back up as he started to doze off, his chin headed toward his chest. He'd spent the last twenty-four hours in this little room and he'd fallen asleep occasionally in the chair he felt had become an extension of his body. Bizzy had come to relieve him a little while ago, and he'd gone back to Lydia's for a shower but returned immediately after. There was no way he could sleep. Time travel. The ramifications staggered his imagination—this was an historic moment, one that would change human experience forever. And he was right here to see it firsthand.

Mixed with his awe and the adrenaline of ambition, however, was worry. Tesla had been gone since the night before and there had been no sign of her since. He hadn't fully comprehended what it would mean to send someone back in time and then just sit and wait. He'd wanted to go himself, of course, but it would never have occurred to him to wonder what it might be like for the person left behind—he had virtually no experience with that kind of connection or empathy. He was a family of one, and he liked it that way—with the possible exception of Joley, of course. And, increasingly since he'd moved back here, Keisha as well. Tesla, he barely knew, but this *worry*—

He might, just possibly, have started to care about her, and he was far from happy about it.

He ran his fingers through his untidy curls and closed his eyes wearily.

"They've got *you* manning this contraption?"

Finn's eyes flew open at the sound of Keisha's voice. "What are you—how did you get in here?" he demanded.

Keisha smirked, loving this rare moment when she had the better of her cousin. He was far too smug, in her opinion. "Bizzy let me in—wait, before you say anything against that sweet, but let's face it, hair-and-make-up-challenged girl, I tricked her."

Finn rubbed his face hard and then stood up to face whatever disaster Keisha had wrought. "What have you done?"

"I have simply been me, and outsmarted your friends, who obviously think I'm an idiot," she said, savoring each word. "I went to your place and hung around until I caught Bizzy alone. And then I just pretended that I knew more than I do. I pretended I was mad, and that I thought it was her fault that T had gone missing, and I demanded that she get her back here, right now." Keisha grinned broadly at him. "She jumped to it. It was awesome. I was totally vague, and the next thing I know she's stammering out an apology, telling me you're down in the 'Bat Cave' waiting for Tesla to 'jump back to our time,' and that she's just sure everything will turn out okay, that even though this is the first time a human has time travelled—and I'm like, what the hell did you just say??—she's got every confidence in Tesla's dad, and who knows what else. I didn't understand it, frankly, but I got the gist. 'You better take me down to that cave and my cousin right now,' I said. And, so, here I am."

Finn stared at her, incredulous. In ten minutes she had not only gotten Bizzy to tell her about time travel, about Dr. Abbot's work, this secret facility, but that Tesla had actually jumped back in time herself.

He was just about to impress upon her—well, attempt to impress upon her—the seriousness of these matters when there was a sudden, brilliant flash of light, white-hot, from the monitors in the control booth, and he was out of his chair and on his feet. One glance at the screen directly in front of him revealed Tesla's curled-up form in a fetal position on the floor and he was out the door, down the metal stairs and into the Bat Cave, with Keisha on his heels.

"Is she dead?" Keisha yelled behind him.

Finn threw open the heavy metal door and knelt on the floor beside Tesla, and he tentatively touched her shoulder. "Tesla?"

She opened her eyes and looked at him, and the smile that broke across her face was like another laser flash.

"Hey," she said. "I guess I'm back."

"I guess you are."

She sat up, a little slower than she would have if she'd had two good arms, but for all that she looked just fine, and Finn could feel himself start to relax, finally.

"T, what the hell—are you okay?" Keisha asked, skidding to a stop right beside Finn.

"Yeah, I'm good—what are you doing here?"

"I'm in the inner circle with you geeks now," Keisha said proudly.

Tesla turned to Finn, her surprise apparent. "Lydia agreed to this?"

"Hardly. I don't think she even knows. Keisha made Bizzy think she already knew, and bullied her into bringing her down here."

"Nice," Tesla said, holding her hand up, palm facing them. "Up top."

Keisha, finally getting the recognition she felt she deserved, high-fived her best friend. "You should've told me, though," she admonished Tesla.

"I really didn't know until yesterday. Literally. When I told you I thought I'd hallucinated all that stuff in the hospital, that's what I really thought it was. Hey—is Max okay?" Tesla asked, turning back to Finn.

"Max is fine, everyone is." He paused a moment, but he couldn't resist, he wanted the story. "So it worked. You went back? Same place?"

"Yup," she said, and the triumph in her voice was unmistakable. "Piece of cake. Wound up in the coffin, in the lab, same time of night there as it was here when I left."

"So time runs parallel here and there."

"Far as I could tell," she said. "From what Sam said, the same amount of time had passed there as had passed here since last fall when I stumbled into the Bat Cave with my concussion."

"You talked to the janitor kid about time travel?" Finn asked, incredulous.

Tesla responded hastily. "I didn't tell him. He works there— he knew it was a time machine before I ever showed up. But yeah, he was there in the lab. He'd waited for months, I guess, hoping someone would come back in the time machine."

Finn nodded. "I guess I can't blame him for that. It is pretty incredible. Still, Lydia won't be happy that you had that conversation."

Tesla merely shrugged. In light of her successful return from the past—not to mention the fact that Lydia wasn't here—she didn't feel overly concerned. She turned to Keisha. "Hey, maybe it'll take the pressure off you and Biz. Cat's out of the bag all over the place."

"But Tesla, I still don't get why you did this," said Keisha.

Tesla sobered immediately and explained quickly about her father. "Is there any news of my dad, Finn? Any word from Jane?"

"Lydia is on it, of course, but she hasn't updated us directly since you left last night. If she's heard from Jane I'm not aware of it."

"But Jane knows I took the jump, right?"

Finn hesitated. He didn't want to tell Tesla that he sensed Lydia didn't quite trust Jane; the woman was practically her aunt. "You'll have to ask Lydia," he finally said in a tone that did not invite questions. "We should probably head to the house. Everyone will want to know you're back, and hear the whole story—you were gone a full day, you must have a lot to tell us. And your bag looks pretty full—did the mouse...?"

"Schrödinger," Tesla corrected. "And yes." Tesla reached into her bag and pulled out the tiny traveler, who blinked enormous black eyes at Finn.

"He made it," Finn breathed. "Do you know what this means?"

"It means we need some Purel, stat," said Keisha, backing away from Tesla.

"It doesn't mean anything until we can repeat it," Tesla answered Finn, too well schooled in the scientific method to let excitement lead her to a hasty conclusion.

Finn took the mouse and put it in a little wire cage that sat in a dark corner of the larger cave outside the time-machine room before they left the cave for the stairwell that led up and out into the world again.

"I brought some stuff back, but it's unclear to me how valuable it is. Bizzy will be able to help figure it out, I think," said Tesla as she climbed. "And I thought, you know, besides the technical aspects, you're probably the one to help me dig into the past. Seems kind of journalistic."

"It is that," said Finn easily. "Plus, of course, that's what my paycheck is for, as Lydia will happily remind me."

They climbed the stairs in single file, Finn leading the way. Tesla, walking just behind him—her torso was twenty-six inches from his—vividly recalled the way he'd kissed her, right outside the door they were headed for. They'd stood in the light rain, a perfectly damp, warm summer night, and though she'd made the first move, his response had been—well, responsive. She flushed, suffused from head to toe with a warmth that was unmistakable. She glanced at his back, noted the way his T-shirt stretched taut across his shoulders, and her eyes traveled down his body, over his narrow hips, the fitted jeans, muscled thighs...

She wanted to kiss him again. And more.

"Tesla, geez!" Keisha complained when she ran smack into Tesla, who had unconsciously stopped on the stair, staring at Finn's ass.

"Sorry," Tesla mumbled, trying not to laugh as she started climbing again.

A few minutes later they rounded another bend in the seemingly endless metal staircase, which echoed loudly with every step they took until they reached the exterior door that led to the quad. Happy to have climbed out of the bowels of the Bat Cave, and anxious to breathe the fresh night air, they picked up their pace until they were at the door. Finn opened it to reveal the darkness just beyond where the light spilled out from the stairwell.

Tesla walked outside with Keisha, Finn right behind them, but before he could grab the door as it shut and cut off the only source of light in the darkness, they caught a glimpse of the man who emerged from the shadows only a few feet away and moved purposefully toward them. The door clicked shut behind them, their escape cut off, and they turned to face whoever it was that waited for them.

"Tesla," the man called softly, as Finn pulled the girls back and stepped in front of them protectively.

"What do you want?" Finn asked.

The man ignored Finn. "Tesla, don't be afraid. You know me."

Tesla peered around Finn's shoulder and stared at the shadowy figure in front of them. Her scalp pricked eerily at the sound of his voice. She *knew* that voice, though she couldn't place it.

"I'm sorry to startle you," said the man. "I've got a flashlight, I'm going to shine it on my face."

He brought the flashlight up and turned the beam on his features. They stood like that for an interminable minute, as Finn, Keisha, and Tesla looked at him, and he stood patiently while they did. He wasn't quite as tall as Finn, but he was harder, with a bigger, more muscular build. His thick, black hair was cut short, an almost military style, and he looked at Tesla intently with dark, liquid eyes—

"Sam?" Tesla suddenly said, her voice hesitant with disbelief.

"Yeah," he replied, his voice still soft, as if she were a skittish colt he did not want to startle. "It's me."

"Oh my god," she whispered, and then she was out from behind Finn before he could stop her and had flung herself into the arms of the dark haired man.

Sam's arms went around her and held her tightly, her feet several inches above the rain-wet grass. He'd dropped the flashlight to catch her and it landed just in front of him, tipped up at an angle on a small hillock of grass to illuminate the tableau of Tesla's arms around the handsome stranger's neck, a self-assured man, older than Finn but, without a doubt, young enough.

"That's hot," said Keisha with warm approval.

Tesla moved, pulled away from him just slightly, and Sam released her immediately to set her gently down on the ground.

"I can't believe it," Tesla laughed breathlessly. "I just left you, I just saw you like, twenty minutes ago! But you were—"

"Yeah, I know, it takes a while to get used to the idea." He bent down to retrieve the flashlight and turned it off, which plunged them all back into darkness. "But it was eight years and twenty minutes ago for me."

"Eight years," she whispered. "But…"

And then Finn spoke. "Of course," he said. "You've had to wait all this time." Finn's and Sam's eyes met and, despite the gloom, they saw each other quite clearly.

"Oh, sorry," Tesla said. "Sam, this is Finn and Keisha."

Sam stuck his hand out and Finn grasped it with his own. "Good to meet you guys."

"Likewise," said Finn easily.

"Yeah, very, very good to meet you," said Keisha, expertly elbowing her cousin aside to shake Sam's hand as well.

"We should get to the house," said Finn. "Lydia will want to talk to you, too, if you'd like to come with us."

"Yeah, I would," said Sam. "Thanks."

They began the trek across campus, toward the library, as they made their way to Lydia's old Victorian house.

"So, you work in Dr. Abbott's lab?" Finn said, the first to break the awkward silence.

"Well, I did," said Sam. "But I haven't worked for him for six years."

Tesla still struggled to grasp what had happened, how much

time had passed. "So you must be—what?" she asked Sam. "Twenty-four?"

"Almost," he said, and she could hear the grin on his face.

"Right," she said with a laugh. "Twenty-three and three-quarters."

"Exactly," he chuckled, as Finn walked silently beside them.

"And what do you do now?" asked Tesla.

"I'm in my second year of med school," he said. "Cardio— that's the plan, anyway."

"Specializing in arrhythmias?" Finn asked evenly.

Tesla glanced quickly at Finn's profile but in the dark she saw only polite, casual interest on his face.

"Not exactly," Sam said. "My father had a heart attack and died when I was eighteen, and since then I've planned to be a heart surgeon."

"That's rough," said Finn evenly, genuine sympathy in his voice.

"It was," Sam agreed. "Thanks."

Keisha took over at that point, grilling Sam about med school, while Finn and Tesla walked in silence until they arrived at Lydia's, where Finn walked up the front steps, opened the door, and stood aside to let the others precede him.

Tesla sat on the sofa next to Keisha and finished off the peanut butter and jelly sandwich Max had brought her almost immediately.

"Thanks," she said to her brother after she'd washed it down with the last of the milk in her glass.

"Sure." Max smiled at her from his place on the floor, where he sat with his legs crossed, obviously at home in Lydia's house. "I figured you'd be hungry."

"Yeah, I didn't realize how much," she said.

"Those eggs didn't tide you over?" asked Sam, but Tesla only smiled in return, uncomfortable with this strange collision of worlds, with this Sam who was all grown up, incredibly handsome, even well-dressed. His white button down, with the cuffs open and turned up twice, revealed strong arms, and the open top button created a perfect setting for the column of his tanned neck, his chiseled features, those smoldering black eyes.

"Shall we get down to business?" asked Lydia, and though there was no overt criticism in her words or tone, Tesla sensed that she found this sandwich break—not to mention the pervy once-over Tesla had just given Sam—a waste of valuable time.

"Of course." She colored slightly and glanced around the room, still shocked to see Keisha, to know that she was fully informed—at least in a general way—about this whole time travel thing and the fact that her dad had been kidnapped. It was a great relief to have her there. Apparently Bizzy had told Lydia that she'd inadvertently told Keisha, and though Lydia was still grumbling about the lax security she was forced to accept with teenagers on the payroll, she seemed to have resigned herself to the growing number of them in her midst.

Beckett and Lydia each occupied a chair, with Bizzy perched on the arm of Lydia's while Joley and Finn stood in front of the fireplace, like some sort of united-guy front. Sam sat on the sofa, next to Tesla.

"Tesla, why don't you begin from the moment you made the jump twenty-four hours ago," Lydia ordered as she peered at Tesla from over the tops of her half-glasses, her yarn and knitting needles forgotten in her lap.

Tesla tried her best to remember every detail as she spoke, though she deliberately left out the freedom and excitement she'd felt on the motorcycle, her uninjured arm wrapped tightly around Sam's waist. Irritated, somehow, that she seemed to want to avoid Finn's eyes as she mentioned the motorcycle, she looked deliberately at him, defiantly.

Finn's only response was to look amused.

"I trust you wore a helmet," Joley said.

"Gonna sue someone, counselor?" Keisha teased.

"Of course she did," said Sam from beside Tesla. "I put mine on her before she even got on the bike."

Keisha made a small sound of approval that everyone heard, a sound that she somehow managed to pack with sexual innuendo, and Tesla closed her eyes. *Thanks, Keish.*

"Go on, please," Lydia said.

"Well, then we went to his house—it was like six a.m. by then—got some food—"

"Did anyone see you?" Beckett asked, and Tesla looked at her quickly, amazed that the girl could immediately zero in on the worst possible question to ask.

"No," said Tesla. "There was no one else there."

Beckett smiled a very little smile.

"As soon as the library was open we headed back to campus," Tesla continued. Reluctant to confess she'd lied to Sam, she looked at her cast and picked at a loose edge of plaster with her other hand. "And I went to the physics department instead."

Tesla turned to Sam. "Sorry, but I lied to you. It wasn't that I didn't trust you, but I thought if I told you too much about the future it might, I don't know, cause problems."

Sam smiled and covered her hand, briefly, with his own. "Of course."

"So I went to the physics department and just walked in, went to my dad's office to see what I could find."

"How did you get in?" Joley asked.

"She brought a key, I'll bet," said Keisha. "You brought your dad's spare key with you, didn't you?"

Tesla smiled at her. They'd once taken that key and gone to her father's office on a Sunday afternoon, to do who knows what. They'd been twelve at the time, and when her dad caught them and called Keisha's mom, they'd both been grounded.

"Yeah, I did," she said. "I had planned to give it to Finn for his jump, but somehow I forgot, and didn't even remember it was in my bag until after I made the jump in his place.

"Nice," said Beckett. The approval was grudging, but it was there, and Tesla glanced at her in surprise. "What?" the blonde girl said defensively. "Don't get excited, it's not really a compliment. It turned out well, but only because you screwed it up and forgot to give Finn the key."

"True enough," Tesla admitted with a shrug.

"Did you find anything?" Lydia prodded.

"I did," said Tesla as she opened the messenger bag that sat on the sofa beside her. She reached inside and brought out several manila folders and extended them toward Bizzy, who walked over and took the folders out of Tesla's hand. "These appear to be early work my parents did on the time machine, as well as some evidence that Sebastian Nilsen actually did steal data from my parents' lab and use it to write the article that got him in trouble."

"You know Sebastian Nilsen?" Sam asked.

"Do you?" Lydia countered.

"Not well," he said slowly, "and certainly not in a good way. I met him once, and saw him one other time, a few years later."

"Can you be more specific?" Beckett asked.

"Yes, of course," Sam said quickly. "When I worked the night shift in the Abbott's lab—I think I was sixteen—a man approached me outside the building one night after I'd clocked out. I asked him what he wanted. He told me I was clearly a 'go-getter,' that kind of B.S., and he could help me out. I asked him what he meant, how he knew me, but all he would say was that he was interested in the work that went on in that lab, and that if I would give him access at night, just so he could look around, he would pay me. A lot."

"And did you do it?" Bizzy asked.

"No, I didn't," said Sam, gently but firmly. "I told him I was not interested, and I got on the bike and left."

"How did you know that was Sebastian Nilsen?" Joley asked.

"I didn't at the time," Sam said. "But a few months later I saw him again when I was on campus—I had run into Dr. Abbott on my way back to his office, and he stopped suddenly. A man stood by the side entrance with a young woman, a student I guess, and they were obviously in a heated argument. The man looked angry, and so did the young woman. I said something like, 'I can't believe he's back!' and your father grabbed my arm and took me—none too gently—into the nearest classroom and demanded that I explain. I felt guilty because I hadn't told him earlier, I'd thought somehow it might reflect badly on me, but I told him then. The man we saw with that woman was the same guy who had tried to bribe me to let him into the lab a few months earlier."

"What did my dad say?" Max asked from the floor.

"He said, 'That's Sebastian Nilsen, and he is a very dangerous man.'"

Lydia nodded. "I'm not surprised."

A faint sound, a movement of air from the front door, and everyone in the room turned to see Jane Doane standing in the doorway, her small black bag at her feet.

"What did I miss?" she asked as she shut the door behind her.

"Not much," said Lydia before anyone could answer. "I haven't heard from you," she said casually. "Any luck across the border?"

Jane smiled at the older woman, but without warmth, and Tesla felt again the inexplicable tension when the two were together.

"Some," said Jane with a noncommittal shrug. "We're certain Nilsen was there, but it appears he crossed back over into the States. He and anyone else who was with him. We lost the trail, however, in Buffalo."

Tesla had become aware of Sam beside her because his body was tense and he was so focused. She glanced at him, surprised to find him fixated on her Aunt Jane. Jane followed Tesla's glance and looked appraisingly at Sam as she tucked her short dark hair behind her ear and smiled at him.

"Hello. And you are?" she asked briskly.

"I'm Sam," he said, his voice a little tight. "But we've seen each other before—or at least, I've seen you."

"Really?" Jane looked exactly the same as she had before Sam spoke, yet she was clearly, somehow, more alert.

"Yes," he said. "I saw you once, about seven years ago, on campus. You were with Sebastian Nilsen."

CHAPTER 21

Every eye in the room turned to Jane then, and Tesla marveled at her aunt's composure. Jane walked into the room and stood next to Beckett's chair. She said nothing, but after a moment the badass-ninja-girl got up meekly and went to sit on the floor beside Max.

As Jane settled into the chair Beckett had vacated, the tension in the room grew palpable as everyone waited for her to answer the unspoken question inherent in Sam's revelation. They all assumed that Lydia would take the lead, get to the bottom of this, but Lydia remained silent.

Jane smoothed a nonexistent wrinkle in her fitted dress pants, tucked her hair behind her ear again, and looked up, surprised. "Oh, sorry, was I supposed to respond?"

"I think you'd better," said Tesla quietly.

"Well, of course I know—knew—Sebastian, he and I and Tasya and Greg all did our undergraduate degrees together. Tasya and I were roommates our freshman year, I met Greg in the first semester, the same time Tasya did, and we were all fast friends before Spring Break rolled around. We all knew him, and he knew us." Jane was wide-eyed and guileless, happy to prove that this scrutiny was no more than a mild amusement.

Tesla felt the hot flush of guilt wash over her for her suspicions. Jane Doane was like family, the closest friend her mother ever had, but then Lydia spoke.

"That is, of course, true, Jane," she said, her voice very serious. "But that doesn't explain why you were with Nilsen only seven years ago, long after the friendship had ended and he was completely estranged from the Abbotts. By then he had stolen data from their lab and published his infamous article, and he no longer worked for this university."

As if they watched a tennis match, all eyes turned from Lydia back to Jane.

Jane smiled. "Yes, you're quite right," she said smoothly. "I hadn't had any contact with Sebastian in years. But he waylaid me on campus that night to persuade me of his innocence. He asked me to intercede on his behalf with Tasya, to convince her that he had not stolen her work. He missed us all, he said, and wanted his good name back."

Lydia merely waited for more.

"Of course I said no," Jane said, annoyed for the first time. "And though I was brand new to the job—I'd only just been recruited, and hadn't officially begun my work with the agency—I made a full report. Feel free to check on that," she added to Lydia.

"I would, Jane, but of course you know I don't have access to your internal reports. I work for a different shop, and we all hold our cards very close to the vest."

Jane shrugged. "Oh, well."

After a moment, Lydia turned to Tesla. "Perhaps we should continue this later," she said, as if no one else was in the room.

"After I've left?" asked Jane, one eyebrow raised. "Please, Tesla, continue with your story."

Tesla pulled the cassette tapes from her messenger bag and held them out to the room at large in the palm of her hand. "I also found these, but I haven't listened to them," she said.

Joley moved from the fireplace to the sofa where Tesla sat, took the tapes from her, and left the room.

"I'm sorry, I missed some of this," said Jane. "You found those tapes where?"

"In Dad's office," Tesla said.

"Tesla, how did you get in there—that whole side of the building is shut down, your father's office is nothing more than a crater from the blast. That was a very foolish thing to do—the engineers haven't begun to assess the structural damage—the floor could have collapsed!"

Confused for a moment, Tesla suddenly realized that Jane didn't know she'd made the jump back in time. Her aunt assumed that Tesla had gone to her dad's office now, in the present.

"No, Aunt Jane," she said. "I went back. I used the time machine. I got this stuff from Dad's office eight years ago—yesterday, but eight years ago."

Startled out of her calm demeanor at last, Jane sat forward on the edge of her chair and leaned toward Tesla. "I thought you had all agreed Finn would go," she said, clearly displeased.

Lydia jumped in to spare Tesla. "The technology does not appear to work with Finnegan. We're not sure if it works with anyone except Tesla. She is two for two, you might say."

Jane turned on Lydia. "You don't have the right to make these decisions without me, Lydia. She's a child. And I'm family."

"Well, she is a minor, but hardly a child," Lydia said. "And you're not actually family, are you?"

Jane flushed and sat back in her chair, her lips pursed tightly together. Lydia was correct: she had no rights where Tesla and Max were concerned.

Joley came back into the room then, and they felt his excitement like an electric current that crackled and sliced through the room.

"What is it?" Keisha asked.

"These are audio tapes of a heartbeat."

"What do you mean?" asked Beckett.

Joley held out the small tape player he held in his hand and pushed Play. The speaker was small and weak, but they all heard it clearly: the sound of a heart as it pumped blood through a body.

Joley went to hit the off button but Sam put up a hand to stop him. "Wait," he instructed. They all listened for another minute and then Joley turned it off and the room was silent once again.

"What is it?" asked Lydia.

"That heartbeat is irregular. And a little fast." Sam looked at Tesla then, and he took her right hand in his. "Tesla, the heartbeat on that tape has an arrhythmia."

Tesla could feel her own heart beat in response. "So, w-what does that mean?" she asked with a slight stammer.

"I think it means that given where you found the tape, the heart we just heard is likely yours. Your heartbeat, recorded at least eight years ago."

"But, why?" she said, completely confused. "I don't understand." She pulled her hand away from his.

"Isn't a heartbeat a kind of biological signature?" Finn asked slowly. "You know, like a fingerprint, or DNA?"

Sam frowned as he thought about this, his black eyes fathoms deep. "I suppose it's possible," he said slowly. "But a heartbeat wouldn't be a unique signature, one that you could identify as one person's, and not anyone else's."

"Even if the heartbeat in question was arrhythmic?" Finn

pressed him, and everyone in the room seemed to hold their breaths.

"You'd have to have an enormous amount of data to determine if there was, over a long period of time, any discernible pattern, let alone a singularly unique pattern," Sam said. "I mean, it's called arrhythmic for a reason: there's no rhythm. No pattern. The beat is random, at least for the duration of the tests we use to monitor hearts."

"But what if a heart was monitored for a lot longer?" Tesla asked. "For a much longer period than any medical test would require? Would you find a pattern—an individual biological signature?"

"Is that possible?" asked Beckett. She turned to Bizzy, as they all did with technology or science questions.

"I don't know," Bizzy admitted. "This certainly isn't my area." But before everyone could turn back to Sam, Bizzy added, "What I do know, though, is that Tasya Petrova was heavily involved in chaos theory—randomness and pattern—in her work right before she died."

"And—" Tesla began, stunned as she saw exactly where Bizzy was headed.

"And her journal, which is focused on the time machine they developed, refers to *the Tesla effect*," Bizzy finished for her.

The room was deadly silent. No one moved.

"Someone has to say it," Beckett said, her voice strained.

And then, much to everyone's surprise, it was Max who said it. Max, who knew essentially nothing about quantum physics or the human cardiovascular system but could put the disparate threads of dramatic narrative together, unravel the tangle of complex plots with multiple characters and conflicted motivations and see the entire trajectory of the story before anybody else ever did, spoke the words first.

"It's Tesla." His eyes blinked behind his battered, wire-framed glasses. "Tesla's heartbeat is unique, and our mother figured out its pattern, and it's that pattern—that heartbeat—that makes the time machine work."

"*Ho. Lee. Shit,*" Sam said softly, and Tesla noted, as if from very far away, that he still used the same expression, with the exact same inflection, that he had as a kid.

"Indeed," Lydia added, as they all sat and absorbed this idea. And then, as usual, she took charge.

"Alright everyone, listen up," she began. "We've got work to do. It seems clear that the files Tesla brought back confirm the theft by Nilsen many years ago, and the reason for the destroyed friendship. This is not new information, but it is always good to reaffirm what we already know. It also seems likely, given what was in the first locked drawer, that the second one Tesla did not open might also contain important information, maybe even a direct clue as to where Dr. Abbott is being held." She turned to Tesla, who sat on the sofa looking a bit shell-shocked. "You'll have to go back, dear."

"I know," Tesla said. She had already figured that part out. "I'm so pissed at myself. I can't believe I panicked and raced out of the building like that. I should have waited until I'd checked the other drawer."

"I wouldn't be too hard on yourself," Lydia consoled. "It's difficult to imagine how any of us could have done better, set down in the middle of our own lives almost a decade in the past. I'm sure it will be easier this time."

"Probably," Tesla agreed. "Guess I'll get ready to head back to my little coffin."

"Wait, I almost forgot," Sam said. He put his hand, very

briefly, on Tesla's leg, just above her knee, and didn't even seem to realize it. Startled by his touch, Tesla turned quickly to face him and wondered if everyone else in the room had seen his intimate gesture. If Finn had seen it.

"Remember that second time you made the jump?" Sam began.

Tesla had to laugh, and Sam was dazzled by the deep dimples, the glitter-green and blue of her eyes. "Yeah, I remember," she said. "It was, like, yesterday."

"Right," Sam grinned sheepishly. "It's all so weird, even though I've had years to get used to the idea."

"You said you forgot something?" Finn asked, and Tesla could not mistake the coldness in his voice.

"Yeah," Sam said immediately as he turned to Finn with an open, friendly face. "Just before Tesla made the jump back—earlier tonight—she made a similar comment about how small and tight the early time machine was. The coffin, I guess you guys call it. So the next night, when I came in for my shift, I made an offhand suggestion to Dr. Petrova about how cool it would be someday when her prototype actually worked and how, from what she had told me, people from the future could come here, to her time machine. It would have to be bigger, though, I told her, because nobody would be able to fit in that little box."

"Nicely done," Beckett said with admiration.

"Yes, it was," Lydia agreed.

"Well, they acted almost immediately on the suggestion I planted. I had no idea how they got the funding so quickly, but a little less than a week later, the coffin had been replaced by a time machine that was roughly the size of a walk-in closet."

"So the coffin is no more?" Tesla asked.

"Not for another week," Bizzy answered. "You know, a

week from now, eight years ago."

"So we have to wait a week?" Tesla asked, the alarm in her voice apparent to everyone. "What if in the meantime there's no clue here, in our time, to my dad's whereabouts? We don't have—he doesn't have—that kind of time. I can still go now, the coffin is tight, but it's obviously doable for me."

"No, no, it's not a problem," Bizzy hastened to assure her. "I can adjust the calculations and reset the destination equation—to a point."

"Oh," Tesla said, taken completely unawares. "I assumed the two points on the closed time loop were fixed; that our time was connected to exactly eight years ago by the wormhole the machine created. You can change where the connection is?"

"Yeah," Bizzy said. "In theory, anyway. I mean, I think I can do it. You know, without losing you somewhere. Somewhen."

"Then why," Tesla asked slowly, "haven't we planned all along to simply go back to the night my dad was taken by Nilsen, the night Finn and I were attacked and my arm got broken, and just prevent all of it in the first place?"

Bizzy dropped her eyes to her lap where she twisted her favorite skull ring that she wore on her index finger. "Because I don't know how," she said, so softly the others barely heard her.

"But—" Tesla began.

"Bizzy is an incredible resource, I'm sure we'd all agree," Lydia cut in smoothly. "But we should remember that she is sixteen years old, an undergraduate student, and while certainly Dr. Abbott has offered her unparalleled access to his work, and shown great confidence in her abilities, she does not know what he knows."

"I wish I could do it," Bizzy said miserably. "I don't want you to think I didn't think of this, it's so obvious. But I have to use the time machine as it is currently set—and it's actually a huge risk to make even this small adjustment of one week. There is no way for me to even consider the massive changes in calibration necessary to shift the timeline connection to just a few days ago. I wouldn't even know where to begin, and with Dr. Abbott gone, as far as I know there is no one on the planet who would know how to do that. I'm really, really sorry, Tesla."

"Bizzy, don't be ridiculous!" Tesla said. "The agents haven't been able to locate Nilsen and my dad, haven't even found a clue as far as I can tell. The only reason we even have a shot at all is because of all you *do* know, and Max and I are really grateful. We'll just have to stick to the plan and see what was—is—in that other drawer eight years ago."

"I don't like it," Finn said from his position by the fireplace.

"Why not?" Lydia asked.

"Yeah, Finn, when I said it was risky, I really just meant that I could be a few hours, maybe a day off in the destination," Bizzy said. "You can trust me."

"I know I can, Biz," Finn said. "That's not the problem." He walked behind the couch and paced while he spoke, which made Tesla very tense. She felt and heard him directly behind her, felt and heard Sam breathe beside her, both of them uncomfortably close. And of course, she knew exactly how close.

"We've figured out that the time machine operates only when Tesla is physically inside it," he continued. "It's coded to operate, somehow, by a pattern her mother discovered in the seeming chaos of Tesla's heart's arrhythmic beat."

"We know all of this, Finn, please get to the point," Lydia said, her gentle patience clearly near its end.

"If we've figured it out, others can, too," he said quietly, right behind Tesla. The skin on her neck pricked as he spoke. "She's in imminent danger the moment anybody else realizes that if they have her, and they have Dr. Abbott's lab—here and now, or ten years ago, or anytime in between—they have access to time travel."

There was silence in the room, until at last Aunt Jane spoke. "Well, I think we know what Sebastian wants," she said quietly. "The key to Greg and Tasya's time machine." And then she turned to Tesla and said what they all had just begun to realize. "But Finn's right—you are only safe as long as Sebastian doesn't realize that you are that key."

CHAPTER 22

"You don't really know what you're talking about here," Finn said to Sam. The discussion of whether Tesla should jump again was still underway half an hour later, but in the past five minutes it had become an argument, and the only two who were still at it were Finn and Sam.

"I know enough," Sam said. The two stood near the sofa where Tesla still sat, and everyone watched to see how it would play out.

"Do you have any idea how ruthless this guy is? The lengths he would go to for this?" Finn was furious, but he'd so far kept his temper in check, and while Sam seemed calmer, it was clear that he, too, was angry.

"Yes, I have a pretty good idea. But try to hear me on this. I am not suggesting that Tesla isn't in danger, or that time travel itself doesn't pose any sort of risk. My point is that the sooner we get her father back and take Nilsen into custody, the sooner she'll be out of danger—and whether we like it or not, at this point Tesla is the only one who can go back in time. Whatever is in that drawer may be the only evidence in existence that will lead us to Dr. Abbott. We have no choice."

"We do have a choice," Finn said, his jaw muscles clenched. "We keep her here, safe, and we figure out a way to code her heartbeat into the machine so that it will work without her. Then someone else can go."

"You say that like it's easy!" Sam said, his voice raised for the first time.

"I didn't say it was easy," Finn snapped. "Think about it. It's not as though we've tried to do it and it hasn't worked. No one had any idea until just now that Tes's heartbeat was a part of this, and so *no one has tried*! For all we know, Joley could step into the time machine, play that old cassette tape of her heartbeat, and he'd make the jump himself! Don't you think it's worth a try?"

"Oh, mate, I'm not going. Just to be clear," said Joley quietly.

Sam ran his hands through his hair, almost as if he still had the boyish haircut Tesla knew, thick and blue-black, the too-long bangs that fell in his face, instead of the bristly, short hair he now wore. "I don't know," he said, and it was the first time he'd hesitated since he'd stepped out of the shadows to find Tesla.

Tesla, who, like everyone else in the room, had sat silently as the two men argued, could not have said why she suddenly looked at Lydia, but she did. Lydia's expression revealed how torn she felt, how unable even she was at this moment—she, who was so completely and irrevocably in charge, no matter what the circumstances—to decide on the right course of action.

Lydia sensed Tesla's scrutiny and their eyes met. After a brief moment, in which neither of them said a word, Lydia smiled a small, inexplicably sad smile, and Tesla stood up from the couch. Sam and Finn became quiet, and all eyes in the room were on the red-haired girl, her arm encased in turquoise.

"Finn, I appreciate the concern. And if these tapes allow someone else to make the jump, fine. But it has to happen immediately. I won't spend another day of the time my dad has left—and it might not be much, let's please be honest about that—in an attempt to fool the machine when I can just do it. I'm sorry."

Finn looked at her, and without a word turned and walked out of the room.

"He looks really mad," said Max.

"He's not mad, don't worry," said Joley. "Having to include other people in decision-making is still rather new to him. I've known him for a long time, but that doesn't mean it's easy to figure him out. Trust me, it takes some time. He just doesn't share everything until he's ready."

Max thought about that. "Okay."

All of the energy and drama of the moment seemed to have left with Finn, and within moments people started to drift away, to get a few hours of sleep though the sun had just come up.

"Tesla, I'm not sure at all that this is the way to go, but I believe it was your decision to make," Lydia said.

"I agree," said Jane. She turned to Tesla and smiled. "Your mother would be proud of you."

Tesla nodded, suddenly unable to speak past the lump in her throat, and Jane, always observant, stood up. "I assume there will be no activity today?" she asked Lydia briskly.

"You know as much as I do," Lydia said serenely. "We'll move on this later tonight. Tesla needs to sleep."

"Good. In the meantime, Tesla and Max, let's head back to the house, shall we? I imagine it'll be nice to sleep in your own beds. You must both be exhausted."

Max nodded and moved toward the door, clearly relieved, but Tesla found herself oddly reluctant to go with Aunt Jane. She felt that quiet, breathless sensation you get after an explosive event, when there's nothing to really say or do in the calm that follows. It had descended upon her when Finn left the room; she knew she couldn't have made any other decision, but she was filled with a sad, hollow emptiness, nonetheless.

"I'll take you over there later if you're not quite ready to go yet," Sam said quietly to Tesla.

"Aunt Jane, you and Max go ahead. I'll be home soon," Tesla said immediately.

Jane noted the pale cheeks, the suggestion of shadows under Tesla's eyes. "Sure," she said. "You need to sleep, though. You look tired, and you should be rested and ready when you go."

When Jane and Max had left and the sound of her aunt's SUV had faded, Lydia said she, too, was off to get some sleep and excused herself from the room as the others filed out as well.

Tesla and Sam were left alone.

"Do you want me to take you home now?" Sam asked.

"No, not yet. I don't think I could sleep. I feel...I don't know. Like I don't have anywhere to go."

"What do you mean?" he asked.

"I thought all I wanted was to go home, but now I don't really want to. My dad's not there...it's all different now...." She trailed off, and then laughed at herself, but the sound didn't hold any humor. "Forget it. I'm being ridiculous."

"No, you're not," he said. "Come on." He took her by the hand and led her out the front door, down the steps, and back toward campus in the soft gray light of dawn. They walked for ten minutes in silence until they reached the lot where Sam had parked his motorcycle. He unlocked the storage compartment in the back and took out two helmets, laid one on the seat and put the other one on Tesla's head.

"Chin up," he said, and when she tilted her head back, he fastened the strap under her chin.

"You've upgraded," she said simply as she took in the black and chrome Harley while Sam fastened his own helmet.

He grinned at her, and then swung his leg over the bike and sat down. "Get on," he said, and she did, and when she put her right arm around him and leaned forward, just enough to comfortably rest her broken arm in between their bodies, she closed her eyes and leaned her head against his back, the warmth and solidity of him against her cheek.

The sun, risen just enough to illuminate the ribbon of road that stretched out in front of the motorcycle, began to shimmer in the air with a soft golden light. Tesla was lulled by the steady throb of the Harley and the nearness of Sam, almost to the point of falling asleep. She was so tired. She sat up a little straighter and looked around her, somewhat surprised to find that they were in the country, on a narrow, two-lane road.

Sam felt her shift away from him and break the contact they'd shared as she had leaned into him for the past half hour, and he felt the loss of warmth against his back where they had touched. He slowed the bike and turned his head to the side to ask over the sound of the motor, "Recognize where we are?"

Tesla looked more carefully around her, at the sunlit summer grass, thick stands of oak and maple, and masses of wildflowers that undulated like yellow and lavender waves in the sea of fields all around them.

"Isn't this...is this where we were last night?" she asked.

The bike had slowly decelerated until they moved so slowly they could have walked at the same pace, and Sam pulled the bike off the right shoulder of the road, rolled to a complete standstill, and turned off the ignition.

"Yes, but for me it was eight years ago that we came here,

after that brief encounter with your father—and yourself—at your old house on Webber."

Tesla slid off the bike, undid the clasp on her helmet and removed it with her uninjured hand, while Sam took his off as well.

"Why did you want to come here?" Tesla asked.

Sam shrugged. "I remember that you were upset when we saw your dad, and we wound up here, and you felt better. Simplistic, I know, but I've always thought this place had a good vibe. It's kind of special to me."

"Oh." Tesla wondered if she was supposed to say more. Feel more. "So, you've come here again, since then?"

"Yeah, you could say that," Sam said with an odd smile she could not read. "Come with me, I want you to see this." He held out his hand to her, and after the briefest hesitation she took it. They walked across the field, through purple flowers that reached past their knees, toward a thick copse of enormous pines about one hundred yards ahead.

They didn't speak until they reached the trees, where Tesla peered into the shadows beneath their thick, leafy boughs. She could just see the shape of a small structure nestled between the trunks of three huge old pines.

"What's this?" she asked as she paused and pulled back on his hand when he continued to walk.

"What's what?" He turned back, her hand still in his and a grin on his face.

"This. This field, this house. Why are we here?" She didn't want to sound suspicious, but she didn't know him, not really. She had felt close to the boy Sam, despite the short period of time they'd spent together, but this Sam—this grown man, so sure of himself, so determined, so gorgeous—seemed different, and Tesla was suddenly very aware that they were alone, out in the middle of nowhere. She felt completely out of her depth, and she never had learned how to tread water.

"Okay, I can see that you're nervous," he said and immediately let go of her hand to face her where she stood at the start of a vaguely marked path through the trees. "This is no big deal. This is the meadow we stopped at back then. I love this place. I own it. I built a little house here, it's where I live. I thought you might like to see it, especially since you were at a loss as to where to go, where you fit in, just now."

Tesla looked again, tried to make out the house that stood in dappled sunlight and shadows beneath the trees.

Sam watched her. "We can leave right now and go back to your house, or wherever you want. Just say the word."

"No," she began, hesitant at first. "It was nice of you to think of it. I want to see your house. It's cool that you built it here."

"Okay, let's go." He picked up the pace as they entered the path and the cool shade, where a soft carpet of pine needles cushioned each step.

Sam took her hand again and gently pulled Tesla along behind him. "It's not much, you know—an apartment, really. But it's so quiet out here, and you should see it when it snows—here, come look at this." They had reached a small clearing, just in front of the house, that Tesla hadn't realized was there—she'd assumed the trees grew close and crowded the house, but that wasn't it at all. The house had plenty of open space and air, and even sunlight around it, but it was all so subtle, so uncontrived. Instead of planting things around the house that needed to be trimmed and shaped and manicured, like some suburban dreamscape, Sam had opted instead to work with only the materials that he found on the site. Sandstone, and some fairly large, warm-hued boulders had been carted to a spot in the clearing where the early sun broke through the trees in brilliant shafts of light that contrasted starkly with the shade all around. He had shoveled rich black topsoil into all the crevices between the rocks and boulders that formed a mound almost five feet tall, a mound of rock that looked like nothing so much as an avalanche that had occurred millennia ago, and then within and on top of those mostly hidden crevices, now filled with rich nutrient soil, he had strewn seeds from the wildflowers that grew in the meadow. The warmth and light of the summer sun had brought forth an explosion of color, petunias and periwinkles, marigolds and dahlias, snapdragons and more, velvety purple, yellows and oranges so bright it hurt your eyes to look at them, soft pinks and the cinnamon and reds of the autumn that would eventually change everything, as autumn always did. The flowers grew in and around the rocks, at various heights, and looked as though they had sprung fully-formed from the rocks themselves. It was gorgeous, and wholly natural and, as Sam pointed out, required zero maintenance. He just had to let nature do its work.

He spoke with a quiet pride and a hesitant hope that she would find it charming. And she did—but he didn't realize that the place he had created here told her much more about him than he would ever have been able to tell her, even if he could have seen himself in this way. It was a place of beauty: she saw his appreciation of color everywhere, the comfort of balance and proportion that seemed accidental, unstudied, unaffected. The little fence that edged the back of the clearing, just behind the house before the trees became dense again, was made from found branches of different colors and woods, chosen and placed for maximum interest as white ash and birch contrasted with weathered, dark oak. Each piece of wood was bound to the next by what looked like copper bands that had begun to turn green in spots as they oxidized in the open air.

"Wow," Tesla breathed.

"Do you like it?" Sam asked. "Really?"

"Yeah, of course. Who wouldn't?" she asked, a little scornfully, the sincerity in her voice unmistakable.

"Come see the inside," he encouraged, and led the way up to an arched oak door set in a wall of stone. There was a small window in the door, framed in the same greening-metal as the hardware on the fence.

As they walked in the front door, Sam watched Tesla to catch every expression as she took it all in. The huge logs that made up the exterior of the house were visible on the inside, as well; he had not covered the walls with plaster or sheetrock. Instead, the stained wooden beams, with some hardened white material between each one, made the walls airtight and were their only ornament. Just inside the door was a coat and boot closet, and on the opposite wall a small mirror and the portrait of his family that Tesla had seen at his parents' house.

There were two steps down to a sunken room just big enough for a round table and four straight-backed chairs, a cherry-red sofa and a comfortable old chair and hassock. Open bookshelves lined the walls behind the sofa, and what were probably medical books, notebook and pen littered the rough-hewn coffee table where Sam no doubt studied. Instead of a TV, there was a stone fireplace, and to the left of the entry was a small but open kitchen, with a sunny garden window over the sink where clay pots of herbs grew. The roof was steeply pitched and open, the structural beams revealed, and the entire back wall was solid glass, with French doors that opened onto a small deck. Tesla gaped at the view. The land behind the cottage in the woods fell away to a spectacular valley, and from the glass wall one could see for miles the beauty of the natural world.

"Sam, I've never seen anything like this," she began as she turned to him, her eyes bright with appreciation and excitement. "It's so beautiful! You're actually an artist, you know—"

Sam was kissing her before she could finish her sentence. He had taken one purposeful step toward her as she told him how much she loved the place, taken her face gently in both his hands, and covered her mouth with his own.

CHAPTER 23

Startled by the sudden kiss, Tesla paused for a fraction of a second, her unspoken question, *yes or no*, clear to both of them. She reached up with her right hand, placed it on top of his that cupped the side of her face, and kissed him back.

Yes.

He wrapped her in his arms and pulled her in close to him with unexpected intensity. He made a low, soft sound, and she pulled away, her heart hammering.

"Sam, I—"

"I know, I know, I'm sorry," he hastened to say, both hands up in surrender. "I hadn't intended that, I swear. That's not why I brought you here."

"I didn't think that," she assured him. "It's just that...I'm a little confused...I'm not sure...."

"I understand," he said. "I don't want to scare you away, but I won't pretend that I haven't waited years for this." His eyes were direct and without pretense, and Tesla felt a shiver roll up her back as his gaze held hers. "You, on the other hand, have not. Believe me, I am nothing if not patient." He smiled, and while she knew from the tightness around his mouth what the admission cost him, she also believed he meant exactly what he said.

"Okay," she said, uncertain if that was the appropriate response. "Thanks."

They stood there, awkwardly at first, and then he said, "Let's not let a simple kiss ruin the day. C'mon, let me show you the rest, and then I'll get us a cold drink."

Fifteen minutes later Tesla nodded on the red sofa, her glass of lemonade tipped precariously in her hand. Sam reached over and gently took the glass from her and set it down on the coffee table.

"I'm sorry," she mumbled as she fought to keep her eyes open. "I'm so tired all of a sudden."

"So take a nap," Sam said. "It's barely eight a.m. Just tell me what time you want to be out of here and I'll make sure you wake up in plenty of time."

"I don't know...." She hesitated, looked longingly at the comfy couch, and then back at Sam.

"I've got some stuff to do around here, so you're free to sleep." He got up from the sofa and headed toward the kitchen. "You won't bother me."

She needed no additional encouragement. Tesla pried off her running shoes and lay down on the sofa, a soft feather pillow, covered in some deep, dark green fabric, under her head. She closed her eyes, breathed out in one long, deep exhale, and was sound asleep.

Sam sat in the worn, overstuffed chair across from the couch where Tesla slept. Slouched down low in his chair, he watched her, a brooding, unguarded look on his face. It freaked him out, that she looked the same after all these years. She *was* the same, he reminded himself, because no time had passed. He had grown up, and the vision of her he had carried in his head all these years was right in front of him—but now she was the kid, not yet eighteen. Christ, he could be arrested for what he was thinking. He knew he should walk away, but he didn't know if he could. When it came to Tesla, he still felt like that awkward teenager who would've given anything—anything he had, or would ever have—to be with her.

Sam tensed when Tesla stirred. She rolled, just slightly, from her back onto her side and faced him in his chair only a few feet away. Her breath slowed and deepened again, and she slept on. He realized that he held his breath, and shook his head, a silent laughter in his mind. *You're such a fool*, he thought, though he never took his eyes from her face. The tangled mass of her hair shone brilliantly in the sun that streamed in through the wall of glass beside her and turned it from a deep blood-orange to honey-gold as it curled over her shoulders and spilled across the green pillow and halfway down her back. Her lashes were thick auburn fringe against her pale, smooth skin, cheeks with the barest hint of pink echoed in the slightly deeper hue of her lips. Her small, round breasts were outlined by the tight little T-shirt she wore, with its swirls of psychedelic blue-green-purple-white that rode up just enough to reveal two inches of her taut, flat stomach above her low-rise, somewhat tattered jeans. She had kicked off her shoes, and he saw that her toenails were perfectly lacquered with hot-pink polish, a note of unexpected whimsy that somehow broke his heart.

He must have sensed some change in the room, a lessening of the power that an unchecked gaze focused on someone else's body always affords. His eyes leapt back to her face and her eyes, remarkably, devastatingly blue and green, stared back at him.

"You're awake," he said unnecessarily.

"Yes," she said, her voice low and soft with sleep.

Neither of them moved.

"It's still early, not even noon," he said. "You can sleep

longer if you like." He wanted her to get up, to ask him to take her back to her father's house, to Lydia's, to Finn. He wanted this impossible situation, which he had worked to achieve for almost a decade, to be taken away from him so he didn't have to decide. To decide to give her up, wait for her to grow up and hope that she would want him, too, or to win her over and make it happen now. He knew he could do it, not because he was so irresistible or she was so malleable, but because he was twenty-three years old, and she was seventeen. Some things are just that simple.

"Can I stay a while longer?" she asked.

He swallowed. Exactly, and not at all, what he wanted.

"Of course," he said. "You can stay as long as you like."

CHAPTER 24

Tesla looked around the small control room again, as if Finn might have magically appeared since the last time she checked.

"Tesla, it is imperative that you pay attention," Lydia said.

"Yeah, I know, sorry. I'm distracted," Tesla said guiltily. "Where is everybody?" Sam had dropped her off just after two o'clock in the afternoon at Lydia's house but it had been unusually silent. Finally Lydia herself had come downstairs and they'd walked over to the physics building, and down into the Bat Cave, together.

Lydia relented—as much as Lydia ever relented. "Beckett is with Max back at the house—I believe they're in the basement, which I have turned into a training facility-slash-media room. Something about pizza and *The Matrix* and some basic judo lessons, I believe. Joley has to study for a midterm, but you're to offer him no sympathy, since he insists on an overload of summer classes so he can take the bar exam before he's twenty-three, thus besting his older brothers in some he-man-lawyer contest. Jane has been called into her office. And I haven't seen Finnegan all day. Now, can we get back to work? The stakes are considerably higher now, you know. We've got to try and prepare for every possible contingency."

"You're right, Lydia." There was no one else in the room save Bizzy at the control panel, who checked and rechecked her calculations and equipment and ignored them both. The audio recording of Tesla's heartbeat had failed to trigger the time machine, and preparations for Tesla herself to make the jump were underway.

Lydia paused and looked hard at Tesla. "Alright then," she said briskly, but not unkindly. "As I said, now that Elizabeth has adjusted…well, whatever it is that she needs to adjust, you need to get ready. I have some items for you to take when you jump this time."

"Spy stuff?" Tesla asked eagerly.

Lydia flashed a smile, but it was gone before Tesla could congratulate herself on cracking the woman's stern exterior. "Yes, spy stuff," she said as she looked down at the box on her lap.

Tesla sat down in the chair Lydia indicated and waited expectantly. "This is awesome," she said to the older woman. "It's like you're Q and I'm Bond."

"I assure you, I am much more than your quartermaster here."

"Oh, yeah, of course," Tesla hastened to agree, unsure if Lydia was kidding or not.

Lydia pulled out a slim black device that fit neatly into the palm of her hand. "This is a smart phone."

"Yeah," said Tesla, unable to hide her disappointment. "I've seen 'em."

"No, my dear," said Lydia conspiratorially. "You haven't seen this one."

That got Tesla's attention, and the older woman went on. "This is not yet available to the public, and when it is, it will not be *this* version. This one was designed especially for our industry."

"What's it do?" asked Tesla eagerly.

"Well, it's a phone, obviously, and a digital camera, with wifi and network capabilities—capabilities, I might add, that utilize government satellites and towers, not commercial ones. Quite a difference."

"So, there'll be no 'can you hear me now?'" Tesla asked.

"It won't work," Bizzy said. She continued with her work and did not turn around.

"We've been through this, Elizabeth," said Lydia, who kept her back to the goth girl as well.

"I know, but it won't work. None of today's hardware was in place then, communication networks have changed drastically in the last ten years. Do you have any idea how many more cell towers and satellites we have, how quickly equipment becomes obsolete and is replaced? And the smart phone itself—"

"Yes, dear, so you've said already. Humor me anyway."

Tesla hid a smile as Lydia focused on her again. "I'm sure she's right, but we have to be careful with our assumptions. We really don't know how, or in what ways, time travel affects us, or our technology, or what new possibilities are opened up, perhaps for the very first time, by these jumps. I think we should experiment."

"I agree." Tesla reminded herself that she and Finn had already begun to experiment with Schrödinger, and that she would need to surreptitiously pick up the mouse before she jumped to see if they could repeat their initial success.

"How lucky for us that you do," Lydia said dryly. "As soon as you arrive, I want you to call me—I've programmed a number into the phone, under my name in the contacts, a number that has been in service continuously for over ten years. I want you to email and text as well. It may not work, but there's only one way to find out."

Tesla held the iPhone in her hand, turned it over and looked at its reflective, obsidian surface. "What else does it do?"

Lydia pursed her lips, "Nothing that you are qualified to use, so its other attributes have been disabled for now."

Tesla was clearly disappointed, but Lydia ignored her.

"Here is your driver's license," the woman said as she handed Tesla the hard plastic card with the usual holographic images and seals.

Tesla looked at it. "Wow, it looks legit."

"Yes, of course it does. This is not the first time we've created an identity for someone."

"Ellie Foster?" Tesla read.

"That was my idea," said Bizzy as she spun around in her chair to face them. "Remember that movie with Jodie Foster, the one where she's the very first human to travel through a wormhole, and she has some freaky trip with aliens? And Matthew McConaughey is a hot young missionary?"

"Uh…." Tesla had no idea what Bizzy was talking about.

"*Contact*," Bizzy said impatiently. "The movie was *Contact*."

"Yeah, I don't know that one," Tesla admitted.

Bizzy rolled her eyes. "I live in a cultural wasteland. Jodie Foster's character was named Ellie Arroway. Your jump-name is Ellie Foster."

"Oh," Tesla said. "Okay. Cool?"

"Forget it." Bizzy turned back to her work.

"Your name is Ellie Foster, and you have legal identification. You also have money," Lydia said, and handed Tesla a credit card from her box of goodies.

"Sweet!" Tesla exclaimed. "What's my limit?"

"Tesla, you are not going shopping. If you get in a predicament where you have to show identification, or make a purchase—in an emergency—you can do so. We don't want you to wind up in jail, or out on the street without food or shelter. Remember, we can't get to you; you are on your own once you jump. This is just a little security to send with you. Both this credit account and this driver's license are active in 2004."

Tesla realized she hadn't really thought about how vulnerable she was when she jumped. She couldn't rely on anyone but herself. She looked again at the I.D. in her hand, at her actual driver's license photo. Just as she was about to ask Lydia how they'd gotten her real DMV photo for the fake license, she noticed the birthdate printed right next to it.

"You made me eighteen!" She looked up at Lydia with a huge grin on her face. "I can buy a car—or order a beer in some states…. And I'm done with high school!"

Lydia closed her eyes and summoned the strength to continue. "Tesla, please try to focus, dear. You're as bad as the boys. Which is not a compliment."

"Right. Sorry." Tesla schooled her features into her serious-face, and tucked the I.D. and credit card into the outside, zippered pocket of her bag. "What's next, boss? Can I call you M? Or Mum, in my best British accent?"

Lydia looked at her, but did not answer—nor did she reach inside the box. When she spoke, it was clear she was not joking. "As you know, Nilsen is alive eight years ago, and he may very well be in town where—when—you will arrive shortly. He doesn't know what has transpired in subsequent years, of course, but he has already begun to attempt, at that time, to gain access to your parents' work. And that's only what we know for certain."

Tesla sat silently and waited, Lydia's tone and face driving all humor from her mind.

"I want you to be able to protect yourself," Lydia said. "I want you to take this with you."

When Lydia pulled her hand out of the box, she held a small, darkly metallic gun. Lydia deftly pulled the top of the barrel back. It slid on its well-oiled mechanism, and Tesla heard a click that sent her heart beating wildly. "It's loaded," Lydia said, her eyes on Tesla's. "The safety is on, here—see?"

"Oh, no way." Tesla stood up quickly, a sudden sheen of sweat on her upper lip. "I don't do guns." She had begun to back away from Lydia, though she did not realize it.

Lydia cocked her head slightly, noting the girl's widened eyes, the quick rise and fall of her chest as her breathing quickened. This was panic, clearly—a panic whose origin was unclear. "Tesla, I understand. And I'm glad that you aren't comfortable with this: a gun is certainly not a toy, and I am reassured you understand that. What you must also understand, however, is that Nilsen—and whoever else works for him—will not hesitate to use a gun against you, someone you care about, or any unlucky person who simply gets in their way. I insist that you take this. You must be able to protect yourself."

"I can't do it, Lydia, I'm sorry," Tesla said as she continued to shake her head. "I understand about Nilsen, and I don't disagree about the potential for danger, but I will not shoot anyone. Now or ever." Tesla knew instantaneously that she was absolutely immovable on the point. Her agitation at the sight of the weapon in Lydia's hand should, perhaps, have generated some questions in her mind, but it did not. She simply knew what she knew: no guns.

Lydia looked at her for a moment, and the sudden sag of her shoulders told Tesla she had won. "I was afraid you'd say that," Lydia admitted. "You're very much like your father in that."

"Really?" Tesla asked, surprised. She and her father had never discussed guns—why would they—and in general she tended to see her father as very, very different from herself.

"Yes. He was reluctant to accept any security measures at all, and adamantly refused to carry a weapon himself. I thought you might be cut of the same cloth, so I've brought you this as well." Lydia handed Tesla a small spray canister, metal and unmarked.

"Pepper spray," Lydia answered Tesla's unspoken question. "I presume your ethics will allow you to make someone who has attacked you somewhat uncomfortable for about an hour, with no permanent damage to your assailant whatsoever?"

"Yeah, that would be okay, I guess," Tesla said quietly, and she added the pepper spray to her bag.

"Good," Lydia said, brisk again. "All I have left for you are a bottle of water and an apple."

"Seriously?" Tesla asked, unable to make the leap from deadly weapon to fruit.

"Well, yes," Lydia said, mildly defensive. "Apples are quite good for you, and you've got to stay hydrated."

"Everything on this end is set," Bizzy interrupted. "Whenever you guys are ready."

Tesla looked at Lydia. "I guess I'm ready."

"Have you still got your father's office key?" Lydia asked.

"Yeah." Tesla patted the messenger bag that was slung, as always, across her chest and down by her hip.

"See you tomorrow night, Tesla," Bizzy quipped as Tesla moved toward the door. "Oh, I've decided to poke around in the thrift stores for an outfit to wear to the Physics Institute event Saturday. I'll look for you, too, if you want."

"Oh, okay. I forgot about that. Maybe my dad will be back by then—we're supposed to go. Thanks," Tesla said, just before she closed the door to the control room and headed, alone, down the metal stairs and into the Bat Cave. She marveled at Bizzy's ability to pause in her work at the controls of a time machine to think about what to wear to a party. The girl was unusual, to say the least.

Once she was in the time machine chamber, with the now-familiar mirrors at each corner of the room, Tesla wondered what Sam was up to, where he was—he had certainly been unhappy when Lydia denied his request to be here for the jump. Would she see his younger self when she arrived, she wondered? *I should have asked him,* she thought, as she suddenly realized that of course he already knew the answer to that since this jump today was in his past—

"Ready?" asked Bizzy through the mic, and Tesla nodded from the center of the time machine.

"In five...four..." Bizzy began.

Out of the corner of her eye, Tesla thought she saw movement....

"Three...."

She turned her head to look....

"Two...."

And Finn stepped out from behind one of the mirrors, sprinted to her side, and grabbed her hand, hard....

"One!"

The brilliance of the lasers eclipsed Tesla's world and blotted out all that was real in a brilliant flash, including the feel of Finn's hand in hers.

CHAPTER 25

Tesla opened her eyes and saw herself reflected in the pupils of Finn's.

"What the hell?" She jerked her hand free and stepped back from him.

"I decided to see if someone else could jump along with you," he said with a grin that was calculated to irritate Tesla. "What?" he asked with a shrug, his hands raised to suggest he didn't know what all the fuss was about. He laughed when she glared at him.

"That's what Schrödinger is for!" she said.

"Well, you forgot to put him in your bag," he pointed out, taking a step toward her. "Just think of me as another adorable creature you can pet. But you should know up front, my whiskers may tickle...."

"You could have been killed, you absolute moron! Or, or ripped to shreds at the subatomic level, or—"

Her sentence was cut short by Finn's mouth, which he had suddenly pressed to hers. "Cut it out!" she said as she pushed back from him again.

"Thanks for worrying about me, Abbot. It's really sweet,"

Finn said, but Tesla was too angry to respond. "So, you're the old hand at this," he continued, his eyes amused, as usual. "What do we do next?" He rubbed his hands together, so obviously pleased with himself it set her teeth on edge.

Tesla was determined to stay on task and not let Finn get under her skin—who did he think he was, anyway? He'd treated her like crap since Sam arrived, ignored her after she'd made the decision to jump, and then snuck into the Bat Cave to jump with her, without anybody's permission—and now kissed her, again, as if she had no say in it!

"Um, hello?" Finn said quietly, eyebrows raised.

On task. Right. Tesla took a deep breath, blew it back out, slowly, and turned from Finn to look around them. The new coffin was, indeed, more like a big closet now. Eight and a half feet square, with a nine foot ceiling, Tesla calculated with a glance. Mirrors sat in each corner, semi-translucent, just like the ones in the Bat Cave.

"First, we get out of this box. Then we get to work," Tesla said with an authority Lydia would have recognized.

"Here's the door," Finn said as he spied a recessed metal handle on what looked to be solid wall. He pulled the handle toward him as the door swung silently inward on unseen hinges, and they saw that it was a seamless, perfect fit, visible only after it was opened. He stood aside and allowed Tesla to look cautiously through the door.

She pulled her head back inside and spoke quietly. "We're in the lab, and I don't see anyone. There's a light outside the lab door. This is how it looks every time I jump."

Finn nodded and stepped in front of Tesla and into the lab. He looked around, noted the work areas, the cabinets, the chalkboards and desks, and began to walk toward the door.

"Wait, let's stop and think a minute," Tesla whispered. Finn turned toward her and waited. "I've only ever been here when Sam was here," she began. "I'm not sure if I can find my way to the exit, and I'm pretty sure Sam always used a security key card to get outside."

Finn frowned. "A key card, even from the inside?"

Tesla nodded.

"I guess we have no choice, then," Finn said. "Let's go find your boyfriend."

Tesla rolled her eyes but said nothing, and followed Finn out the door and into the brightly lit hallway. They moved along the hall cautiously, ears strained for the sound of anyone else. At the first point where they had to make a decision on whether to go straight or turn left or right, Finn stopped.

"Look familiar?" he asked.

"Maybe... yeah, but give me a minute." She paused, closed her eyes, and tried to remember when she had walked out of the lab with Sam, headed down the hallway and made their way to the—

"Left," she said. She turned confidently down the adjacent corridor. "The break room and snack machines are down here. We've walked essentially the same number of steps Sam and I did before we changed directions, even given the probability of a slight variation in stride length."

"Wicked smart," Finn said quietly behind her as he shook his head.

They walked another thirty yards and were suddenly aware of the sound of footsteps from the hall that now opened up on the right. Tesla froze, pressed her back up tightly to the wall and looked frantically around as she realized that there were no doors for them to duck into, and not time enough to return the way they'd come and hide in the lab. She opened her bag and felt around for the canister of pepper spray. Finn caught her eye and put his finger to his lips. The footsteps grew louder. Finn stepped in front of Tesla, fists clenched by his sides, to face the corner where the owner of those footsteps would emerge in seconds.

It was Sam.

"Oh my god," Tesla exhaled and leaned heavily against the wall.

The boy made no sound as he came around the corner and found himself face to face with Finn, who was quite a bit taller and obviously stronger and more athletic than Sam was at fifteen. His eyes had widened a bit, and he'd stopped dead, but he stood his ground.

"Tesla?" Sam ignored Finn and rushed over to Tesla.

Finn, preoccupied with their safety, had not seen Tesla slump against the wall. He turned and put his hand on her shoulder and leaned toward her, alarmed. Her eyes were closed, though she remained upright.

"Tesla—is it your heart? Tesla!" Finn felt a surge of adrenaline course through his body, almost as if he himself were in mortal danger, and it shocked him to his core. He was *afraid*!

Tesla opened her eyes. "I'm fine, Finn, geez. I'm relieved— you scared the crap out of us, Sam!" She pushed off from the wall and Finn's hands dropped to his sides. Shaken and confused, not to mention irritated by the implication that he was overprotective, Finn's jaw set hard when Sam laughed, oblivious to whatever that bizarre moment was.

"Hey, you're the time traveler," he teased Tesla. "You're the one who sneaks around inside a high-security facility. You better get used to the rush."

Tesla laughed with him until she glanced into Sam's smoke-dark eyes and suddenly remembered the feel of his mouth when he'd kissed her earlier…. No, that hasn't happened yet, she reminded herself, unconsciously touching her mouth with her fingertips as she stared at the boy in front of her.

"Okay, we're here, we found our guide, now how about we get some work done?" Finn asked pointedly.

Grateful to drop her head and break the unexpected and startling connection to Sam—which of course he knew absolutely nothing about—Tesla fished in her bag until she found the smartphone Lydia had given her. She dialed Lydia's number and she got a click and then dead air, not even a recorded not-in-service message. She emailed and texted, but received an error message each time: delivery failure. Tesla put the phone back in her bag. "Well, Bizzy was right."

"Bizzy usually is," Finn acknowledged.

"Who's Bizzy?" asked Sam.

"Long story," said Tesla. "Should we head right over to my dad's office?"

"Tesla, it's early—just after six a.m.—which is one of the reasons I was so surprised to see you," said Sam. "You've come at night, early in my shift the other times. I'm usually gone by now—you're lucky you didn't run into anyone else. I'm pretty sure your mom—Dr. Petrova—is in her office right now, catching up on lab reports and stuff. And her office is right next to your dad's."

When Finn looked at him, a puzzled frown on his face, Sam explained. "Since I met Tesla, I've been sort of keeping an eye on her folks," he said, clearly embarrassed. "Not in a big way, but, you know, she could come back at any time, and I wanted to be able to help her steer clear of them, fill her in on how they were. You know. Stuff like that."

"Thanks," Tesla said as she put her hand on Sam's shoulder for a moment. "I guess we have to wait to have another go at my dad's desk. Anybody object to Dodie's Diner for breakfast? I'm buying—oh, wait, is it open in this timeline?"

"It is, and I'm definitely in," said Sam. "Lemme just change and clock out. I'm starved."

"You're buying?" Finn said. "Do you even have a job?"

Tesla waived the credit card Lydia had given her. "Just call me Ellie."

"I think that's for emergencies only," he teased her.

"Well you heard Sam. Starvation certainly qualifies as an emergency. I am a humanitarian."

Sam returned, dressed now in faded jeans, black boots and a red T-shirt, a motorcycle helmet in his hand. "Ready?"

Tesla looked at Finn, who winked at her. "Lead on, Ellie."

After they'd eaten their fill—Tesla had been appalled at what it took to fill Finn and Sam up—they sat at their booth and made a plan. Sam slurped the last drops of chocolate milk through his straw as both Tesla and Finn watched him.

"Dude, you can eat," Finn said. Tesla could never understand guy-admiration for the ability to eat gross amounts of food.

Sam shrugged. He tried to look humble but grinned like a champ. "Yeah, I guess."

"Seriously," Finn said. "Eggs benedict and a club sandwich. With fries and chocolate milk. Impressive."

"Yeah, impressive," Tesla agreed, by which she meant exactly the opposite. "So what do we do now?"

Finn answered her, without hesitation. "I think we should split up."

"Why?" Tesla asked, concerned. At least she could get back on her own, as long as she could get to the lab, but Finn needed her physical presence to jump. What if he got stuck here, without ID or money?

"Because we'll be more effective if we separate. I want to go to the library, as well as the courthouse. We might as well play to our strengths. I know how to follow a paper trail, put a story together, talk to people and charm them out of information they don't want to divulge," he said. "I am very, very charming."

"So you keep telling me," Tesla retorted. "But I was raised by scientists. I can't just take your word for that. I need evidence, and so far, I've seen nothing." Gratified when Sam laughed, Tesla continued. "What about us?"

"You need to get into your dad's office, and Sam can monitor your mother's movements and not raise suspicions. You'll need Sam's help—you should stick together, and when the coast is clear, get inside, look around. See what's in that drawer—Lydia gave you a camera, right? Take pictures, then get out."

"It'll take Finn a little while to get back here since he'll have to walk," Tesla pointed out. "We have to factor that in when we decide when to meet back up." She and Finn had walked the seven eighths of a mile to Dodie's while Sam had ridden his motorcycle and met them there. But luckily the lab, the library, her dad's office in the Physics building, and the courthouse were all downtown, very close together.

"Sam, why don't you run Finn over to the courthouse, it should be open soon," Tesla suggested. "I'll pay the check, and you can swing back and get me, and we'll go see if my mom is still in her office."

"Sounds like a plan," Sam said. "Should we meet back at the lab, same door we left from, at nine o'clock tonight? Everyone should be gone by then."

"Do we need the whole day?" Tesla asked. "I'd rather we meet up earlier. Just in case."

"Just in case what?" Sam asked.

"I don't know," Tesla said. "Just in case. The whole point of just in case is that we don't know what might happen, what might come up."

"I agree," said Finn. "Why don't we meet back here at six. All the government facilities will be closed by then anyway."

"Okay," Tesla said, and Sam nodded. "So we'll meet back here at six."

Finn leaned toward Tesla and spoke quietly. "Stay safe, Danger Girl." He stood up before she had a chance to reply.

When Finn and Sam both stood and moved toward the door, Tesla signaled to their server that they were ready for the check.

"Finn," Tesla said quickly, before the boys were out of earshot. She felt nervous, twitchy, with an odd feeling of tension in her body that left her a little breathless. Finn turned around and looked at her from thirty-two feet away, standing amid the crowded booths, waiters delivering food, Sam by his side, but Tesla saw only him. "Be careful."

"Just this once—for you." He smiled, and then they were gone.

CHAPTER 26

"Her car's still here," Sam said. "She hasn't left." Tesla leaned against him, straining to hear him. Both their bodies vibrated as the motorcycle idled in the university parking lot.

"What do we do now?" she asked.

"What do you want to do?"

She thought for a moment. Even with the morning sun warm on her back through the thin black hoodie she wore, and the comfort of Sam pressed up against her, she hadn't been able to shake what she'd felt as Finn had walked away from her in the restaurant, a feeling that she was being—*stretched*, she thought. *Weird. Not to mention uncomfortable.*

She needed to be busy, distracted. "Let's go by my house," she said.

Sam didn't answer and Tesla wondered if he would try to talk her out of it, point out that it had upset her the last time, and that despite the fact that her father had not recognized her then, it was still a risk. But he put the bike in gear and headed for the Abbott house on Webber.

They drove slowly as the house came into view, and then they rode past it. At the end of the street, where the road curved and the house was no longer in sight, Sam pulled over to the curb and cut the engine.

Tesla took off her helmet, relieved to feel so calm. The tension was still there, that weird feeling in her chest she couldn't quite define and had certainly never experienced before, but she didn't feel nervous or anxious anymore. She felt okay—maybe she was just getting used to everything, and that was good, right? Of course she would still feel the freak-out factor of actually traveling through time, she reasoned, and that would account for the feeling she'd had at the diner. Now, she wanted to see her house. She would do this—and she knew before she spoke that unlike Finn, Sam would not try to stop her, even if he was so inclined.

She really liked that about Sam.

She got off the bike, took the helmet off and handed it to Sam.

"Tesla…" he began.

"I'll just take a look," she said. "I promise I'll be careful."

"You can't be seen, Tesla—make sure of it. Without the helmet your hair and eyes are too unique. Someone could figure it out."

It wasn't exactly an endorsement of her plan, but she'd take it. "You're right, I'll put my hood up. I won't be seen, and I'll be really quick." Before he could respond she turned and walked toward the house where she once lived. Where they all had lived.

She walked leisurely, her hood dousing the flame of her hair, but her eyes were glued to the house as soon as it came in sight. She could see no movement—it was possible that no one was home, and Tasya was clearly at work—but the tall privacy fence that enclosed the backyard seemed to beckon. As she came to the house itself, she made a spontaneous decision and walked up to the gate of the fence, lifted the latch, and walked into the backyard. The side of the house had two windows near the back, a small one, five feet up, probably a bathroom, and a larger one that began three and a half feet up from the ground. Tesla couldn't remember the layout of the rooms—her memory of her life before her mother died was vague, at best. She moved to the side of the house and walked slowly toward the larger window, then ducked below the small bathroom window when she got to it. She knew she couldn't be seen from the neighbor's house, because the privacy fence would have to be at least eighteen inches shorter for the neighbors to see her from their property, unless they were on the roof, which was unlikely. Similarly, the sightline anyone inside her house would need to spot her as she crept along the outside wall of the house was impossible—they would literally need to stand inside the wall to get the right angle. In this moment, at least, she was grateful for what Finn called her "gift."

She stopped at the edge of the window and listened. The warmth of the summer morning worked in her favor: the window was open, a soft breeze blew blue and white striped curtains, curtains with rocking horses printed on them.

Max's room, she thought.

She heard a baby's gurgling laugh and knew instantly that she had to look, so she moved just enough to get one eye past the window frame. There was baby Max in his crib—he slobbered and talked gibberish to some stuffed toy he clenched in his chubby fist.

Gross, she thought, as he brought the toy clumsily to his wet mouth. But she couldn't sustain the revulsion, and actually made a just-audible *Awwww* sound when he squealed happily, though she would have denied it if anyone had accused her of it.

Suddenly the door to the baby's room opened and Tesla pulled quickly back, out of sight.

"Maxie!" came a childish voice. "You're awake!"

Her stomach dropped, and she trembled uncontrollably. She groped in her bag, pulled out the smartphone, and tapped the camera icon. Slowly, carefully, Tesla positioned herself at the edge of the window and raised the camera. She held it in front of her and watched the screen as her six year old self said good morning to her baby brother through the bars of his crib.

The girl wore a Spice Girls T-shirt and pink shorts, with white socks and pink sneakers that had *glitter* on them . *Good god,* Tesla thought. *Who used to dress me?* Her nine-year old self bent down a little until she was eye level with Max, who screeched in delight at the sight of her. She smiled at him and poked her finger through the bars, and Max moved his own hand, shiny with spit, toward his sister's. When the tips of their fingers touched, the baby squealed and the little girl laughed.

Tesla took pictures, the camera both an extension of herself and a buffer, a way to shield herself from the raw emotions that coursed through her. Suddenly a mock, stern voice boomed from just outside the bedroom door, "What's all this?"

"Maxie's awake, Daddy!" the little girl shouted as she ran to the door and flung herself into the arms of her father, who stood in the open doorway.

"So he is!" Greg Abbott said as he hugged Tesla's tragically pink-clad self. Then he put her down and turned to his son.

"Hi, buddy," this young and rather rumpled version of their father said gently as he bent to lift his son from the crib. "You ready to get up?"

Nine-year old Tesla jumped up and down. "Let's do the sandbox, let's do the sandbox!"

"Okay," said her father. "Let me get Max changed, and we'll go out in the backyard to play for a while. But your mother will be home soon, don't you want to wait for her?"

The girl shrugged, and with the brutally pure disregard for others' feelings that only children have, said, "No. Just you, Daddy." And she followed her father out of the room and out of Tesla's sight.

Tesla sat down in the grass against the wall of the house, a frown on her face. She didn't remember this. Had her father been her favorite? How was that possible? Her dad was a huge irritation in her life, and sometimes she couldn't get out of bed for wishing her mother was still alive. What had happened in the last eight years to change so drastically the way she had felt about her parents?

The screen door closed with a bang around the corner at the back of the house—an eerily familiar sound—so Tesla got up and made her way to the corner, where she peered into the backyard. Her younger self was in the sandbox and had already begun to pour sand into differently shaped molds. She dumped the sand onto a pile in front of her and shaped it with her hands, intent and focused while her father stood by and watched, with Max in his arms.

The little girl's red hair was electric in the summer sun and clashed perfectly with her pink clothes. The skin of her arms and legs was milky white, and Tesla wondered as she watched from the shadows if her Dad had put sunscreen on her.

"What are you building?" Greg Abbott asked his daughter.

"The town. This is your office," she answered without looking up.

"That looks very realistic. You have a good memory," he said.

"Yup," she said simply, all concentration.

Her father watched, along with her older self with camera in hand as the sand structure took shape. The L-shape was an exact replica of the three-story physics building on campus, the longer wing that housed the labs, the shorter, perpendicular piece that formed the base of the L where the offices were.

It was a perfect scale model. Greg Abbot watched as his daughter made holes with her index finger to indicate the three horizontal rows of windows. "How do you know how many windows to make?"

"Cuz that's how many windows there are," she said simply. "And look, here's your window. She pointed to the third window from the left on the shorter base of the L.

"Tesla…" her father said. "That *is* my window. How do you know that?"

Tesla squinted a little in the sun's glare as she looked up at him from her sandbox. "I don't know. I've been in your office. It's your window."

"Did you count them?" he persisted.

"No," she said after she'd thought it over. "I don't think so. But there's fourteen of them."

"And why aren't there any windows in the other part?" he asked as he pointed to the longer section. "You've never been in those rooms."

"There is one," she said, and pointed to the very end of the wing, the highest point of the L. "This is the stair's window. All the rest is for those rooms with no windows to the outside."

"That's right," he said, speaking very slowly now. He stared at his daughter with an odd expression. "Tesla, do you know how many diapers your brother has left in the house?"

"Twelve, not counting the one he has on," she answered without hesitation, her hands busy with her shovel as she poured sand into the bucket by her side.

"And how many steps is it from your sandbox to the back door?"

"Thirty-six, unless I take giant steps, and then it's thirty-one," she said.

"How many little girls, just your size, could sit in the sandbox with you?" he asked, his voice oddly tense.

She thought for a moment. "Are the girls all sitting Indian style, or with their legs out like this?" she asked as she demonstrated the two positions.

"Indian style," he said, choking a little on the last word.

"Twenty-five, and they'd have to be touching each other," she said with absolute confidence. "But there wouldn't be room for any toys, or for sand castles. We'd all be squished, and bored."

Her father could only nod, and watch his daughter as she returned to her task.

At the corner of the house, Tesla's hand shook so badly she had to put the camera back in her bag. Her mathematical skills, her strange, intuitive grasp of the spatial realities around her, were old news in her family. It was too weird to watch her father as he recognized them for the first time. Way too weird.

Tesla felt like she'd already pushed her luck, so she walked quickly and quietly back to the gate, slipped out, and closed it again. It took her only a few minutes to make her way back to Sam, who paced nervously next to his bike.

"What the hell took you so long?" he hissed as soon as she was close enough to hear him.

"It wasn't that long," she said defensively. She took the helmet from his hand and put it on. "I was looking around. Like I said."

Sam exhaled in exasperation, a scowl on his face, and got on the bike without another word. Tesla climbed up behind him, and before she was fully situated he gunned the motor and they took off like a shot. She had to grab him quickly around the waist to stay on the bike, and for a brief moment this Sam, and an older Sam, a taller, stronger Sam, who had pulled her to him, his mouth on hers, were one and the same.

He drove too fast, took the on-ramp to I-76, and they flew. The wind tore at their eyes, their cheeks, pushed its way into their nostrils, made conversation impossible. Sam drove for ten minutes, then slowed and took the next exit. Only when they'd stopped at the first traffic light in town did Tesla loosen her grip around his waist. She'd had to hold on for dear life.

"Sorry, Sam," she said, her chin on his shoulder so he could hear her.

"Yeah. Me, too," he said, but he did not turn around. "Let's go see what your mom's up to—and try not to do anything stupid, okay?"

"Okay," she said. "If you try not to kill us in a fiery motorcycle crash."

"Okay," he said, and they moved forward as the light turned green.

They found Tasya Petrova's car—a faded old Peugeot with rusted-out wheel wells—in exactly the same spot.

"What now?" Tesla asked, crestfallen. "We've got to get into my dad's office, but my mom's is right next door, we can't risk it as long as she's in there."

Sam thought for a minute. "I'd be really surprised if she's still in her office," he finally said. "She hates paperwork, and she makes as quick a job of it as she can. Your dad teases her about it all the time."

"It's so bizarre that you know my parents better than I do," Tesla said, and the jealousy she felt was apparent in her voice.

"I don't, not really," he assured her. "I maybe just know

more about their work habits, and only right now, not in your time."

Tesla grinned. "It still makes my head explode when I try to think about it," she said. "Time travel. Me."

He smiled, too. "I know. It's so tight."

"So what should we do? We don't have all day. Literally."

"True," he conceded. "I guess I should go check. I'll bet she's over in the lab by now, but we can't be sure."

"And it wouldn't be too weird if you showed up?" Tesla asked hopefully.

"No, not really. I'm around sometimes before my shift, and it's Friday—I could be here to pick up my check. Actually, I do need to pick up my check."

"So let's go in, and you can make sure she's not in her office," Tesla agreed readily. "I'll hang back, and as soon as you confirm that she's in the lab, we'll let ourselves into my dad's office."

They stowed Tesla's helmet, locked the bike and went inside. There were a few people in the corridors, what looked like a grad student or two who spoke with great animation. Their hands flew about as they argued about some obscure piece of data. *Boring*. Sam led the way as though he belonged here—which of course he did. Tesla found two comfy chairs by a window, just outside of the department offices but around a corner, and Sam agreed that she should be fairly safe there. He would be back momentarily, anyway.

Tesla sat down and clutched her messenger bag in her lap with both hands. She sat straight up, her back about four inches from the upholstered back of the chair. *Calm down*, she thought. *You must look like you're about to jump out of your skin*. She made herself relax, slouch down a little in the chair, lean back. Just another student on a much-needed break from classes.

She waited patiently. And then a little less patiently. She chewed on a nail, drummed her fingers on the arm of the chair. Crossed her legs and shook her foot furiously back and forth. One person walked by, some woman with gray hair and a lab coat on, and she smiled absently at Tesla. The minutes dragged on.

Where is he? Tesla thought. *Talk about how time slows down for a ticking clock!* Finally, she couldn't take it, got up and walked purposefully toward her mother's office.

The door was slightly ajar, and she heard the murmur of voices from inside. No one was in the hall. Tesla stopped just outside, pressed herself against the wall, and listened.

"That sounds really cool, Dr. P," Sam said.

Tesla heard a woman laugh. "Well, I don't know about cool, but it could turn out to be important—or at least useful. It's not the direction I had thought to go with my work on chaos and pattern, but I am intrigued."

Sam replied but Tesla couldn't hear him. Her ears buzzed loudly and there was a strange constriction in her throat. That was her mother's voice, her mother's melodic, Russian accent. Her mother—the mother she missed so badly it was a physical pain—sat at her desk and laughed and talked about her work only a few feet away from where Tesla now stood, silent and still. Did she stay hidden because she knew she didn't have the right to alter the world—what would happen if she took that one small step into the office and revealed herself? Or was it because the voice she had wanted to hear so badly didn't sound familiar, not the way her dad's had as he'd chatted with her younger self in the sandbox?

Either way, Tesla felt sliced wide open, all that had held her together suddenly gone, her insides exposed.

Tesla was startled when the door suddenly opened and Sam

almost walked right into her. His face registered shock, but he didn't speak, merely pushed her ahead of him, back down the hall. They didn't stop until they reached the stairwell and went inside. The door clicked shut and the sound echoed off the concrete walls.

"What the hell—I thought you said you wouldn't do anything stupid?" Sam asked, clearly angry.

"You took too long," Tesla said, unable to conjure any anger of her own. "I'm sorry. I know I said I'd wait. But then I couldn't." She looked at the ground, miserable.

Sam didn't answer, but his expression softened.

"It's no big deal," he said. "She didn't see you. I tried to leave sooner, but she wanted to talk about some new pattern experiment with audio."

Tesla still hadn't looked up, and Sam heard her sniff.

"Hey, really, it's fine," he said, alarmed. "She'd already packed up her briefcase when I got there, she's on her way to the lab right now. We can go to your dad's office. Tesla?"

Tesla looked up then, and Sam saw her blue-green eyes awash. She blinked hard. "I didn't recognize her voice."

"Oh," said Sam. "It's probably just been too long."

"That's what I'm afraid of," she said as she swiped at her nose with the sleeve of her hoodie. "What if it's been so long, and I've changed so much, that she doesn't really mean anything anymore?"

On instinct alone, because he certainly had no experience with distraught teenage girls—he steered clear of his sister whenever she had a meltdown—Sam took her shoulders in his hands and forced her to look at him. "Tesla," he began. "It doesn't matter how long it's been, how much you've changed, or what you can't remember. She's your mother. Nothing can ever change that, or how important that fact will always be. Nothing."

Tesla gulped and nodded, then flung her arms, cast and all, around Sam's neck. She held him tight and drew one deep, ragged breath. After a quick beat, Sam put his arms around her, and they stood like that for a full, long minute. Tesla thought about the loss Sam would have to bear when his father died in just a few years, and she could not tell him. The bond they shared, she realized, ran deep.

Sam, for his part, would never again think of Tesla as beyond his reach. No matter how foolish it might be, how badly he could be hurt, he knew as he held her, his black hair brightened as it mingled with her red-gold curls, felt her breathe against his chest, so warm and soft and achingly lovely, that he would never want anything as much as he wanted this.

And then she pulled away from him and smiled. "Come on, let's go see if my dad has any secrets we can steal."

CHAPTER 27

Five minutes later they were safely inside Greg Abbot's office, the door closed and locked behind them.

"Okay, first to the drawer I didn't get to last time," Tesla said. She moved the chair back from the desk and crouched down on the floor. She got her dad's flashlight out of the drawer again and worked quickly on the lock, thankful that her father had apparently not discovered the theft of papers and tapes and changed the combination when she heard the tumblers fall into place and the drawers in the front of the desk click open.

"Nice," said Sam, who stood off to the side by her father's overstuffed bookshelves.

Tesla opened the drawer she'd abandoned last time and felt a rush of disappointment when she saw that all it contained was a single, large yellow envelope.

"What is it?" asked Sam, who'd taken a step closer to the desk and peered over Tesla's shoulder.

"Just an envelope."

"Well, see what's inside it," Sam said, clearly excited.

She laid the envelope on the desk in front of her, opened the flap, reached inside and slid the papers out. It was a meager stack—

only a few pages. Tesla pulled the desk lamp on its flexible neck closer. A page of handwritten notes. She moved it aside and quickly glanced at the other two sheets, both of which appeared to be sketches of a building, one an exterior elevation, the other an interior layout. She took out her camera, took several shots of each page, then slid the papers back inside the envelope, in the same order she'd found them, and shut it back in the drawer. She spun the combination lock and stood up.

"Ready?" asked Sam.

"Yeah, I think so," Tesla said. But on their way out of the office she glanced to the left and saw three framed photographs on top of the filing cabinet beside the door. She'd been in such a hurry to leave last time, she hadn't noticed them.

The first was a picture of her mother and Aunt Jane, probably from their undergraduate days, before her parents had married. Aunt Jane's hair was long, like her mother's, but where Tasya's smooth, fine auburn hair was flawless against those incredible cheekbones, an elegant, sophisticated young woman, Jane's thick brown hair hung in great hunks, uncombed and a little frizzy, and she'd made the classic mistake of cutting bangs into her wavy, otherwise all-one-length hair. Tasya sported a wise little smile, while Jane's mouth was stretched wide in mid-laugh and her frumpy sweatshirt clashed with the tailored, silk blouse that Tesla's mother wore. They both held ice cream cones, but Tasya held hers awkwardly, as if she wasn't quite sure what to do with it.

The second picture was her parents' wedding photo that Tesla had seen a million times, the same photo that sat on the mantel at home. She turned to the final frame—a photo of both her parents, and Tesla and Max—and stared, not exactly sure what fascinated her about this fairly ordinary family photo. Her mother sat in a chair outside on a summer lawn. She looked beautiful in a simple, sleeveless green dress, and she held a very tiny Max in her arms. He couldn't have been more than a month old when the photo was taken, Tesla thought. Her father was turned away from the camera because he was looking at her—at Tesla as a little girl— and little Tesla, who ignored whatever commands the photographer had given her, stood upon a crumbling garden wall made of stones. Greg Abbot had his arm near her, probably to steady her or catch her if she fell, but he did not touch her. The little girl stood on the narrow wall, on one foot, arms crossed over her chest, her red hair held back with a lacy, flouncy, flowery headband of some kind, a robin's egg blue dress with a big skirt puffed out around her like a parachute. She scowled ferociously, right at the photographer, in defiance of everyone.

What the hell kind of a brat was I? Tesla wondered. *Geez.* She looked at her father's face in the photo, his eyes on her, the edge of his mouth just starting to turn up—

He had liked her, she realized. Felt some pride, even, in her stubborn rebelliousness, her obstinate, combative nature.

I bet he doesn't like it anymore, she thought, surprised by her own wistfulness. She hadn't known she cared, one way or another, what he thought of her now, and the million small ways she chose to punish him.

"Tesla?" Sam whispered as he stuck his head back in the door from the hallway.

"Yeah, coming," she said and closed the door quickly behind her, anxious to put some distance between herself and the past, courtesy of Sam's motorcycle.

Tesla and Sam were early, but the server at Dodie's had agreed to let them have the table for the rest of the afternoon, if only because the place was dead. Tesla had a coffee, and Sam ordered one too, but he hadn't touched it, which amused Tesla enormously.

"You can order a different drink," she said as she looked pointedly at his now-cold mug of coffee.

"Yeah, I know," he said, cool as he shrugged with studied nonchalance. "I don't like it as much when it's hot."

"So why didn't you order an iced coffee?" she said. She had found that making him feel young and inexperienced helped her to feel less so regarding the kiss they'd shared. Would share.

Whatever, she thought, exasperated by the confused timelines.

Sam blushed a little, but Tesla had already turned back to her smartphone to scroll through the pictures she'd taken earlier. Sam watched her for a minute, and then he noticed that her expression had changed dramatically.

"What's wrong?" he asked.

"I don't know," she said slowly, as she moved her finger across the touch-screen to look at the pictures in quick succession. "But—"

"But what?" he asked.

"I don't know. It's weird. You know, like deja vu."

"So?"

"So that's impossible."

Sam shrugged and manfully sipped his tepid, black, diner-quality coffee and pretended he liked it.

"Well you did used to live in that house. I mean that was you that you were watching, you that you were taking pictures of, so it seems reasonable that you—"

"What did you just say?" Tesla demanded.

"What?" Sam asked, startled and a little confused. "About what?"

"You said 'it was you taking pictures of you.'"

"Huh?" Sam said.

"These pictures," she said, her eyes riveted to the twenty or so shots she'd taken. Her finger swiped the screen obsessively, the photographs on a continual loop.

As the truth of it hit her, Tesla felt the blood drain from her face.

"I'm not sure how to explain it," she began haltingly.

At that moment Finn walked in the door, and his pace quickened considerably the moment he caught sight of them in the booth, though he had the presence of mind to arrange his face in a look that suggested amusement and boredom. The intensity of the relief he felt at the sight of Tesla, however, ran alarmingly deep.

"What'd I miss?" he asked, as he slid into the booth next to her.

She turned to him then, and away from Sam, pulled toward Finn, she realized, because Finn already knew the past—which was actually the future—and didn't need her to explain it to him. "Remember those photos that somebody sent my dad for his birthday? The photos none of us had seen before?"

"Yeah," Finn said, inexplicably wary.

"I took those pictures," Tesla said, slowly and clearly. "I took them today."

CHAPTER 28

"Tesla, you look great in that, you have to wear it!" Bizzy sounded every bit as exasperated as she felt.

"I don't know, it's not exactly my style," Tesla said as she stood awkwardly in front of the full-length mirror in Bizzy's room, which was neat to the point of sterility.

"You have a style?" Beckett asked from the doorway, where she stood fully dressed—stunningly, of course—for the Physics Institute Gala. Her blonde hair hung straight and shone like glass as she leaned seductively in the doorway. She wore a silver-beaded white dress, fitted and slim to the floor, where just the tips of her silver sandals peeked out from below the hem. She shimmered when she moved. Hell, she shimmered when she breathed, Tesla thought, as she noted the deep neckline and impressive cleavage. She looked like a hot—albeit lethal—mermaid.

Bizzy shot Beckett a nasty look. "Don't undo my work here, Beckett," she said, then turned immediately back to Tesla. "You *do* have a style," she assured the girl who looked skeptically at herself in the mirror. "And this is a part of that style, it's just the dress-up version and you're not used to it."

Tesla considered that as she looked at this unfamiliar self.

Her wild, curly hair was caught in a loose knot at the nape of her neck, with a few long curls that escaped near her face. Bizzy had found the dress at a vintage boutique, and Tesla had to admit it was beautiful as she touched the fabric of the skirt again, though she wasn't generally fond of dresses. It was a simple design, with cap sleeves, a deep, round neckline and an empire-waist skirt that fell easily, without embellishment, to mid-calf. But its simplicity was a deception; this dress was all about the fabric. It was some kind of satin, she thought, a heavy, watery dark-chocolate color—at first glance, anyway. When she moved it gleamed subtly in the light to create a suggestion of metal: brown became copper, bronze, gold, the sharp and indestructible became molten, forced into shapes and uses with hammer and fire. Bizzy had lent her a pair of boots that alone would have persuaded Tesla to wear whatever the other girl wanted, they looked 19th century, straight out of an Alcott novel, actual bronze boots with tiny stacked heels, a dozen grommets up the front of each boot for the laces that ended at mid-calf to meet the hem of the dress.

Tesla turned a little left, then right. She loved the colors that moved through the dress and interacted with the light they absorbed, reflected, and changed. Where Beckett was all in-your-face fantasy, Tesla was more smoke and mirrors, illusion that allowed her to feel a little hidden. She realized that Bizzy was right, this did suit her. The deep color of the dress turned her hair into smoldering embers, her skin a silky alabaster that fairly glowed. A dust of pink blush on the apples of her cheeks, a little black mascara, and barely-tinted lip gloss was all the make-up Tesla would allow, and she had refused all jewelry until Bizzy had come up with a simple, brown velvet ribbon which she had wrapped with some kind of thin, pliable copper wire and tied around Tesla's throat, with a bow at the back.

Copper wire, Tesla mused. *Who has uninsulated wire in their jewelry box?*

"Yeah, I guess I like it," she said as she met Bizzy's eyes in the mirror and smiled at her. "Thanks, Biz. Although I feel sort of naked without my messenger bag."

Beckett snorted. "Don't be ridiculous. Steampunk is totally hot. You look fantastic." When Tesla blanched in surprise at the compliment, she added sweetly, "For you."

"There's the Beckett we all know and love," Bizzy murmured as she put the last touches on her own costume. She had opted for black tights, black ballet slippers with wide, pink satin ribbons that criss-crossed up her calves, a short black tutu that stuck out straight in every direction with layers and layers of tulle, and a very—very—tight, long-sleeved black T-shirt with AC/DC written in shiny silver letters across the front. She had removed all the jewelry from her piercings, except the tiny silver studs in her ear lobes and one to match in her nose, and she wore fingerless black lace gloves, and a studded black dog collar. Instead of her usual spiked hair she had slicked it back with a severe side-part, and it lay close to her skull, bone-straight, tucked behind her ears in a kind of Garbo-gone-Black-Swan. Carefully smudged black eyeliner and nude lipstick completed her ensemble, and she looked, astonishingly, beautiful. She had managed to suggest a delicate, fragile femininity that was emphasized, rather than negated, by the severity of her hair and the heavy-handedness of the dog collar and make-up. Unexpectedly sweet, wistful and vulnerable, Tesla thought as she began to realize that there was an artistry to this stuff.

"If we're finished admiring ourselves, we should probably get downstairs," Beckett said. "The boys were reluctant enough to get dressed up. I suspect that if they have to wait much longer they'll revert to their usual grunge in no time."

In the second-floor sitting room Finn and Joley sat in the club chairs by the fireplace and chatted easily, as if they were both accustomed to formal clothes. When the girls walked into the room, they stood up.

"Hello, you stunner," said Joley in response to Beckett, who led the way in the girls' grand entrance.

"Thanks," she said sweetly and further dazzled him with her smile.

"You all look fabulous," Joley said magnanimously, though he only gave Tesla and Bizzy a glance.

Finn remained by his chair and looked at each of them in turn. "Absolutely true, you do," he said easily as his eyes returned to Tesla.

There was a knock on the front door below, and Bizzy left quickly to go down and answer it while Joley and Beckett flirted quietly by Lydia's favorite chair.

Finn sauntered over to where Tesla stood, his eyes never leaving her, and it made her nervous. "Nice dress."

Tesla fidgeted and smoothed the fabric over her abdomen. "Well, I'm not sure—"

"You're perfect," said Finn.

Tesla blushed, felt her pulse in her throat, but as soon as she realized it was a struggle to meet his eyes, she made herself meet his eyes. "Thanks," she said brightly. "You look pretty great yourself."

Both he and Joley had opted for simple, elegantly tailored black tuxes. While Joley had worn the traditional bow tie, however, Finn had opted for an unusually high-collared white shirt with a black pearl button closure at the throat, and no tie at all. His long curls were caught loosely at the nape of his neck and tied with a thin black silk ribbon, and the sharp points of his collar jutted out from just under his chin. He looked like the rakish young lord from the cover of one of those heaving-bosoms romance novels.

And it was totally working for him.

"I do what I can," he said as he gazed slightly upward and off into the distance, his idea of a *GQ* pose.

Tesla laughed—they clearly had different ideas about what sort of cover he should grace—and then turned at the sound of Keisha's voice.

"Tesla, get over here and let me look at that gorgeous dress!"

"Keish!" Tesla squealed as she ran to her friend, who had come up the stairs with Malcolm. Bizzy stood next to them and beamed proudly, as though she had produced them from thin air just for Tesla's pleasure.

"What are you guys—wait, are you coming to the party?" Tesla asked as she finally registered Malcolm's monochromatic, dove gray suit, shirt and tie, the exact color of his eyes, and Keisha's little black dress, her sheer hose, the four-inch heels and fire-engine red lipstick.

"I got them press passes," Finn said, his hands in his pockets, ruining the line of his jacket, which somehow made him look even more attractive.

"He said they should come," Bizzy interjected, breathless and talking fast. "He said you should have some fun for a change. He said it would make you happy."

"Biz," Finn growled.

"Oh, get over it," Keisha said to her cousin. "Your secret is out. You're a nice guy."

"Slander," Finn said, feigning outrage.

Keisha gave up. "Fine—you're not that nice." She turned to Tesla. "He finally forgave me for crashing his stupid party. I told him he could buy me a new dress for tonight to show he really meant it, but he just laughed. I had to spring for this myself. You like?" She turned gracefully and all eyes went to her legs.

"I like," said Joley with unabashed enthusiasm from where he still stood beside Beckett, who had begun to scowl as soon as Keisha and Malcolm arrived.

"We'd better go," said Bizzy. "Lydia's already there, and she said not to be late."

"Who's got Max?" Beckett asked.

"He's home with Aunt Jane," Tesla said. "He said he wouldn't wear a tie unless he absolutely had to."

"Off we go then," said Finn as he opened the door and ushered everyone out and down the stairs like a herd of cattle through the front door. "Anyone wearing heels that they can't walk two blocks in will be left for dead, the vultures will pick their bones clean, and they'll have no one but themselves to blame. You know who you are."

Keisha and Beckett looked at each other and raised their eyes to the heavens, sisters for just that moment as they wondered why they hadn't been blessed with escorts who understood that a limo was always in order for a swanky party.

The Institute of Experimental Physics held its twenty-fifth anniversary Gala, carefully planned to wine and dine its generous donors and, simultaneously, introduce and welcome its new Director, Dr. Erik Van Alden, in the grand ballroom of the University President's mansion. The mansion was one hundred and fifty some years old. It sat atop the county's largest hill on the north side of campus and overlooked the university and the town in which it resided. Tesla had seen the mansion from the street a million times, but she'd never seen it like this: each window brightly lit, small twinkly lights in the branches of every tree that bordered the broad, circular drive from the street up to the front of the house and back out again. Cars lined the nearby streets, parked there by red-jacketed valets who met guests at their cars as they pulled up to the massive, double front doors of the residence.

Keisha still grumbled because they had to walk to a party of this caliber—uphill, no less—and Beckett's unusual silence when there was complaining to be done suggested her complete agreement. The others ignored them both and took in the splendor of the place as they approached the entrance, manned by two men in dark suits who carefully checked invitations and IDs before they let anyone inside.

"Really?" asked Malcolm, amused as they waited in a short line at the door. "At a science gig?"

"Yes," Bizzy said. "Dr. Abbott told me there would be tight security. The Institute does some highly classified work, not to mention all the government contracts. Some of these quirky old professors with tape on their glasses are doing groundbreaking work. There are plenty of people who'd like a chance to chat with them, for whatever reason."

Too bad my dad didn't have this kind of protection, Tesla thought, then forced herself to smile and join the banter that had of course ensued after Bizzy's serious statement.

"You're not just a geek, you're a geek-fan-girl," Malcolm said to Bizzy, who immediately punched him in the arm.

"Awww," said Keisha quietly in Tesla's ear. "Baby's first flirt."

Tesla laughed, and then they were at the door, their invitations scrutinized by the guys in suits who, once they were close enough, Tesla could see had some kind of transmitter wire that ran from their earbuds into the collars of their suits. She was dying to see them talk into their watches, but they refused to oblige her.

Inside the massive front door a formal hallway with gilt mirrors on the walls led them, along with the crowd, about thirty feet into the interior and through a tall arched entry to the left that, once they walked through it, proved to be the ballroom. It was a spectacular space, with high ceilings, molded plaster, enormous chandeliers, and more mirrored panels on the walls. A band played some kind of old-fashioned music, but it was kind of cool, Tesla thought. Both sides of the enormous room were lined with long, linen-covered buffet tables that sported china plates, crystal stemware and punch bowls. The tables groaned under the weight of massive fruit bowls, mounded plates of cheeses, meats, and tiered towers of tiny, bite-sized desserts. Small tables were scattered around the room, with comfortable chairs for intimate seating, so guests could eat, converse, or simply rest and watch the dancers in the middle of all the splendor.

There were dozens of couples on the dance floor already. Most of the men wore tuxedos, though a few wore elegant white dinner jackets with black trousers and bow ties. The women's clothes were as varied as they were. Tesla saw several brilliant, jewel-toned saris, sparkly, modern cocktail dresses, ball gowns, slinky, form-fitted dresses that couldn't possibly have had underwear underneath, and even a few poufy, frilly numbers that looked like giant wedding cakes.

It was awesome.

Keisha left immediately to dance with Joley and Tesla watched them twirl away.

"We're going to get food," Malcolm said, and he and Bizzy left, too.

"I'm certainly not hanging out with you wall flowers," Beckett said dismissively and made a straight line for a group of young men in tuxes that looked, collectively, like a Ralph Lauren ad. Every last one of them turned to watch Beckett approach, and she was surrounded in just under twenty seconds.

"Well, that leaves us," Finn said cheerfully. He grabbed Tesla's forearm and headed toward the nearest table with her in tow.

"I guess," she said lightly. She had sworn to try to match his cool, noncommittal tone.

"Are you okay now?" he asked quietly as they sat down. "Leaving the photos with Sam? You were kind of freaked out yesterday."

At Dodie's yesterday—was it only yesterday?—she had explained to Sam and Finn about the déjà vu she'd experienced when she looked at the photos on her phone, and her realization that these were the very same photographs that had arrived for her father's birthday, in an album, only a few days ago. Photographs that no one remembered. She couldn't get her mind around it. The photos were of Tesla and her family, eight years ago. She and Max were little kids then. Her mother had been alive. And none of them had remembered the photos when they'd arrived a few days ago, because they *hadn't yet been taken*. It had all become just a little much, what with future events that were actually past events, and the past that now happened in the present when they jumped back in time.

"Yeah, I guess I'm okay with it," she answered hesitantly. "I'm not really sure what choice I had."

"Good," Finn said. "We all agreed that what we do now can affect the past, which can then change the future, and that sort of obligates us to make what has already happened, happen."

"Yeah, I know," she said. "But doesn't it bother you? I mean, this is a pretty simple, insignificant example of that. My dad got the photo album a few days ago in our present time, and since then we've travelled back, and it turns out I took the photos, and so I left Sam the pictures, back in the past. I bought the album, gave him money and my future address and the date for him to ship them, from me. I even described the picture of my mother in her lab, the last one in the album, and asked him to take that picture and include it. That guarantees that the future event of my dad's birthday—the one that happened a few days ago—will happen the same way it's already happened."

"It's almost impossible to even talk about, isn't it?" Finn asked. "At least in a way that doesn't make us sound like morons."

"Thanks," Tesla said dryly.

Finn laughed. "You know what I mean." They sat at one of the round tables and their chairs faced each other instead of the table. Their knees almost touched.

"I like that thing around your neck," Finn said suddenly, his eyes narrowed slightly as he studied her, his expression unreadable. "It's—rough. Utilitarian. Bizzy's got talent—the contrast with your skin is—"

"I found you," said a deep voice just beside them.

Sam towered over them and his black hair and eyes shone. His shoulders looked enormous, his white dinner jacket no less brilliant than the teeth he flashed when he smiled and held out his hand to her. "Dance?" he asked.

Tesla glanced at Finn, who shrugged, a clear indication that it didn't matter to him one way or another. "Sure," she said, stung. "I would love to dance."

CHAPTER 29

They walked out onto the floor without a glance at Finn, who sat and watched them go, his expression unreadable. Tesla turned to Sam, who gently took her into his arms, one hand on the small of her back, the other holding her hand firmly in his own. On the beat he whisked them off, and Tesla gasped. "I don't really know how to dance to this music," she stammered.

Sam laughed. "It looks to me like you know how."

It kind of did, Tesla realized. Sam was sure of the steps and knew how to guide her. She relaxed, then, and began to understand the pattern and the rhythm. Her confidence increased and she began to enjoy it, unconsciously aware of exactly how many inches separated her from the other couples that twirled around them on all sides.

"Too bad we don't dance like this anymore," she said. Her dimples flashed as she smiled up at him.

"We can dance like this anytime—every time—you want to," he said, mesmerized by her eyes. And just like that, he knew he could be reckless.

Tesla's cheeks flushed pink. "I could get used to it." She felt sophisticated, older, maybe even a little dangerous as Sam's arm tightened around her waist. She'd felt in charge with the younger Sam, like she was the one who would or would not make things happen, and somehow that feeling lingered, even though this older Sam was anything but a pushover. *Be careful,* she thought. *That kind of attitude is trouble and you know it.*

"I didn't know you would be here tonight, Sam," she said quickly. "I haven't seen you since before the jump."

"I've been busy—I am in medical school, you know. And I'm here because all the science-related departments were invited. I'm certainly glad I decided to come—you look beautiful."

They danced for a while in silence, and then Tesla said aloud what had bothered her since she and Finn had jumped back to the present last night. "Sam, why didn't you tell me before I jumped that Finn would come too, and that I would give you those photographs to send to my dad eight years later?"

Sam considered before he spoke. "Because what the three of us talked about at Dodie's all those years ago—last night, for you and Finn—is true, and I think right. We have an obligation not to interfere, as much as we're able to, at least. What would have happened if I'd told you? Would you have stopped Finn? Would you have taken no pictures, or different ones? Would you have decided not to send the album? So many choices, and all of them seem so small, but we can't know the ripple effect they might create."

Tesla missed a step, but Sam caught her when she stumbled and pulled her in close. She picked up the steps again, and he let her go.

"Finn and I were just talking about that," she said. "I have so many questions about this—you're right, the photo album isn't important but other things are. I lie awake at night over some of them. I wonder what I could change—what I could fix—with this ability to move around in time."

"Your mother?" Sam asked as the music stopped, and they stopped. The couples around them clapped and smiled, but Sam stood, his arm still around Tesla's waist.

"My mother," she said softly, so softly he barely heard her.

"Tesla," he said, his voice somewhat strangled. When she looked up at him in surprise and noted with concern the inexplicably tortured look on his face, he immediately smiled at her. "Try to enjoy yourself," he said.

She smiled a sad little smile and they made their way back to the table, where Lydia, Keisha, and Joley now sat with Finn.

"Tesla, you look lovely," said Lydia as they approached the table.

"Thanks," Tesla said, somewhat subdued.

Finn's sharp eyes took in the change from the exuberance she'd displayed before she'd danced with Sam, and he didn't like it. What he did like, however, was the discovery that as Sam had led Tesla out onto the dance floor he had not experienced that strange pull, the tightening in his chest he had begun to associate with her not being near him. Because that sounded like—well, like she had begun to mean more to him than he wanted. He had watched them dance, though, and while he didn't especially like Sam, he had felt none of the pulse-quickening adrenaline rush he had before.

And that could mean only one thing: he was back, and with no annoying complications to contend with.

"You look great, too, Lydia," Tesla said.

Startled out of his self-congratulatory thoughts, Finn really looked at his employer for the first time since they'd arrived. Lydia was dressed in a deep purple, full length sheath dress with some pale lavender, translucent material that floated all around her shoulders like some sort of gossamer wrap. She wore her hair styled, a little tastefully applied makeup, and diamond drop earrings that twinkled with each movement of her head. She was actually pretty, he thought.

"Thank you, dear," said Lydia with genuine warmth. "It's always nice to have a reason to dress and present one's best face to the world. One brief bit of business, however," she said, her words suddenly clipped and determined. "The jpeg files you sent me earlier today are with the analysts, along with Finnegan's notes. When they have anything concrete to tell us about the drawings and the text you photographed, they'll let us know. Have you destroyed the originals, like I asked? We can't have copies of what may be sensitive information on your phone."

"Yes, I deleted them right after I talked to you," Tesla said quickly, though that was not quite true. *Damn*, she thought. *I forgot. I'll do it as soon as I get home tonight.* The phone Lydia had given her was still in her messenger bag at the house, but Tesla had been so tired after the jump, so glad to be home, that she'd just fallen into bed and slept until Jane woke her up and told her it was time to go to Lydia's and get ready for the party.

"Why aren't you going, Aunt Jane?" Tesla had asked.

Jane had shrugged. "I'm not really in the mood for a social event tonight. I'll stay here with Max, and after he goes to bed I'll go over the files again that we've compiled about your dad's kidnapping."

"I'll stay home with you," Tesla said immediately, and she meant it. "I can help with the files, and I'd much rather do that than go to a party. I'm worried about Dad." Her voice broke a little on the last word.

Jane put her arm around Tesla's shoulder. "I appreciate that, and I would accept if I thought it would help your dad. But I don't think it will, and besides, he would want you to go. He was kind of excited about it—despite the whole tuxedo thing—and you can be his proxy tonight. He would be glad to know you were there to represent the family and have a little fun with your friends in the midst of this whole ordeal."

Tesla bit her lip, not sure what to do. She didn't care about the party and would skip it in a heartbeat if she could help find her dad. But if Jane was right, and there was nothing she could do tonight, she did not want to just sit around the house, pacing and worrying. It sounded horrible. She'd much rather be distracted by the Institute party.

"Good," Lydia was saying. "Thank you for taking care of that immediately."

Tesla felt herself blush. She looked up and saw that Finn watched her closely.

"I'm going to get some food," she announced abruptly, but Sam stepped in.

"Why don't I go fix us both a plate, and get some punch. I'll bring it back here and we can relax before we dance again."

Before she could respond he had walked away, toward the long tables of food and drink.

"He's well-trained," said Finn, amused.

"It's called manners," Tesla snapped. Finn laughed and pushed a chair out with his foot.

She hesitated a moment, then sat down. She would only make herself look like a child if she refused. She needed to take a lesson from Finn—nothing ever got to him.

Bizzy and Malcolm wandered over, and they both sat down. "Good eats," said Malcolm. "I may have to go back for seconds."

"You mean thirds," said Bizzy, her enormous, black-ringed eyes narrowed in laughter. "You can eat more than anyone I've ever known."

"Thanks!" said Mal brightly.

The music had slowed to a deep, throbbing tempo, the melody carried by a saxophonist who had stepped to the front of the stage. The song had a slightly melancholy feel to it, not sad, exactly, but thoughtful and full of unspoken desire.

Malcolm cocked his head as he listened to the opening notes. "I do believe I could dance to this." He turned to Bizzy. "I can put my arms around your waist, and you can put your hands up around my neck. I can sort of shuffle back and forth, and try not to step on your ballet shoes. But I am not Sam, so let's kill that dream right now."

"Who could resist such a romantic invitation?" Bizzy laughed as she stood up and headed for the dance floor and Malcolm, who shot Tesla a thumbs-up, hurried after her.

"Oh my god," Tesla said, laughing. "What an unlikely pair."

"I think it's sweet," said Lydia.

Finn looked at Tesla, an exaggerated look of earnestness on his face. "I can shuffle my feet around and hold you awkwardly, but you're on your own in terms of your shoes. Shall we join the children?"

She couldn't help it. She knew Finn was likely to laugh at her at the first opportunity, but it was a party, and she was all dressed up, and…. And it was Finn, she admitted to herself. She got up, he took her hand, and they walked to the dance floor.

They turned and faced each other and Finn put his hands on Tesla's waist, just as he said he would. But it was far from awkward. Tesla's pulse raced, and she sensed that Finn drew in a breath and held it, just for a minute, when she stepped in close to him and put her good hand high on his shoulder, her fingertips just touching his neck above the collar of his white shirt.

"Sorry about the cast," Tesla said as she adjusted her

turquoise-plastered arm on top of his.

"What cast?" Finn asked without a trace of mockery.

She felt the warmth of his hands through her dress. He held her lightly, his thumbs on the flat of her stomach, nothing but the soft, watery satin of her dress between his skin and hers.

They danced, but Tesla wasn't certain they moved at all. With Sam, she had felt excitement, exhilaration. It was another thing entirely to dance with Finn. The world was reduced down to the deep, resonant notes of the saxophone, and Finnegan Ford's eyes, his lips, and the curls against his neck, which had somehow become twined around her fingers.

He leaned down, slowly and deliberately, and touched her mouth with his, softly, intimately. She felt a rush of warmth envelope her as his hands tightened and pulled her in closer. She closed her eyes as his lips brushed feather-light across her cheek, and she felt his soft breath against her ear just before he whispered, "Why did you lie to Lydia about destroying the jpeg files from your dad's office?"

The world righted itself, and Tesla's face was guarded again. "I don't know what you're talking about," she said evenly as she stepped away from him and he was forced to drop his hands to his sides. "Jack-ass," she added as she turned away from him, pretending she'd been unaffected by his nearness, the slow, sexy music, his lips and his hands, his hands, those hands....

He cocked an eyebrow and grinned at her and she blushed because he could read her so well. He was impossible, infuriating. She walked back to the table, no idea whether he followed her or not. She didn't care, she told herself.

"Sam, you're back!" she said, more enthusiastically than she felt. She wondered if everyone at the table—including Beckett, who had reappeared sans her groupies—had seen their intimate embrace on the dance floor.

"I am," Sam agreed, polite but a little remote. *Well, I guess he saw, at least,* she thought to herself.

"What'd you scavenge for us?" Finn asked, right next to her again, as he rubbed his hands together in greedy anticipation.

"I brought Tesla a variety. I wanted to make sure she got whatever she wanted," Sam said stiffly.

Finn laughed. "I'll bet." He scanned the room, his interest already elsewhere. "Oh. Hello," he said suddenly, quietly, as he pulled his cuffs out from his coat sleeves and headed toward a tiny brunette in an alarmingly short red dress.

"He. Is. Awesome," said Malcolm as he watched Finn make his move across the room.

"Hardly," said Tesla, her voice brittle, as she crumbled a tiny puff pastry in her fingers. Suddenly she flashed a brilliant smile at Sam. "Would you like to dance again?"

"Sorry," he said. "I promised this one to Beckett." Beckett and the dress she'd poured herself into stood up in a graceful, fluid movement. She took the hand Sam offered her and disappeared onto the crowded dance floor.

Tesla sat, miserable and confused.

"It's your own fault," said Keisha cheerfully.

"What is?" said Tesla, her voice sharp.

"Here you sit, all alone and with a big pout on, and not two minutes ago you had two hot guys vying for your attention."

"I have no idea what you're talking about, Keisha," Tesla said in an edgy voice as Lydia tried unsuccessfully to hide a smile behind her napkin. Joley quickly escaped to the buffet.

"You've handled this badly, is all, but it's fixable." Keisha scooted over to take the chair next to Tesla and, thankfully, dropped her voice so everyone in the tri-county area couldn't hear her.

"They both dig you, obviously," Keisha said, her doe eyes sultry as they reflected the candle light from the table. "And they're both jealous of each other. Please," she said quickly as she put her hand up to stop Tesla's protests.

Tesla conceded and waited silently for the rest of it.

"Back off and slow down," Keisha advised. "Enjoy them, enjoy the attention, but be real—don't play them off each other, that's just not right."

"I didn't mean to do that," Tesla said, but she realized as she spoke that regardless of her intention, that was exactly what she'd done. "Gross," she said, her self-disgust apparent. "I'm *that* girl."

Keisha laughed. "No you're not, you're *this* girl."

"Wait a minute," Tesla said. "You're the biggest flirt I know, and pretty regularly have multiple boyfriends at the same time. How come I get this advice?"

Keisha shrugged, very French—at least in her own mind. "Because I'm me. You're you, and you gotta recognize that. You don't like to make people uncomfortable, you're too nice for that. When you play Finn, when you try to use Sam to make Finn jealous, you're obvious, and it just pisses them both off. You're bad at it because it's not who you are."

"Huh," said Tesla. "Makes sense, I guess."

"Of course it does," Keisha said. "End of the day, you always go home with you, which sucks if you don't like what you've been up to."

"Miss Abbott?" said a smooth, older male voice.

Tesla looked up at the man who had approached their table so quietly she had not noticed him until he spoke. "Yes?"

"My name is Erik Van Aldan. I'm the new Director of the Institute of Experimental Physics. Would you care to dance?"

"Um, sure," Tesla murmured as she threw a quick glance at

Keisha that said, *What the hell?*

"Marvelous," he murmured and stepped back to give her room to stand. "Lydia, you look lovely this evening," he added with a slight bow.

"Thank you, Erik," Lydia said warmly. "Congratulations again on being named Director. I know the faculty consider your appointment a great coup, and the start of a brilliant new chapter for the Institute."

"My goodness, how kind! Shall we?" he asked Tesla.

He held the tips of her fingers in the crook of his elbow and led her to the dance floor, and then laid his hand lightly on her waist and took her other hand in his, exactly as Sam had done, but without any of the attendant excitement she had experienced with the younger man.

They danced, neatly and efficiently, and Tesla was glad to have had the practice with Sam first. The steps were the same, and Dr. Van Aldan was adept, if not particularly inspired.

"Are you enjoying yourself?" he asked.

"Yes," she said. "It's a great party. Oh, and congratulations on your appointment."

"Thank you," he said as he turned them expertly to follow the other couples on the floor. "I had looked forward to meeting your father—I've followed his work for many years now."

She smiled politely but said nothing.

"I knew your mother's work, as well," Van Aldan said.

"Really?" Tesla asked quickly.

"Yes. She was brilliant—truly a remarkable woman, I understand. Her death was a tragedy."

"Yes," Tesla mumbled into the awkward silence.

"I'm terribly sorry for your loss," he continued. "Yours and your brother's. And now, of course, your father—"

"My father's not dead," Tesla said, shocked. She stopped abruptly and felt the brush of someone's dress against her own.

"No, of course not," Van Aldan assured her as he moved them forward again. "Forgive me, that was poor phrasing on my part. I simply meant that it must be hard for you and your brother, after the tragedy you've already suffered, to have your father disappear."

Tesla followed his steps as the music played on, but she relaxed. He was actually pretty nice, and it felt good to get a little sympathy for a change. The whole spy thing surrounding her dad's kidnapping meant that all the people who knew he was missing were actually on the job, working the case, and nobody had time to think much about her and Max's feelings.

Her silence only made him feel worse. "I only meant to offer sympathy, my dear, and to tell you that if there is any way I can help, you have only to let me know. I'm aware, of course, that your father's, ah, current status is not public information, but of course as Director I've been apprised of the situation. This is clearly related to his work. And I wanted you to know, personally, that I'll do whatever is in my power to have him returned unharmed."

"Thank you," she said warmly. "That's really nice of you, and I'm sure both my parents would appreciate it. My brother and I appreciate it. It's just difficult to talk about—we're very worried."

Van Aldan smiled. "I understand completely. So tell me, Tesla, what have you been doing with your summer? Something exciting, I hope?"

Nice guy, Tesla thought again. *Changed the subject immediately when I said it was hard to talk about. Dad will like him.* "No, not at all. I mostly just hang out. It's kind of a small town, I'm afraid."

"Pity," he said. "Although that cast looks relatively new—some small adventure perhaps?"

"Yes, a spelunking accident," she said, smiling. "Broke my arm saving the others from a wicked crevasse."

Van Alden laughed with her and she thanked him for the dance when the song ended. He escorted her back to her table and left.

"Well that was certainly a high point of the evening," Lydia said. "Sought out by the Institute's director for a dance!"

"I guess," said Tesla. "He really just wanted to say something nice and supportive about Dad. I guess you guys have had to tell a few university officials about the kidnapping. But yeah, Aunt Jane will get a kick out of me dancing with the big celebrity."

"Yes, I'm sure," Lydia said. She ran her finger around the rim of her punch glass, apparently deep in thought. "You know I thought Jane would be here," she added. "I can't imagine what would keep her away."

"She's home with Max," Tesla said.

"Of course, dear," Lydia said smoothly. "In a town filled with college-aged boys and girls, most of them in need of money, it's impossible to find a sitter."

Tesla was suddenly tired. Tired of the weirdness between Lydia and Jane, tired of the tension between Finn and Sam, tired of Beckett's barbed comments, even Keisha's criticism. She was especially tired of the Jekyll and Hyde routine from Finn, intense and romantic one minute, then headed for the nearest Lycra miniskirt the next. She wouldn't be made a fool for anybody.

"I've got a headache, I'm gonna head out," she said abruptly and left the table for the ballroom door before Lydia could respond. Tesla recognized the familiar, dark mindset that was descending fast, the sense of loss and loneliness that always preceded it, and she didn't want to be here when it really hit and overwhelmed her. That feeling crushed her periodically, with the accumulated weight of the never-ending desire to have known her mother, to have her here and now. Tesla knew exactly how the rest of the night would play out, as it did each time her grief built up to this point: the desperation for a sense of herself that she knew, she *knew*, would be so much stronger if she only had her mother.

How *I wish you were here*, she thought, rocked to her core to find that it wasn't her mother at all that she wanted this time. It was her father.

CHAPTER 30

Tesla walked in the front door—after she'd opened it with the key she now had to carry everywhere, thanks to Finn. He'd told Aunt Jane that they never locked their doors and she'd made a huge deal out of it. Tesla stood in the doorway to the living room and watched Jane, who clearly thought she was alone.

The TV was on, a sappy Lifetime movie by the looks of it, although Jane paid no attention to it. She looked instead at the photograph she held in her hands, a framed picture of Tasya and Greg, taken on their wedding day, the one that usually sat on the mantel.

The look on Jane's face was what gave Tesla pause. Some war clearly waged within Jane as the play of emotions changed the expression on the woman's usually placid, unreadable face. Tesla saw anger, then tenderness, watched Jane close her eyes briefly as she flung the photo away from her onto the sofa. A look of disgust distorted her pretty features, and then it was gone as her eyes flew open and she looked right at Tesla.

"Tesla," she said lightly as she placed a magazine over the photograph on the sofa next to her. "You're home earlier than I expected. How was the party?" Jane deftly picked up the magazine—with the framed picture of Tesla's parents safely hidden beneath—and moved them to the coffee table. She patted the sofa cushion next to her. "Come tell me all about it."

Tesla sat and bent down to unlace her boots. "It was fun," she said, her voice somewhat muffled. After she'd kicked off her boots, she sat back against the cushions, faced Jane, and curled her legs up under her. "Really fancy—it's a gorgeous place—and everybody was all decked out."

"Did you dance?"

"Yeah, a couple of times. The music was old, but I liked it. No vocals, just jazz. Big Band, Lydia called it."

"She'd know," Jane laughed. "What is she, a hundred and eight by now?"

Tesla laughed, but felt a little uncomfortable. Lydia was really very sweet to her. And to Max. "I danced with the new director. He said some nice stuff about my mom and dad. You know, professional stuff."

Jane nodded. "That doesn't surprise me. Your parents are actually pretty well-known in their field, you know. Your dad's work is widely read around the world, it's considered very important."

"Yeah, it seems weird, though. You know, he's just my dad."

Jane smiled. "I know, and I think that's how he wants it. To just be your and Max's dad to you guys."

"I miss him." Tesla looked at her hands in her lap.

"I know. Maybe you could tell him that when he gets back."

There was no condemnation in Jane's tone, no reproof, but Tesla felt it nonetheless. "It's not just me, you know," she said, defensive despite her efforts. "If we don't get along, it can't just be me."

"I'm sure he would agree with you," Jane said. "But in order to figure out what happened between you two, and figure out how to make it better—you actually have to have a conversation."

Tesla said nothing, and Jane refused to help her out.

"Yeah. I guess." That was as much as Tesla would admit, and Jane was wise enough to let it go.

"Your dad's absence is tough on Max," Jane said. "I'm a little worried about him."

Tesla looked up again, alert and no trace of sullenness left on her face. "What can I do?" she asked quickly.

"I'm not sure there's anything you can do," Jane said immediately. "He doesn't remember his mother, and his father is gone, possibly in danger, and now you're the one who has to jump each time. He's still just a little boy. He's scared."

"God, could I be any more of a shit?" Tesla wailed suddenly.

"This isn't on you, Tesla. You've been brave to go, and you've done what you've been asked to do. I'm here at night, but I have to work. And frankly, even when I'm here, it's not the same. I'm not really part of the family."

Tesla opened her mouth to assure Jane that she was, indeed, part of the family, but then she closed it again. There were too many unanswered questions. Why Lydia was so suspicious of Jane. Why Jane seemed so evasive when Sam identified her as the woman he'd seen with Sebastian Nilsen. Why she'd looked angry and disgusted at the photograph of her parents.

The truth was, Tesla had to admit, that she didn't trust Jane. Why would she hide information about her dad, about Nilsen, if it wasn't because she was somehow involved?

Tesla excused herself then, said she was tired and wanted to go to bed, and she went upstairs, closed her door, and uploaded from her camera to her laptop the photos she'd taken at her dad's office. While the files transferred, she tossed the bronze boots into a corner, thankful she had become adept with her cast. She pulled the dress over her head and prepared to send it in the same direction as the boots, but instead she stood in the middle of her room, looked at the dress for a moment, and then hung it up—on a hanger—in her closet. *Whoa*, she thought, a wry twist to her lips.

She left the velvet and copper wire choker around her neck, but not because Finn liked it, and her hair still loosely gathered in what Beckett had called a *chignon*. She pulled on an old brown T-shirt—it actually said "Brown" on it, from the university in Providence—and her crumpled boyfriend jeans, which she picked up from the floor. She sat on the bed with her laptop until the early hours. She studied the images, read and reread the one document she'd found with the drawings, blissfully unaware that at least two people watched her lighted window from outside and wondered what, exactly, she was up to.

There didn't seem to be any mystery at all about what she'd found in that last drawer in her father's office. The one-page letter, on Institute letterhead, merely confirmed her father's appointment to the board of the organization, and thanked him for his service on the *ad hoc* committee for Facilities Development. Whatever that was. And the two architectural drawings were pretty easily decipherable, at least to Tesla. The exterior elevation appeared to be set on the university campus, on the quad, but it certainly didn't exist there now. Tesla knew the campus too well not to recognize the setting, and in particular the L-shaped physics building adjacent. The plan was for a small structure, at least for a university, with a few offices and classrooms, an auditorium, a posh conference room on the second floor, and not much else. The elevation suggested it was an important structure, though; its classical lines, fluted columns, and other ornamentation suggested a formality and a solemnity usually reserved for high level administrators or alumni, the ones who either raised lots of money, or gave lots of money to their alma mater. The edges of the hospital sat to the left of the property, the physics building, clearly marked, to the right. But oddly, the new structure—had it existed—would have sat in the center of a very large piece of land that, at least in the drawing, would essentially go unused. It would have been unusual, to say the least, for the university to allow so much green space, unless it was dedicated to student-use, like the quad, which was what this piece of land had eventually been used for. On the drawing, however, all that undeveloped property was heavily landscaped, filled with trees and bushes, but without paths or benches or open spaces, like the quad, where students could study, or play ultimate Frisbee, or lay out in the sun with friends.

The other drawing, Tesla realized within minutes, was surely a blueprint of the Bat Cave. At first she was confused by the lack of windows—there wasn't a single one—but when she realized that the majority of the space was dedicated to one enormous room, she knew. So her father had been a part of the Bat Cave from its conception, or at least privy to it, but she didn't see how that could be significant.

Tesla sat quietly, a worried frown on her face, and wondered what, if anything, either Jane's or Lydia's agencies had found. Had they found any new leads? Had they heard from Nilsen? There must be a way for her to help move things along.

She was frustrated, and suddenly she just couldn't sit around any longer and wait for someone else to keep her informed and give her some chore to keep her busy. She pressed her lips into a hard, unyielding line her father would have certainly recognized, and with swift, assured movements she shut down her computer, pulled on her Teva sandals, and snuck out the front door and into the cool dawn air.

"Has there been any progress in my dad's case?" Tesla asked without preamble.

"Nothing concrete as of yet. I'm sorry," Lydia answered, her hands folded on her desk.

This was the first time Tesla had been in Lydia's private office. She'd arrived at the old house just as the sun began to light the sidewalks outside, and Bizzy, rumpled from sleep, had answered the door. Lydia had appeared, fully dressed, before Biz had even shut the door behind Tesla. The older woman had taken one look at Tesla's face and ushered her into this room.

"You'll just have to be patient," Lydia said. "We've all got to be patient, and trust the professionals—they work around the clock, my dear."

"Okay, but we maybe need to approach this differently," said Tesla.

"What do you mean?" Lydia asked.

"I mean, let's look at what we found the last two times I jumped."

"Alright, let's," Lydia said.

"First, we found audio tapes of my arrythmia," Tesla said. "Then we found evidence of Nilsen's theft of my mom's data, and a copy of the article he published from it that ruined his career."

"Yes, Tesla, I'm aware of all this," Lydia said.

"I know, but wait," Tesla said hurriedly. "Next, I find blueprints of the Bat Cave."

"I thought you deleted those files," Lydia said sternly.

"I did," Tesla replied smoothly, without even a twinge of guilt for the lie. "But not before I looked at them." She had decided she was under no obligation to tell anyone what she did or thought.

The others all seemed to have agendas, not to mention secrets, so she'd keep her own counsel from now on.

"And what did you find?" asked Lydia as she took her hands off the desk and put them in her lap.

"Not much," Tesla said, a little deflated. "At least not at a glance. It seems pretty clear the interior blueprint is of the Bat Cave, and that it was originally intended to be underneath a building that was never built."

"Yes, Finnegan's research has already uncovered that part of the story."

"Oh," Tesla said, surprised. "Why didn't he tell me?"

"Perhaps because you don't sign his paychecks, dear."

Tesla bristled. "Yeah, fine, but this is about my dad, and it's not like you've changed your mind and decided to keep me out of the loop, right?

"That is true, but Tesla, you both just returned, he had to write up his report, and he turned that report in yesterday just before the gala—and you left early, so there was no time for conversation later, I might add. I was up at four a.m. to read his report. You'd have been filled in this morning, whether you had marched over here to demand it or not."

"What did Finn find out?" Tesla asked. She refused to be sidetracked by Lydia's attempted guilt trip.

"It appears the building that was supposed to be over the Bat Cave, where the quad now sits, was intended to house the Institute, but the necessary funds were never procured and they came up short."

"What does that mean—and how is it important to us?"

"What it means is that the Institute's board—which, by the way, included both your parents—approved the plans, oversaw fundraising, acquired all of the necessary permits and so on, but in the end there simply was not enough money to complete the project. The Bat Cave was constructed—obviously—but the plan for the Institute's home—the public façade—had to be abandoned."

Tesla's disappointment was obvious. "So none of this is relevant to my dad, to Sebastian Nilsen? All that work, and the additional jump back in time, were for nothing?"

"That, I'm afraid, is mostly what we do in this business," Lydia said, her voice sympathetic. "We chase leads, we do the research, we dedicate untold man—and woman—hours, and most of the time we hit dead ends. It's often an agonizingly slow process, and filled with disappointment. We learn not to get our hopes up."

"But why would my dad have this stuff locked up?" Tesla asked. She stood up and began to pace, no longer able to sit still as the days went by and they seemed no closer to an answer.

"I wish I could tell you, but I can't. It doesn't make sense to me, either," Lydia said smoothly. "Have you discussed this with your Aunt Jane?"

"No," said Tesla absently. She knew it was obsessive, this focus on why her father had locked up these particular documents, when it seemed they could have sat out on the coffee table for all they were worth.

"Good. I think it's best to let her do her work, not distract her with these unproductive avenues. And you should try to get some rest, dear. You look tired."

"I'm not going to go lie down," Tesla snapped. "My dad's been kidnapped, and you obviously think my aunt is somehow on the wrong side of all this. I've got too much to worry about and try to figure out to think about a nap, for god's sake."

Lydia looked at her, one eyebrow raised, and Tesla felt the heat rise to her face. "Sorry," she mumbled. "I didn't mean to take it out on you."

"I understand completely," Lydia said. "Some rest would help, though."

Tesla nodded. Afraid of what else she might say if she opened her mouth again, she walked out of Lydia's office, tears of anger and worry welled up in her eyes.

As Tesla rounded the corner of the hall, where early morning sunlight reflected off the walls and made her way toward the parlor from Lydia's office, she heard voices she recognized and stopped.

"—I don't see how this is any of your business, Ford," said Sam, his voice pitched to a conversational volume, but cold and steely in tone.

"This kind of thing is everybody's business," Finn said easily, casually. *Too casually*, Tesla thought in alarm. Couldn't Sam hear the controlled anger in Finn's voice?

"And what, exactly, is 'this kind of thing?'" Sam asked, his voice now equally dangerous.

"Abusive, creepy. You know, restraining-order worthy."

"What the hell do you mean by that?" Sam demanded, angry but clearly confused.

"Where were you last night, after the party at the Institute?" Finn asked.

"What?" said Sam, startled. "Who do you think you are?" He switched to offense. "Are you spying on me?"

"Hang on, mate, take it easy," Joley said, and Tesla heard the sound of hurried footsteps. *What is going on?* she thought as she inched closer to the doorway of the parlor so she could hear more clearly.

"I asked you a question," Sam said, his voice like a whiplash.

"Yes, you did," said Finn, unfazed. "And I asked you one.

Where were you last night?"

"It seems you already know the answer to that question. Which means you were there, too. Maybe you should tell us why."

"Finn doesn't answer to you," said Bizzy, her sweet voice uncharacteristically aggressive.

"And I don't answer to him, either," said Sam.

There was silence for a moment, and then Finn said, "I was there, you're right. I'm there most nights."

"And you have the nerve to accuse me?" Sam said, his voice much louder now, and accompanied by the sound of hurried steps, perhaps even a brief scuffle punctuated by Joley, who shouted, "Both of you, bloody calm down," with such authority that all the other sounds ceased.

Tesla's heart pounded, and she recognized the fight-or-flight response coursing through her body, the adrenaline, that new tautness in her body, a sense of being pulled. She knew she shouldn't eavesdrop, but there was pretty much nothing she could think of that would make her stop at this point.

"I was there, and I'm frequently there, because it's my job," Finn said, his voice deliberately calm and matter-of-fact. "What's your excuse?"

Sam waited before he spoke, and when he finally did, Tesla understood why. His voice now matched Finn's in its quiet, calm delivery.

"I keep an eye on Tesla, too, though I don't get paid to do it," Sam said. "And I followed her over here because I was worried about her. I don't know you people at all. I intend to make sure she's safe."

"That's your explanation?" Finn said, his voice now pitched, maddeningly, to suggest amusement. "You're just here to serve, to make the planet safer for everybody? Nothing personal in this for you?"

"No more than there is for you," Sam said, his words heavily weighted.

Finn laughed. "At least I know the difference between liking a girl and stalking her."

The sounds of a struggle, an incomprehensible shout from Bizzy, all in a split second, sent Tesla around the corner and into the room before she'd thought it through, her body acting on instinct alone as her entire being was reduced down to one coherent thought: *protect him.*

"Stop it!" she shouted at the sight of Sam and Finn desperate to get their hands on each other, Joley in between to keep them apart. Bizzy stood nearby, wide-eyed and horrified.

They all stopped and turned toward Tesla, and then Beckett walked in, right behind Tesla, from the same doorway where she'd hidden only moments before.

"Just when it had started to get fun," Beckett said just before she turned to Tesla. "Didn't you want to wait and hear the rest of it?"

Tesla could have scratched Beckett's face off, and she felt her own face burn with shame as she glanced guiltily at Finn and Sam.

The moment had passed.

Sam shook Joley's hand off, turned and walked out the front door without a word. Beckett hesitated, then went after him. Bizzy, Finn, and Tesla looked at each other.

"Well, that was fun," said Finn lightly.

"No, that wasn't fun at all," Tesla said, an echo of Finn's words to her the first night they'd met, here in this very room. Then she walked out the door, too.

"Tesla, wait!" she heard Bizzy shout, but she shut the door on them all and began to walk home, her only thought to get away from these people and the undercurrents that followed them everywhere they went. All she wanted was to find her dad, get her life back to normal. If she couldn't do it with them, she'd do it without them. She turned the corner, onto her street, her gaze fixed resolutely straight ahead. Had she looked the other way at the corner, however, she would have seen Sam and Beckett, who stood beneath the big oak that had sat on that particular corner for at least eighty years, deep in a conversation that animated both their faces.

CHAPTER 31

Tesla finished her braids and pulled on her black hoodie over a slate gray tank, with the hood up to cover her too-bright hair. They thought they could spy on her, keep tabs on her, tell her what to do. *'Just go dancing,'* she thought angrily. *'Don't worry, go take a nap'*. Well screw that. Her dad had been kidnapped by some lunatic and the only thing everyone agreed on was that Greg Abbott would soon run out of time. Tesla was done with the drama, done with these boys and their bowed-up macho crap.

Done with feeling like she had to watch out for them, protect them—but was that about both of them, or just one? And which one? Either way, it was a new development she neither understood nor appreciated. Besides, despite Lydia's insistence that Tesla should just let the so-called professionals handle this, they didn't seem to be getting anywhere.

She pulled on her black skinny jeans and running shoes, pulled the messenger bag strap over her head, checked inside to be sure she hadn't forgotten anything, and then she turned the stereo up.

She couldn't help but smile as she glanced at the window of her bedroom, wide open to the night, light and music pouring out for all the world to see and hear. Just another Tuesday night for your average teenaged girl, who certainly would be up in her room, Adele cranked up, while she wrote bad, angst-driven poetry.

Tesla felt rather smug as she slipped out of her bedroom door and into the hall, crept down the stairs in the dark and skipped the step that creaked. Max had gone to spend the night at Dylan's, happy to be a normal kid for at least tonight, and Aunt Jane was "on the job," as she had said wryly. Tesla walked across the tiled kitchen floor, her thin, rubber-soled shoes completely silent. She didn't have to think at all as she walked through the darkness, despite the lack of moonlight. Tesla knew this space, and that knowledge was better than night vision. She knew to the eighth inch where, exactly, the doorknob to the back door was located, and her hand moved forward with confidence, grasped it, and turned it quietly.

She slipped out the door, thankful that no one in her family had thought to replace the bulb in the outside light that was supposed to illuminate the backdoor at night, though it had burned out months ago. She stood against the wall of the house, in shadow, and looked around, a wild creature who listened, smelled and tasted the air. Alert to danger, and the presence of predators. All was quiet, just the whisper of leaves that moved in the soft breeze. She slipped easily across the lawn to the big hedge that separated the Abbott's property from their neighbor's and wriggled through it, at the bottom. She had to get on her belly and crawl a bit, and when she came up on the other side, dirty and a little scratched up, she was immensely satisfied. She travelled through several consecutive backyards like a wraith, but once she was a block away she felt safe. Anyone who watched her house, if they'd missed her initial escape from the back door, would never spot her now. She came around to the front of a house down the block from her own and hit the sidewalk at a light run as if she were an insomniac out for a jog, and headed toward the university hospital.

Tesla knew she'd lucked out when she walked up to the main entrance of the hospital, the automatic doors opened smoothly, and she found the information desk unoccupied. It was way past visiting hours, and she'd been prepared to argue with whoever stopped her, plead with them to just let her go up quickly to see her grandmother, she'd only stay a moment, cross her heart. Spared that performance, she headed straight for the elevator, got in, and pushed the button for the sixth floor. She planned to retrace her steps from the hospital room she'd been in months before, in order to make her way down to the Bat Cave without the need to go through the Physics building, which would most certainly be under surveillance by Lydia's people, probably Jane's as well. Not to mention whatever bad guys lurked about.

She wasn't sure what she hoped to find, but Tesla couldn't get past the conviction that the underground facility was at the center of everything. Her father had kept the plans under lock and key before it was even built, and there was no indication on those plans that anything top secret would be housed there. This was, in some way Tesla could not pin down, never about time travel. So why the top-secret routine from her dad, who didn't even lock the doors of their house at night? Clearly there was something about the Bat Cave, beyond the time machine that it now contained, that had warranted secrecy even before it was built.

The elevator *pinged* softly and the doors slid open. Keisha stood just outside, in the wide hospital corridor, dressed in black with a vase of flowers in her hands.

"Have any trouble?" Tesla said as she stepped out of the elevator.

Keisha shook her head. "Not really. I did have to use the sick grandmother story, but I'd grabbed these from my house on the way out, for a prop. The old man at the front desk downstairs said I was sweet."

"Good thinking on your part," Tesla said. "Bad judgment on his."

"Yeah, well. My mom's gonna be pissed. This is her favorite vase."

"Ready?"

"Yep," Keisha said as she set the flowers carefully on the floor outside of the private room just across from the elevator. "Somebody might as well enjoy these."

"Let's go," said Tesla as she turned to the stairwell just past the elevator, the same stairwell she had used the night she'd come here with a concussion.

They slipped inside, closed the door softly behind them, and began the long descent. Tesla was a little worried because she didn't feel the familiarity she'd expected, but figured that was because she'd had a concussion at the time, and wasn't quite in her right mind. It made sense that her memories of that night would be a little fuzzy, she assured herself. They continued down without conversation, save for Keisha, who said, "Dude, is this *Journey to the Center of the Earth* or what?" at about the midway point.

Once they'd reached the bottom and set off down the interminable hallway that Tesla remembered, if a bit vaguely, they picked up their pace. When they got to the door with the security pad—which was shut firmly this time—Tesla finally spoke.

"Here's the first trial," she said grimly. "Let's hope it works."

She'd watched Bizzy carefully the last time they'd gone to the Bat Cave, seen the sequence of numbers she had pushed to gain access to the underground facility, but Tesla didn't know if it would work now. Or here. Bizzy had taken them in through the Physics building, not the hospital, and Tesla didn't know if they used different codes for each entrance, or if the code was regularly changed. Still, she had to try, even if it meant that this was as far as she and Keisha would get.

Tesla pushed the seven buttons that Bizzy had pushed, and then tried the door. It opened easily, without a sound.

"We're in," she said unnecessarily as she looked at her best friend with barely suppressed excitement.

"Yeah," said Keisha, "but what, exactly, is your plan of action now that we're here?"

They entered the hall, shut the security door behind them, and Tesla walked quickly on. "Unclear," she said without embarrassment. When they got to the next door—the one that led to the last hallway before the Bat Cave, with doors on each side—she opened the door without hesitation.

"I guess we open some doors," she said, and Keisha nodded. Tesla reached into her messenger bag and pulled out the canister of pepper spray that Lydia had given her.

Keisha stared at Tesla, who looked about thirteen with her red hair braided in pigtails. "I am completely freaked out right now," Keisha said. "You're *armed*?"

Tesla shrugged. "It's a tool," she said firmly. "You never know what you might need." She walked into the hall and Keisha followed close behind.

"Tools," Keisha repeated. "Whatever you have to tell yourself."

Tesla was about to give Keisha a hard time for giving her a hard time, but before she could open her mouth they froze as a *click* from the door at the end of the hall reached their ears, and it began to open slowly inward. The girls moved closer together, and Tesla raised the pepper spray as someone walked through the door.

It was Beckett.

Beckett saw Keisha and Tesla—and their tiny can of pepper spray held out in front of them—the moment she stepped through the door. Her ninja-stance relaxed immediately, and she turned her head and spoke to whoever was behind her, still unseen by the two girls in the brightly lit hall.

"Found them."

Beckett moved aside, and Finn, Bizzy, Joley—and Malcolm—followed her out into the hall.

"What the hell are you all doing here?" Tesla demanded, determined to ignore the just-perceptible slackening of that stretched feeling that seemed to be her constant companion these days.

"I'm just along for the ride," Malcolm piped up. "I was at Bizzy's when this went down and, well, you know how I hate to be left out."

Beckett silenced him with a glance.

"Lydia said there's been a breakthrough in your dad's case," said Bizzy. "She sent us to your place to get you."

Finn looked accusingly at Tesla, struggling to sound light, to hide the fear he'd felt when he'd found her room empty, the unmistakable *pull* he could not ignore that led him to the Bat Cave, to Tesla. "I was at my post, across the street from your house, when Bizzy and Malcolm found me. I went to your door and knocked, but you didn't answer. *Probably can't hear me over the music*, I thought. So I went in, went up to your room, and found that you'd left. Snuck out. And seriously? The pillows under your covers, like it was you in there? What do you think this is, an *I Love Lucy* episode?"

Tesla felt a sudden, nameless exuberance. She was feather-light. *A breakthrough in your dad's case*, Bizzy had said.

"What?" she asked Finn, her voice effervescent, bubbles of laughter discernible in every syllable she uttered. "I don't have to check with you every time I leave my house. Right Ethel?" she asked Keisha.

"I figured you'd come back here," Finn went on as though she hadn't spoken. "So we went straight to the physics building and came down here from the other side."

"We went all *Mission Impossible* from the hospital side," said Keisha. "I had to charm a geezer at the information desk."

"I have complete confidence that you looked amazing doing it," Joley said suggestively.

"Could you be any more inappropriate?" Beckett asked him.

"Of course," Joley said with a grin, and Keisha laughed.

"Hello, the breakthrough in my dad's case?" Tesla said as she stared pointedly at Keisha.

"What?" Keisha said. "He's funny. You know I like funny."

"Let's go see what Lydia's found out," Finn said, and Keisha turned to head back through the hospital side, the way she and Tesla had come in.

"Wait, Keish, if we go up that way we'll be two hundred yards farther from Lydia's house."

Keisha stopped and rolled her eyes, but she turned around and walked back the other way.

"What?" Tesla asked, her hands raised in supplication as she fell in behind her best friend. "I can't help it if I know where we are. After all these years you should be grateful. If we left this sort of thing up to you we'd find ourselves in Hoboken, and you know perfectly well you couldn't stomach New Jersey."

Finn laughed. "It's true, she couldn't."

"Yeah, maybe we could admire Tesla's wit later," Beckett said. "I don't like it down here, never have. The sightlines are short, and there are too many closed doors for my taste. Makes me jumpy." Suddenly Beckett broke into a sprint, caught up with Keisha, and said, "Hold up, Finn's cousin, let me go first. The rest of you, stay covered until I check this out."

Keisha bristled, but Beckett ignored her, and ignored Joley, as well, who said, "What is it, Beckett?"

"Beckett leads," said Tesla as she put her hand on Keisha's arm. "It's not personal, it's smart."

"True," said Beckett. "Though you're clearly in the lead in the number of guys you keep on the line."

"Jealous much?" Keisha asked.

"Whatever, tag-along," said Beckett dismissively. She motioned for everyone to stand back and off to the side so only she was exposed as she gently pushed the levered door handle down. The door swung inward a few inches, but revealed only darkness. Beckett moved forward—maybe she meant to close the door again, or even go inside, find a light switch, investigate further—and then there was a flash of light and a deafening explosion, a stifled scream from Beckett, who spun around with a grimace of pain on her face, and pandemonium ensued.

The breath exploded from Tesla's lungs as Finn tackled her to the ground. He scrambled up off of her while Bizzy screamed. Tesla saw Finn reach out and slam the door shut again, and they all heard the shooter race up the metal stairs away from them and into the physics building.

"Get them out of here, Joley!" Finn shouted. Tesla's breath had been knocked out of her and she tried to pull air into her lungs. She got to her knees, saw Bizzy grab Malcolm's arm and drag him toward the hospital side, while Keisha and Joley each took one of Tesla's arms and pulled her to her feet. They all ran, but not before Tesla looked back and saw Finn drape one of Becket's arms around his neck while she hissed through gritted teeth, "Amateurs! Not a single one of you took cover like I told you to."

"Shut up, Beckett," said Finn lightly. "You're bleeding all over my favorite shirt."

Tesla finally got her legs under her. She sucked air into her lungs gratefully and ran alongside Joley and Keisha, but the stretched feeling got stronger with every step. They caught up to Bizzy and Mal, who had stopped at the door that led to the hospital, and everyone paused, wide-eyed and breathing hard.

"It's locked," said Malcolm.

"I've got the code," said Bizzy breathlessly. She pushed the seven numbers with fingers that shook, but nothing happened. No click, and the door wouldn't budge.

"The code's been changed," she said, after she'd tried it for the fourth time. "It's set to randomly change at automatic intervals, and we have to log-in—those of us with clearance—to get the new code. I'm sorry."

"We have to go back," Tesla said. "We shouldn't have left them there in the first place." She was already backing up, her body moving in the only direction that would ease the now-unbearable tension she felt in every inch of her body.

"That's where the shooter went," Keisha said.

"Come on," said Joley. "We have to go back anyway to go out the other side."

In two minutes they were back. Finn had propped Beckett up against the wall and she sat with her legs stretched out on the floor in front of her, while he ripped the bottom four inches from his T-shirt, which he'd pulled off as soon as he'd gotten Beckett settled. He glanced up once, saw Tesla, then started the tear in his shirt with his teeth. He ripped the cotton fabric with his hands, his biceps knotted as he tore through it, his abdomen flat and hard and well-defined.

"Yeah, I look pretty much just like that without a shirt on," Malcolm said with a nervous laugh.

"This is gonna hurt," said Finn to Beckett as he pulled her forward, as gently as he could, from where she sat, slumped against the wall. "Somebody come help me," he said, and Tesla and Joley stepped forward immediately and crouched down beside him.

"What do we do?" Tesla asked.

"I need something I can cut with," he said.

"You're gonna operate on that girl?" said Keisha, but Finn ignored her.

Tesla reached into her bag and pulled out a utility knife and held it up. "I have this," she said.

Finn turned to her, took the knife and pushed out the blade.

"Huh," said Beckett, who had opened her eyes and looked at Tesla. "That's a surprise."

Tesla shrugged. "You never know what you might need when you're a spy." Becket smiled and closed her eyes as Finn sliced through the strap of her Lycra camisole and pulled it down just enough to reveal the black, bleeding bullet hole in her shoulder.

"Oh my god," said Bizzy, her voice a sepulchral whisper.

"Shut up, Biz," said Beckett, her eyes still closed.

"Sorry," Bizzy whispered, her own eyes wide.

"Joley, hold Beck's arm out away from her body. And be careful."

Joley did as he was told, hesitating only when Beckett gasped, her eyes shut tight against the pain the movement caused her. "Oh bloody hell," he said. "I'm so sorry Beckett."

"Tes, take my T-shirt, wad it up over the wound, and press hard on it."

Tesla swallowed and moved closer, just past Joley who held

Beckett's arm out of the way. She got inside, close enough to Beckett and Finn that she brushed against both of them, and pressed the shirt to the girl's bloody shoulder. A groan escaped Beckett's tightly-shut lips and Bizzy whimpered softly from behind them.

"Keep the pressure on," Finn said quietly beside Tesla. "Just like that."

He reached across Tesla, his bare chest against her arm, and said softly to Beckett, "The bleeding has slowed from the pressure, Becks, and now I'm gonna tie it up. It's got to be tight, so get ready."

Beckett exhaled once, slowly and thoroughly through her mouth, and then inhaled, long and steady through her nose. She nodded once, her eyes still closed, and began another long exhalation of air through her mouth as Finn ran the 4-inch wide strip of cloth under her arm and against the rest of the shirt Tesla still held tightly against Beckett's bloody shoulder. As he drew the fabric in tight to the wound and then pulled it even tighter into a square knot, Beckett slumped forward against Tesla, who had removed her hand from the makeshift dressing at the last second. Tesla caught her, carefully avoided her wounded shoulder, where a small spot of red had already appeared through the cloth, and looked at Finn.

"I think she's fainted."

"No she hasn't," Beckett said weakly, her eyes still closed. "She's just regrouping."

"You are one tough blonde," said Finn affectionately.

"Don't forget it," Beckett said weakly as she leaned against Tesla, who actually smoothed her hair back tenderly. Beckett opened her eyes, looked up at Tesla, and raised an eyebrow. Tesla smiled at her and shrugged.

"We need to get you out of here," Joley said. "Think it's safe to head back up?"

"We don't really have a choice," said Finn as he looked at the blood that already seeped through the T-shirt bandage on Beckett's shoulder. "We can't stay here."

"True," said Joley. "Plus, I'm hungry."

"Don't make me laugh, it hurts," said Beckett, her voice a little stronger.

"Okay," said Finn. "Joley and I will get Beckett up the stairs, you guys go ahead of us. If there's any sign of trouble—and I mean this—the rest of you haul ass up those stairs and get to Lydia's. No turning back." He looked at Tesla, spoke to Tesla, and she could not look away. "Understood?"

Everyone nodded, and they went through the door and up the metal staircase that would lead them out fairly close to Lydia's house. Finn and Joley got Beckett up and moved as carefully as they could. Beckett was able to carry some of her own weight, but it was clear she couldn't have walked on her own. The rest of them tried not to look back as they climbed, listening for the smallest sound and watching for any movement as their eyes swept the darkness at each corner they rounded in the stairwell.

They finally made it to the top, and the door loomed ahead of them. Tesla was there first, and she took a breath and opened the door to whatever awaited them in the dark.

CHAPTER 32

"Clearly, I will have to rethink this entire operation," Lydia said, her fury barely contained. "I expected a minimal level of professionalism from each one of you that you have *all* failed—miserably—to meet. All of my efforts to effect Dr. Abbott's safe return were geared for maximum safety. We could—and should—have been able to navigate this case without *anyone* getting hurt."

They had gathered in Lydia's second-floor sitting room—even Sam, who had arrived only minutes after the rest of them—and awkwardly stood, sat, or paced around the room. No one was able to meet Lydia's gaze. Without ever saying so, they all knew they would remain until the doctor had taken care of Beckett, and emerged to tell them just how bad it was, despite the fact that at this moment they would have all preferred to be elsewhere. All the doctor had said when he arrived with his nurse, who carried a large black roller bag, was that Beckett had lost a lot of blood. Then he closed the door to her room, and they waited.

Lydia fumed for a few minutes, silently, and the clock on the mantel ticked loudly. Finally the older woman looked up and over the top of her glasses and focused on Finn.

"What, exactly, were you thinking?" she asked.

"We went to get Tesla," he said, though they'd already explained at least twice. "She had snuck out, we thought we knew where she'd gone. So we went there to get her. Those were your instructions."

"As you know perfectly well, Finnegan, my instructions were to bring her here from her house. When you found she was gone you should have texted to inform me, and waited for further orders." Lydia's fingers drummed on the arm of her chair nervously, and Tesla was surprised to see her so agitated. She must feel horrible about Beckett, maybe even responsible, to have employed such young, inexperienced operatives.

"And what about you, Tesla?" Lydia asked sharply. She had turned to the girl so suddenly that Tesla jumped.

"Me?" Tesla squeaked.

"Yes, you. Why would you go off on your own like that?"

"She wasn't alone." Keisha spoke for the first time from the seat next to Tesla on the sofa. "She was with me. I knew about her escapade below the hospital before any of you got involved. My only allegiance is to T—of course I'm gonna be with her. You'll just have to get used to it."

"You are not trained—either of you—and there is a chain of command that must be followed, or—or this kind of thing happens," Lydia said with a wave toward the closed door of Beckett's bedroom.

"Look, no offense, Lydia, but I don't know about your chain of command, or why you think I should follow it. I don't work for you, and neither does Tesla." Keisha said it politely enough, but she held Lydia's gaze and it was, shockingly, the older woman who looked away.

"That is an excellent point," Lydia said after a moment. "And it serves to remind me that Tesla should not have been brought into this at all."

"But Lydia, you don't have the right to keep me out of the picture when it's my dad who's been kidnapped," Tesla protested. "And why, exactly, have I been here for half an hour and been told absolutely nothing about this breakthrough in his case that was the reason you sent them after me in the first place?"

Lydia looked at Tesla, who glared back at her. "You're right, of course, dear." To everyone's surprise, she sounded suddenly very old, and very tired. "Forgive me. I knew it would be an unpleasant conversation, and with Beckett injured, well.... I suppose I was relieved to postpone this."

"Postpone what?" Tesla sat up straight on the couch in sudden alarm. "Is my father hurt—or dead?" she asked, her voice low and carefully controlled.

"I cannot answer that with any certainty," Lydia said calmly as she held Tesla's gaze. "But Jane Doane has disappeared, and—"

"What? Aunt Jane's been kidnapped, too—but why? And how?" Tesla stood up, looked wildly around and took a step away from the couch toward the door, ready to—well, she didn't know what. She felt a sudden helplessness, a fear and vulnerability that paralyzed her, and then Lydia spoke again.

"Tesla, you don't understand—listen to me."

The woman's sad, gentle tone—the lack of any semblance of urgency—immobilized Tesla. "What don't I understand?" she asked, though she knew before she'd even finished the question that she didn't want to know the answer.

"Tesla, we have evidence that Jane has been in league with Nilsen the entire time. Probably from the start, all those years ago. I said she was missing, dear. Not kidnapped." There was a pause, a beat that lasted an eternity.

"I'm sorry," Lydia added.

"I don't believe it," Tesla said. She pulled free from Keisha, who had stood when she did and had her hand on Tesla's arm just above the cast. "I've known her my whole life, there's no way."

"Yes, but have you really known her?" Lydia asked sadly. "Think about it, Tesla. Did you know what her real job was? Did you know, until Sam accused her, that she had maintained her relationship with Nilsen long after your parents broke ties with him?"

"No," Tesla said quietly, tears in her eyes. "But that doesn't mean—"

"Tesla, if she kept all of that from you, what else has she kept from you?"

Tesla walked to the fireplace and back, desperate to find a way to refuse this. She was glad Max wasn't here, glad he was spared this, but at the same time she missed his particular gift, his insights about people, stories, motivations—of course, she thought. *Motivations.*

"Why would she work with Nilsen?" Tesla asked as she whirled back to face Lydia. "What could she possibly have to gain? I know her, I know how she lives, she doesn't care about money, she lives simply, and she could have made a lot more money in the private sector, but she chose government work. So why?"

"You really don't know?" Lydia asked.

"No." Tesla felt her braids hit her shoulders as she shook her head. "I really don't know."

"Jane loves your father," Lydia said gently. "She's always loved him."

"That's crazy," Tesla said, but her voice had lost the strength of conviction it had held only seconds before.

"Is it?" Lydia asked. She rose wearily from her chair and walked toward Tesla while the rest of them watched other people's lives unravel. "Is it crazy that she would have fallen for him in college, so smart and handsome and kind, fallen for him even before her more attractive and sophisticated roommate had met him? Crazy that he would have fallen for the roommate instead, that Jane would be forced to watch the love and the life your parents built together, relegated to just the old college friend, the aunt and godmother to their children, forever the outsider?"

Tesla had backed up to the fireplace until she had nowhere else to go. Sam, who stood nearby, took a step nearer to Tesla, who didn't look at him because she couldn't take her eyes off Lydia.

"Leave her alone," he said.

Lydia ignored him. "Tesla, this may be hard to hear, but it's the truth. You told me once, in this very room, that even if it was hard you preferred to know the truth."

"I know," Tesla said. "And I still prefer the truth, but Lydia, this doesn't make *sense*." She turned to Finn, "Does this make sense to you?" she asked, and he recognized it as much more than the question she'd asked—it was a plea to leave her some small scrap of the foundation upon which her world had always rested.

"I don't know," he said as gently as he could. "It's possible that she loved him—that she still loves him." He shook his head lightly, tried to clear the wave of grief that threatened to drown his attempt to think this through, confused by how strongly he felt her pain. With an enormous effort of will he set the overwhelming emotions aside.

"But Lydia," he said, turning to the older woman. "Why would Jane work with Nilsen to steal the time-travel technology, why would she participate in, or even just cover-up, Nilsen's kidnapping of Dr. Abbott? How does that help her if what she wants is Dr. Abbott for herself, finally, after all these years?"

Tesla, who had stared at Finn as he spoke, whipped her

head around, back to Lydia, her mouth slightly open, her eyes desperate and bright.

"Because as long as Dr. Abbott continues to work on time travel, he will never truly leave his wife—she was also his partner, his colleague. This is their work—perhaps even more fully hers than his—and as long as Greg Abbott continues that work, Jane Doane has no hope of taking Tasya Petrova's place in his life."

Lydia turned to Tesla. "I am sorry, my dear. I understand how crushing this kind of disillusionment can be."

Sam stood right next to Tesla, put both arms around her and she buried her face in his chest. Finn and everyone else in the room stared at the sight of her, broken and alone, when the door to Beckett's room opened and the doctor walked out.

Tesla and Sam stood by the bed in Beckett's room, the last two to file inside and speak to her. She lay on the bed, the covers pulled up over her chest and tucked underneath her arms. She had a fresh dressing over her bullet wound, and her face was peaceful, her eyes closed.

"She looks better," Sam said quietly, and Tesla nodded. She was glad for Beckett, but the day had become surreal, a dreamscape she occupied, with full knowledge of what it was. She felt nothing—about any of it. It just wasn't real.

"She's also awake," Beckett whispered.

"And still talking about herself in the third person," Tesla whispered back.

Beckett smiled.

"Sorry, did we wake you?" Sam asked as he took a step nearer.

"No, I'm just laying here."

"It doesn't hurt anymore, now that the bullet's out?" Tesla

asked.

"Couldn't tell you," Beckett said. "Good drugs."

"I guess I missed all the excitement," said Sam. "I saw Finn and the others race away from Tesla's house, but I couldn't get into the physics building to follow them. It must have been pretty crazy down there. You were lucky, I guess."

"Yeah, lucky," Beckett said dreamily, her eyes still closed. "I guess they told you about your aunt, huh?"

It took a second for Tesla to follow. "Lydia said they suspect her of working with Nilsen," she said reluctantly.

"Not to mention shooting me," said Beckett.

"What?" Tesla reeled, and just when she thought she couldn't be shocked by anything else, ever again. "Why do you think that?"

Beckett's eyes were open now, and looking—with actual sympathy—at Tesla. "It all fits," she said quietly. "Motive, opportunity, skill set. And now she's disappeared. Not a coincidence, I think."

"God, Beckett," Tesla said softly, horrified. "My Aunt Jane shot you? I—I don't know what to say."

"Why should you say anything? It's not like you're responsible," she said dismissively. "In fact, you were not bad down there. You had a cool head." Her eyes closed again. "I actually thought I might die. Kind of puts it all in perspective, you know?"

No one answered her, and the room was silent. Just as Tesla thought the injured girl had fallen asleep, and that they should leave her to rest, Beckett spoke again.

"Makes me feel bad about our little deal," she said.

"Our deal?" Tesla asked, confused.

"No, idiot. Him," she said. "Our deal to keep you and Finn

apart."

Tesla turned and looked at Sam, who met her eyes but stood rigid, resolutely silent. Tesla turned back to Beckett. "You and Sam are trying to keep Finn and me apart?"

"Well, we hadn't really started yet," Beckett said as she opened her eyes and returned Tesla's look. "But we agreed to try."

"Why?" Tesla demanded, the question for Beckett alone. She didn't want to hear Sam's answer to that question.

Beckett shrugged, and the movement caused her face to contort in pain. "Shit," she said softly, and waited until the pain passed. "I don't really know," she admitted. "I guess I'm just a bitch."

Tesla took a deep, shaky breath, and then let it out, along with her anger. "No, you're not," she said, which surprised them both. "You try, but you're not as good at it as you think you are."

"Great," Beckett said. "Way to make me feel even worse."

Tesla smiled, and then Beckett smiled, too.

"I guess I'm glad you're not dead," Tesla said.

"I guess I'm glad you're a spy now, too," Beckett said.

There was no more to be said after that and Tesla, utterly exhausted, did the only thing that was left to her: without so much as a glance for Sam, she slipped out of the room and out of that house before anyone could stop her and made her way down the streets of the town she knew, the life she thought she knew, and she didn't stop until she was alone, as it was apparently meant to be.

Tesla tried to sleep, but after an hour in which she tossed and turned and punched her pillow into shape it was clear that sleep was not in the cards. She got up and walked downstairs in the soft, stretchy tank and boxers she liked to sleep in. Maybe some mindless TV would help.

She was twenty minutes into some ancient, post-apocalyptic *Twilight Zone* episode, where some book nerd guy was delighted to find himself the only person left on Earth, with the public library now his, forever, when there was a soft knock on the front door—so soft that Tesla wasn't sure she'd heard it the first time.

She sat up straight to listen, and then she heard it again. *At this time of night?* she thought. She checked herself just as she was about to open the door wide. *It's not that kind of a world anymore.* She went to the window first and moved the curtain aside to peer out into the darkness.

Sam.

She leaned her forehead against the glass for a moment and closed her eyes. This was not what she needed, but then again, she couldn't sleep anyway. *Might as well get it over with,* she thought.

Tesla opened the door and stood back, the open space a clear indication that Sam could come inside. He did and, like Tesla, he did it in complete silence.

She shut the door and then led the way to the sofa, where she'd been camped out before he arrived. They sat down, and Tesla looked at him expectantly. She would not speak first.

At first he couldn't say anything at all—he could hardly look at her. Like storm clouds moving in a high wind, expressions of embarrassment, shame, and anger came and went across his face. He knew, of course, that the anger was born of the embarrassment and shame, that it was an attempt to deflect the responsibility of this whole thing away from himself, focus it on Beckett, or Finn, or even Tesla herself, but he refused to let himself get away with that.

"I came to tell you that I'm sorry," he began.

She waited.

"Tesla, I don't expect you to just say, 'Okay, no problem Sam.' I know it will take a while. I know that I have to earn back your trust."

"Earn *back* my trust?" she said. "I don't know you. When did you earn it in the first place?"

His deeply tanned face seemed to pale a bit, and she steeled herself against the hurt she saw in his dark eyes.

"Fair enough," he conceded. "But I think it's safe to say you were surprised and disappointed, and you wouldn't have felt that way if you hadn't thought well of me before Beckett staged her little confession."

Tesla studied his face. "Look, Sam. I don't want to be mean, but…this just isn't really on my radar right now."

He looked confused, and she gave up the effort to spare him.

"I don't care as much about this as you think I do."

He seemed to draw away from her a bit though his back was up against the couch cushions. "Wow," he said quietly. "I was prepared for anger, and hurt feelings, disappointment and a lack of trust. I didn't expect indifference."

"Look, it's not that I don't like you, it's just that my life is crazy right now—I mean, really, Sam. My dad, my aunt, my little brother, some mad scientist-kidnapper who apparently hates my family, suddenly I can jump backward in time, I've been, like, six feet away from my mom—and that's just this week. Did you really think that you trying to keep me from getting close to another guy—who I also just met—would be front and center for me right now?"

He looked at her a bit more sharply. "So I'm wrong that Finnegan Ford—and me, to some extent—have not been on your mind at all this past week?"

Tesla blushed, a little less in control of the situation than she'd thought. "No, you're not entirely wrong," she finally said. "But I won't be distracted by this stuff anymore. Not right now."

He nodded, thoughtful. "I think that's wise," he said. "And I really am sorry about that whole ridiculous plan with Beckett. It was very high school of me. I'm embarrassed."

"Hey, as a high school student, I resent the implication—it was very seventh grade of you."

Sam smiled, a bit tentatively at first, but then broadly, relief apparent in his expression. "You can't be that mad if you're joking around already," he said.

She shrugged. "I guess not. I mean...," she struggled to articulate what she felt, forming the thought fully for the first time. "I guess I'm flattered. But jealousy and emotional manipulation aren't what I want to want—I don't want to find those things romantic. Does that make sense?"

"Yeah, it does," he said quietly. "But unfortunately, it just makes me wan—like you more," he quickly amended.

Tesla leaned toward him and her wild hair fell below her shoulders to obscure the little straps of her black camisole. "Can we just take it a little easier?" she asked. "Let's be friends, and just let it happen. Or not happen. Whatever. And focus on the more pressing issues. Okay?"

He nodded, and she sighed just a little, because his heart was so completely in his eyes.

"I can't help it," he protested. "Yes, we'll be friends. We'll spend some time together—without the intensity. But I won't pretend I don't feel this way, Tesla. And I won't pretend I don't see Finn as a rival, or that I don't plan on winning—you'll just have to live with that. But I won't be an ass about it, and I won't be dishonest again, you have my word on that."

"Okay," she said, and visibly relaxed. "I mean, we're going to know each other a long time, right? It's not like there's any rush here.

Sam's eyes lit up at that, and he smiled a very strange, very little smile.

"What?" she asked, confused by that smile.

"Nothing," he said, as he picked up the TV remote. "I just have to remember that everything can happen."

"You mean 'anything can happen?'"

"No," he said. "I mean everything." He slouched down comfortably on the sofa like he planned to stay awhile. "So what are we watching?"

CHAPTER 33

Finn got up again from his favorite chair in the parlor, a peacock blue, velvet wingback. He wasn't sure why it appealed to him—it wasn't that comfortable—but he liked the contrast of the formal lines and the outrageous color, the sensual fabric. He was drawn to contradiction.

Like this thing with Jane Doane. In all the confusion tonight, Lydia had not had a chance to fill them in on any details, and it all felt very incomplete to him. He didn't like loose ends, and the notion that Jane was a double agent was nothing *but* loose ends, at least at this point. What kind of evidence did they have against her? And, perhaps more importantly, where was Jane now? Lydia was out again, no doubt to gather all of her resources to locate Jane and, thus, find Dr. Abbott and Sebastian Nilsen, but he hated to be out of the loop. After Tesla left, Finn had gone in to check on Beckett again before he got back to work, but by the time he'd come out Lydia was already gone and he was left to pace the floor and wonder what was happening elsewhere.

Clearly he would get no sleep tonight, and that stretched-thin feeling didn't help. His mind was a merry-go-round that spun endlessly; the same pieces came around again and again, but they were gone so quickly that he never could grasp what connected them.

He finally got up and went to Lydia's office. He'd already been in there twice tonight, but he came back on instinct alone, like some mindless swallow to Capistrano. He sat down at the desk and pulled the full-size hardcopies of the blueprints toward him that the analysts had delivered, the ones Tesla had photographed in her dad's office. He had pored over them already, and he did so again now, more out of a need to do something than an expectation that he would find anything new. He traced with his eyes the route Tesla had described to them when she told the story of her first encounter with the Bat Cave, the night she was in the hospital with a concussion. The sound of her voice was in his head as his eyes followed her route from the hospital to the first security door, which had stood open, oddly enough, then the second door and down the long hallway that ended at the door she then passed through into the Cave….

Finn suddenly sat up straight, his breath caught in his chest. He retraced her path, this time with his finger on the page, and followed the lines that indicated her route. Down the stairwell, the security door, the long hallway, the door to the Bat Cave—*Goddamn it*, he thought as he sprang to his feet. *I should have seen this before.* He rolled up the blueprint and tore down the stairs and out the front door, racing to Tesla's house just as the sun rose above the treetops.

When he rounded the corner to Tesla's street and her house came into view, Finn felt the strange, tight feeling in his chest begin to ease, but before he could examine that feeling, wonder at the change and what it might mean, he saw Max on the sidewalk headed toward the Abbott's front door.

"Max!" Finn yelled. "Wait up!"

Max turned, saw Finn and waved.

"I need to talk to your sister right away," Finn said. "Hey, you okay?" he asked. He realized only now how early it was, and here was Max, out and about with a backpack slung over one shoulder.

Max turned and they walked toward the front door. "Yeah," he said. "I spent the night at Dylan's, but he has a piano lesson today so I had to leave early. His mom said he had to practice."

Max opened the door with his key and they walked inside and moved straight into the living room, where they could hear the TV. Then they stopped dead in their tracks.

Tesla was asleep on the couch, curled up, her head on Sam's chest. Sam, too, was asleep, with his arm around her. He had slid down low on the sofa, and his head was tilted toward Tesla, his chin settled lightly on the top of her head.

"Geez," said Max.

Finn said nothing as the sight of them hit him like a truck, and he heard the *click* of all his defenses settle back into place. Tesla looked so peaceful as she slept that he realized for the first time how consistently worried and anxious she had looked lately. Her hair was a tangled riot of red curls, and her skin looked like the magnolia petals he'd seen once on a trip down south, creamy white and soft to the touch. He'd never seen so much of her skin before, her long legs and feet bare, her pink-polished toenails. She wore only a tiny black shirt with thin straps, a shirt that hugged her body intimately, beautifully, and black silk boxers that shone softly like a slippery seal in water.

"Tesla, what are you doing?" Max asked, both amused and a little shocked.

Sam woke up first, and all at once. His eyes flew open and

his arm tightened protectively around Tesla before he even registered that Max and Finn were in the room. When he did, he gently moved Tesla off of him and sat up. "Tesla," he said as he touched her arm and gently prodded her. "Wake up."

Tesla opened her eyes and looked at Sam. "Wha—?" she began, clearly confused. "We fell asleep? What time is it?" She turned her head to find the big clock by the front door and saw Finn and Max in the doorway.

"Oh, hey," she said, and then she blushed as she began to grasp the situation. "We were watching TV," she said. "I guess we fell asleep."

Sam stood and spoke to Max, ignoring Finn completely. "Sorry about that, Max. We were watching some *Twilight Zone* marathon and I guess we both fell asleep. I'll get out of here, give you and your sister your house back." He looked at Finn then, his meaning clear: they should *both* leave.

Finn looked back at him, unmoved. "See ya," he said, and stood his ground.

Sam flushed, clearly unhappy, but mindful of his promise to Tesla. "I'll call you later," he said to her, and left.

Max whistled as he walked into the kitchen to rummage for breakfast, and the front door closed behind Sam.

"I should go get dressed," Tesla stammered as she rose from the couch and pulled what there was of the legs of her boxers down a bit, then tugged at her camisole, all too aware of what they revealed.

Finn raised his eyebrows suggestively. "Suit yourself," he said casually, "but there's no need to on my account. Why should Sam have all the fun?"

She was stung, just as he'd intended. "What do you want?" She forced herself to stand still, refused to fidget or cover herself up.

She had nothing to be embarrassed about.

He looked at her for a moment, torn between the vulnerability that made him angry, even mean, and an intense desire to move closer to her, touch her skin, talk this over in hushed, intimate tones while she reassured him.

She stared back at him, defiant.

"I think I found something. I came over to convince you to go back to the Bat Cave with me, to see if I'm right, because I think your dad is out of time, and no one wants to say that to you. So I came over here to say it."

"Will you please tell me what you found, and why, exactly, we're down here?" asked Tesla as they began their descent down into the bowels of the hospital, down the metal staircase that was by now all-too familiar.

"Of course. I just thought we should get started first, not waste any more time." Finn's tone was impersonal, matter-of-fact, but at least he was talking to her.

"Well, we certainly have time now," she said. "It takes a while to get down to the bottom."

"I brought the enlarged copies of the photos you took of the blueprints in your dad's office," he said as he opened the flap of her messenger bag and took out the rolled-up paper he'd placed in there. While she had gotten dressed upstairs Finn had picked up her bag from the floor, wandered down to the basement, added a few items, and slung it over his own shoulder.

He stopped on the stairs in mid-descent. "Here, take a look at this."

Tesla came in close, aware of the warm brown skin of his hands that held the paper up for her to see. She looked, immediately oriented to the diagram on the page, and placed her index finger on the page at a point about three inches from his thumb. "We're here," she said with absolute authority.

"Right," Finn said. "Let's go the rest of the way, and I want you to keep in mind when you were down here before."

"Which time?" she asked. "The one where I had a concussion, or the one where Beckett got shot?"

"The first one," he said grimly. "I don't want to be reminded of the second time, especially since we're down here alone."

"And why is that?" Tesla asked. "Where are the others— does Lydia even know we've come down here?" She wasn't sure why this hadn't occurred to her earlier, she had just thrown on a pair of shorts and a semi-clean T-shirt, pulled on her running shoes and left with Finn, no questions asked.

"Beckett's out of commission, and Lydia is away, probably assigned to bring in your —bring in Jane. The others have a lot to offer, don't get me wrong, but mostly in terms of research. Not so much in terms of, um, a more physical situation."

"And you and I do?" Tesla asked, skeptical.

He laughed, more relaxed than he had been since they'd left the house. "Yeah, well. We're what we've got."

They continued to follow the stairs down, each of them lost in their own thoughts. And then they rounded another bend and found themselves at the bottom, the security door in front of them.

"I forgot," Tesla said suddenly, her hand on his forearm as she turned to him. "The combination didn't work on this door yesterday, when we tried to get out after Beckett was shot."

Her hand on his arm burned and he moved it, breaking contact. He wasn't an imbecile—touch a stove once, and that's enough for a lifetime. He was happier and more effective, more focused when he was alone.

"No, it's fine," he said. "Biz gave me the new code." He

punched in the seven-digit number, the door clicked open and swung inward.

"Here we go," said Finn. He exchanged a sober look with Tesla, then led the way down the hall. "Leave that door open," he said over his shoulder.

At the end of the corridor, just as Tesla remembered it from months ago, and just as she and Keisha had seen yesterday, was the second metal door without the security key pad, the door that led into the Bat Cave.

Finn had stopped and turned to face Tesla. The look on his face was strange, and she could not read it.

"What?" she said, agitated. She supposed the blood on the floor right by Finn's feet—Beckett's blood—was enough to explain it. She felt jumpy, she supposed he did, too.

"That night you first came down here," he said. "When you had a concussion. When you told us the story, you said that the hall dead-ended at this door, and you went through it."

"Yeah," said Tesla, confused. "Same as yesterday, same as right now." Her hand indicated the space they both stood in. "There's the door."

"I've only ever been down here from the physics building side, never from this side, never from the hospital," he said, and her skin prickled at the suppressed excitement she heard in his voice. "But I remembered the way you described it."

"So?" Tesla asked.

"So, look at the plans." He held the blueprints out for her to see again. "What do you see?"

Tesla looked, and then stepped back to look around her. "This hall dead ends here, at this door. But in the drawing, the hall goes on, that way," she said as she pointed at the solid wall immediately to their right.

"Exactly," Finn said. "You had a concussion, and you were confused, you said, but you never mentioned that you had to make a decision here that night, about whether to open this door or continue down the hall to the right. I wondered why, and I started to suspect that it's because there was no decision to be made at all. And what that might mean."

Tesla looked up at him, as excited as he was now. "It might mean that they built it like this," she said, and tapped the blueprint. "It might mean that this is a false wall, and the hallway continues behind it, with the rooms shown here hidden away."

"Exactly," Finn said. "And why would anyone want to have hidden rooms that nobody knew about?"

Tesla's breath was caught in her throat, and she had to attempt twice to get the words out. "Because they have something that they don't want anybody else to find."

Finn looked at her and nodded. "Yes. I think your dad might be down here, behind this wall somewhere. But you have to be prepared, Tes. We don't know what we'll find."

Tesla nodded, and couldn't seem to stop, or even blink her eyes.

"Breathe," Finn said quietly.

Tesla closed her eyes and exhaled, long and slow, as she'd seen Beckett do to prepare herself for pain. If Beckett could do that, with a bullet in her shoulder, she could do this.

She opened her eyes. "How do we get in?" she asked evenly.

Finn's face broke into a wide grin. "Glad you asked."

Before Tesla could speak he opened her messenger bag that he had slung across his chest. "While you were upstairs I raided your basement. I borrowed a few things."

Tesla looked at him, surprised, as he handed her a short crowbar and took a hammer out for himself. He walked over to the smooth, solid wall to the right of the door and, hammer in hand, began to tap along the wall until they both heard the change in sound. Finn turned to Tesla, and they both spoke at the same time.

"Hollow."

Finn continued to tap the hammer on the wall in a horizontal line, and Tesla confirmed that there was a hollow space behind the wall that was the standard height and width of a doorway.

"Ready for some demolition?" Finn asked with a rather wicked smile.

"Absolutely," Tesla answered as she weighed the crowbar in her right hand.

Finn swung and the drywall gave way with a puff of plaster dust as his hammer went right through the wall. He had to pry it out, and his second hit, just inches away from the first, made the hole bigger. He repeated this two or three times, until the hole was about six inches across, and then Tesla stepped up.

"My turn." She inserted the crowbar into the hole, set the lip of it firmly against the edge, braced her feet and gave a mighty pull. A big chunk of the wall broke off and hung by its plastered surface. They continued to pull the broken chunks off with their hands until the hole was big enough, they estimated, to climb through. They breathed in the fine white dust that filled the air as they looked through the hole into an identical hallway, softly lit by the same fluorescent lights that illuminated the one they stood in.

"Ready?" Tesla asked. She handed the crowbar back to Finn, who put it in the messenger bag, along with the hammer.

Finn ducked his head and stepped over the piece of wall they'd left intact at the bottom and into the newly-revealed hallway. Tesla climbed through behind him, and they walked cautiously down the hall. They passed four identical, unmarked doors on their right, about ten yards between each of them; the wall to the left was smooth and unmarked. They could see that the hallway ended up ahead with another door directly in front of them. Finn stopped, and so did Tesla.

"What do you want to do?" he asked.

Tesla frowned. "I'm not sure. It's not like I've seen the whole facility. I have nothing to compare this to." She thought for a moment as she unconsciously pulled at her bottom lip with her teeth. Finn watched her and waited, willing himself to be detached.

"I think we should try these doors," she said after a moment. "There's a reason why this section is hidden away, and even if there's a bad guy behind every one of these doors, there's no way I can leave before I've checked to see if my dad's here."

"I agree," said Finn. "Are you ready?"

"Wait, Finn," she said, her voice soft, hesitant.

He turned back, prepared to hear her say that she was with Sam now. He was braced for it, had already convinced himself it would be for the best—for both of them.

"When you don't want anyone to find what you've got, a secret room is useful. But it would also be useful if you don't want anyone to find *you*."

Sam forgotten, Finn sucked in his breath. "Of course," he said quietly, as if to himself. "Brilliant."

"Yeah, he is," she said. "In an evil-mad-scientist kind of way."

"I didn't mean Nilsen," Finn said. "I meant you. It all makes sense now. He was here from the start. Nilsen probably still worked here when this facility was planned and built. And all these years, no one's been able to track him, he just shows up here and there, and then he's gone again. Because this has always been his home base, and it's completely off the grid."

"That's what I meant," Tesla said. "He's completely unprincipled, but he's smart. You've got to give him that. His hiding place actually has a built-in, state-of-the-art security system developed and installed by the US government. No wonder no one could find him. Including the US government."

Finn shook his head in admiration, however begrudged. "Unbelievable."

"So," Tesla said. "We want to find my father—alive and well—but we have to be prepared to also find Nilsen. And if this has been his base of operations for years, I think it's safe to say he's got home court advantage."

Finn opened up the messenger bag, gave her back the crowbar, and took the hammer out for himself.

"Ready?" he asked, and when she nodded, they walked to the first door and turned the handle.

CHAPTER 34

It was locked. Tesla tried to relax as she and Finn stood on either side of the door and he had reached out to open it. They remembered all too well the sudden gunshot, the blood and chaos, and the painful recovery that still lay ahead of Beckett.

"Should we try to force it open?" Tesla wondered if her father might be just a few feet away, separated from her by only a locked door.

"Let's try the other three before we decide," Finn said, and Tesla nodded.

They moved to the next door and took up their positions, pressed up against the wall to take advantage of what little cover was available. Finn tried the door, and the handle turned and swung inward without a sound. They looked at each other, drew a breath, and Finn led the way inside the dark, silent room.

He felt the edges of the wall until he encountered what he'd hoped to find: a light switch. He flipped it on and the buzz of a fluorescent light sounded faintly as the room was flooded with a harsh white light. They stepped a little further in, and had just begun to register the military cot, the canned goods, unmarked cardboard boxes stacked high to the left to form a kind of wall, the huge maps pinned to the wall, when Tesla stopped dead in her tracks at the last sound she expected to hear.

"Who's there?" asked Aunt Jane.

The unmistakable voice of Jane Doane had come from behind the boxes. Tesla watched Finn move purposefully behind the wall of cardboard, hammer in hand, and then someone grabbed her from behind and covered her mouth and nose with a thick wad of fabric. She couldn't breathe. Her heart racing, she flailed about, desperate and terrified, kicking at the legs behind her, hands trying to pry off the arm that now held her around the waist. She screamed but heard only a muted, muffled sound escape her throat as the arm that pinned her to her assailant's body held her captive, and the wet, heavy cloth that cut off her air supply as well as her voice made it impossible for her to warn Finn. As the wooziness set in she realized the cloth was soaked with some kind of drug and she wondered, with her last conscious thought, what had happened to Finn and how her parents could have been so very wrong about Jane.

Before she actually knew she was awake, Tesla was aware of the awful, slightly metallic taste in her mouth.

I was drugged, she remembered. *Knocked out.* She opened her eyes and squinted against the bright light above her as her eyes slowly focused. She moved to sit up, only to find that her hands and feet were tied. She fought down the wave of panic that threatened to engulf her, aware of that feeling of being *pulled* again, which made no sense at all. She paused for a moment, taking stock: *is it my heart? Some effect of the drug?* She couldn't say for sure, but her instinct told her it was neither of these things. It was physical, the tension was very real, like a wire pulled so tight it was almost vibrating, but it was also, equally, an emotional feeling.

Move toward the pull, she thought, without the slightest understanding of what the hell that even meant.

Tesla looked around, took stock of her situation. She lay on her back, on the floor of the room she and Finn had entered. She had been grabbed, drugged unconscious. Her hands were bound in front of her with some sort of flexible plastic band pulled tight—too tight to work them free. Her ankles were similarly bound, but she used the abdominal muscles she had worked all year, with crunches and planks, to sit up so she could look around.

The cot had a pillow and a blanket on it, neatly made. A small refrigerator hummed at the foot of the bed. Shelves held canned goods, bottled water, a few plates and bowls and utensils. An open door on the opposite wall revealed what looked to Tesla like a small bathroom.

Her head was still fuzzy, but better, and her heart no longer pounded, Tesla noted, when she heard a soft moan from somewhere behind her and the pull she had felt grew stronger, followed by a faint wave of nausea. She used her feet to turn her body toward the sound and realized it came from behind the stacks of boxes that filled half the room.

"Who's there?" she said softly, tentatively, with the exact inflection she'd heard in Jane's voice just before she had lost consciousness.

"Tes?" came the groggy reply, and she immediately began to scoot toward the boxes, around the stack that effectively divided the room in two.

It was Finn, and it seemed to take Tesla forever to get to him. She couldn't move fast enough, she had never wanted anything so much, to get there, to already be there, even if all she was able to do was press her arm up against his. She felt that pull, and it was almost as if a line connected them and it felt so real she wanted to reach up and grab it and by simply putting one hand over the other drag herself to him by the thing that connected them. As she got closer she saw that just as she had been, he was bound and lay on the floor, but unlike her, he was on his side, and he was clearly injured.

"Finn," she said breathlessly as she finally got close, her shoes at last touching the fabric of his shirt as another, stronger wave of nausea washed over her and her head began to ache. "Are you hurt? What happened?"

"Shhhh," he said quietly, his face scrunched up in pain, his eyes barely open as he squinted up at her in the harsh glare of the overhead lights. "World's. Worst. Hangover."

"What happened to you?" she asked again, alarmed.

"I heard a voice behind these boxes," he said, his voice a little slurred. "I walked back here, heard a sound from you and—weird, I sort of got dizzy and my vision blurred—but before I could turn around someone hit me—hard—on the back of my head. Now here I am, all trussed up. I started to come to and didn't know where you were or what had happened...it felt—are you okay?"

"Yeah, I'm fine," she assured him. "Somebody grabbed me and put a cloth over my nose and mouth. Knocked me out. Chloroform, maybe—I think that's what they use in the movies." She paused, wanting to tell him about the strange pull she'd felt, the oddly *physical* need to get to him, the nausea and headache, but figured it was all part of the drug still in her system.

"Did you hear Aunt Jane?" Tesla asked, so softly Finn barely heard her.

Finn nodded.

"I guess it's true, then," Tesla said. "I had hoped that Lydia was wrong."

"Good people do bad things sometimes," Finn said.

"Don't do that," Tesla said firmly. "I'm not a little girl. I don't have to hide from the real world, or be protected from it."

"I know. And that's good, Tesla, but it's still true, you know. We can try to understand—that's not the same as excusing, or even forgiving. We don't know the whole story yet."

"Sometimes all that matters is what someone does, not why they do it."

Finn couldn't argue with that. He hated to see her bitter and shut down, but he knew it was sometimes necessary in order to grow up and move on with your life. He had certainly had to do his share of it and knew perfectly well that where his father was concerned he was incapable of following his own good advice.

"We need to get out of here," Tesla said. "We have to assume that Nilsen—or Jane, or both of them—will come back, and I don't want to be here when they do."

"Agreed," said Finn. He took a deep breath, rolled onto his back and sat up and the pain in his head exploded, made even his eyes hurt.

"Whoa, shit," he said through gritted teeth at precisely the moment Tesla said, "Oh God, my head," in a voice tight with pain.

They looked at each other in shocked silence, her shoes now touching his pant leg, her bound hands thrust forward, clutching at the sleeve of his T-shirt, though she didn't remember reaching out and touching him. His breath was shallow and fast, and hers matched his, like two galloping horses, side by side, who've synchronized in some way, without any overt communication, the rhythm of their pounding hooves, the flex and strain of muscle, the flow of blood and oxygen.

Tesla let go of his shirt, leaned against the wall and closed her eyes, willing the pain and dizziness to recede. *What is going on?* she wondered. *Something has happened—to both of us.* "Are you okay?" she asked in a shaky voice

When he opened his eyes he met hers, two brilliant spots of beauty in this awful hole in the ground. He smiled, just a little, at the concern apparent in her voice. "Yes. My head hurts."

"Concussion," she said forlornly. "Been there."

"Okay, doc, you can prescribe something for me later. Maybe a sponge bath."

"Yeah, you're okay," she said disgustedly, letting go of his shirt and leaning back away from him. "At least as okay as you ever are."

"Come closer," he said suddenly, and without hesitation she scooted in toward him again until her knees, bent and pulled in close to her body, were pressed up against his shoulder. "Can you reach into your bag?"

"They didn't take it?" she asked, surprised to see that he still wore it.

He didn't answer—he didn't need to—and she awkwardly got her hands inside the bag's main compartment.

"Empty," she said, as she felt around in the bag.

"So much for my genius in packing for this little adventure," he said.

"Wait," she said suddenly and turned the bag sideways with her tightly bound hands. "There are other pockets." She fumbled with the zipper on a small side pocket that wasn't immediately obvious. He waited, turned a little to the side to make it easier for her.

"Ha!" she said, loud enough to startle them both, and then she leaned in close to him. Her eyes shone and her cheeks dimpled. "Who's the genius now?"

Finn shook his head slowly, both to clear his concussion-rattled brain and to force himself to focus on the rather dire situation they were in instead of her very full, very soft lips that were at the moment so close to his own.

All he could manage was a vague, "What?"

"This!" she said triumphantly as she held up the utility knife he had used to cut away Beckett's shirt where she'd been shot.

"You are, clearly." He held out his bound hands to her.

In moments they were both free. They rubbed their wrists and ankles to restore blood flow and then Tesla stood and gave Finn her hand—which he needed—to help pull him to his feet.

He took stock: the nausea was better, but he was still dizzy and could not be completely certain that he wouldn't just fall down again. "How do you feel?" he asked.

"My head's better," she announced.

"Mine, too," he said, but stopped short. "Although I don't get why I started to feel dizzy and nauseous before I got hit."

"You're a copy-cat," she said lightly. "Sympathy pains for my drugged state, maybe."

They went quickly to the door and, naturally, it was locked from the outside. They began to take stock of what was in the room—they wanted tools, but they wanted weapons as well, and Finn, unlike Tesla, would use them if needed. All they found, however, was a fork, and it was made of such soft aluminum that even had they wanted to stab someone with it, there was little doubt that it would merely bend on impact. Tesla's utility knife was all they had going for them.

They sat on the edge of the cot, unsure what to do next. "I really wish right now that I had told someone where I was headed," Finn said, grateful that he felt a little more steady.

"Yeah, your maverick-ness doesn't seem quite so appealing at the moment."

"So you're saying it usually does?"

Tesla ignored him, got up and walked to the door again. Just as she got close enough to reach out and touch the door handle, they heard the click of the lock and the handle slowly turned.

Finn was up and moving immediately, pulled to her as though his body was doing the thinking for him. He grabbed Tesla's shoulder and drew her back toward him, toward the cot and the boxes, away from the door. His head still swam but he managed to push Tesla partly behind him as the door swung cautiously inward and Lydia walked in the door.

"Well, of course you managed to figure this out *and* get yourselves caught," she said as she eyed them both and shook her head. "Teenagers as agents. It's insane," she muttered.

"Is this a priority extraction—leave no man behind—or are you here to ground us?" Finn said sarcastically, but relief was plain in his voice.

"The first for now," she said. "But don't rule out the second."

Finn grinned and turned toward Tesla, no doubt to make some other cute remark, when Jane Doane walked in the open door and, immediately behind her, Dr. Van Aldan, Director of the Experimental Physics Institute.

Lydia moved into the room, her eyes on the two newcomers. She seemed coiled, tensed to spring, and Tesla thought *she's definitely got a plan* before she turned to look at Jane.

"Aunt Jane." Tesla felt stricken now that she faced the petite, dark-haired woman, despite her calm and cynical conversation with Finn about the woman's betrayal. "How could you—where is my father?"

"He's here," said Jane Doane as she rubbed her wrist, her voice strong, but infinitely sad. "He's been here all along. You figured it out."

"Dr. Van Aldan," said Finn coldly. "Or Dr. Nilsen. Which do you prefer?"

Tesla's head whipped around and she stared, horrified, at the man she knew as Erik Van Aldan. "You're...you're—"

"Sebastian Nilsen," he said smoothly. His hands hung by his sides, he looked and sounded as relaxed as if they'd bumped into each other at a coffee shop in town.

"But..." Tesla stammered, unable to form a coherent thought.

"You kidnapped Dr. Abbott to get him out of the way before you took your new position as head of the institute," Finn said, talking fast as the pieces, finally, fell into place. "You had to avoid him when you interviewed for the Director's job because Abbott would have recognized you immediately, despite the years that have passed and the changes you've made to your appearance. He knew you too well to be fooled."

"Indeed," Nilsen said smoothly. "I would have preferred a less messy solution, but he left me no choice—again. The opportunity to head the institute, to have access to this facility and Tasya's work, well, it was too great to pass up. I sacrificed far too much to create Erik Van Aldan to let it go for the sake of an old college friend."

"You were never their friend," Tesla spat. Her tone introduced a dangerous level of intensity and venom into the conversation that had felt perfectly civil up until this moment. "You stole from them, you were jealous, you were a cheater and a liar all along."

"Oh, my dear, you know nothing at all about it," Nilsen said quietly as he advanced toward Tesla. He actually sounded sad.

She felt Finn tense, but he did not move. "I know enough," she said, defiant.

"I was very much their friend," he continued smoothly as he stopped a mere ten inches from Tesla. Too close, she thought, but she refused to back up. She could see the blood vessels in his eyes, the pale blonde stubble on his unshaven chin.

"Liar," she said simply.

He looked at her then, his head cocked slightly to the side as he considered the girl in front of him, the shape of her face, her long orange and gold hair, those incredible eyes. "You look like her, you know," he said. "And you're quite intelligent, too, I understand. Your mother was a brilliant woman—did you know that it was I, not your father, who began the work on time travel with her? That's right," he said softly, in response to the incredulous look on Tesla's face. "She chose to work with me. For years we were in the lab together. It was I who realized what she was, where she would lead us—your father never understood her abilities—he always underestimated her."

"Shut up," Tesla said viciously, unable to bear his oily voice or hear him talk about her parents.

"Such volatility," he said, clearly amused. "Your mother was a passionate woman, too. Brilliant and passionate—qualities I fully appreciated—personally as well as professionally."

"You're revolting," Tesla said, her voice raw.

Nilsen considered that. "Perhaps. You *do* look remarkably like her," he said again as he reached out and took her chin gently in his hand and tilted her face up, searching—for what?

She sensed, rather than saw, movement from Finn at her side, but he was checked immediately as Lydia's voice rang out like a gunshot.

"Finn, don't!"

It was enough, and he became still again.

Tesla scowled angrily back at Nilsen. She breathed hard and

concentrated on her anger, fanned its flames—anything to hold on to the rage, lest it be replaced by fear. She would not give him the satisfaction, she vowed, as she stared him down, his face only inches from her own. Unexpectedly, he flung her face roughly aside and she staggered into Finn, who caught her and steadied her.

"But there, you have more than a bit of your father in you, too," he said coldly. "Your moral outrage is so very pedestrian—and completely misplaced."

"Shut up about my father!" Tesla shouted.

"Time to grow up, little girl," Nilsen snapped. "Of course you've idolized your father, children always do, but you've decided to play with the adults now, and you no longer have that luxury. You've willfully forced together the few pieces of this little puzzle that you think you know, to create the pretty picture you want, but the pieces *don't fit*! You've already begun to see that, though, haven't you?"

He faced Tesla, as angry now as she was. "It was never true—that I stole their work, published it as my own. It was *my work all along*! Hers and mine, from those early years. She started to date your father, and his work began to evolve, moved more closely to hers, and somehow I was eased out, your father in her lab, and in her bed." He paused, breathing hard, but mastered it to continue more calmly. "It's always a sad day when you are faced with the toppling of your heroes. Your father is hopelessly flawed, my dear. In ways you cannot even imagine."

Tesla stood, her hands clenched in fists by her side. She was only vaguely aware of Lydia, of Jane, of Finn beside her, her entire being focused on Sebastian Nilsen, whose face suddenly changed from controlled anger to cunning—and something else.

"It is *your* flaws, however, that make you so very valuable, eh?" he said softly as he moved even closer and forced Tesla to lean back into Finn. "That flawed heart of yours—"

Tesla gasped as he suddenly reached out and laid his hand on her chest, his fingers curved to cup her left breast, right over her heart. She jumped involuntarily, her stomach lurching, nauseated that he had actually touched her, just as Finn pushed her aside, lunged forward, and shoved Nilsen hard in the chest.

Nilsen staggered back but recovered immediately and laughed. "How amusing. Young love." He chuckled to himself for a moment while they all stood, barely breathing. "Enough," he announced with finality. "Tesla, you're coming with me, I'm afraid."

"I'm not going anywhere with you," Tesla said through gritted teeth.

"Oh, but you are," he said in a voice like steel. "I know everything—I have someone on the inside, as you now realize. I know how the time machine works, and I know someone can jump with you as long as you are in physical contact with them. I hold all the cards here, and I believe you're smart enough to understand that. You're the only one in this room that I have reason to keep alive. And that includes, of course, your father."

He paused a beat, let his threat sink in, and then glanced at Jane and Lydia. "Time to wrap this up," he said casually to the two women. "Kill her. We can certainly do with one less government agent."

CHAPTER 35

Tesla gasped as she turned in horror to Jane, bracing for the gun in her hand, the shot that would end Lydia's life.

Jane looked back sadly at Tesla. "I'm sorry, Tesla. Sorrier than I can possibly tell you."

"Aunt Jane, you can't!" Tesla cried.

"Oh Tesla, really," Lydia said, thoroughly exasperated. "She's sorry she failed her mission, sorry she could not save your father—sorry she has to die. Honestly, for a bright girl you can be a little slow."

"Lydia?" said Finn, clearly shocked, and he and Tesla saw at exactly the same moment the gun she held—the cold, gray handgun Tesla had refused—pointed right at Jane.

"All our cards, finally on the table, eh Lydia?" Jane asked coldly.

"Indeed, though I suspect you have a few still up your sleeve," the older woman said serenely. "You're very good, as I've said all along. I want you to know that I know that. For what it's worth."

"Very little, actually. When did you turn?" Jane asked quietly.

"When it became clear to me that all we do is tilt at windmills. When my meager pension and that rickety old house became unacceptable compensation for a lifetime of putting myself in harm's way, while others got rich."

"Isn't that every traitor's rationale?" Jane asked contemptuously.

"Careful," Lydia said, pleasant and menacing.

"Get it done, Lydia, and the boy, too," said Nilsen as he moved toward the door. "I'll make the preparations. Bring the girl to me when you've finished," he said over his shoulder.

"Lydia," Tesla said when Nilsen was gone. "I don't understand, you've been so—"

"So nice?" Lydia finished for her. "So kind, so motherly? Well, why not?" She glanced at Finn. "I feel a great deal of affection for you all, actually. How absurd to assume I like Nilsen, and dislike you—it's not true, but completely beside the point. He is clearly despicable, but he is a means to an end, and I did what I could to protect you from him, though I suppose it would be a bit much to expect you to appreciate that now."

Finn snorted. "Bullshit."

Lydia shrugged, a small, sad smile on her face. "Well, up to a point of course. I knew Jane would have to die, but I am sorry about you, dear."

Lydia raised the gun toward Jane, her arm steady, as Finn reached into his pocket and found the utility knife he'd put there after he'd cut Tesla free. He knew they had a couple of seconds, at best, and he also knew that Tesla was their only hope. He withdrew the knife, pushed the blade out as far as it would go, and pressed the handle firmly into Tesla's hand, which hung beside his own.

He felt an unexpected current run between them as their hands touched and she closed her fingers over the knife without hesitation. She did not turn or start in surprise. He felt, rather than saw her weigh the heft of it in her hand, glance up at Lydia, and then she moved, a wide, powerful movement of her right arm, just as they heard the terrible sound of a gunshot, the boom and echo of it deafening from only a few yards away. It happened so quickly that all he registered was that Jane stood and Lydia had fallen to one knee, the handle of the utility knife protruding from the back of her hand, the blade buried up to the hilt in her flesh.

Lydia cried out once in pain, the gun fallen from her hand. Finn raced to it and picked it up just as Jane reached Lydia and pulled her to her feet.

"You have the right to remain silent..." Finn heard Jane begin to intone as he raced out the door, his head still pounding, and into the Bat Cave after Sebastian Nilsen.

Tesla took a step nearer to Jane, who had not-too-gently sat Lydia on the edge of the cot, where she cradled her injured, bloody hand in her lap.

"Aunt Jane, I'm so sorry. There was so much left unexplained, so many coincidences, and when Finn and I came down here, we heard your voice. I thought..."

"I know what you thought, Tesla," Jane said, neither anger nor pity in her voice—for herself or for Tesla. "I understand. Lydia told you I was in on your father's kidnapping, that I was with Sebastian. And you believed her. And then when you heard my voice—of course I was tied up, just as you were shortly after. One of Nilsen's goons forced me down here at gun point, and I've been down here ever since." She held Tesla's gaze, and Tesla's eyes filled with tears.

Jane smiled a little, and her kindness made Tesla feel even worse. "It's not your fault," Jane assured her. "I learned a long time ago that you can't live this life, in which you keep everyone at arm's length, lie about what you do, where you go, and why, and expect them to really know you. We make that impossible, eh, Lydia?"

Lydia looked, for the first time, Tesla thought, old. So much smaller than Tesla had always perceived her to be. The woman looked up at Jane and she, too, smiled.

"It's not an easy life," Lydia conceded. "You've suspected me for some time, haven't you, Jane?"

Jane considered the question. "Not as long as you might think. I didn't like you much, of course—you've always seemed a bit off to me—but I didn't have any evidence. So I watched and waited. I knew you searched Greg's house, rifled Tesla's room weeks ago, but I assumed it was a questionable method in your effort to protect the family. My mistake."

"Yes," Lydia said. "That was sloppy of me, but frankly we had gotten nowhere with Tasya Petrova's 'Tesla effect' reference, and Nilsen is not exactly a patient man. He was in favor of taking Tesla, actually, and I tried to forestall that. My hope was that we would learn what we needed and Nilsen would be gone before the gala, and then none of this—the kidnapping, whether it was Tesla or her father—would have been necessary. But that was before we knew Tesla herself was necessary to jump. Given that fact, this really couldn't have ended any differently."

"Was it you who shot Beckett?" Tesla asked.

"No, dear, it wasn't," Lydia said. "Neither did I set the explosives in your father's office to play for time, nor attack you in your home and break your arm. I assure you that Nilsen has other employees who are far more capable—and enthusiastic—in that department than I."

"Lydia," Tesla said then, too exhausted to accuse her, too filled with anxiety about her father and Finn, who'd gone after

Nilsen, to rail and shout her outrage, "Where's my dad?"

"He's here," Lydia said without hesitation, not because she wanted to help, Tesla realized, but because it just didn't matter anymore. She had lied, she had stolen, she had put them all in danger countless times when it served her purpose. Lydia indicated, with a sideways movement of her head, the mountain of cardboard boxes behind Tesla. "In there."

"Dad?" Tesla called as she moved toward the boxes. Jane scrambled right beside her, though she kept one eye on Lydia. They heard nothing, sensed no movement, not a whisper or a breath, and Tesla felt the panic begin to rise in her chest. "DAD!" she screamed, suddenly desperate.

She and Jane began to remove boxes, which turned out to be empty, tossing them aside quickly. It took less than a minute to reveal that the boxes had been stacked over and around a low, sturdy structure made of some kind of smooth, solid metal with a latched lid, not unlike an oversized freezer. With the boxes gone, Tesla and Jane unlatched the lid and opened it wide, hope and fear warring for supremacy in their minds.

Dr. Abbot lay on his side, elbows and knees slightly bent. He was bound at the wrists and ankles just as Tesla and Finn had been, with similar plastic ties. He was motionless, though, and his eyes were closed. He had some kind of a mask on his face, a clear plastic cup over his nose and mouth, and the contraption it was attached to was strapped to his head.

Tesla was sure her heart had stopped. She heard a strangled little cry and started, only to realize that she had made the sound herself.

Jane looked closely at Greg Abbott, deep inside the metal chest, and put her hand on Tesla's arm. "It's okay, look—he's breathing."

Tesla looked again, focused on the clear cup over her father's nose and mouth, and she saw that the cup misted up with his breath every time he exhaled.

She exhaled herself, finally, and climbed into the box with Jane's help. Jane handed her the utility knife she'd extracted from Lydia's hand, and Tesla quickly cut the plastic that bound her father as she noted rather grimly that she had become somewhat accustomed to this stuff already. She pushed the blade back into the handle and locked it, slipped it into her pocket, and looked at Jane, a question in her eyes.

Jane turned to Lydia. "Is he injured or has he been drugged?" she asked coldly.

"I honestly don't know," Lydia replied. "I wasn't privy to all of it, not by a long stretch."

"It looks like a simple oxygen mask," Jane said after a moment. "Go ahead and take it off."

Tesla gently removed the straps that held the canister with its clear plastic cup to her father's face. He continued to breath, she noted with relief, but his eyes remained closed. He might have been asleep.

"Dad?" she asked tentatively. Tesla was about to turn to Jane, insist that they call an ambulance, when she saw his eyes begin to flutter.

"Tesla?" he asked as his eyes came slowly into focus and he tried to turn his head toward her.

"Yeah, Dad, it's me." Tesla laughed and cried simultaneously, her hands flitted about him, touched his face, his arm, his shirt collar. "Are you okay? Are you hurt?"

He began to move then, rolled over slowly, painfully, and sat up in the box. Both Tesla and Jane reached in to help him.

"Jane," he said once, clearly. Simply. Tesla saw Jane smile at him, a tremulous little smile, and then she said, her voice strong, "Good to see you, Greg. Happy belated birthday."

He laughed—a little exhalation of breath, really—and then stood up. "I'm all right, I'm all right," he said, irritated by the fuss. "I'm just stiff, I haven't moved much in—how long has it been?— feels like weeks. Sebastian came in a couple of times every day, let me out to use the bathroom. He gave me food and water, and then back in I'd go, and whatever was pumped through that mask would put me right back to sleep. At least I'm well-rested."

Tesla threw herself into his arms and hugged him as tightly as she could. His stupid jokes, his matter-of-factness—God, she'd missed him.

He seemed surprised, but after a few seconds, his arms went around her, too, and they held each other for a minute as Greg and Jane exchanged a look over Tesla's head.

When he gently stepped back from her, Tesla let go. "Dad— there's so much to tell you—" she began.

"Yes," he said, oddly grim now that everything was fine. "There is a lot to say, a lot to explain."

"Right," Tesla said, "but first I need to go find Finn." She was already through the door before they could stop her, and though she heard Jane's shout—"Tesla, wait! That's exactly where Nilsen wants you!"—she sped down the hall, through the door, and across the vast, open space of the Bat Cave, following the persistent pull in her chest as she headed straight for the time machine, and Finn.

"Mildly impressive," Nilsen said calmly as he stood in the control booth, his hands loose by his side and in plain sight, as Finn had ordered. Finn was tense and hyper-aware, the gun Lydia had dropped on the floor now in his hand and pointed right at Nilsen's chest.

"Thanks," Finn said. "It's always nice to be appreciated."

"I have to ask, though," Nilsen went on conversationally. "What do you imagine will happen here?"

"Well, I know I have the gun," Finn said. "And I know Lydia is now out of the picture, which would suggest that you're finished. I guess we just sit here until the cavalry arrives."

Nilsen smiled—actually smiled, Finn thought. He had to give the bastard credit for having a pair. "And do you suppose that a man of my means and intelligence has only one middle-aged woman on his payroll?"

Finn's face was impassive, but inside he cursed himself for his carelessness. This could be a bluff, but it stood to reason Nilsen had others here, or at least nearby. *Shit*, he thought. *He even had two men at that stupid keg party, and that was just a fishing expedition.* Surely Nilsen's people would arrive soon, and to Finn's knowledge, none of the good guys had called this in.

There would be no back-up.

Finn shrugged. "I've got all day," he said. "And plenty of bullets. The only way into this room is up those stairs, single file, and in plain sight."

Sebastian Nilsen merely smiled, and Finn forced himself not to react. The seconds ticked by, then minutes, and then a sound, the last sound Finn wanted to hear right now: Tesla's voice, on the staircase, her feet pounding up the metal stairs to the control room, as she shouted his name.

"Finn!"

"Tesla, no!" he yelled as he moved toward the open door in an attempt to slam it shut and lock her out, anything to keep her away from Nilsen, but it was too late, she was through the door, out of breath, and then Finn felt the cold metal of Nilsen's own gun pressed against the back of his head, just at the base of his skull.

Tesla's eyes were wide with fear, and Finn had no choice but to let go of his gun when Nilsen reached out to take it from his hand, that cold, hard circle pressed firmly against his head to remind him that he was a flick of the man's finger on the trigger away from his brains spattered all over Bizzy's shiny control panel.

Nilsen took a step back as he motioned with his gun for Finn and Tesla to step further inside the room and away from the door.

"You see, my boy?" Nilsen said. "Things always change."

"It might be wise to remember that while you gloat," Finn replied.

"Touché," Nilsen laughed, but was immediately serious again. "I've a colleague who will arrive momentarily. Lydia was supposed to operate the controls, but he'll have to act as understudy. Tesla, you and I are taking a trip—eight years back in time. Straight to your parents' lab—and, incidentally, to the scene of the crime. The first crime, I should say."

"I think I said this earlier, but *I'm not going anywhere with you*," Tesla said slowly, insultingly.

"Well, in fact you are," Nilsen said. "I'm tired of these games. You can tie this one to the chair, and walk with me down to the machine, or I can shoot him now and drag you by the hair, as you kick and scream, down those stairs and to the machine. Either way, this will happen. The choice is yours—I couldn't care less if you are battered and bruised and grief-stricken over the loss of your boyfriend when we make the jump. I don't even care if you're conscious. All I need is for your heart to beat, as only it can do."

"My life's mission is now to see you rot in prison for the rest of your life," Finn said quietly. "And if you touch her, I swear to God I'll kill you."

Nilsen didn't even bother to respond, he merely looked at

Tesla, both his question and his impatience plain on his face.

"I'll go," said Tesla, unable to bring herself to look at Finn, whose intensity as he'd threatened Nilsen had shocked her. "I need something to tie him up with."

"Improvise," Nilsen said as he motioned with his gun for Finn to sit in one of the two chairs in the room.

Despite the technology and hardware, the blink and beep of readouts on the panels, the metal-encased equipment everywhere, Tesla quickly realized it was all anchored down. She scanned every surface and found only a couple of pens and a few wireless mics on stands. She moved to the one metal cabinet in the room and opened the doors wide, then pulled out a bundle of electrical cord and held it up.

"This?" she asked.

"Fine," he said, his voice clipped, authoritative. "Tie his hands behind his back—tightly—over the back of the chair. And I mean tight—I'll check it before we go downstairs." He looked at his cellphone, nodded once, satisfied. "My man is here. And, incidentally, another is on his way to intercept Jane, since Lydia is clearly incompetent."

Tesla stood behind Finn's chair and wrapped the insulated extension cord in a figure eight, around and over and under Finn's wrists, her fingers tingling every time they brushed his skin. She wrapped the cord tightly, just as Nilsen had told her to. When she finished, she palmed the utility knife she'd slid out of her pocket and slipped it into his hand. His fingers closed around it and she stood up.

"Done." Her voice suggested her complete subordination. "Sorry, Finn."

"Don't do this, Tesla," Finn said, playing his part, his voice catching at just the right moment, filled with emotion.

Nilsen walked over to tug on the cord that bound Finn's wrists. "Well done," he said, pleased and surprised. "I like competent people. I may decide to keep you once we jump." He chuckled then, a sound of pleased surprise.

"You will see me again," Finn said, his voice tight.

"I'm afraid that's not possible," Nilsen said as he opened the door for a giant of a man with a receding, blonde crew-cut. "I will no longer be in the world with you, nor will Tesla. Say your goodbyes, children."

Tesla glanced at the guy who towered over her in the doorway and recognized him as the man who'd tried to drag her out of the party at Lydia's.

He grinned at her. "I guess we get to have that conversation after all, huh?"

"How's the wrist?" Finn said, and Tesla shivered at the look the man shot Finn.

"After I push a couple of buttons for him," Nilsen's man said softly, "You and I are gonna have a little fun."

"I have to insist that you buy me dinner first," Finn said, his voice steady. "I'm not as easy as I look."

"Tesla?" Nilsen said as he held the door open. "You have your instructions," he said to the blond man who stood near Finn. "Carry them out—to the letter."

"Understood," the man replied. He turned from Finn and sat in the other chair at the control panel.

Tesla walked down the metal stairs with Nilsen behind her. She did not look back as she walked into the room with the mirrors and took her place in the center of the room. Nilsen grabbed her hand and held it tightly, the gun in his other hand held firmly and pointed at her hip—not her heart, she noted, as she paled at the thought of what he would do to her if she fought him.

"Are you ready for our little adventure?" he asked. His voice quivered with excitement. "You know, I've waited for this moment all my life. Your mother should have been here—and it's your father's fault that she's not. You do know there was no car accident, don't you? You're a smart girl—have you figured it out yet?"

Before she could say a word, a deep male voice began the countdown and she braced herself as she shut her eyes against the lasers, the fear, and whatever truths might lie behind Nilsen's ugly words.

"Three…two…one."

She saw the flash against the back of her eyelids, but before she could open them again she heard a woman's voice, oddly familiar, as it inexplicably repeated the count.

"…two…one."

Another flash, and though she felt slightly disoriented when she opened her eyes, she was resigned to what she would find: the new closet-sized coffin around her, Nilsen by her side with his gun trained on her, everything in her life as she knew it, gone.

But she saw instead the big time machine, the mirrors in the corners where they were supposed to be, and Nilsen…gone, just as her father burst through the door from the Bat Cave to gather her in his arms and hold her tight.

EPILOGUE

The watcher hung back at the edges of the crowd, adept by now at going unnoticed. The place was crowded, as it always was, but the group the watcher was interested in had commandeered several tables and pushed them together in the small pizzeria. It was obviously the redhead's birthday, they had just sung a horrible rendition of *Happy Birthday* to her and presented her with a slice of pizza with a candle in it. She was a little subdued, perhaps, but otherwise she seemed fine. Her cast was off and her left arm appeared to be completely healed.

They were all there—well, most of them. Keisha, tall and lovely, and her cousin Finnegan, with his perfectly pitched nonchalance that fooled everyone in the group. Finn—like the watcher—kept his eye on the redhead, and he was impressively subtle about it. The blond boy, Malcolm, sat next to Elizabeth, whose spiky black hair and piercings did little to hide her sweet, wounded nature, despite her efforts, and the watcher felt both pity and admiration—not for the first time—for all the girl had endured as a child, all she worked so hard to hide from the world. The ever-flirtatious Joley and the deadly Beckett Isley, up and about for the first time since she was shot, sat on either side of the redhead's little brother, Max. And Sam, quietly and authoritatively by Tesla's side, spoke occasionally with a lightness that belied the intensity the watcher could read on his face, a deep love and longing masked by the ridiculous story he was telling about having invented the redhead's favorite pizza when he was fifteen years old.

Unable to resist the celebration, the emotional undercurrents that swirled and eddied around and within the group, the watcher moved in closer.

"I'm still stunned about Lydia," Joley said. "We should have bloody known, shouldn't we? We're supposed to be good at that."

"How could you have known?" Max asked. "Real people aren't like old Westerns, with good guys and bad guys you can spot by the color of their hats." The boy took another bite of his pizza and pushed his bent wire glasses up higher on his nose where they sat, crooked and smudged. "Real people aren't like that at all."

"Well, thanks for that compliment. Hopefully I'm not that simple-minded," Joley laughed.

Max blushed a little. "That's not what I meant. I just think Lydia was kind in a lot of ways, and I think she did love you guys. It's more complicated than whether she was good or bad."

"I agree," said Finn. "I don't think she wanted anybody hurt."

"But they did get hurt," said Beckett.

"I know, but her part in this doesn't erase the good stuff she did," Finn insisted. "It just makes her harder for us to understand. We want it to be easier."

"We want not to have been betrayed and shot," Beckett said.

"She's right," Tesla agreed. "Sometimes it is black and white."

"And sometimes people talk about themselves in the third person, or the first person plural, and it's really, really annoying," said Keisha in an attempt to restore the mood—the insult to Beckett was just gravy. "Seriously, people. This is a party. T is finally eighteen, so I have to give her grief about something else. I need suggestions."

"She's a huge slob," Max said helpfully.

"Old news," said Keisha with a dismissive wave of her hand.

"What about her newly-discovered, apparently badass knife-throwing skills?" Beckett asked.

"We want to make fun of her here, Blondie," said Keisha as she rolled her eyes.

"Yeah, I know. I couldn't think of anything," Beckett said.

Tesla laughed and the sound did indeed lighten the mood. "Why don't we not mock me and instead focus on the good news." She raised her glass. "To the bizarre but totally awesome development of Lydia transferring ownership of her house to Aunt Jane, who is now assigned here, and your new landlord."

"And your boss, love" added Joley. "You're officially on the team now."

"You and Dad get along better," said Max. "We should drink to that." He raised his cup of root beer and clinked it with Beckett's. Tesla touched his glass and drank too, despite the questions she could not quiet, the questions that Nilsen had raised and that kept her awake nights. She had never questioned her father's account of how her mother had died, had always assumed his refusal to discuss it was because he couldn't bear the pain of remembering. But what if that wasn't it at all? She would ask those questions now, she knew, and hope the new-found closeness with her father would survive it.

And of course, at the center of it all now, there was this thing—The Tesla Effect—that she still didn't understand. She was the girl who could jump back and forth through time, and that fact disturbed her greatly. It also, she admitted, excited her, and in her most private moments she allowed herself to imagine the possibilities. For herself, and for everyone else she loved.

As if he had read her mind, Sam stood up. "And let's drink to Sebastian Nilsen, who made the jump back and left Tesla here, safe and sound. We don't know why, or how, but we'll take it."

Finn raised his glass and drank with everybody else, silent amid the happy chatter, but he could not forget that if Nilsen was not here, he was somewhere—some where, and some when, and up to God knew what. Finn could not follow Sam's lead and just write off the inexplicable with a shrug. That's not how Finn was made. Things always made sense, you just had to dig, and think, and dig some more, and do the work, until the patterns fell into place.

As Tesla leaned forward to touch Sam's glass with her own, her face lit up by her dimpled smile, those blue and green eyes crinkled up in laughter, Finn resolved then and there that he would dig, and think, and work until he knew exactly what had happened—to Nilsen, and to himself and Tesla, who seemed now to have some sort of connection he could not understand or explain, their physical and emotional realities... *tangled up*, somehow. The one thing he knew for sure was that this was far from over.

The watcher studied Finn's face for another moment and then, finally satisfied, got up and walked away, out into the summer evening, just as dusk began to fall upon the town square and the last fiery edges of a spectacular sunset faded, inevitably, into night.

THE END

.

ABOUT THE AUTHOR

 Julie Drew is Professor of English at The University of Akron in Ohio, where she teaches creative writing, cultural studies, and film. When she and her family are not in Akron, they are in RI, in a delightful little roundhouse in the woods.

Julie's first novel, *Daughter of Providence*, was published by Overlook Press in 2011 to enthusiastic reviews, after which she jumped right into *The Tesla Effect* trilogy. *Glimpse* will be followed quickly by *Run* and then *Breathe*.

Learn more about forthcoming books and communicate with the author at www.juliedrew.com.

RING OF FIRE PUBLISHING

www.ringoffirebooks.com

Made in the USA
San Bernardino, CA
14 October 2014